# ROSES
# HAVE THORNS

Center Point
Large Print

**This Large Print Book carries the
Seal of Approval of N.A.V.H.**

# ROSES HAVE THORNS

## A NOVEL OF ELIZABETH I

# SANDRA BYRD

CENTER POINT LARGE PRINT
THORNDIKE, MAINE

This Center Point Large Print edition is published in the year 2013 by arrangement with Howard Books, a division of Simon & Schuster, Inc.

This book is a work of fiction. Names, characters, places, and incidents either are products of the author's imagination or are used fictitiously. Any resemblance to actual events or locales or persons, living or dead, is entirely coincidental. All Old Testament Scripture quotations are taken from the King James Version. Public domain. All New Testament Scripture quotations are taken from *Tyndale's New Testament*. A modern-spelling edition of the 1534 translation with an introduction by David Daniell. Translated by William Tyndale. Copyright © 1989 by Yale University Press. Used by permission.

The text of this Large Print edition is unabridged. In other aspects, this book may vary from the original edition. Printed in the United States of America on permanent paper. Set in 16-point Times New Roman type.

ISBN: 978-1-61173-747-9

Library of Congress Cataloging-in-Publication Data

Byrd, Sandra.
Roses have thorns : a novel of Elizabeth I / Sandra Byrd.
pages ; cm.
ISBN 978-1-61173-747-9 (library binding : alk. paper)
1. Elizabeth I, Queen of England, 1533–1603—Fiction.
  2. Great Britain—History—Elizabeth, 1558–1603—Fiction.
  3. Large type books.  I. Title.
PS3552.Y678R67 2013
813'.54—dc23

                                          2012043059

Roses have thorns, and silver fountains mud,
Clouds and eclipses stain both moon and sun,
And loathsome canker lives in sweetest bud.

—"Sonnet 35," William Shakespeare

# Henry VIII Family Tree

Henry VII
*King of England*
B. 1457

Elizabeth of York
B. 1466

Arthur Tudor
B. 1486

Mary Boleyn Carey
*Mistress*
B. 1499

Katherine Carey
B. 1524

Henry Carey
B. 1526

Henry VIII
B. 1491

2. Anne Boleyn
B. 1501

Elizabeth I
*Queen of England*
B. 1533
Stillbirths: 1534, 1536

3. Jane Seymour
B. 1508

Edward VI
B. 1537

4. Anne of Cleves
B. 1515

5. Catherine Howard
B. 1520

6. Kateryn Parr
B. 1512

1. Katherine of Aragon
B. 1485

Stillborn

Henry, Prince of Wales
(Died in Infancy)

At least 4 stillbirths and/or miscarriages

Mary I
*Queen of England*
B. 1516

Elizabeth Blount
*Mistress*
B. 1502

Henry Fitzroy
*Duke of Richmond & Somerset*
B. 1519

1. Louis XII
*King of France*
B. 1462

Mary Tudor
B. 1496

2. Charles Brandon
*Duke of Suffolk*
B. 1484

Katherine Willoughby
B. 1520

Margaret Tudor
B. 1489

James IV
*King of Scotland*
B. 1473

# Dudley Family Tree

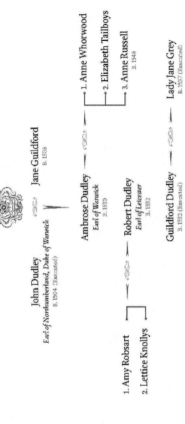

John Dudley
*Earl of Northumberland, Duke of Warwick*
B. 1504 (Executed)

Jane Guildford
B. 1508

Ambrose Dudley
*Earl of Warwick*
B. 1570

1. Anne Whorwood
2. Elizabeth Tailboys
3. Anne Russell
B. 1548

Robert Dudley
*Earl of Leicester*
B. 1532

1. Amy Robsart
2. Lettice Knollys

Guildford Dudley
B. 1532 (Executed)

Lady Jane Grey
B. 1537 (Executed)

Mary Sidney
B. 1550

Sir Henry Sidney

Other Issue

Sir Philip Sidney
B. 1554

Mary Herbert
*Countess of Pembroke*
B. 1561

Robert Sidney
*Earl of Leicester*
B. 1563

Other Issue

# PROLOGUE

There once was a strong, benevolent lady who was walking through a frozen rose garden in the grievous chill of winter when her slipper brushed against something on the cobbled path. She saw that it was a snake, stiff with cold and nigh on dead, having run the fool's errand of leaving its own nest to seize a better one.

Forswearing her initial hesitation, the lady placed the serpent close to her bosom, where it quickly warmed. When it revived, the serpent resumed its natural nature, bit its benefactress, and poisoned her with a wound unto death.

"Why have you done this?" she cried. "I have sought only to assist you!"

"You knew full well what I was when you drew me close to your heart," replied the cunning viper.

"I am justly rewarded, then," the lady sorrowed, "for pitying a serpent."

—A retelling of Aesop's fable

# ONE

November: Year of Our Lord 1564
Tre Kronor, Stockholm, Sweden

Winter, Spring, and Summer:
Year of Our Lord 1565
At Sea and Over Land

I may have been a maiden just shy of seventeen years of age, but I was no simpleton. I recognized beard burn on the fair face of my sister when she emerged, breathless, from a small closet off one of the king's galleries.

"Have you been with someone?" I asked. By *someone,* she knew I meant a man.

She would not meet my gaze. But she answered, "Don't be foolish, Elin." She looked at my gown, plain cotton. "You'd best be preparing for the evening. The king is not likely to be pleased if we are not present when he commands the festivities to begin." At that, she turned, held high her head, and proceeded down the long wooden hallway toward our mother's palace apartment.

My stomach grew unsettled, as it always did when I was fed an untruth and forced by custom to compliantly digest it. Karin was right, though, that King Erik would not look kindly upon a late arrival. Everyone at court sought to keep the king

11

placid and happy; he was a cart with three wheels, unsteady and liable to collapse at the slightest bump in the road, spilling his load on whoever was near. I turned and began to follow Karin into our mother's lodgings when I heard a noise behind me, the quiet shutting of a door.

I turned to look back and saw a figure hurrying down the hallway in the other direction. "Philip?" I called after him.

My fiancé, Philip Bonde, was heir to the great Bonde mining fortune, and his face was as well favored as his purse. Before my father died some months earlier, he had finalized my betrothal to Philip. I was ever so grateful; my father had never expressed love or affection for me, preferring instead Karin, the baby, who resembled him in her blonde, blue-eyed beauty.

"Elin!" Philip stopped, turned to walk toward me, and then drew me into a quick, stiff embrace.

"Where are you going?" I asked, puzzled.

"Rather, whatever are you doing hanging about in the gallery when we're to see the king within the hour?"

I was taken aback for a moment, recognizing, perhaps, that he sought to put me on the defense rather than account for his own presence.

He grinned and gently kissed my cheeks one by one in the French fashion, his beard lightly scratching my face, the unique spiced-herb blend of his wash water surrounding him, his lips

12

freshly warm and soft though the hall was chilled. "I shall see you downstairs, soon."

Then he turned and left.

I walked, slowly, to dress myself for the evening, unsettled, unhappy, confused. When I arrived at my mother's chamber, my married sisters, Gertrude and Brita, were already fully gowned, and the lady maid was assisting Karin as she slipped into a stunning gown of green and silver. "Where have you been?" my mother clucked. I kept trying to catch my sister's eye, but Karin kept her chin up and studiously avoided my gaze in the looking glass.

I knew.

"I'm here now," was all I answered. After Karin was gowned, the lady maid turned to me, pulled out a gown of gold-stamped gray crushed velvet, and then shook it twice before bringing it toward me. After helping me dress she weaved gold threads through my long red hair.

I would be leaving on the morrow for England, with Princess Cecelia. So my gown had been most costly, a gift that was a dear sacrifice for my widowed mother and a token of her affection and esteem. I kissed her on the cheek, and we four girls followed her down to the great hall where Erik and his new mistress would arrive.

The hall was ablaze with torches and candles; flickering gold light, rolling fires, and the heat of hundreds of noble bodies warmed the cold Swedish night. I soon lost my family in the crowd of others and danced while the king's court musicians played on. After an hour, I sought to rest and spied Karin Mansdotter in the corner, splendidly dressed and bejeweled but forlorn and alone. Although Sweden was collectively grateful for the opiate she was upon our sovereign, she was lowborn, the daughter of a tavern-keep, and had been, only months before, a lady maid to the king's sister. Stunned by her beauty, Erik had plucked her from the rushes and made her his own.

"May I sit near you?" I looked at the red-covered chair next to hers, which was backed against a gilded wall.

"Oh, yes," Karin Mansdotter said, breathless, then composed herself. "I mean, assuredly." She smiled, and I smiled back at her.

"Are you afraid to sail tomorrow?" she asked. "I know I would be. Those ships are so small and the sea so vast!"

I found her forthrightness refreshing and laughed. "I am not afraid of the seas," I said, catching Philip and my sister dancing together, again, out of the corner of my eye.

"Do the English speak German or Swedish?" she asked.

"No," I answered. "But the princess has had Master Dymoke, Master Preston, and Master North teaching us the English language and customs for nigh on six years, since His Majesty decided to offer his hand to their queen."

She looked at her lap, and I chided myself for bringing up so indelicate a topic.

"I hope they have lingonberries," I said, and at that she looked up. I smiled but said nothing more, she watching the king as he made merry with the ladies of the court and I watching my sister and my fiancé entangle their hands. I wondered about the king's mistress, born low and raised high so quickly, instantly forced to adjust to a court and a manner of life utterly different from her own, and no friend to help smooth the transition. My sister Gertrude had told us that when the king first took Karin Mansdotter as a mistress, she had been engaged to someone else. The king had asked his new paramour to send for her fiancé, and when he arrived, Erik had him killed.

Within a few minutes, Philip came to collect me and lead me to dance. "I've been seeking you!" he said.

"And now I have been found," I said, cheered that he'd been looking for me. He took my hands in his own and, after we had danced for a while, led me into the long gallery next to the hall. The ceilings were painted with images of the king's father, Gustav Vasa, and victory against the Danes, with whom we still fought. Torches along the gallery lit the room, but dimly, as they were few. We sat on a long bench, softly cushioned.

"You leave on the morrow," Philip said.

"I don't have to go," I replied. "Princess Cecelia has five other maids ready to serve her on the journey and in England, and I am sure she would not miss me." That was probably untrue, but I felt I must make any attempt to reach out to Philip before I left, given what I had seen earlier.

Surprise crossed his face, and perhaps irritation, too, before he blotted it with a smile. "After these many years of English lessons?" he teased. "And it is a singular honor to serve the princess and perhaps make connections with the woman who might soon be our queen. England is also a seafaring country, and I know my father is interested in making himself known to mutual interests."

"Perhaps I can assist with that," I offered weakly. I looked up to see my sister Karin, shimmering in the candlelight, near the doorway from the hallway to the gallery. She spoke with one of our cousins. Philip glanced up at them, transfixed, and then back at me.

"There is no other reason for me to go . . . or stay?" I lightly probed. I recalled a Swedish proverb that said it was not safe to leave the kitchen while the fires were lit.

"Not at all," he replied smoothly. "And while you are gone, I will speak with my father about the . . . missing dowry portion."

I blinked. "What missing dowry portion?"

"You do not know?" he asked.

"I know nothing of this."

"Before your father took ill he had been gambling with the king and some other noblemen. I understand that he took a fair portion of your dowry money, as yet unpaid to my father, and bet it as a bid to earn a dowry for your sister Karin as well."

I shook my head, speechless and incensed. He had gambled my dowry? He would never have gambled Gertrude's or Brita's dowries. But for Karin . . . he'd lost mine.

"Your father did not pay the last quarter of your dowry before he died. My father was negotiating with him about it, but it is, as yet, unsettled, which may void our engagement. I shall see if I can speak with him about this and settle things while you are gone."

I nodded, dull. I had a partial dowry. Why had no one as yet brought this matter forward?

He took my hands in his own and kissed them. "I shall find a solution, do not worry. I already have an idea in mind."

"I hope so," I said. None of us relished a winter voyage in rough seas or the overland portion upon the ice and snow, but Princess Cecelia had insisted we go. The king, I suspect, was glad to be rid of her persistent fault finding and allowed the journey to move forward in spite of the weather. "Will you miss me?"

Philip perfunctorily kissed my hands again. "Of course!" He bowed to me before returning to the group that included my sister and my cousin. I watched them for a long while, but nothing seemed outwardly improper. Perhaps I had misunderstood the earlier situation in the closet. Or perhaps not.

A small crowd gathered at the ship the next morning as the wind spat ice. My trunk had already been loaded into the suffocating cabin that Bridget Hand and I would share for the sea portion of our journey. The Englishmen were already on board, eager, I supposed, to return to queen and country. With the exception of our princess, we Swedes were reluctant travelers.

I stood near my mother, sisters, and brothers, and a few of my young cousins. One, seven-year-old Sofia, broke away and impudently ran toward the end of the dock. Only quick thinking on the part of my brother Johann saved her from an icy journey heavenward. Princess Cecelia soon approached us, and we all curtseyed.

"Do not worry, Lady Agneta," the princess soothed. "I shall be as a mother to Elin Ulfsdotter. She shall be in my constant care, as will all of my ladies, and I will return with her safely, and soon."

My mother, still beautiful, bowed her head, a tear trembling in the corner of her eye. "Thank you, my lady."

Princess Cecelia then left us to our parting sentiments while she went to bid farewell to her own family. Her new husband, the Margrave of Baden, waited for her on board, having no Swedish family to part from.

My mother had already given me her gift earlier in the day, a golden locket necklace with a sketch of her on her wedding day, and a recent one of me, inside. Each of my sisters came to me in turn. Gertrude pressed a jar of dried lingonberries into my hand, then softly kissed my temple, as we sisters did out of affection. "Good-bye, dear sister," she said. "I shall pray for you."

Brita came next and held out a new needle for my lacework. She kissed my temple and murmured her affection before stepping aside for Karin. My head snapped up as I saw that she wore one of my gowns, a favorite of rose pink.

"You shan't need it for a few months," she said without remorse. I held my temper and my tongue in front of the others; my mother disapproved of outward displays of emotion, finding them low-bred. Karin, too, kissed my hairline and bade me a safe journey and a speedy return. I noticed, as I held her near, a faint aroma of the spiced scent of Philip's wash water. I looked at her, alarmed. She had betrayed me, she had! I did not want to leave, and yet it was too late; Princess Cecelia was motioning us all toward the ship.

It did not occur to me until later that Karin alone

had offered no gift upon my departure excepting, perhaps, a Judas kiss.

The ship wound its way through the fjords and into the open ocean. What should have been a journey of perhaps one unpleasant month turned into a nightmare of nearly ten. There was no ill weather that did not bedevil us, from ice storm to windy squall that threatened to scupper the ship nearly every week. The seas churned, gray trimmed with foamy white ribbons like an old man's beard, and most days we kept to our cabins.

When the seas were not unwelcoming, the Danes were. They proved to be the hellhounds we expected them to be, harrying us from one coast to the next and forcing us to travel over ice-sheathed land by horse-drawn sleigh to friendly noble homes before boarding ship again. If it weren't for the loyalty I knew I owed my king, I might have wondered if he'd signaled our route to distract the Danes from his brother Johan, whom he loved, in Finland.

"Why complain of cold when we are on our way to see the wonderful queen of England?" our princess cried in joy. Although I saw the irony in her warm pleasure while we numbed with frost, I was truly happy for her. For many years, since her brother Johan had visited England and returned to tell of its wonders, Cecelia had prepared herself for her own journey of diplomacy, mastering the language with only English merchants as teachers.

Within a few months it was clear that Princess Cecelia was with child, and we all gave a portion of our foodstuffs so she and the babe would not suffer. "I have to look away when she is sick over the side of the ship," Christina Abrahamsdotter confided in me. "My innards pain me for lack of food, and then I watch as my supper lurches from her stomach into the sea."

We began to run out of wood, too, with which to warm ourselves. Princess Cecelia sat shivering in a corner chair. "I need more coats!" She looked at us by turn and we reluctantly shed our warm outer clothing, and she took them one by one and layered them upon herself. From then on we ladies went about with our thinner inner garments. We often danced about in our light dresses to keep ourselves warm while the princess, now comfortable, sang English sea songs and English hymns. This did not endear any of us to royal service, but we were well trained enough to say nothing.

It was also clear that Princess Cecelia had been turning her husband away from their marital bed. Master Preston sternly warned the ship hands from even looking upon us, but he was not of a rank to speak thus to the margrave. One night the margrave appeared in my cabin as Bridget was attending to the princess.

"Hello, *schön* Elin," he said, his German tight-toothed and proper. "I have been waiting for the right time for us to become better acquainted. You are the most beautiful girl at court."

I moved away from him, steadying my feet with the constant pitching of the ship. "I think we know one another well enough already, sir."

"But I do not, Elin," he said. I could not even account his behavior to drunkenness, as he appeared to have all of his wits about him. He drew closer, and I grabbed hold of the feeble chair in the corner of our cabin to steady myself. As he advanced again, I feigned that I was losing my balance and pushed the chair in his direction, aiming a wooden leg for the part of him where he would feel the most pain.

He doubled over and cried out.

"I'm so sorry, my lord, I lost my balance," I said. But I did not draw near to help him, and my voice was not falsely contrite. He left my cabin muttering and did not return again. I smiled when I thought upon it and Bridget did, too, when I told her.

Winter warmed to spring, which then unfolded into summer. We became truly alarmed that my lady would give birth before we reached London, and there was not a married woman among us, much less a midwife. Cecelia had no such concerns. Her greatest joy was that her firstborn would be birthed in the land of the queen she'd so admired for her autonomy and freedom.

One night in late summer we were happily

informed that we were nearing Calais, from where they would send a message ahead that we were nearly to England. I sat that evening with Bridget; we had become as sisters during the journey and there was no thought too private for me to share with her.

"I should have married Philip by now," I said with regret, speaking aloud the relentless thought I'd pushed back a dozen times over the months past as I lay abed wondering what he and Karin were doing in Stockholm. "It is September. Autumn."

"Do not fret," Bridget said. Her voice did not convey the confidence of her words.

"Perhaps they will marry him to my younger sister in my stead, as Gustav Vasa did with Princess Cecelia's first fiancé," I worried.

Bridget lowered her voice. "There will be no need to marry your sister to your fiancé, because your father did not find you willingly in bed with another man, drag you out by your hair, and unman the culprit."

I agreed, and we smiled bemusedly together in the pitching cabin. The king had a coin struck with Cecelia on one side and the virginal Susanna from Holy Writ on the other, circulating the idea of his daughter's innocence every time the coin was used. I didn't know if the coin had made it to Baden, but the margrave had not hesitated to take Cecelia as his bride.

"There may be other reasons for Philip to desire to wed Karin," I said, twisting the ring on my third finger, which had grown bony during our long journey. "We have been so very long gone." *She took my gown. She took my fiancé. In truth, he desired her before we'd even left.* "And my dowry was not paid, which makes our engagement uncertain. Or void." *He's always preferred her to me. Who would not?*

" 'Tis nothing to think upon now," Bridget said sensibly. "We are far from Stockholm, and near to England. We must act upon that which is here, and we do not know what lies just ahead."

"Are you unsettled by that?" I asked her.

She, who was typically calm and self-assured, merely nodded but didn't speak. I, too, was anxious and unsettled, though I didn't understand exactly why.

We were thin and weary and our teeth hurt in our heads, but we were here; within days England beckoned on the horizon, green and gold and holding out her arms to welcome us, I hoped, like Freya, the mythological Norse goddess of beauty and love.

# TWO

September, October, and November:
Year of Our Lord 1565
Dover, England
Bedford House, London
The Palace of Whitehall, London

November: Year of Our Lord 1565
The Palace of Whitehall

A small party awaited us, splendidly dressed and accompanied by the finest horseflesh I had ever seen. I was anxious to make a good impression on the English; I hoped that they liked us and would welcome the princess as a royal sister. The princess disembarked from the ship first, all health and cheer as one might expect after her fine diet and warm clothing. She and the margrave were shown the honor and welcome befitting their royal status. We ladies stood to the side so as to give the princess precedence, but it soon became clear that something was amiss.

Christina Abrahamsdotter moved forward and then came back to tell Bridget and me, "A bee is harrying the princess."

The princess was deathly afraid of bees, having been stung by a small swarm of them as a child. Her husband must not have known this, as he stood to the side looking chagrined. The princess continued to bat the air around her and cry out in a most undignified manner. *"Hilfe!"* she shouted, her belly making it hard for her to move away. "Help!" she tried in English.

Perhaps the Englishmen were unaware of the bee and simply saw her batting the air. Perhaps her brother Erik's reputation as an unbalanced man had preceded her. But they stood still, which I thought very unchivalrous indeed for a country that prided itself otherwise.

I stepped forward impatiently, stood next to my lady, and when the bee hovered close, I clasped both hands around it. The margrave hurried his wife away just as the bee slipped its needle deep into the soft flesh of my palm. I said nothing, but grimaced. The other ladies ran to help Cecelia, as was proper. I unclasped my hand and let the bee fall away while my hand swelled in anger.

As I turned I noticed a tall, elegant man standing next to me. By his dress, his manners, and his silver-marked horse, he was clearly the highest-ranked gentleman present.

"Marquess of Northampton, my lady," he said, bowing. He offered his arm, which I took with pleasure, drew me near, and to the astonishment of both English and Swedes, escorted me to the litters that awaited. Perhaps chivalry yet lived among the English.

"Elin Ulfsdotter," I said, using my Swedish

patronym first, as a good daughter would. "Lady Elin von Snakenborg," I concluded, because my heritage was noble and I was proud of that, too.

He held my gaze, not overlong, but much longer than with any of the other ladies in waiting to whom he was introduced, and I blushed. Bridget smiled at me behind his back and, though weary from the journey, I felt it was a bright spot and a warm welcome and I smiled at her, and at him.

The Marquess of Northampton, or Lord Northampton, was not only the highest-ranking man in our welcoming party but one of the highest-ranking men in all of England. Princess Cecelia soon found this out and made it her business to be most attentive to him as he journeyed with us to Bedford House in London, where we would stay. The queen had sent some of her own hangings and tapestry for our warmth and pleasure, and they were rich indeed. I enjoyed needlework and marveled at the tiny stitches that joined so tightly as to almost be painted.

"Are you well?" A warm woman with a long brown gown came to me and made inquiries.

"Yes, my lady," I said.

"Call upon me, Lady Sussex, or my husband, Lord Thomas, if you or the princess should need anything," she said. I dipped a short curtsey and thanked her for her kindness. Aside from Lady Sussex, none of the other women had spoken to us at all, and when they did, they used loud, slow

27

voices, though we assured them we understood English. It was disheartening, as we had come to offer warm friendship but found cool acceptance and reserve except for the Sussexes and our hosts, Lord and Lady Bedford. Within days, the queen herself came, from the Palace of Whitehall, one of her many royal residences.

Princess Cecelia had dressed for the occasion in a black velvet robe with a mantle of black and silver; a costly gold crown graced her blonde head. She looked magnificent. We ladies wore crimson taffeta that shone in the candlelight and rustled quietly as we walked. Although she was regal, our princess had not been trained by my mother and therefore was not given to with-holding her emotions. As Queen Elizabeth approached, Cecelia reached forward, full body notwithstanding, and gave her a long embrace. The queen seemed genuinely moved by it and indicated by word and motion that they should retire to Cecelia's receiving chamber.

I stood close enough to attend my lady when she required, but not near enough to overhear their conversation, which left me able to observe. The queen was splendid beyond what anyone had imagined—she smiled often, and when she did, there were tiny wrinkles upon the corners of her black eyes, like the splaying of a fine paintbrush. Her skin was poured silver—no, rather moonlight, because it was ethereal. And yet there was no question of the power that rested completely in her hands, sheathed by pretty gloves. At age thirty-two she was nearly thirteen years older than I, and seven years Princess Cecelia's senior, but looked no older than Cecelia whatsoever.

We were all taken with the queen, with the exception, perhaps, of the margrave; he had noticeably slipped away. He'd once been proposed as a suitor for Queen Elizabeth. I wondered, at this rich court, if he felt that he'd settled for less than he should have.

"Do you find your quarters comfortable, Lady Elin?" A voice came up from behind me, and I saw that it was the marquess. His hair was silver but carefully groomed. He smelled faintly of pine; perhaps he scented his wash water with marjoram. All Swedish ladies learned to work with herbs so 'twas easy for me to recognize.

"Very, Lord Northampton," I said, comfortable and safe in his presence, honored to have been singled out by him. "Lord Bedford and his wife have made us exceedingly welcome, and I know my mistress is overjoyed to meet yours after these many years."

"The queen shared how pleased she is to have Princess Cecelia, and her entire retinue, here," Lord Northampton said. "Come, will you accompany me at a walk in the garden? The countess has an exceptionally lovely autumn display."

I looked at my mistress, who nodded her

permission, and I gladly slipped away. As I did, I noticed Bridget smiling in my direction, but the other ladies in waiting, and quite a few of the English ladies, frowned. I tucked my hand into Lord Northampton's proffered elbow and tried to ignore them. As we walked through the gardens, I asked him how long he had known the queen.

"Nearly all her life," he said. "My sister Kateryn was the sixth and final wife of Her Majesty's father, King Henry, whom I also served." I tried to hide a smile, but Lord Northampton caught it and smiled with me. "I see that you know of our king," he said.

"Somewhat," I answered with a teasing smile. I wasn't going to cast the first stone on behalf of Sweden's royal family, with its own checkered past.

"I next served the queen's brother Edward, when he was king, as Lord Chamberlain and Master of the Hawks. When the queen's sister, Mary, took the throne, my wife and I were convicted of treason. I was imprisoned in the Tower and sentenced to death, though, as you see, the order was not carried out."

I laughed. "And it's a good thing that it was not. Please, continue!"

"Soon came the glorious day Her Majesty became queen. She was returning from the Tower of London when she spied my pitiable self locked up behind one small window. She stopped her palfrey, called out to me, and asked after my health. Her Grace had been especially close to my sister Kateryn and remembered that, and me, when she came into her power. She freed me and restored my titles, to my everlasting thanks and gratitude."

I smiled, and a cool autumn breeze rustled through the trees, coaxing some of their burlap cupules to the ground. It reminded me, with a pang, of my home, where beech grew freely. "I find it difficult to believe that you were ever pitiable. And what of your wife, Lord Northampton?" I asked. "Was she pardoned, too?"

"Oh, yes," he answered. "She was a great friend of the Queen's Majesty as well. Sadly, she died April past after a long illness."

"I'm sorry," I said. He seemed like a good man who had sorrow etched on his handsome face, and I felt moved with the desire to lift his countenance if I could.

"And so am I," he answered. "But that is not talk for a comely lady on a beautiful day. Tell me of Sweden. Is it wild? Are there yet Danes harrying every port?" he teased.

"Indeed there are," I replied. "They are a pestilence."

At that he laughed, as I'd intended, which pleased me, and said the English cared little for Danes as well. We sat in the garden and talked of Sweden and of my family, and I spoke to him in

French as well, which I had also been tutored in, as our king and his brother Duke Johan had had French tutors along with Latin.

As darkness fell he indicated to me that we should return to the house, as Princess Cecelia would be wondering after me. "I should like to teach you Italian sometime," he said. "If you'd like."

"I'd like that very much," I said, thinking that this was my first happy day in well over a year. "If I see you again."

"You shall," he said. "I can promise you that."

The very next day the princess began her pains; we ladies rushed to assist, and I prepared a mixture of lady's bedstraw and applied it to a linen. I held it next to her nose, and as she breathed in, her pain became more tolerable and she quieted enough to calmly deliver of a son, Edward Fortunatus. The name Edward had been chosen for Queen Elizabeth's brother, the former king, and Fortunatus because he had made it safely through many perils on the journey to England. My duty done, I stood back, pleased, but noted with confusion the querying look the English midwife directed toward me. Was she upset that I had stepped in to help my lady? Surely that was my place. Feeling awkward, I withdrew to my own room.

The queen herself stood as godmother some

days later when young Edward was baptized at the Royal Chapel at the Palace of Whitehall. Queen Elizabeth had spared no expense for the child of her Swedish "sister." The Archbishop of Canterbury, Matthew Parker, blessed the font before the child was brought in by our Bridget. She handed the babe to Lady Margaret Howard, who stood in front of the Earl of Leicester, the queen's favorite, and the Earl of Sussex, an especially trusted friend of Her Majesty but sworn enemy of Leicester. My Lord Northampton held the towel with which to dry the babe.

"Why the pelicans?" I asked him after the ceremony, nodding to the many fine linens upon which were stitched those delicate birds.

"A pelican is the symbol of self-sacrifice," he said. "When there is no other food available, she will reach down and with her beak wound her own breast to supply blood for her children to sup on. This is a figure of our Lord and His passion. And also of our queen, who readily sacrifices herself for her realm, England."

"I learn something new from you each day!" I teased, but it pleased me, the interest he took in me, and I wanted to offer a return. "So now I shall have to try to teach something to you as well."

I tried to teach him a few words of Swedish, but he could not readily grasp them and, after a moment or two, lost interest, though he was gracious about it. I suspected he found our language guttural. We reverted to smooth French, which was comfortable for both of us, or in the main, English.

That evening, Anne Russell, in whose home we stayed, came to visit with me. We'd become quick friends, and I enjoyed her wit and kindness. So I found it odd, then, when she approached me with hesitation and perhaps a little fear. "The Englishwomen, we're wondering—what did you give to Princess Cecelia that quelled her birth pangs so readily? I told them I would ask you and share the secret."

"Lady's bedstraw," I said. "Mixed with some other herbs from the north."

She remained quiet for a moment before shaking her head, and laughed, but uneasily. "Those strange northern herbs seem to have worked . . . wondrously!"

I reached out and squeezed her hand; she was to be married very soon and I suspected that was the seat of her curiosity. "I shall readily assist you when it's your turn to bear a child if we have not yet returned to Sweden!"

She smiled, but I noted that she did not say she would be happy to have me do so. I sighed a little and wondered if we'd make any friends here at all before we returned home.

Some days later, as my lady was recovering from childbirth, Lord Northampton asked if he might take Bridget and myself to show us his estates in London. "You may," the princess said, waving her small hand in the air. "But I have sworn to be their mother on this journey, and I'll expect you to care for them thusly."

"I shall," Lord Northampton replied with an easy grace. "The Queen's Majesty would have it no other way." He brought around a fine litter with foot warmers and furs, and Bridget and I spent a glorious day at his large estate, waited upon by a dozen servants, eating pheasant and other delicacies as Lord Northampton spoke warmly of England. We passed the hours in charming, pleasant companionship and conversation, and I was sorry to leave his happy home.

That night, in our chamber, Bridget asked me, "Is Lord Northampton wooing you?"

"I do not know," I said. And then after a minute, I said, "Perhaps. He says I favor his late wife. But he is kind and attentive to me for my own sake, too, I know that as well."

"What about Philip?" she asked me.

"I do not know," I said, not wishing to think upon it. For all I knew, he was cozily partnered with my sister. "If things progress, I shall ask our lady what I must do."

"Do you care for him?" she asked.

"Philip or Lord Northampton?"

"Either . . . both," she responded.

"Yes," I said. "Yes, I do." I rolled onto my side

to forestall further questions, even from my dearest friend, so I could think, and pray, about what I must do.

Some weeks later, the margrave and Princess Cecelia held a large, lavish banquet to celebrate the birth of Edward Fortunatus. After the rich meal of nearly one hundred courses, a masked herald arrived in the hall, and as the room hushed, he trumpeted three times and then spoke up. "A messenger has late arrived with tidings from a strange country, with greetings and an invitation for Her Majesty Queen Elizabeth and the Honorable Princess Cecelia of Sweden."

The crowd began to clap and all seemed delighted with perhaps the exception of the margrave, who had not, noticeably, been included in the greeting.

A second man strode into the room attired in heavy boots and spurs and knelt before the queen. "In honor of the marriage, next month, of the Earl of Warwick and the Lady Anne Russell, four foreign knights challenge any comers of Your Majesty's kingdom. Shall this challenge be met?"

A great ripple of laughter, shouts, and cheers went up. Lord Robert Dudley, the Earl of Leicester, called out, "I shall meet these strange comers. Who rides with me?" Many men stood to meet the challenge. Lord Northampton cheered and clapped with the rest of them, but he did not offer to joust.

The queen raised a hand and instantly the room grew quiet. "We heartily thank you, Master Herald, Master Messenger, and we shall be most pleased to look upon these strange knights and the defenders of our realm," she said. "And we are most pleased to attend the wedding of our dear friend Lord Ambrose and his betrothed, Lady Anne." She turned to Princess Cecelia. "If that seems right to you, too, my good sister?"

Cecelia nodded and smiled, and then the room burst into cheers again and music echoed throughout the hall. I was instantly chosen to dance, as were Cecelia's other maids of honor, which pleased us all and brought happy, high color. The night was joyous and festive, and I admit I enjoyed not only the playacting and playfulness of the queen's court but the pleasant manner of the queen herself.

After some time I noticed Lord Northampton approach Princess Cecelia. I didn't have to wait long to find out why. She called me into her chamber, alone, the next morning. "Elin," she said, "sit with me." She indicated a plush low stool near her feet. "Lord Northampton, the Marquess of Northampton, approached me last eve," she said. "He said he had fallen in love with one of my ladies. I asked of whom he spoke, though I could but guess. He spoke of you and wished to know if he had any hope of winning your hand."

"But . . . I am engaged, my lady," I said, vexed. Even if Philip did not love or desire me, I understood that there had been some arrangement that I could not set aside without permission or a refutation on his part. "To Philip Bonde."

She raised an eyebrow. "Are you, indeed?"

"Am I not?" I asked wonderingly. Did she know about the partial dowry, and had it canceled our engagement? Or had news reached her regarding Philip and my sister Karin? Would I want to stay here in England after the others returned home? Worse, perhaps, would be to return home with no dowry and my fiancé in love with my sister.

The margrave came in then, and the princess dismissed me. I would have to wait until she raised the matter again.

It has been said that every wedding puts a woman in mind of her own nuptials, whether or not they have yet to transpire; therefore we ladies were a happy gaggle. Bedford House was the Russell family home, and we Swedes were particularly fond of the bride. She was of an age with most of us and, in fact, shared my exact day of birth and had her apartments across the hall from Bridget and me. So I felt closer to her, perhaps, than to the other Englishwomen. And of course William's request to Princess Cecelia for my hand was much on my mind.

One afternoon I helped Anne Russell stitch a rip in her train and asked, "Are you happy to be marrying Lord Ambrose?"

She nodded. "Yes, of course, he's very kind."

"Do you . . . do you mind very much that he has been married before?"

She didn't rebuke me for my impertinence. I think she knew I was airing my concerns about my own potential situation with Lord Northampton.

"No. I believe he loves me, as he loved the others."

I smiled at her and she smiled back, warmly. In spite of her odd and somewhat unresolved comments regarding the lady's bedstraw and other herbs, she continued to kindly befriend me. In that, she was alone among the Englishwomen.

Later, we gathered at the Queen's Great Closet for the wedding of Lady Anne, whom her new husband had nicknamed Amys, to Ambrose Dudley, Earl of Warwick, twenty years her senior. We ladies thought it romantic that her husband had a special name for her, and I hoped, for myself, that my own husband would lovingly do likewise. Lady Anne wore a kirtle of silver mixed with blue and a gown of purple embroidered with silver. Upon her fair hair she bore a golden caul, and her train was borne by little Catherine Knollys.

Lord Northampton invited me and my friend Christina Abrahamsdotter to be his guests at his banqueting table, and we gladly agreed. I noted that he was served more quickly, more attentively, and with better dishes than the other guests. His benches were also cushioned. There were some long looks toward me from the others at the table, but soon enough talk reverted to the events of the day, and the week ahead.

"Do you celebrate weddings in Sweden with banquets and jousting?" one woman asked politely.

"We do banquet often," I replied. "Vadstena Castle has a beautiful and ornate galley called the Wedding Hall. But we hunt and hawk perhaps more than joust."

"Which is a pity," Christina said, "as your knights in their armor are compelling to look upon."

The others at the table laughed and began to speak of other tournaments they had witnessed, arguing the valor of one man over another. I smiled at Christina's sentiments, heartily agreeing; the jousters were strong and fine-looking, and cast an air of manliness, but I said nothing. Lord Northampton's gout prevented him from jousting.

"You speak English well," a young man sitting next to me said. "With a pretty accent."

"Thank you," I said. "*Danke*, or *tack*—thank you in German and Swedish, too," I said with a wink.

He grinned and struck me up in another conversation, but soon enough Lord Northampton stood behind my chair. "Would you and Lady Christina like to see the Royal Library?"

"Oh, yes," I said, and Princess Cecelia nodded her assent. We followed Lord Northampton from the banqueting hall through a long gallery and up a sweep of stairs. At the top of the stairs the gallery led either left or right. We took the right, and as we did, I caught sight of a couple out of the corner of my eye. The man, splendid in purple, was the queen's handsome favorite and her lifelong love, the Earl of Leicester, also known as Robert Dudley, whom I recognized from the christening.

What would it be like to have a lifelong love? Highborn women did not expect to marry for love, but one had only to read Greek or Roman mythology, or attend a masque or performance at court, to know we all wished we could.

Lord Robert was accompanied by a heavily pregnant, beautiful woman perhaps ten years younger than Her Majesty and looking remarkably like her. It was a tribute to the power of her charm, I supposed, that even while so pregnant she seemed able to enchant Lord Robert.

"Who was that?" I asked Lord Northampton as he led to the library.

"Lord Robert Dudley, Earl of Leicester," he answered.

"Nay, the lady . . . accompanying . . . him."

"Lady Lettice Devereux," he answered gruffly. "Sister to the little girl who bore the bride's train this morn. Cousin to the queen."

Two days later we were seated at tournament to watch the jousting. Princess Cecelia sat with the queen, of course, her husband the margrave beside her. The margrave was splendidly dressed in new garments, as was Princess Cecelia, and they had been handing out lavish gifts to our new English friends, which was worrisome and the focus of much discussion among us ladies. The journey had taken many months more than we had anticipated, and gifts and remunerations had to have been paid along the way. I wondered that King Erik had funded his sister so lavishly, especially since any and all talk of a potential marriage between the king and England's queen had come to naught since our arrival and the idea, for the most part, had quietly died. If she spent all of our money, how would we get home?

Lord Northampton asked me to sit with him, and after ascertaining that this was all right with Princess Cecelia, I happily agreed. There was no need for a chaperone, as we were among all the others, so Lord Northampton did not invite anyone else to accompany us to his viewing area, which was very close to the action. I could have reached out and touched the jousters as they kicked up dust in the arena.

"Some weeks ago I spoke with your princess about my affections for you."

"Indeed, she mentioned that to me, Lord Northampton."

"Please, call me William," he said, smiling. His smile, as always, put me at ease.

"William," I said. "But then you must call me Elin."

"I had told her that I found you beautiful, Elin, a delightful, rare flower. I had wondered if there was any hope of your remaining in England and, perhaps, marrying me."

"What was her answer?" I, of course, already knew, as she had told me, but I wanted to let him speak for himself on this delicate matter.

"She said there was an engagement in Sweden that she believes was set aside due to the lack of a dowry, and that she was to act as your mother while in England. She would also send a letter to your mother with some of Geoffrey Preston's merchant friends. In the meantime, dear Elin, I should like to know your mind on this matter."

Princess Cecelia knew about the dowry problem and assumed that it had canceled my engagement—or perhaps she knew that it had already been canceled, and I was the only one who hadn't been told for certain.

I was angry and yet . . . I knew now that I did not

truly love Philip, and I would never be able to trust him. But if we were legally betrothed, then there was no more to be discussed. William made me laugh, he clearly adored me, we had rousing discussions, and while he knew more than I in every matter, he never made me feel lesser for it. I felt good with him. I felt safe. I was truly fond of him even if there was not the passion found, perhaps solely, in poetry.

"I am honored that you would wish to take me as a wife." I took his hand, which seemed to please him, thrilled that he'd concerned himself with my opinion. "I find great pleasure in your company and enjoy our times together very much," I said. "Perhaps I may think upon it while we wait to hear from my mother."

"Of course," he said. "Of course you must. I would provide everything you need, should you agree, of course. Maids of honor and servants and lady maids of your own, fine houses and your clothing and jewels. No woman will ever be more treasured than you, Elin."

"I know your character, William," I said. "I feel treasured by you already." And I did. I had never felt so valued by a man.

He placed his hand over mine and I allowed it to rest there. I prayed silently for a quick response from my mother; the Danes sometimes let through the English ships, so a letter and response might be forthcoming.

44

Once the challengers rode into the tiltyard, my mind set aside thoughts of marriage and letters and focused on the match. The horses twitched with energy, stamping at each end of the arena, and though the men were wrapped in metal I could sense their readiness to battle. I watched and cheered as much as the next person. Lord Robert rode for the queen's favor; the gossip was that there had been a loud and public quarrel between Lord Robert and Her Majesty after the queen had seen him close together with Lettice Devereux. I had difficulty believing that, as the queen seemed so calm and dignified. And today, when she smiled upon him, it was certainly with the look of a woman deeply in love. I looked but did not see Lady Devereux among those watching. I wished that one day a man would ride for my favor, but then I looked at William, so kind, intelligent, and caring, and thought perhaps that didn't matter so much after all.

After the contests were complete and the crowds began to thin, William led me out toward the litters returning to Bedford House and then stopped to talk with someone while I proceeded on. As I reached the end of the tiltyard, one of the comers lifted off his helmet and then turned and looked straight at me. His longish blond hair was pulled back in a queue and he had a smear of blood on his cheekbone. His blue eyes held mine. I was taken aback by his strength and his frank interest. "Thomas Gorges," he said before bowing to me, metal clanking.

His words startled me out of my reverie, and I nodded. "Lady Elin von Snakenborg."

"Are you new to court?" he asked.

"Yes." I nodded. "I've come with Princess Cecelia from Sweden." At that, I felt a presence beside me. William looked at Thomas for just a moment and then put his hand behind my back to guide me on. Thomas bowed his head toward me and turned to leave.

"I know Her Majesty enjoys the tiltyard, but it can be a bloody and, perhaps, unrefined sport," William said as we walked. "I shall take you hawking."

Later that night, in our chamber, Bridget and I discussed the day's events. "William spoke to me himself of marriage," I said, shrugging into my sleeping gown.

"William? Not Lord Northampton?" she teased, already snug under a thick coverlet.

"Yes, William," I said with a soft laugh. "Princess Cecelia has written to my mother to ask her permission. Since things are unsettled, or perhaps void, with Philip . . ." I let the sentence dangle. In spite of his ill treatment of me, I did not want to dishonor him.

"Has Cecelia truly written to her?" Bridget asked.

I stopped brushing my hair and turned toward her. "What do you mean?"

"If you were to marry the marquess, you would be nearly as highly ranked as she. I suspect she would like that not at all. Perhaps one way to forestall that is to lack the agreement of your family."

I found that unsettling for a moment, but then simply refused to believe that the princess would do ill by me. She had promised to care for me as a mother would. Hadn't she?

# THREE

Winter: Year of Our Lord 1566
The Palace of Whitehall
Bedford House, London

Spring: Year of Our Lord 1566
The Palace of Whitehall
Parr's Estates, London

The Queen's Majesty was keen to hunt all winter long. In preparation for my first hunting party with her, William invited me to his estate and the mews wherein he kept his hawks and falcons.

"I don't sew their eyes shut," he said as we strode down the center of the long building. I found it to be a mark of his gentleness. "I have hoods made for them instead, to quiet them until the hunt." He showed me one of the tiny caps, fitted to his thumb, stitched delicately in red leather. He called twice, and a large brown hawk came and landed on his outstretched wrist. It nodded and bobbed its head before looking at me, unblinking.

Not to be outdone, I took a lure and boldly called, too. To William's pleasure, a young red falcon swooped down and landed on my gloved wrist.

"I've never seen them come for anyone but me!" he exclaimed. I laughed lightly, delighted to have pleased him. I visited the mews with him several times after that before riding out with the queen and her party some weeks before Christmas.

"Are you certain I may take your leave?" I asked Princess Cecelia.

"Indeed," she said. "The tailors and seam-stresses are coming this afternoon to measure me for new gowns, and I have plenty of *attentive* ladies should I require assistance." She waved me away without another word or look in my direction.

I pondered that for a moment. Was she irritated at not having been invited? I didn't believe so, as she did not care to hunt.

We left from the Palace of Whitehall on the queen's horses, of which Lord Robert was master; he rode at the head of the party with the queen. I had never ridden so magnificent an animal, and at first it sensed my hesitance and tried to get the better of me. Everyone was mounting their beasts, and I grew aware of the eyes upon me as I struggled to get my horse under control. A combination of sharp spur and soft word given at the same time made her understand that I was her mistress and she settled obediently. As I watched the queen interact with her courtiers, I saw that she employed the same method with them.

The queen, of course, had the finest hawks, and one flew from her wrist to take in a quarry nearly twice its size. It brought the bird down; afterward, the queen rewarded the hawk with a small bit of raw pigeon flesh. Others flew their hawks one by one, and William's birds appeared to be the best trained. I knew he took great pride in that. Soon enough we approached the clearing where the queen's men had set up a tent for our midday supper.

I sat near William, and then came a tall, boorish man with a loud voice. "Lady Elin, you've hawked before, I see."

"Yes, Sir—"

"His Grace the Duke of Norfolk," he corrected me.

"Yes, Your Grace. I have."

He tried to cow me with his considerable bearing, but I held my back firm against his wind.

"Northampton is quite a master of falcons," he said. "He's told us that the best birds come from Norway."

At that several men in the crowd guffawed, and the ladies politely looked down. I had no idea what the intent was, but clearly *bird* had more than one meaning to the English, and the one he intended was impolite. William opened his mouth to speak, perhaps in my defense, but the queen silenced him with a slight lift of her leather-gloved hand. I was not about to let this highborn but ill-mannered man best me.

"I'm uncertain of that, Your Grace, as I am from Sweden and not from Norway. However, my noble mother is descended from King Haakon of Norway, so perhaps I can write to her and ask if she knows." I continued sweetly, "I could also inquire as to whether some Norwegian birds could be sent to England for your pleasure."

At that the men who had laughed at me roared at Norfolk. I held my head and gaze steady, though I felt my neck tremble with tension and a bead of sweat slipped down it. The queen clapped her hands in pleasure and called to me, "Lady von Snakenborg, come and sit by us."

She ate lightly and had finished her small portion; she pressed me to take some of the marchpane she was savoring off a small gold plate. I took one and thanked her profusely before eating of it. I couldn't hide my astonishment and pleasure as it fairly melted on my tongue.

She laughed. "We trust you find our English confectionaries to your pleasure?"

"Indeed, Your Majesty, indeed I do!"

"We watched you handle Northampton's falcons today. You have a fine hand for the birds. We enjoy birds, too, especially birdsong. We keep cages of them in each of our palaces to enjoy their sweet music throughout the day."

"I am sure they are happy to sing for so fine a

queen in so fine a place," I said. "I know I would be!" After I said it, I wished it back, because it sounded so young and ill timed.

But the queen laughed. "We should be glad to have your song in our court, my lady," she said. "And at Northampton's estates, too." Her eyes twinkled at me. She knew! But of course she knew.

When I returned to Bedford House that evening, there was a letter for me. "Geoffrey Preston brought this," Bridget said.

"Did he have any mail for the princess?" I asked.

"He didn't tell me," she said. "But I did not see him stop to speak with her."

My hand shook as I clumsily opened the letter. It was not from my mother but from my sister Gertrude instead. After sharing some tales of her family and news of the court, she drew her letter to a point. I read it aloud to Bridget.

" 'And now, dear sister, I must share ill tidings. Our sister Karin has somehow grown close to Philip Bonde in your absence.' " I took a deep breath before forcing myself to continue. " 'They are scarce apart from one another when at court . . . or away. Karin denies it, but I have heard of Philip's request that his father transfer the dowry portion already paid to marry Karin in your stead. Our lady mother believes none of it, of course, ready to defend your honor and arrangement. You must hurry home.' "

I folded the letter and smoothed it over and over again with my hand until Bridget put her hand upon mine to stop it. "What shall you do?" she asked.

"I know not," I said. As I lay there quietly, a passage of Holy Writ returned to my mind.

> For I know the thoughts that I think toward you, saith the Lord, thoughts of peace, and not of evil, to give you an expected end. Then shall ye call upon me, and ye shall go and pray unto me, and I will hearken unto you.

*Hearken unto me, Lord,* thought Elin. *Please hearken unto me.*

I lay awake that night, praying and thinking, and I confess, it pained me some that I was not worth three-quarters of a dowry, but Karin was, if indeed my father had lost the dowry portion at all. But did I want to marry a man who was in love with another? And with my sister at that?

Then the answer came to me: I was worth marrying to a gentle, highborn man who, unbelievably, was demanding no dowry at all. Instead, he promised a house full of servants, a comfortable, honest life. He was an honorable man who treasured me. And here in England was a queen, I could admit in my heart if not aloud, worthy of devoted service. In the morning, I wrote to William and told him that I would be delighted and honored to marry him if my princess would give her permission in my mother's stead. I sent the note with a messenger and awaited his reply.

Within hours, I could hear someone arrive at Bedford House. "Look and see who it is!" I told Bridget.

She peered out of our courtyard-facing window and nodded. "Yes! It's Lord Northampton!"

Fifteen minutes later, Christina Abrahamsdotter knocked on our chamber door. We opened it and quickly let her in. "He's speaking to the princess about you," she whispered.

"And?" I asked, clasping my hands in anticipation.

"At first the princess refused to give permission for your hand. She said she was commissioned to act as your mother, but she did not know if she could do without your service on the journey back to Sweden."

"And his response?"

"He offered to pay fifteen hundred pounds of her debts. And she agreed!"

Heat rushed to my cheeks. I was to be married!

Bridget held herself steady, however. "The princess has that many debts?" she asked.

"And more," Christina said. "I've heard her speaking with the margrave. He's to slip out of England soon, to Germany, escaping his English debtors and finding a way for us to return home."

Both Bridget and I were shocked at that. Fifteen hundred pounds was an unimaginable amount of money, and I did not want the payment of the princess's debts to be the manner in which I started married life. William would have to pay a dowry, of sorts, rather than receive one. But I quickly moved to thinking of my wedding, and what I should tell my mother, and if she would receive a letter if it were quickly sent.

I sent that letter off to Sweden, telling my mother that I would be married here, begging for her approval, and steeling myself to tell her that I was giving my blessing to Philip and Karin should they choose to marry. I was to remain in England! I would become an Englishwoman. The thought terrified me, and thrilled me, and I tried not to think upon the fact that I may never see my mother or sisters again but rather that I would be the beloved wife of a marquess and would make my way, somehow, at the Queen of England's court. William could not have been more kind. He was attentive and presented an expensive necklace and a new gown to me as New Year's gifts. I made a fine ruff for him and did the lacework on a delicate pair of gloves for the queen.

One of the queen's men arrived at Bedford House with a New Year's gift for me from Her Majesty.

"For me?" I said. "Are you certain?" I hadn't

attended the New Year's ceremonies, as the princess had pled illness.

"Yes, my lady," he said. "I'm certain." He unloaded the gift from the cart and brought it into the great hall, where he took the satin sheet off it with a flourish. It was a gilded cage with a pair of lovely songbirds.

The other Swedish girls tittered politely behind their hands while I stuttered out my thanks. After the queen's man left, we all let free our laughter. They knew, though the English didn't, that I cared not at all for songbirds. I hadn't, of course, informed the queen, who'd assumed I shared her love of them.

"These you must care for, no matter what," Bridget said.

"Indeed, I understand that," I said. "I shall write to Her Majesty immediately, offering profuse thanks." I took the cage to our room, held at arm's length. Songbirds. *Milde makter.*

To my utter dismay, Princess Cecelia had rather another kind of gift in mind for me, and it was an unwelcome surprise of a much stronger sort. She called me to her chamber one morning in March after the margrave had fled for the Continent.

"I have changed my mind," she said.

"About what, my lady?" I asked.

"About your marrying Northampton. I'm revoking my permission. You will return home to Sweden with us."

I hid my anger and feigned willing obedience as I sank to my knees on a cushion before her. "Madam? Surely you cannot mean that. I have already written of this to my mother and given my blessing for my sister Karin to marry my, er, former fiancé, Philip Bonde. I have given Lord Northampton my answer, my word. As have you," I dared to point out. Of course, I said nothing about the £1500 debt as I did not desire to be slapped.

"The Lord Northampton may be a marquess, but I am a princess, and I shall write to the queen. Shall you act as my secretary, as I have been deprived of my own?"

"Indeed, I shall, if you wish it," I said, though I could scarce keep my wits about me with this news. With one half of my mind I was thinking how to untangle the knot in this delicate thread and with the other I was putting to paper the words she spoke.

We do not doubt, most gracious and powerful Queen, that you remember how we once complained to your Majesty of wrongs done to us by certain of your subjects, who until now have gone unpunished, which fact has caused us great grief of mind. This grief has been further increased today by a great wrong done to us by Ephippiarus, who, not satisfied with any of the reasonable terms which the other creditors have accepted, has arrested and detained our Secretary, and has spread a false report about us through the whole city, that we are planning a secret departure from here. . . .

May it please your Majesty graciously to call to mind our love toward you, and that we came into this kingdom for no other reason than to declare the same. Therefore we do not doubt that your Majesty will equally reciprocate our love and ward off from us every harm, and kindly restore to us our Secretary out of arrest; and this kindness we will labor to deserve by our love toward you, whatever injuries we may receive.

"There now, quickly seal it and hand it to a court messenger," the princess said. I did as I was bade, but I knew there were mistruths therein and it disgusted me. It was indeed true that the princess was planning a quiet escape; the margrave had cut his beard and disguised himself to reenter the city with plans for the Swedish party to meet him at Dover, where he would have a ship from the Continent waiting. Christina Abrahamsdotter had told us that not only the jewelers and the tailor but the butcher, the poulterer, the grocer, the baker, the butter man, the fishmonger, the brewer, and the grocer had all petitioned the Queen's Privy Counsel for overdue payments. The margrave had also fallen in with some unsavory persons to whom he owed great gambling debts.

That night William came to call for me and conveyed Bridget and myself to his manor to dine. One of his friends took Bridget from hall to hall to show her some of the statuary while William spoke with me privately. "You do know that Princess Cecelia would like to revoke her permission for our marriage."

I nodded. "I do. I'm distraught about it. I wish to remain here, and to become your wife."

"Must you do as she insists?" he asked.

"I have had no word from my mother. I shall write her again tonight and tell her of my affection for you and my desire to remain. But the princess is likely to sail before I hear back."

"I shall write to your mother, too, to reassure her of my protection and care, and enclose my letter with yours," he said. "In the meantime, perhaps you could speak with the queen?"

"She would be interested in so mean a matter?" Hope rose within me. I had already begun to imagine a sweet and meaningful life with William.

"'Tis not a mean matter to me," he said with deep emotion, taking my hands in his own. "And therefore it is not to her, friend that she is."

A messenger came from court the very next day. Princess Cecelia was vexed when it was not the expected letter returning her secretary and promising to pay all her debts, but rather a summons for me to appear before the queen. "Go, then," she barked at me.

I did not take her bitterness to heart. I knew she was greatly disappointed that the queen she had nearly worshipped for many years would not come to her royal defense. As for me, I sided with the queen. Silently.

When I arrived at Whitehall, the queen was in her receiving chamber with a few of her women. I clamped my jaw to stop my teeth chattering and willed my knees firm under my rich, gold-stamped gown, thanking my mother, in my heart, for the gift of it before I'd left Sweden, and asking the Lord Jesus to help me be strong and courageous.

"Lady Knollys, please inquire after the mending of the blue gown we wish to wear this evening," she said to a woman who smiled back at her intimately and warmly. Lady Knollys was a softer, gentler version of her daughter Lettice, whom I'd seen in the hallway with Lord Robert. When Lady Knollys departed, the queen and I were left alone, with the exception of a page or two on the fringes of the room and a maid of honor silently sewing.

"We understand that your princess is shortly to return to Sweden," she began after she bade me rise from kneeling.

"Yes, Majesty." I neither confirmed nor denied, simply acknowledged the queen.

"She has extended her permission for you to marry Northampton?"

I nodded, then apologetically explained, "She extended permission, then withdrew it, Your Grace."

"And what is your mind upon this matter?"

"I wish to stay and marry Lord Northampton," I said, fervently hoping she could assist us. "And I believe that my mother would wish it so as well, as she desires happiness and contentment for all of her children." Even Karin, I supposed.

The queen nodded and thought for a moment. "We like you well, Lady von Snakenborg. You have a quick wit and will be a charming ornament to our court. You may stay at our leave, if you wish, and serve as one of my maids of honor until such time as Northampton takes you as his wife."

I crumpled to my knees again. "Oh, thank you, Majesty, thank you. You shall never find a more dedicated lady. I should forgo eat and drink if that was your wish!"

She laughed at that. "We have been accused of eating lightly, but we do not starve our ladies," she said. "We heard that, while at Dover, you suffered an injury while protecting your princess. From that, we know you understand what it means to wait upon a royal mistress."

"I should not only clasp a bee for you, Majesty, but would walk into the very den of lions ahead of you and shut their mouths on your behalf should no angel appear to do so!"

She laughed again and waved her hand. "I doubt you not, mistress. But remember that promise, for someday that very well might be required of you."

I deeply curtseyed again and backed from the room, then ran into William's arms. He'd been waiting nearby. "I stay!"

He reached his arm around me and kissed me, lightly, which was welcome and lovely and I kissed him back of my own accord for the first time.

I waited until morning to approach Princess Cecelia. There were agents at Bedford House carrying off items that might be sold to partially pay for the margrave's debts; it was humiliating, and most Swedes kept quietly to their chambers, packing for the journey home.

"I have spoken with the queen, at her command, and she has offered me a position with her ladies until I can soon marry Lord Northampton," I said. "If you will allow it."

She abruptly stood up. "No, no, I will not allow it. It is utterly traitorous when this realm has stolen from your own crown and refused to treat me with honor. Do you think you will be well looked upon after we leave? Indeed not. These people do not care for any but themselves. You will always be an unwelcome foreigner among strange people, and they will not hold faith with you. Mark me in this."

I stood before her, head bowed. I had not thought of it before, that I would be utterly alone, so taken was I with the idea of marrying Lord Northampton.

"You saw what the journey here was like; none is likely to undertake that again. There will be no way for you to return to Sweden." She sat down again; in the distance I could hear someone quieting the wailing Edward Fortunatus.

"I understand, my lady," I said. With so much money owed, it was unlikely anyone would return from Sweden to England in my lifetime. "I am sorry this journey did not bring you the happiness with the queen you had hoped it would."

At that, she heaved a heavy breath. "The queen is by no means who I understood her to be. She is unkind, she is selfish, she is vicious. Do you know that she has kept her cousin Katherine Seymour in exile for nigh on six years, and she with two young sons, for marrying a man the queen did not approve of? I think, mayhap, it is the sons and the husband the queen covets and not the protection of her honor and law."

I took a deep breath before speaking. "I did not know that."

"Katherine's sister Mary Grey is now likewise detained, a young woman who is"—she pointed at her temple—"not complete. Hardly a threat."

A bit of dismay must have crossed my face because Princess Cecelia smiled for the first time in our conversation, but wickedly. "Perhaps this queen is not all you understand her to be, either. So stay, stay if you insist. I give my permission. But by the time you figure out who this queen really is inside, my dearest Elin, it will be too late."

She dismissed me with a wave of her hand and went back to directing those who were helping her pack her considerable number of trunks and coffins.

Within two weeks the entire Swedish delegation had packed and was leaving Bedford House. I had told William that I would remain there to see them off, and he promised to send a litter for me and my things later that afternoon. I said good-bye to the ladies one by one, feeling especially torn to be parting from Christina Abrahamsdotter and Bridget.

Bridget and I held one another's hand until she needed to get into a litter to depart. "I shall miss you desperately," I said. I did not want to let go of her hand. Had I made a grave error? If so, it was not too late to join them for the return journey. I was homesick already. I might never see Sweden again, nor hear my native tongue spoken, kiss my mother good night, or eat of the small strawberries Brita and I collected each June on the hillside near our summer home.

"You've rightly chosen," Bridget reminded me, seeing, I supposed, the fear cross my face. "Karin and Philip are likely already married. And William loves you well."

I nodded. "Write to me." She agreed, and I kissed her on the hairline.

The princess came up to me and I curtseyed before her one last time. "Thank you, my lady, for everything you have done for me," I said, voice trembling.

She nodded, holding her head erect, and then began to walk away. Before she'd taken more than three steps, though, she turned back to me and spoke with no trace of kindness. "Lord Northampton won't marry you. He can't. He's already married."

# FOUR

Spring and Summer:
Year of Our Lord 1566
The Palace of Whitehall
Windsor Palace
On Progress

Year of Our Lord 1567
The Palace of Whitehall
Windsor Palace
Stanstead Hall, London

What did she mean? She was telling the truth, of that I was certain. I had made a mistake. A terrible mistake. It took all of my strength not to race after them, gown held in my hand, as they departed Bedford House. Instead, I paced the great hall and wandered outside from time to time to see if William approached. He arrived several hours after the delegation left; he rode a fine horse, as all in his stable were, and had a manservant ride another one for me. Another set of horses conveyed a litter for my belongings, such that they were. They were so few that, had it not been beneath his station, we could have carried them in saddlebags instead. The day's cool mist mingled with hot tears to blur my view of his face as he drew near.

He greeted me with kisses but then withdrew. "What is it?" he asked.

I was not yet a practiced dissembler, though I had come to believe 'twas a skill I must learn. "Come to the great hall," I said. "The fire is still warm and we can talk there." I led him in by the hand and we took our seats.

"Have they gone?" he asked.

I nodded. "Yes, they have. And on the way out, the princess took care to share a most distressing thought with me, one that I, of course, do not believe but must ask you."

He shifted his body and his gaze away from me. My heart fell. I knew before I even asked him that it was true. "She says you are married. I know this cannot possibly be true because you told me yourself that your wife died one year ago, last April."

He took my hands in his own. Although they were smooth and well groomed, they were also a bit frail. I became aware, perhaps for the first time, of the chasm of years between us. Thirty.

"I promise you that I have been honest, but perhaps not complete," he said. "First, I would have you know that King Henry, the queen's father, called me his integrity, his incorruptibility. It was true then, and it's true now. If I can be trusted to be forthright with my sovereign—and I can—how much more will I be with you, my own true love?"

I softened then. "Yes, I believe you."

"My belief," he said, "is 'love does no wrong.' "

"But . . ." I sensed there was more.

"I have a wife. Of sorts."

I forced myself to breathe, uncomfortably aware that the Swedes were too far gone for me to catch up with them now, had I willed it.

He went on to explain that he had been married young, at his mother's urging, to a great heiress. They were both children at the time, so they did not live together for twelve more years. Within a short time, his wife left him for another man, with whom she bore children.

"According to the Scriptures, I was free to remarry," he said. "And after . . . courting . . . some women, I came to know Elisabeth Brooke, and with her faithfully spent twenty-two years, until her death. Parliament had declared my first marriage void; I wed Elisabeth in all honor and rightness."

"And so?" I asked.

"Queen Mary declared my first marriage valid, and my second null, and imprisoned me in the Tower for treason, as you knew. When that queen died, there came a new government, which declared my marriage to Elisabeth valid. She, of course, died. But the current government is not sure but that there is a cloud over my marriage. My first wife still lives, and as the marriage has been valid and void, valid and void, there is some confusion."

"I see," I said. I dwelt in the silence for a

moment before speaking. "Neither my faith nor my honor will permit me to live with you as husband and wife while unmarried."

He nodded and spoke softly. "I would not have it otherwise. I had thought to have this righted by now, but it is not. I understand the queen has offered you a position among her ladies."

"Yes," I said. "I hadn't understood then why." I did not look at him but at my hands. I heard the queen's birds singing mournfully in the distance. "What shall become of me?"

He drew near to me, and I leaned into him. "It shall be quick work to make right. And then we will marry and you will be mistress of all my property as you are now of my heart. Meanwhile, I shall see that you want for naught while at court or in my homes."

We rode to the palace, which gave me time to think. I trusted him implicitly, and yet he hadn't told me of this while I still had the chance to change my mind. Perhaps it was an oversight, and, truth be told, I wouldn't have changed my mind anyway. I was aware anew, though, of how vulnerable I was. I was in a strange land with no family to protect me or my interests. The queen had seemed pleased with me, but I knew as well as any how fickle royal favor could be.

We arrived at court, and William promised to be back within a few days. I felt alone, nervous, and perhaps somewhat abandoned as I watched him ride away. He had his own quarters at all of the queen's residences, of course, so we would see one another often. But I would also have duties waiting upon the queen. William had told me that it had been but a year since Kat Ashley, the woman who had raised the queen, had died. Since then, Blanche Parry, who had also been with the queen since childhood, had become the queen's "mother at heart," and she was very motherly indeed. Her Majesty had asked Mistress Parry to see that I had everything I needed.

"Her Grace has given you apartments near her own lodgings," she said, showing me to a small suite of well-appointed rooms close upon the Royal Suite, and with an enchanting view. She lowered her voice. "The other maids of honor share chambers and maids, so it's a singular honor that you'll have your own rooms, a lady maid and servants, and a horse of your own. You are also excluded from the sumptuary laws, so you may dress in a manner which will befit accompanying Lord Northampton."

"Oh, thank the queen for me, please," I said. "I am overcome."

"You can thank her yourself, Elin."

"Helena, please," I said. "I am an English-woman now. My name is Helena."

I soon learned the queen's daily routine and my part in it. We ladies were never to interfere in her politics or her court. At first I was downhearted about that, thinking that though I loved cards and games and needlework and horses, exercising my mind and my mouth was more to my pleasure. I soon learned, though, that the ladies had considerable power to influence, often heard Her Majesty's speeches well ahead of the men as she practiced them in her chambers, and were able to persuade effectively by softer manner. The queen was never alone; we ladies trailed her, like purebred spaniels might trail a lesser woman, no matter where she went. She loved us well, though, and although it was always clear that she was the mistress, it was often clear that she was our loving friend as well.

The queen began her day with six or seven galliards, for exercise, and we ladies were expected to dance along with her. If she chose not to dance, she and we oft took a quick walk in the gardens. She said she was no morning woman but she was always back at her rooms very early to attend to her devotions and then to her correspondence. After we dressed her, her counselors came to see her in her Presence or Privy Chamber. She attended to paperwork for a while, then walked in a garden or a gallery with her ladies or Lord Robert. Afterward, she might ride in open carriage, so her people could see her, to a nearby park to hawk or hunt, often with Lord Robert, her Master of Horse.

When she was with him, the breath of life was breathed into her. Bliss.

William had provided my lady maid at his own expense. Although the queen had offered to provide one, she was glad to save the cost and William told me, quietly, that it would be better if he provided her for me.

"If I hire her, she knows that she is to carry out what I tell her to do as her primary responsibility. I've told her to answer any questions you may ask that would assist you to understand court, or England, our history, and the courtiers. She was educated somewhat before her family fell upon difficulties and she has served in noble house-holds, so she will be a source of knowledge for you."

I kissed his cheek. "Thank you, dearest William, for thinking of things I might not have even considered."

My first difficulty arose within the first few days after I moved in. I asked Clemence, my lady maid, if she could arrange for a large urn of hot water and an empty one, too, to be delivered each evening.

"Of course, my lady, but if I may ask, why?"

"To bathe!" I said. This had not been a problem at Bedford House, occupied as it were by Swedes, but I had noticed since coming to court that the English did not all hearken to the northern habit of daily baths.

Clemence, bless her, did as I asked, and each night I bathed in water that I scented with my own herbal preparations, oftentimes rose but also marjoram. The Queen's Majesty called me to her.

"Lady Helena," she said, clearly pleased by the Anglicization of my name, "you always smell sweet and there is a fresh air about you. Why is that?"

"Swedes bathe daily, Your Majesty, in scented water, and I have continued that custom though I am now an Englishwoman."

She nodded approvingly. The queen was known to have a sensitive sense of smell; even the leather her books were bound with was not to be cured with anything pungent. From that day on I became one of the queen's bed warmers. At night, before Her Majesty retired to her bed, one of her ladies climbed into the royal bed to warm the linens that Blanche had keep over; then the maid of honor left the bed just before Her Majesty climbed in. That lady usually spent the night sleeping on a small bed at the foot of Her Majesty's great one. I didn't mind. There were always two or three ladies in Her Majesty's chamber, day or night, to protect and assist her as well as defend against malicious gossip.

One night, after the torches were snuffed in the bedchamber and Squires of the Body quietly prowled the hallways to keep watch for her security, Her Majesty was abed, with only me and

Mary Radcliffe, another of her maids of honor, in the room, and she spoke quietly. "Lady von Snakenborg?"

"Yes, Majesty?" I said sleepily from the trundled bed at the foot of her bed of state.

"I prefer the marjoram-scented water you bathed in this evening. It leaves a soothing scent upon my linens and I believe I shall sleep most soundly."

"If it pleases Your Majesty, I shall ensure to use it each time I am called to serve you in this manner," I said.

Mary Radcliffe had had nary a word for me before that, but that night she sent a smile in my direction, visible by moonlight. The next day, I asked Blanche Parry if I might ask Mrs. Morgaynne, who was the queen's apothecary, for some essence of marjoram to add to my own store of herbs and essences. "I shall sprinkle some upon Her Majesty's linens each night whether or not it's my turn to warm the bed." Blanche Parry readily agreed.

There was no comfortable rest to be found in the week after, as we waited upon her in her Privy Chamber, where she was haranguing some of her councilors ahead of her presentation to Parliament. "Though I be a woman, yet I have as good a courage, answerable to my place, as ever my father had," she scolded them all.

"Majesty," Lord Robert began, "Mr. Molyneux has suggested that the money you have requested should be given only upon the contingency that Your Grace makes a declaration about your successor. This motion was very well approved by the greater part of the House!"

"It would be wise to consider it, Your Highness," William said softly. "They mean it for your good, and the good of the realm. They want a successor named."

"Was I not born in the realm? Were my parents born in any foreign country?" she demanded. "Is there any cause I should alienate myself from being careful over this country? Is not my kingdom here? Whom have I oppressed? How have I governed since my reign began?"

She sat down upon her chair of state, her stomacher pressing into her, bosom heaving. "I will marry as soon as I can conveniently. And as to the succession—I stood in danger of my life, my sister was so incensed against me. I did differ from her in religion, and for that I was sought for diverse ways from plotters and overthrowers. So I shall never name my successor, who may will to unseat *me!*"

She calmed and continued. "Some would speak for their master, some for their mistress, and every man for his friend. But my very life would become a target. Men foment about the second when the second is known. I know this better than any in the realm. As your prince and head, we must be left to judge the timing of the move, without prompting from our subjects. For it is monstrous that the feet should direct the head."

No reassurance was forthcoming from those "feet" she trusted most. She waved to silence Cecil, her secretary of state and most trusted principal advisor, who'd begun to speak, then turned to my marquess. "Northampton," she said to my great horror, "methinks you had better talk about the arguments used to enable you to get married again, to yon lady"—she looked toward me—"when you have a wife living, instead of mincing words with us."

She rounded toward Lord Robert and said, "We had thought that if all the world abandoned us, you would not have done so."

"I am ready to die at your feet, madam!" Lord Robert protested. He, more than any, would press her to marriage. With himself, if it could be!

"That has nothing to do with the matter."

She loudly banned them entrance to the Presence Chamber and stormed off, calling for the comfort, of all persons, of the Spanish ambassador. We ladies, of course, said nothing at all, as was our place, but quietly slipped down the corridor.

By June the storm seemed to have lifted and the queen was dancing and making merry after dinner when Cecil took her aside and whispered something in her ear. Her face, normally pale, waxed into a death mask. She left the room immediately, and we ladies followed her.

She dismissed all but Lady Knollys, Blanche, Anne Russell Dudley, Mary Radcliffe, and myself.

As we helped her undress, silent tears slid down her face, coursing through the light powder she'd been made up with, streaking the faint sheen of whipped egg white that held said powder in place and smoothed her first wrinkles.

"Our cousin, the Queen of Scots, has given birth to a fair son," she said. Our hearts broke for her. Queen Mary had provided her kingdom, and if the plotters were satisfied, perhaps Elizabeth's kingdom, with a prized heir, which meant stability, continuity, surety. A male heir was what the English desired but which our queen was as of yet unable or unwilling to provide.

As I readied myself for bed that evening, I, like the queen, wondered if I should ever have a child of my own, something I had greatly desired since my own girlhood. I had recently realized that William had been married twice and had not yet sired a child.

Almost every summer, barring illness or plague, the queen would journey through and stay at some of the towns and estates in her kingdom, greeting the common people she held with motherly affection and being entertained by her courtiers.

That summer on Progress, we stayed for some time at Lord Robert's estates in Kenilworth. Some said that the queen was his wife in all but name, but I, having slept in her room and observed how impossible it would be to be in the queen's presence alone, vigorously disagreed. We women surrounded her chambers night and day, and anyone who thought the queen could be expertly redressed by an unpracticed man, alone, had not been present in her bedchamber when the hour-long gowning and pinning was under way.

I would admit, though, that they oft strolled together in the public gardens at Kenilworth unmolested by courtiers or other subjects. One afternoon William and I were arm in arm enjoying the roses when we came upon Robin, as she called Lord Robert, and the queen. I wondered if this Robin was a songbird she would like to cage, and was about to jest about it with William, but stopped myself. I did not think he would find it particularly amusing, as he was not given to either wry humor or to Lord Robert. As we passed them and I curtseyed, I thought I spied a faint bit of beard burn upon the queen's fair and smiling face. Though I could not be certain, I hoped it was true. Every lady deserved to be kissed.

We stayed at many manors and in many towns on Progress. Her people, her "children," came to greet her with poems and poesies at each stop along the way. In Sandwich the good housewives had prepared a feast for the queen of 140 dishes, and to the horror of William Cecil, she tasted of them all without first having her taster test them for poisons. Instead, she indicated loudly enough to bring honor to all who had prepared them that some of them should be reserved for her and brought back to her lodgings for private consumption, which put a satisfied, and adoring, smile on the face of each and every townswoman.

The queen listened attentively to the Latin discourse of a young scholar in Norwich, declaring it to be among the finest speeches she had ever heard. I rather thought that the young man would have taken up arms for her then and there if it had been required. She praised all and berated none.

Late that evening, as we were unpinning her gown, Lady Knollys commented on the time the queen took with each of her subjects.

"In truth, I love them well," the queen responded. "And I am certain they know it. For if they did not rest assured of some special love toward them, they would not readily yield me such good obedience. As it is, they know I have their highest and best interests always in mind."

I spoke of that with William, late in the eve, before the dying fire in his apartment within the home of our host. He sipped his wine thoughtfully and then said, "Yes. But they greatly desire the queen to marry and to bring forth a son, to have the succession settled. They are discomfited by the thought of years of war that threaten a kingdom without an heir. And many feel it is unnatural for a woman to rule."

"Will she marry?"

He lowered his voice. "She must. But whom? No matter the offers, parrying, and diplomatic considerations, I believe that the queen's honor and faith will not let her choose a Catholic prince for herself or for her people. Protestant princes are few, and they are entangled in costly wars that would bring this realm nothing but debt, of which we already have an abundance after the . . . generous spending of His Majesty King Henry and the warring of Queen Mary at the provocation of her Spanish husband, Philip."

"An Englishman, then?" I grinned, truly fond of William. "I find myself much given to marrying an Englishman."

"Ah, that it should come quickly to pass," he said as he kissed me lightly.

"Our marriage or hers?"

"Both. We know whom *you* should marry, my lady." He clasped his hand over mine. "But the queen?"

"Lord Robert?" I asked.

"Mayhap," he admitted. "As she has raised him to earl, making him of sufficient rank to partner her."

"Why do I sense your reluctance?"

"The Dudley family is scattered with traitors who tried, like vines, to circle the royal oak and climb to the throne. Elizabeth loves Lord Robert well, but I am certain she does not forget that Lord Robert's father conspired to keep her from her throne by placing her cousin Jane Grey, married to Lord Robert's brother Guildford, on it in her rightful stead."

"Lord Robert's father and brother Guildford are now . . . ?"

"Executed. I believe Lord Robert well loves the queen, but most others believe he is simply another choking shoot of the Dudley vine. Whether or not the queen, in her great love, will risk being entwined with him, only time will tell. Which nobleman in this kingdom will bow the knee to Lord Robert? I'm sure I couldn't say."

After we returned to London, I made my way to the queen's library. Lady Blanche, also keeper of the queen's books, said I might take any of them back to my chamber to read for my pleasure, and to assist in my English. I was excited to find some histories and some Greek myths and stories, as well as a tiny New Testament in which was written on the forepapers, in Her Majesty's own hand, "I walk many times into the pleasant fields of the Holy Scriptures, where I pluck up the goodly green herbs of sentences by pruning, eat them by reading, chew them by musing, and lay them up at length in the seed of memory by gathering them together so that having tasted Thy Sweetness, I may less perceive the bitterness of this miserable life."

I made my way back to my chamber and, as I did, glanced out the window at one of the turreted towers of the palace. I'd heard that King Henry had quietly, officially, married the queen's mother, Anne Boleyn, here at Whitehall in one such tower, while my lady was already comfortably resting inside her mother's womb. Did she even now wonder about her mother? Was her mother's beheading the beginning of the bitterness of Queen Elizabeth's life? Or was it the lack of a husband, of children? The bitterness of knowing that others greatly desired your death so that they may poach your royal perquisites and power?

I wished I had my own mother nearby to discuss these things, to offer affection and counsel. I yearned to hear from her, but she had not written to me, or if she had, the letters had not made it through the Danes. The thought of home, and of belonging, brought me pain, so I quickly dismissed it. I had thought to be married by now, and perhaps on my way to becoming a mother myself.

I carefully thumbed through the pages of the Scriptures I had just borrowed and noted diverse passages that someone, perhaps the queen herself, had underlined, for it was in the same ink found on the forepaper she'd written upon. One of these, in the Epistle of Paul to the Ephesians, struck me:

> For the husband is the head of the wife, even as Christ is the head of the church: and he is the savior of the body. Therefore as the church is subject unto Christ, so let the wives be to their own husbands in everything.

I plucked from the seed of my memory Her Majesty saying that it was monstrous that the head should take direction from the feet. Should she marry, the example of her sister, common practice, and Holy Writ all declared that she would no longer be head, something she knew very well.

As for my own marriage, there seemed to have been no progress on the matter and little interest except from William and myself.

"I cannot continue to live in limbo," I said to him. "I do not know what I am or who I am or where my place is. Your . . . Lady Anne Bourchier, she could have a long and robust life." At that I noted that one of his servants flicked her eye toward me, unusually, and briefly.

I didn't wish ill upon Lady Anne, but I wished to have my own situation resolved.

"I will take it up again with the council," William promised. "It was not so difficult to set aside a false marriage last time, when I married Elisabeth Brooke. But I need to win new champions to our side, and that takes time."

"By when?" I asked softly, but wearily, sensitive to the fact that this troubled him, too, but needing an answer.

"Within a year."

# FIVE

Years of Our Lord: 1567, 1568
The Palace of Whitehall
Windsor Castle
Hampton Court Palace

At the new year the queen's principal councilor, William Cecil, had drawn up a memorandum titled *Certain Cautions for the Queen's Apparel and Diet* and circulated it among courtiers and ladies. The document suggested ways in which Elizabeth could guard against being poisoned. In it, he spoke against accepting gifts from strangers, which I found odd, as all gifts that came to Her Majesty were entrusted to Lady Knollys, and warned of perfume or scented gloves appointed for Her Majesty's savor. That concerned me, as I knew better than most how vulnerable the queen was to using sweet scents to avoid rank ones. She'd insisted upon rose water in the palace privys for years.

I was a welcomed maid of honor and the queen treated me with politeness, though she kept me at some distance. This was frustrating, as the others followed her lead. It pained me to admit that it was exactly as Princess Cecelia had predicted: I was daughter to no one, sister to no one, as yet wife to no one, mother to no one, and apparently friend only to Anne Dudley and William. I missed the companionship of my sisters and of Bridget. I longed to rectify that and had been seeking a manner in which I might make myself even more valuable to the queen. The queen often appointed me to sew new taffeta into the gowns she wished remodeled so she could pass them along to her ladies and maids, or even the underprivileged, but I wanted to be more helpful. And personal.

After the queen had left for a meeting with her councilors, I approached Mistress Blanche with what I hoped was a wonderful idea that would help me please the queen and earn friends. "I wonder if I might offer my assistance in helping blend perfumes and pomanders," I said, my voice trembling a little with hope and the fear of being told no. "In light of Cecil's concerns, I could provide sweet-smelling respite for the queen while protecting her person from harmful fumes given as gifts." I waited and held my breath till she answered.

"That is a splendid idea, Lady Helena," Blanche said. "I shall instruct Mrs. Morgaynne to provide you with whatever herbs and oils you need, and you may also select plants from any of Her Majesty's gardens."

"Thank you!" I said, reaching over to hug her, and she laughed lightly before shrugging me off. Within the week I had prepared some herbal blends and placed them into small, pink satin pouches. I approached Her Majesty as she was relaxing after a midday meal.

"Majesty, I have prepared some pleasant-smelling pomanders, some samples to choose among. Please, tell me which you prefer and I will blend some fine sachets for you."

"Come, Helena," the queen said, calling me forth to the sumptuously covered chair she reposed upon. I knelt before her, and she indicated that I should instead seat myself at the low stool to the side of her.

I held up the sachets one by one and I could tell from the look on her face which she preferred. Marjoram, of course, and those of rose, and some lavender that had been imported from France. The queen favored all things French.

"I shall personally blend these for you, Majesty, and the sachets will be stitched and laced by my own hand," I said proudly. "Is there any other way I can be of service?"

I was still holding her favorite sachet in my hand, and rather than nod me away, she closed her own hand around mine for just a moment as a gesture of affection and acceptance. "No, my lady. How does Lord Northampton?"

"He is well, madam. He is preparing to under-take the diplomatic journey you'll send him on with the Earl of Sussex. I pray that their, and your, mission meets with success."

She smiled at me. "They are found faithful, as

are you, Lady von Snakenborg. Come, tell me about your time thus far in my court."

She indicated that a cushion should be brought for me, and placed near her, and I chatted about my apartment and my readings and the hawking and chess that William was helping me improve at. She shared with me some Greek translations that she was working on, some of which she found vexing.

"I should not have expected you to find anything vexing," I said with admiration.

"Ah, but we do," she disagreed with me. It made her all the more likable.

She offered some kind words and advice of her own, and invited me to dine with her and William, privately, when they returned from their journey. "I shall look forward to your company and pleasant conversation," she said. "And your herbal preparations, of course."

"Thank you, Majesty." I was exultant. I had a task that set me aside from the others, and a manner in which I might serve the queen and the beginning of real friendship with her.

In February, some of the queen's ladies were in her apartment playing gleek when a messenger arrived and burst impolitely into the chamber. The queen was taken aback, Cecil looked alarmed for her safety, and Lord Robert stood up. The messenger went directly to Her Majesty, and, kneeling before her, said, "I bring ill tidings, Majesty. Your cousin Lord Darnley, the husband of Mary, Queen of Scots, has been foully murdered!"

The room collectively gasped, and even Her Majesty, the ultimate dissembler, allowed some shock onto her face. "Is this true?" she demanded.

"I fear so, Majesty," he said. "Lord Darnley was in a building that was exploded. However, when his body was examined it was found that he had been suffocated to death before the explosion."

"Who has done this?" the queen demanded. "Scots rebels?"

The messenger leaned close to her and whispered, but as I was at her card table I was just able to overhear him. "Majesty, the whispering from Scotland seems to be that his wife, the queen, was involved in the plot."

Her Majesty sat back and waved him away in utter contempt. Perhaps the messenger was familiar with the ancient story of Tigranes's messenger having his head cut off for bearing ill news, but in any case, he stepped clear away from Her Majesty. In respect for dead Darnley, the queen canceled the card games and retired to her rooms. Another maid of honor, Eleanor Brydges, and I gathered Her Majesty's cards from the tables.

"I hope Her Majesty is well," I said. "She looked saddened and shocked."

Eleanor nodded. "Darnley was her cousin, as is the Queen of Scots. It's understandable that she be saddened. But there is no reason for shock. I do not believe that Queen Mary had a hand in her husband's death."

Later, after I was abed, it came to me that Eleanor could not have overheard the messenger mention that the Queen of Scots was suspected, as she had been playing gleek well across the great room.

If Her Majesty was shocked and saddened on that February eve, she was shocked and angry in May when word filtered south that Queen Mary had married the Earl of Bothwell, largely believed to have murdered Lord Darnley so he could marry Darnley's wife, the queen.

"Has she lost all sensibilities?" the queen asked as she paced in her chamber. "She has gambled credibility as well as the affections of her people, which must never be treated lightly."

The ambassador brought news that the Scots were arming themselves against Mary after her marriage to a murderer and that she would soon be deposed in favor of her young son.

That night, I heard whispering at the banquet tables while we ate. As few talked with me, I heard quite a lot. The queen rarely ate in public, which meant that most meals were free for courtier discussion. There was a name infrequently circulated in the banqueting hall that I did not know.

I asked Clemence that night, "Who is Amy Robsart?"

Clemence immediately stopped brushing my hair and caught my eye for a moment over the top of my head, in the looking glass. I had the sense that if she could have avoided the question altogether she would have, but William paid her handsome wages not only to attend to my physical needs but to answer questions such as I might need to know in order to better serve the queen.

"Amy was married to Lord Robert Dudley," she answered.

"And she has now passed away?" I asked.

Clemence picked the brush up. "Yes, many years past. She was found at the bottom of a flight of stairs in a manor home, after all the servants had been dismissed for the day."

It was my turn to be startled now. "Was she murdered?"

"The inquiry says no, ma'am, but the people . . . they think yes."

"And who do the people say murdered Lady Dudley?" I asked.

"Why, Lord Robert himself!" Clemence said. "So as he could marry Her Majesty," she continued, her voice lowered. "Though others say 'twas his noble enemies, because with one wife mysteriously dead, the people would never accept him as king, now, would they? When Her Majesty's sister, Queen Mary, married a man the people did'na like, they turned against her. Though all know the queen desires to marry Lord Robert, she dares not, lest she lose the favor of her people."

I instantly understood that night's whispers connecting Amy Robsart to Mary, Queen of Scots, her dead husband, Lord Darnley, and Bothwell.

"Is that all, my lady?"

"Yes, Clemence. And please rest assured that I will hold to faith anything you say to me. I shall not share what I learn with others, nor speak of our talk."

She relaxed then and smiled at me before helping me polish my skin with a paste of ground almonds and water.

In August William left with the Earl of Sussex to Austria, to present the Order of the Garter to the emperor; in truth, they were also going to offer the queen's hand to the archduke. Within months came a response to Her Majesty that while the archduke was eager to marry Her Majesty, he could not in good conscience agree to forgo his Catholicism and embrace Protestantism, a requirement she was not willing to negotiate. With regret, the discussions concluded without good fruit. Her Majesty sorrowed for days and I noticed her occasionally stroking her stomacher, as if mourning a lost child not yet conceived, perhaps an heir.

William returned home, and we hosted an evening at his manor in London. The queen attended, as did most of the nobility. I had been in England for better than two years, but had not yet eaten of the lingonberries that my sister had pressed on me as I'd left Sweden. I instructed William's cooks to prepare them into a compote with sugar and water. They, like my life in England, were a mixture of sweet and bitter.

Although everyone was unfailingly gracious, few offered me a hand or a smile of friendship, save the queen. She sampled the lingonberries after the others had passed them by. "These are delightful, Lady von Snakenborg!" she declared. "I shall have a second serving." She turned to His Grace the Duke of Norfolk. "Have you eaten of these, Norfolk?"

Norfolk had not, of course, but at that point he had little recourse but to eat them and declare them to his liking. Several other ladies did likewise, and while I appreciated the assistance Her Majesty sought to offer, I found compulsory compliments and feigned affection sharp in my ears. Lady Eleanor Brydges was the only person to offer genuine warmth to me. I made cheerful talk with her and sent some specially prepared comfit cake back to her lodging hoping that would be the flint to a friendship. I wondered aloud that night, to William, if things might be different if I were his wife. He promised to press the matter again.

Before Christmas, final word came that there was no prospect of annulment. William was legally married until death did them part.

I was shocked. I sorrowed. In my rooms at court, I angrily packed up all the gowns and jewels he had given me into a large casket to return to him and shouted in German, and then in Swedish, which I knew no one could understand. Clemence, ten years older than I and familiar with tempers, wisely absented herself.

William should have told me this at the outset! And now here I was, alone, adrift, unprotected.

Later I unpacked them all again. He had acted in good faith. He was kind and noble. He had treated me with affection and dignity. But I would need to think upon this in a different manner now. I would not speak to him of it until my thoughts were clear and a decision made. What would I do should I remain in England an unmarried maid? I did not mind serving the queen, and I appreciated her friendship, but I would never have chosen an unmarried life.

William bought me a magnificent horse as a Christmas gift and a fine necklace of emeralds set in gold, and I bought him some falcons that I arranged to have sent from St. Botolph's fair in Lincolnshire. But our inability to marry was a devastating blow to both of us. Letters still made their way irregularly, and I prayed that I would not hear from my mother and be forced to respond with this ill news. I did not wish to give her information to pass along to Princess Cecelia for her evening's amusement.

In January the Spanish ambassador reported to Her Majesty that Philip of Spain, husband to the queen's dead sister, Mary, had arrested his own son, Don Carlos, and thrown him into prison for treason. Don Carlos starved himself in retaliation. We ladies were gathered in the Privy Chamber, where I sat mending one of the queen's delicate ruffs, when Lady Knollys delivered yet more strange news.

"Lady Katherine Grey Seymour is also refusing to eat, Majesty. She is said to be near death, and in fact, those waiting upon her have said she speaks of going toward God as quickly as she can and begs you to care for her sons."

My heart pained at this tender sentiment from a young wife who had been exiled and separated from her husband these many years—four years, I thought, before I arrived on these shores. She had married for love, but Lady Katherine had also married in folly. She had not only forgone the queen's permission, a penal offense for those closely related to the queen and with a claim to the throne, but had admitted to the Archbishop of

Canterbury that she and her husband had purposed to deceive Her Majesty. Worse, there was no proof of her wedding, as the only witness had died and the priest who had performed the ceremony could not be located. Her husband was found guilty of seducing a virgin of the blood royal, and when Lady Katherine bore a second son after trysts in the Tower, she and her husband were permanently separated.

Bad fortune had certainly chased down the ladies Grey, but if the truth be told, it was the queen's brother King Edward and Jane Grey's father-in-law, John Dudley, who'd set loose the hounds on the sisters by illegally bypassing Henry's daughters for the legal succession.

"We are sorry for her ill health," the queen stated before turning back to the manuscript she was lettering in her own hand. "But we can in no way force our good cousin to eat."

Lady Knollys, also Her Majesty's cousin as the daughter of Mary Boleyn, was ever reluctant to find fault with Her Grace. But even she looked shamed at this seeming lack of compassion. The lesson was clear: no courtier, nor cousin, nor lady should undertake marriage without the queen's permission.

Another cousin, stronger and more dangerous, arrived on Her Majesty's shores that May. Mary of Scots, fleeing the rebel lords in her own land, applied to her "good sister" the queen of England to help her back upon her throne. A pamphlet was circulated, *Defense of the Honor of Queen Mary*, which forcefully claimed Mary's right to Elizabeth's throne, as many English Catholics believed. The author was anonymous but the queen's advisors widely believed it to be John Lesley, Bishop of Ross, and Mary's ambassador to Elizabeth's court, and were not afraid to say so publicly.

"Mary's a plague upon this realm," William told me one night as we dined together. "She murdered her husband and carries with her the vapor of death. The only question yet to be settled is whom shall the death she brings strike down."

Lady Knollys's husband, Sir Francis, was to meet the Queen of Scots and accompany her, with guards to protect his and her safety, to the castle in the north. Our queen had decided Mary was to be her "guest" while the matter of Mary's involvement in her husband's death was investigated. The queen could not send troops into Scotland to restore a tainted Catholic monarch to that staunchly Protestant nation, even if she were so inclined, which she was not.

Neither could she send Mary to France, which would be happy to receive her. France looked upon Catholic Mary as the rightful queen of England and would be only too eager to assist her in regaining the Scottish, and perhaps the coveted

English, thrones. For Mary to stay in England was discomfiting as well. There were Catholic subjects in England who still regarded Her Majesty as illegitimate because they had not accepted King Henry's marriage to the queen's mother, Anne Boleyn, as valid. Instead, they held that of the king's children, only Mary, born of King Henry's Catholic first wife, Katherine of Aragon, and then Edward, born after Katherine of Aragon was dead, were legitimate heirs. The king's will had set forth the order of succession: Edward, Mary, and then Elizabeth. After them came the descendants of his sister Mary. But he deliberately barred from succession the descendants of his sister Margaret, among whom was Mary, Queen of Scots. In some ways, I felt compassion for Queen Mary, exiled from her home in a land that was not quite welcoming to her, unable to act of free will in either place.

Lady Knollys approached the queen in the Privy Chamber. They spoke softly, and yet all could still hear.

"Sir Francis has asked if I may accompany him to Lord Scrope's to carry out your instructions, Majesty," she said. It was clear by the pleading look on her face and the tone of voice she used that she wished to accompany her husband. All understood why her husband desired the happy company of his wife while carrying out such an unwelcome duty.

"I value your companionship above all women, Katherine," the queen said gently. "I cannot do without your comfort and presence just now."

Lady Knollys bowed her head in acceptance, but her eyes, already deeply shadowed, showed her pain. I wondered if her husband or her children resented the many years she attended the queen to their benign neglect. Lady Devereux, whom I'd seen flirting with Lord Robert, bore little love for the queen and the queen for her. I, who understood the competition between sisters over the love of a mother, considered whether their ill feelings may have long centered around the division of Lady Knollys's time and affections, and not first Lord Robert.

The queen patted Lady Knollys's hand fondly and rewarded her soon thereafter with the fees from a license for selling worsted cloth reverted to the crown after its owner had displeased the queen. I wondered if Sir Francis was warmed by these fees during his long, lonely journey to and stay at Carlisle Castle. That decision made it hard for me to serve the queen with anything approaching enthusiasm for several days, though I'm certain I hid it well.

Some months later, Lord Robert approached the queen in her Presence Chamber to speak to her of what had been discovered regarding the Queen of Scots.

"Come, Robin." The queen beckoned him to her

side. He drew near her, near enough to kiss, which he did not, but also near enough to share breath, and I thought that, perhaps, they did.

"They have found letters between Mary and Bothwell declaring their love, describing their physical intimacy, and slandering Lord Darnley, all dated from before Darnley's death," Dudley said after moving back and sitting beside her.

"Why have we not heard of this, Robin?" the queen marveled. "We instructed Norfolk to learn what he will and report back to us."

Robert shrugged. "I've heard it said that Norfolk is particularly keen to keep this quiet, thus protecting Mary's reputation from those who might otherwise be abhorred by her shameful conduct."

At this, the queen sat up. I took the goblet from her hand; she handed it to me without acknowledging my presence. There was only one reason that Norfolk, who was rumored to be secretly practicing Catholicism while acting outwardly Protestant, had to protect Mary. He was plotting on her behalf.

"We will have the next meeting of the council here, at Westminster," she declared. "And then Cecil will attend as well. We will not condemn a crowned queen based on hearsay."

We women looked at one another, all thinking, perhaps, of Elizabeth's mother, Queen Anne Boleyn, convicted and beheaded on whispers and a lone, pitiful, racked confession.

"I shall look upon this evidence myself," she finished. Within weeks, she did, as did many of her courtiers, all of whom were shocked by the unsavory contents. To those gathered the queen sadly pronounced, "The letters contained many matters that cannot be repeated before honest ears, and may be easily drawn to be clear proof against the queen."

She looked tired. In light of the findings, there was no way to receive Mary at court, but the queen did send clothing and finances and promised to underwrite her household expenses, which was no mean amount. It didn't please her vanity, either, when her own courtiers seemed taken with the much younger Mary's beauty and charm. After returning from a visit to Carlisle, one of Elizabeth's courtiers told Cecil, when he was unaware that we ladies were nearby, "Mary has an alluring grace, a pretty Scottish accent, and a searching wit, clouded with mildness. Fame might move some to relieve her of her miseries," he finished, "and glory might stir others to risk much for her sake."

William told me that Norfolk had asked to take some of William's birds on a hawking expedition he was undertaking with Maitland, who had once been secretary to Mary, Queen of Scots, but was now an emissary on behalf of the new Scottish government.

"Do you doubt Maitland?" I asked.

"I doubt him not at all," William replied. "I am certain he is in the employ of the Scots queen and arranging with Norfolk for marriage between them, and then from there to rule England. Norfolk has already pressed the Privy Council to agree that Mary will be freed if she is safely married to an English lord. I'm certain he has just such a lord in mind."

We talked for some time and then I grew weary. "Good night, William," I softly said, preparing to leave for my own chamber. I'd felt increasingly odd kissing him knowing that he was still married, even though his "wife" had not spoken to him for decades and had left him for another man, and so I didn't. He respected that but I know it pained him. He continued to treat me with the utmost respect and affection, and we spent time together at court, hawking, dancing, and studying Italian, but we'd grown distant. I sorrowed that, but I could not give my heart to a man I knew was not mine.

"Good night, Helena," he replied.

We were in *ginnungugap*, the Nordic place of void and in-between. I finally determined that, should another suitor appear while William's wife still lived, I was free to consider him. I had acted charitably and in good faith, but I couldn't allow feelings for a married man to grow, nor set aside my own life forever.

# SIX

Year of Our Lord 1569
The Palace of Whitehall

Just after the new year, Lady Knollys, who had been unwell, grew fainter and more ill. She was confined to her bed and the queen visited her daily, often more than once. The queen was sore vexed and could scarce think of anything else but Lady Knollys and her illness. As I was serving her I noticed that her hands, of which she was inordinately proud, were red from wringing.

"Your Grace, may I apply a salve upon your hands, and some gloves, for your comfort?" I asked.

The queen silently nodded. I rubbed them with a lightly herbed ointment and slipped a pair of the gloves she was known for over her hands. The next day, she called me aside. "We thank you, Lady von Snakenborg, as our hands are less tender and raw."

"I shall salve them each evening, madam," I said.

Within days, Lady Knollys died. Her Majesty could not be consoled for a week or more; her eyes were red-rimmed and every conversation turned to good Lady Knollys. Sir Francis was recalled. When I saw him, I was shocked. He'd aged more than ten years and his gaunt face was stone struck with grief. Blanche Parry asked me to assemble into trunks Lady Knollys's belongings, and to care for Her Majesty's birds, which had been Lady Knollys's responsibility. I readily agreed.

To my shame, I read, while packing, portions of Sir Francis's final letter to his wife. In it he pleaded for her to consider a quieter manner of life, to retire from service and live a poor country life with him.

It was too late for that.

Several days later I was salving Her Majesty's hands before she retired for the evening when I noticed her shoulders were hunched. "You are Atlas, my lady, carrying the weight of the heavens on your shoulders," I said. "Let me rub some valerian ointment into them, as we would do in Sweden."

She agreed, and for the first time since Lady Knollys's death, I saw her uncoil. "You do well," she said. "Tell me, have you been reading about Atlas of late?"

I shook my head. "Not of late, Majesty. I love stories and have plucked some from your library. I must say, your library is rich with myths and tales of Greece and Rome; however, there are no stories in them of the myths from the north. There is much to learn from our legends, too."

The queen smiled, and as she did, the others in the room put themselves at ease.

"Tell us about one of them, Helena," Anne Russell Dudley urged. No hint of the lady's bedstraw awkwardness remained . . . at least between us two. "Her Majesty loves a story!"

I knew Anne was hoping to brighten the queen's gloom, so I eagerly sought a story to do that. I indicated that Eleanor Brydges should come near, and I whispered into her ear. She smiled and took her leave. No one asked where she was going; they expected that we were to amuse the queen and let her go, relishing the suspense.

"I shall tell you of our legendary Idun," I said, continuing to knead the knots from Her Majesty's neck and shoulders. "She is most beloved, the goddess of youth and spring and rebirth, and she lives in Asgard, the mythological home of the gods."

Anne Dudley clapped and bid me continue. She smiled in my direction, confirming that I had chosen the right tale for Her Majesty.

"Because Norse gods are not immortal of their own accord, they need to eat of extraordinary apples, protected by Idun, in order to retain their immortality. One day, the evil trickster Loki was captured by a giant, Thiassi. The giant refused to free Loki until he brought Idun and her apples to him as a ransom. Loki, readily turncoat, agreed."

The room was quiet and Her Majesty began to

relax. I stopped for a moment and she spoke up. "Do proceed, Lady von Snakenborg!"

"Loki sped back to Asgard, and because Idun was trusting and kind, she believed Loki when he told her that he had found better apples that could be of help to both Idun and the other gods. He urged her to trust him and she did, following him into the woods. Once there, Thiassi, who had disguised himself in the form of an honorable eagle, swooped down and dug his talons into well-believing Idun and her basket of apples, and carried her away.

"Without Idun and her magic apples, the story goes, the other gods grew gray, feeble, and old. They gathered together and confronted Loki, demanding that he return Idun and her apples or they would banish him from Asgard. Loki, who had no pride and was willing to barter with either side, agreed. He turned into a falcon, flew to Thiassi, and once there, changed Idun into a nut. He clasped her in his claws and flew back to Asgard, furiously chased by Thiassi, who disguised himself in the form of an eagle once more.

"Loki safely made it within the confines of Asgard, where he dropped Idun and she changed back into a goddess again. Thiassi, the evil giant, did not make it into Asgard. Instead, he crashed into the wall guarding it. The gods lit a fire on the walls and Thiassi's wings caught the flame and he died, a victim of his own treachery."

"And Idun, Lady Helena? What of Idun?" Anne urged me on.

"The goddess was as beautiful as ever, and once she returned to her rightful place, the gods grew young and virile again. She served them her apples and they all dwell in Asgard today, safe from giants and old age."

At that, I bid Eleanor come forth. She handed me the basket of apples, which I had sent her for. I knelt and presented them to the queen. "Idun?"

The queen laughed and clapped her hands. Then she accepted them. After the women scattered again to their sewing and reading, Her Grace called me close to her again. Eleanor looked up, expecting to be called, too, I guessed. When she wasn't, she scowled.

"We understand that you have taken over the care of my songbirds after Lady Knollys's untimely death," Her Majesty said.

"Yes, madam," I said. "I have."

"We thank you," she said. "We shall consider other such things as might keep you occupied."

I curtseyed. "Thank you, Majesty."

"We have shrugged off Atlas's burden this afternoon, thanks to your ministrations, though the valerian has, perhaps, a strong savor."

"My pleasure, Your Grace. I shall find a scent to disguise the valerian next time."

We chatted comfortably then, for a few moments, and I answered her questions about the north myths with authority and friendship as well as humility. I think she liked that, as she spoke to me more as an equal than she ever had. I then went to find Eleanor, to thank her and to invite her to sup with me at William's estate the next week, but she was suddenly, and surprisingly, nowhere to be found.

The following autumn, the trickle of rumors regarding Norfolk's intended wedding to Mary swelled to a river. The queen called him into her Presence Chamber to answer the accusations.

"We have heard that you, lately bereaved of your wife, have plans to take another," she began.

He held his peace. "I know not of what you speak, Majesty," he said. "Did you have someone in mind? I should be humbly thankful to take your counsel in this matter."

"I understand," she said with a sharp tone and a look that matched it, "that you already *have* someone in mind, our cousin Mary, Queen of the Scots."

"Nay, Majesty, those are rumors planted by my adversaries that they might sprout enmity between us. I would not be able to sleep upon a safe pillow beside so wicked a woman, such a notorious adulteress and murderer."

"I was unaware that you had adversaries, my Lord Norfolk," she said. "Pray tell us whom these may be so we may defend you."

Norfolk smiled weakly. "Whoever is spreading malicious lies about me, my queen. Those are my enemies."

"We shall keep our ears, and our eyes, open to better hear and see these enemies of yours," the queen said. At that, Norfolk flicked his gaze to Lord Robert, whom the queen affectionately referred to as her "eyes." Lord Robert smoothed his beard and met Norfolk's gaze with a confident smile.

After Norfolk left the room, the queen remarked to Lord Robert, "I know full well that if that marriage comes about, within four months I shall find myself in the Tower." I wondered how heavy was the burden knowing that from the moment of your conception, there were others wishing for and plotting your death.

Within the month Norfolk had lost his nerve and fled court without the queen's permission. She moved to Windsor Castle, her strongest defensive residence, and then sent for Norfolk to be placed under arrest and taken to the Tower on suspicion of treason.

"Madam," Cecil reasoned with her shortly thereafter, "I cannot see how his acts are within the compass of treason. And if you consider the words of the statute, I think you will agree."

She stood up and shouted, "If the laws of England do not provide for Norfolk's execution, then we will proceed against him on our own authority!" She pounded her fist against the table for effect, and what an effect it had. It ushered in the silence of a corpse, which Cecil looked as if he shortly might become. He bowed and left the room. We ladies trailed after Her Majesty, who paid us no mind.

In the end, though, she would be proved right. Within a month there was a revolt in the north of Catholics who sought the throne for Mary.

"Why don't they love and obey me, for as I live I love them and seek only their best?" the queen mourned.

"Her Majesty has sorrow for her people but rage for her nobles," I said to Eleanor as I sprinkled scented water on the queen's linens and she organized onto tufts of satin the queen's hundreds of dress pins.

Eleanor looked at me for a minute before speaking. "It's true. There is rage for the earls of the north who led this, too."

"Earls led this?"

She laughed. "You don't think peasants organized it, do you? There are those in very high places who had a guiding hand. The Earl of Westmoreland, whose wife is sister to Norfolk. Also Henry Percy, Eighth Earl of Northumberland." She stopped pinning and turned to me. "His father was martyred in the Pilgrimage of Grace, when Her Majesty's father sought to put down a Catholic uprising some years ago. And his uncle Henry

Percy was said to have been Queen Anne Boleyn's first *love*."

Her voice had grown quiet; I couldn't determine if she was implying that Queen Anne had a girlhood affection for Henry Percy or that she had *known* him.

Norfolk was eventually released from the Tower as the queen reminded him to take good heed of his pillow. He promised that he would never again deal in the marriage of the Queen of Scots.

Just before and after Christmas the court was at its most festive. It was the season of revels, and plays were performed for Her Majesty's enjoyment. Many courtiers had their own troupe, of professional players, and sometimes men of the nobility snuck in and took a role upon themselves, to the amusement of the queen and her ladies.

The first week in December, playwright John Lyly had the Earl of Sussex's men perform *Endymion*. It had both romance and comedy, each of which Her Majesty enjoyed in turn. William did not attend; his gout pained him more and more frequently, but the Earl of Sussex had pleasant words for me, remembering me from both my arrival from Sweden and also his friendship with William.

We gathered in the great hall, and the stage had been prepared for us with sumptuous settings and costume. The tale began with poor Endymion complaining to his friend Eumenides of his unrequited love for the moon goddess, Cynthia.

"Come to, man, you have lost your senses!" Eumenides rebuked him. "Cynthia is much too high a reach for an earthborn mortal like yourself." At that, Endymion reached high into the air and made as though he was trying to clasp the moon, just beyond his reach.

The court laughed, but something, or rather someone, had caught my attention. I felt certain that I knew the player who was portraying Endymion. He was well favored and fair to look upon; all the ladies' eyes were trained on him though they feigned not to have such interest. But how and when would I have chanced upon a player? I found his lines funny, touching, and well delivered; I enjoyed watching him perform.

Tellus, a woman who had formerly held Endymion's affections, could not abide his new love interest, so she hired a sorceress to cast a deep sleep upon him from which he could not awaken. Eumenides, too, was in love, but with a woman who scorned him. The true nature of his character was tested when he reached a magic fountain and was allowed one, but only one, question.

"I must think upon this," he said. "Do I inquire how to pick the lock of my own love's heart, or do I inquire how to awake my sleeping friend?" At that, the room hushed; we, used to having to choose between duty to others and loyalty to self, understood his dilemma.

"I must choose Endymion," he proclaimed, as all knew he must.

The fountain spoke, "Endymion can be awakened, but only by a kiss from fair Cynthia."

Eumenides pled on bent knee the case of his friend with the goddess, and she agreed, in her kindness and compassion, to offer one kiss to Endymion to rescue him from a life of sleep.

After a feigned kiss, Endymion awakened and, seeing his love, shouted with joy. He well understood, though, that it was not for him to marry a goddess. "Never before have her lips been touched, nor would they ever again be soiled by such condescension, though could that be true I would then wish to be placed under a spell every day!"

As the play was clearly a reference to the chastity and status of the queen, nearly every eye was upon her and she smiled her approval. The player speaking the lines, however, looked directly at me as he spoke them. I looked back into his striking blue eyes and remembered where I'd seen them before. Afterward, he found and spoke with me. "Thomas Gorges, Lady Elin von Snakenborg," he said.

"I remember you, Sir Thomas," I said, keeping a cool reserve though I felt rather warm. "At the joust. And I am named Helena now, as I am an Englishwoman."

"I've certainly not forgotten you," he answered. "But it's not 'sir'; it's Mr. Thomas Gorges. However, Her Majesty has late appointed me as the watch of Hurst Castle, one of her most important coastal defenses."

I teased him. "A player defending the realm?" He looked taken aback for a moment, so I sought to reassure him. "No, no, Mr. Gorges, I know that oftentimes highborn men slip into player groups for the pleasure of it. Lord Robert is said to do that himself!"

At that he relaxed. "Yes, that's true. I am not often at court and thought to surprise and thank the queen for her appointment by appearing in Lyly's play. Her Majesty," he said with some pride, "is my cousin through her mother, Queen Anne Boleyn. I'm also a cousin of the Earl of Sussex"— he flourished with a hand—"into whose company of players I snuck this eve!" He indicated some chairs nearby. "Would you care to sit and talk?"

"Certainly, thank you," I replied.

He waved down one of the serving men, who brought us some wine, which loosened my tongue the smallest amount, and my heart a bit more. For quite a while we talked about his time spent in troubled Ireland on behalf of the queen and his hobby as an actor; and he recited some humorous lines from plays he had performed with other highborn men at various courtier gatherings. I laughed until I had to stop him from sharing them so I wouldn't draw the queen's ire at my indiscreet displays.

At his prodding, I spoke of Sweden and shared with him a myth of the north, since he'd been so good to share some of his own tales. He asked after my family, and our customs, and my loneliness or well-being in a new land, which was something that no one, not even William, had inquired after, and it brought tears to my eyes, which I quickly brushed away. He helped me recover by asking if I liked to bow hunt. I told him I had not learned how to, and he raised an eyebrow and said, "That must be remedied!"

Within an hour, I could see that the queen was readying herself to leave. We ladies always left when she withdrew. "I must go now, Mr. Gorges," I said. "Though it was a true pleasure to see you again."

"Thomas," he said, with a slightly impish smile. "Perhaps I shall come to court more often. I hope I may continue to call you Elin. It's unexpected and comely, and it befits you well."

I blushed like a girl and nodded my assent.

We followed Her Majesty back to her chamber, where the long process of helping her undress began. Away from the prying eyes of the courtiers, we would carefully take off her makeup and unpin her hair and the ruffs and sleeves, stomachers and undergarments that held together her gowns. She was a real woman, flesh and blood, who grew fatigued and angry, who loved and lost and felt anxiety and pain like the rest of us mortals. But to her kingdom, Cynthia must always remain goddess and queen. Her Majesty had to be the most constant, convincing player of all. I imagined that grew tiresome.

I looked about me, and as the queen readied herself for bed, many of her ladies slipped away. Those who remained were mainly relatives on her mother's side. The queen often surrounded herself with her mother's relatives, including Lady Hunsdon, married to Henry Carey, Lord Hunsdon, the brother of poor passed Lady Knollys and son of Mary Boleyn.

"One of your cousins introduced himself to me this evening, Majesty, after the play," I said while I prepared scented water for her wash.

"Indeed!" she responded. "Pray, who would that be?"

"Thomas Gorges," I said. "He told me he was a relative of your mother, Queen Anne Boleyn."

As soon as the words were out of my mouth, all motion in the room stopped. I myself stopped, due to the reaction of those around me. I looked about me, but all gazes were dropped downward. "I'm sorry, madam." I fell to my knees. "Have I misspoken?"

She took a deep breath. "No, Lady von Snakenborg, you have not. My court is unaccustomed to mention of my mother. As you are not from here, you did not know."

"Forgive me, Majesty. It's only that, well, I *am* here at your court, in which I delight and am greatly honored. But no one speaks of my mother or my sisters, and as time passes by I long to hear their names, to remember that they are, and were. When they go unspoken, it's as though they did not exist." Someone inhaled sharply, but I had spoken my mind, and had been given leave, and I was not going to back away now, nor did I believe that the queen expected me to.

She raised me up then and drew me closer, so much more woman than queen then with her white bed dress on and no makeup. "Just because I do not speak of my mother in public does not mean I do not speak of her at all. You have done no wrong, be not afraid."

The room sighed a relief, and the ladies went back to their tasks. I pulled, from under my gown, a long chain with a locket on the end. "May I show this to you, Majesty?"

She looked curious. "Indeed."

I unclasped the locket and held it toward her. "This one is me," I said, pointing to a sketch of a young girl. "And this is my mother, on her wedding day."

She looked at them for a long time before raising her black eyes to meet my gaze. "So she is kept close, though hidden away."

"Yes, Majesty." Nothing more needed to be said.

"We are sorry that you yearn for your family. Especially as things are not yet settled with Northampton. But that may soon change."

"Yes, Majesty," I said, though I had no idea what she was talking about. She held out her hand for me to kiss, and I did.

Lady Hunsdon came forward then with the evening's devotional books.

"Lady von Snakenborg," the queen said to me in a kind voice, before I withdrew. "The past cannot be cured. But the present can be held, and the future can be grasped."

I curtseyed and backed away.

I could not sleep that night. I rehearsed the lines of the play over and over in my head, and in my heart, and thought upon Thomas Gorges. I was ready to grasp my future.

# SEVEN

Year of Our Lord 1570

Winter: Year of Our Lord 1571
The Palace of Whitehall

F or the new year, the queen gave me a brooch
that was fashioned as a jeweled apple. I could
not hold back my joy and reached forward to
embrace her upon its presentation. She did not
rebuke me but allowed me to show my affection
before kissing her hand, perhaps because Princess
Cecelia had already made a royal precedence of
indiscriminate shows of affection from Swedes. I
gave the queen an elaborate lace ruff I had tatted
myself, starched, and then wrapped around hot
rods to shape it.

"This is marvelous," she said with real
enthusiasm. "I much prefer gifts made with the
hand and the heart to those concealed within
purse strings." She indicated to her Mistress of
Wardrobes that she wished to wear it the very next
day.

Soon thereafter she raised Mary Radcliffe and
me to Gentlewomen of the Bedchamber. I continued to care for the queen's gifts; among them
that year were not only precious gems and those
purses filled with coins but monkeys and, of

course, noisome songbirds in gilded cages. I delivered them to Her Majesty's aviary with great displeasure. They squawked, rather than sang, while under my care. I covered their cages with a degree of smug satisfaction at their displeasure at being snuffed, but I was thrilled to be in charge of something so dear to Her Majesty's heart.

Mary took over the job of tasting each of the queen's dishes before they were served to her. She tasted boldly, unafraid, honored by the position. Though we were raised to the bedchamber at the same time, Mary did not warm to me. I did not know why. Was it because I was a foreigner? Had I misspoken? Was she cool to everyone? I should have to seek a way to win friends, as the time when I was not serving was very lonely indeed. I read, I did needlework, I attended church. I looked out the window and hoped that life would lighten soon, like dawn. I wondered about my mother. I wondered if my sister Karin had children. I turned quickly from that thought, as it pained me.

One Sunday in early January we followed the queen to the Royal Chapel for the morning's worship. Her counselors, some of whom leaned toward Puritanism or Calvinism, disapproved of the fact that she held with her clergy's wearing vestments and had a silver cross and candlesticks near her altar. Her Majesty had said that while she was bred, born, and would surely die in her Protestant faith, she preferred to worship this way and none would browbeat her to change. Too, it was an acknowledgment to her Catholic subjects that she had not stripped away all they held dear.

Partway through the morning sermon, there was a commotion in the hallway. The preacher stopped his lesson and someone came in and whispered into Her Majesty's ear. She nodded mutely, signaled for the sermon to continue, and listened until the end. Shortly thereafter she led us to her Presence Chamber, where she met the Scots' ambassador. The Earl of Moray, the Protestant leader of Scotland, and Mary, Queen of Scots's illegitimate half brother, had been assassinated. The way was now made clear for Mary's return to the throne in Scotland.

In the north of England, many Catholics rejoiced.

Shortly thereafter the French ambassador sought an audience with Her Majesty. "My master has directed me to tell you, Your Grace, that if his cousin Mary, Queen of Scots, is not immediately returned to her throne, he will be forced to declare war against you." He removed his cap with a flourish, then removed his presence from the chamber.

Within a second Cecil spoke up. "Majesty, it would be to your uttermost peril to agree to reinstall Mary in Scotland," he said. "Not only would her, and your, Protestant subjects rebel, but she is discontented with her own throne and seeks yours instead. You would be endangering your own person."

"This is not the moment for me to dither with France, Cecil," she said, holding the back of her hand to her forehead and then staring out the window. "We shall dictate some terms to you under which we would consider assisting our sister to regain her throne."

I saw the look of utter dismay on Cecil's face before we ladies were dismissed to prepare a private chamber for a midday meal for the queen.

I awoke on May 25 to a furious pounding on my door not but a few hours, it seemed, after I had gone to sleep.

It was Clemence. "Her Majesty has need of you to assist her in dressing," she said. I rushed to brush and pin my own hair while Clemence prepared a gown for me to slip into. I raced down the gallery toward Her Majesty's chambers. When I arrived, only Anne Dudley was there, and she signaled to me to help her assist Her Majesty. Many of the other ladies, older than we, took longer to arise in the morning when they were not expected.

"That will not do!" the queen barked at Anne as Anne brought forth a gown. Anne nodded to the maid to run back to a nearby chamber where some of the queen's gowns were stored. She brought back two other choices, and Anne nodded toward one. The queen didn't speak her agreement, but she said nothing to the contrary, so we continued to pin her sleeves and other pieces together. I held open a pair of delicate gloves as she slipped her hands into them. We applied her makeup and powdered her red hair with finely ground diamonds. Without a word, she left and went to meet her councilors in a private chamber.

"This morning a Mr. John Felton nailed a bull from the pope onto the garden gate of the Bishop of London," Anne told me. "In it the pope denies 'Elizabeth, the pretended Queen of England, the servant of wickedness,' her throne. He said that henceforth he was absolving all of her subjects of their allegiance to her."

"Surely not! Her Majesty has always trusted that her subjects would be loyal to her," I said.

"It worsens," she said. "He called on all faithful Catholics to rise up, oust, and, if necessary, murder the 'heretic queen.' I suspect it will be ignored by most of Her Majesty's subjects, Catholics included."

"And yet even if there are but a few who seek to do her harm, and there will be, she shall not know whom to trust."

"She can perhaps trust no one at all," Anne replied.

I returned to my chamber in sorrow. Her Majesty had always desired that her recusant Catholic subjects be allowed to worship, in private, as their consciences dictated. "I have no wish to have windows into men's souls," she'd said on the matter. But now the pope had forced English Catholics to choose between treason or faith.

It would not be a lie to say that, while many recusants yet worshipped quietly, after the pope's decree, the queen's policies of necessity began to change. She outlawed Rosary beads. She had the import of bulls and other communiqués from the See of Rome banned; punishment was hanging, disemboweling, and quartering. John Felton, who had nailed the bull to the garden gate, was tortured and executed, but not before loudly denying that Elizabeth was his queen. His wife had been the queen's childhood friend.

That night, I asked Clemence, "What did Her Majesty do when her sister, Mary, was queen? Mary was most Catholic, is that not so?"

Clemence nodded proudly. "Her Grace told her sister that she would investigate the Catholic faith, having not been raised in it. But my mother served in that household, as Lord Northampton knows, and she told me that all present were Protestants, reading Holy Writ and praying in English and putting away popish superstitions and such."

"So the queen remained true to her faith, though its practice was hidden?"

"Yes." Clemence nodded. "All of Her Grace's friends and household were Nicodemites, after

Nicodemus in Scripture, he who came to the Lord Jesus privately to ask Him questions on matters of faith for which he knew he would be persecuted, perhaps unto death. They worshipped privately and bided their time."

I nodded and said no more. I was a Protestant myself, having been raised in the Lutheran faith and then choosing the Church of England as my own. But I saw little difference between a Nicodemite in Mary's reign and a recusant in Elizabeth's.

I would, of course, keep that thought to myself.

The next day William sought me out, though it had been some weeks since we had spent time together. He looked young and hopeful in a way I'd not seen for some time.

"What is it?" I asked, after inviting him into my apartment. He drew me near the window and then near to himself, into his arms.

"I know I should not take pleasure in this," he said. "And indeed, in the suffering, I do not. But my . . . Lady Anne Bourchier, to whom I am married, has taken ill. She is not expected to live beyond the year."

I smiled at him, wanly, I knew, which I am sure he interpreted as my unwillingness to rejoice over the illness of anyone. But inside, I was mixed. I was fond of William, but I had long let go of the heartstring that tied me to him, thinking we would not marry. And, of course, I had of late joyfully considered handing that string to another.

I did not yet know what to think, or feel, or how to proceed, should her death come to pass.

In November, Sir Henry Lee instituted an Accession Day celebration to commemorate the day the queen had taken the throne. Sir Henry had, with other courtiers, chosen to mark the occasion from this year forward with festivals, jousts, banquets, masques, and all other manner of joyous observation.

"It is," William told me, as we made our way to the banquet on the opening night, "a way to pledge our allegiance to the queen, to rebuke the effrontery of the rebellion of the north, and to respond to the excommunication of the queen by the pope."

Throughout the land were bells ringing and bonfires. Poets from Oxford down to the smallest schoolboy composed verse in honor of the queen, and whenever they were presented to her it was clear that she took similar pleasure, no matter the source. The day was added to the calendar of holy days.

"Does this concern you?" I asked William quietly. "She is, after all, woman as well as queen. The more they beatify her, the more difficult it will become for them to accept her marriage and the bearing of children."

He smiled. "Though she is already thirty-seven

years of age, the people want, above all, her marriage and children," he said. "And, methinks, marriage is much on the mind of someone else." He smiled warmly. Anne Bourchier had grown weaker and more ill, and while neither William nor I desired it, her death would open up the way for us to be married. She had, after all, repudiated him nigh on four decades earlier.

With some effort I brought my heart and mind round again to the idea of marrying William. But I did.

On the second day of the celebrations, Anne Dudley introduced me to Anne, Lady d'Aubernon of Usher. "She is cousin to Sir Henry Lee, the man who organized the Accession Day festivities, and he is the queen's champion," Anne said. "As her mother, Meg Wyatt, was a great favorite of Queen Anne Boleyn, Lady Anne is, of course, a favorite of Her Majesty."

I bowed my head slightly. "Lady Helena von Snakenborg," I said. "I am surprised we have not yet met."

A woman of about thirty, she looked ten years younger when she laughed. "I am about court from time to time, but my husband and I have a large brood of children already and I found I am better suited for the country than for court. However"—she grew somber—"I will be present anywhere, at any time, to support the queen. My brother, William, Earl of Asquith"—she nodded toward a tall man with curly brown hair—"often represents Her Majesty as an ambassador or emissary as well as administering his estates."

We made some small talk, but I soon saw Thomas Gorges walking toward me with purpose. He had no armor on, nor stage paint, but bore himself with dignity. I had not seen him since the performance of Lyly's play and my breath caught in my throat.

Lady d'Aubernon smiled at me. "That man looks intent upon speaking with you. I am sure we'll meet again, Lady Helena."

I murmured my agreement as she withdrew.

Thomas bowed. "Elin," he said, smiling at me. "May I have a word?" He looked about, confused. "You are unaccompanied?"

"No." I shook my head. "I was about to make my way back to the viewing windows before the tilts begin."

"I see. You sit with the queen?"

I shook my head. I greatly desired to leave and say no more, but I knew what he truly asked and I needed to answer him. "I sit with the Marquess of Northampton."

Thomas nodded and gently withdrew his proffered hand—which was strong and as square as his jaw—out of respect, I guessed. "I've heard his wife is ill unto death."

"You're well informed for a man who spends most of his time away from court."

"I am no court creature, but I learn what is important to me," he said. "Shall you marry him when she dies?"

I nodded. "He has cared well for me for five years since I arrived in England."

"Do you love him?"

I could have reproved him for his impudence, but I knew the hurt and loss of hope behind his question and so I did not. "I care for him as he has cared for me. Fondly. And I shall not disappoint or dishonor him." I waited a moment before speaking again. "I shan't ever forget your performance as Endymion, nor the words you spoke to me. I recall them to heart and mind most often."

He held my gaze and recited a sonnet to me, softly. "Then here are some others, which I hope you will not forget. 'You do beguile me; O, that I could fly; from myself to you, or from your own self, I.'"

With great reserve, and the training of my mother, I held back from my eyes and my face the affection and budding passion I felt toward him. I kept my hands at my sides so they did not reach forward for him.

He bowed and walked away.

Shortly after the new year, Anne Bourchier died. William saw that she was buried with dignity, then asked the queen if we might marry in May.

I'd thought that the Englishwomen would more readily yield friendship to me now that I was to be properly married, and to a peer, but they did not. Instead, I heard whispers when they thought I could not hear about my skills with herbs and how useful it was that Anne Bourchier had died before Lord Northampton did, though he was unwell more and more often. If he had died first, of course, I would have no husband. The implications in the great hall, where we dined, was that I'd had a hand in assisting Lady Anne Bourchier heavenward in order to procure a high title and substantial incomes. It cast a shadow over the already cool affections many at court had for me, a stranger among them.

Nothing was directly accused, so nothing could be directly responded to.

I said naught to William.

# EIGHT

Spring: Year of Our Lord 1571
The Palace of Whitehall

Autumn and Winter: Year of the Lord 1571
Kenilworth Castle
Warwickshire

I, a Swedish bride of twenty-three, was to be married in the Queen of England's Closet at Westminster. The queen herself had taken charge of the arrangements that would normally be made by the bride's family; she helped me choose my maids of honor and a lady to stand with me. I chose my dear Anne Dudley, Countess of Warwick, and I know that pleased the queen as well as me. I also chose Eleanor Brydges as a maid, and another small girl, the daughter of one of the queen's courtiers, would hold my train.

"We've ordered yellow silk dresses trimmed with green velvet and silver lace," the queen said, "for your maids and ladies. They shall be delivered tomorrow." She did not ask me if that met with my approval; I do not think the queen asked anyone for their approval. However, she had impeccable taste and knew what I liked, the colors of herbs and gardens, and had planned accordingly.

"I'm very grateful, Majesty," I said, hiding a

smile at her competency in this, and every area. "And I'm also grateful for the banquet you're sponsoring for William and me afterward. I do not know how I can ever repay your kindness in this matter." In truth, as the day approached and I truly began to allow myself to believe I would be a bride, at last I grew more excited. I was to be a wife! Mistress of many manors and, legally, rightly, dearest to William's heart and person. I could not keep back my smiles.

The queen saw and smiled at me in return. "We are pleased for Northampton's sake that this marriage, at long last, will come to pass, but we are also glad for our own sake," she replied. "This one time, I do not so much feel that I am losing a lady as gaining one."

I did not understand, just then, what she meant, but there were many details to attend to and well-wishers to respond to, so I let the comment pass.

"The king and queen of Sweden were present at my mother's wedding," I said. "So I am honored that you will attend my own. My mother also said it was luckiest to be married in the morning."

"Then it's a good omen that you will be married in the morn," she said.

"You must arrange your own wedding for the morning, too," I said, teasing her. She still held hope that she would marry, and her monthly courses were regular, so we hoped, too.

"Impertinence!" she said, but with a light wave

of her gloves. "What should we present to you for a wedding gift?"

I stared at her. "Surely not. The gowns, the wedding dinner in the council chamber, the musicians—that is enough and more."

She was pleased, I could tell, but pressed on. "Nothing at all, then, my lady?"

I thought for a moment. "There is one request, if I might be bold."

"Go on."

"In my family, when something of consequence occurs, we sisters would send one another off with a kiss on the temple, for affection and care, and concern. I have no sister to send me off on this journey, Majesty, but you are setting me off upon it. Would it be overbold of me to ask that you might kiss my temple in such sisterly fashion as I took my leave from your chamber to meet with William?"

For the first time in our acquaintance she appeared to know not how to respond; she opened her mouth to say something and then closed it, appearing to think upon the matter. I grew vexed that I had greatly overstepped my bounds, but instead of a sharp rebuke, which she was not afraid to regularly offer, her face and tone softened and she said, "Yes, Lady von Snakenborg, I willingly send you off thusly."

I steadied myself so as not to let a sigh of relief escape my lips!

The next morning Her Majesty had her own ladies, in addition to Clemence, assist me with my wedding attire. I used my own cosmetics; I preferred to prepare them myself. And just before I was to meet William, the queen bent over and kissed me softly on the temple, leaving a lingering scent of the vanilla perfume I'd blended for her.

That evening there was a grand dinner and the queen danced many times more with Lord Robert than did William and I. William's legs still pained him and I kept close to my new husband to attend to him whenever he needed me, and to shower him with my affection and attention, which was his due, and gladly given. He left to receive the congratulations of some of his highborn friends. The queen came to stand near me with some of her other ladies, who looked at me in a new light. I was no longer simply Lady von Snakenborg; I was the Marchioness of Northampton. As the Duke of Norfolk had not yet remarried, after the queen, I was now the highest-ranking lady in England.

The men stood some feet away from us and I could not help but notice how splendidly attired they were. "They are as richly gowned as the women!" I said without thinking. But the group of women around me tittered an agreement and I smiled.

" 'Tis your wedding night," Mary Radcliffe said slyly. "It's natural that you would be noticing the men and what they are wearing."

There was an undercurrent there, and it didn't take the queen, who loved a bawdy joke, long to pick up on it. "Perhaps there is a particular item of the men's clothing that has drawn your attention, Marchioness?" She used my title with relish and affection, so I knew she jested with me, but she waved her fan about midwaist level toward the men. I knew what she was speaking of; like ruffs, which had started small and tasteful and had grown all out of proportion, men's codpieces had become immodest and prominent.

"There are sometimes accessories made so overlarge that even the eye which would seek to avoid them cannot," I said.

"Are 'accessories' not overlarge in Sweden?" one of the ladies asked unpleasantly. I suspected my new title did not warm her English ears, but the queen looked at me expectantly; not replying was not an option.

"In Sweden, the cobblers fashion the shoe to fit the foot, not several sizes too large," I countered delicately.

The queen burst out in laughter, and even the lady who'd meant to prod me responded with a genuine smile. Anne Dudley reached out and took my arm in hers and I gladly entwined elbows; she was a true friend and I hoped I could repay her in kind.

Her Majesty drew me aside before William and

I left to tell me that she had settled some rents upon me as a wedding gift, the incomes befitting my new rank.

William and I left court that evening and returned to his London estate. He'd had the bedchamber prepared with new linens and though the fire was fresh and warm, the servants were not to be seen. I bathed in perfumed water and when I returned, he awaited. He looked younger, though I did not tell him that, and I was pleased to see him so joyous. I felt neither the fear that some women speak of on their wedding nights nor a burst of passion that could not be contained. I felt fondness, and affection, and satisfaction that what we had longed and planned for had finally, happily, come to pass. If anything, he, older and already twice married, seemed more hesitant than I.

I patted the seat beside me to welcome him close. We talked for some time and drank some wine, and then afterward we tenderly, quietly consummated our marriage. As he had been toward me from the first moment he made my acquaintance, he was gentle and thoughtful and treated me with care bordering on adoration. I treated him with affection and respect, and prayed I would always do so.

Afterward, I lay next to him, noticing that the small hairs upon his skin were like tiny, curled wisps of smoke. I reached over and put my hand upon his chest, which seemed to please him.

"It has been a long time since I have had the touch of a woman I love," William said. "Perhaps until it is restored, one does not realize how one yearns for that touch."

I drew the coverlet around me and looked upon him. "I felt warmed by your touch, too," I said. "I have, of late, begun to think about that as regards Her Majesty."

He looked at me. "What do you mean?"

"She is the queen, and it is nigh on impossible to touch her. The times I have reached out to her, for a quick embrace or to ask for the kiss of a sister, the ladies of the court seemed taken aback. And yet, she has no mother to embrace her, no sisters, no husband, no children. Does she, too, not crave human touch?"

"I would think that to be true," he agreed. "I'd not thought of it."

"It's one reason why she dances so much, so often, I'll wager," I said. "Perhaps that's also why she enjoys ointments, salves, and the ministrations of a caring hand."

He reached over then and took my hands in his own caring ones and we fell asleep in harmony.

We stayed at his London home so I could attend to the queen, still, on a daily basis. When I was not waiting upon her we hawked, played chess, danced, and read Italian poetry and plays. As the summer grew hotter and the days longer, William's energy level grew shorter and his gout more pronounced. It troubled me.

The first weeks of our marriage, the nights passed quietly as we shared a bed. But soon, William began to awaken in the middle of the night.

"What is it?" I asked, shivering in darkness lit only by the moon.

"It's an ache in my feet, that's all," he said. But his face was white with pain.

"Can I help? I have some ointment that might assist." I opened the lacquered case in which I kept my preparations and chose one with mint in it, which would speed the medicine through the skin. I rubbed it into his foot, but that seemed to cause him greater pain. "It feels both burning hot and as if my foot was held in cold water," he said. He pulled his foot away, and I used a clean linen to wipe off what remained of the salve.

He lay back down in the bed and turned about like a bird on a spit. I could not sleep, knowing him to be in pain, so I spent much of the night trying to bring him relief. The next day he told me that he was having his manservant prepare another chamber. "I shan't keep you awake all night," he said. When I protested, he held up his hand and indicated that he was going to sleep elsewhere until he felt well.

He did not return to sleep with me all summer. In October came an invitation from Lord Robert to attend a week at Warwick in which he meant to entertain the queen and her closest courtiers.

"We can decline," I told William, waving for a servant to bring more warm compresses to lay upon his legs. "The queen surely understands that you have been unwell."

"No, we must attend," he said. "I have spent so little time at court already."

"But you can hardly walk," I protested.

"I shall arrange for that."

We packed several trunks, loaded upon litters, and William traveled in the litter rather than ride. I rode alongside him so his pride would not be wounded by my riding horseback. We took the journey slowly and arrived in late October. Although I was able to attend most of the festivities, including a play in which Lord Robert himself starred for the queen's pleasure, William was unable to leave his room and I returned to check on him at every free moment.

He grew steadily worse until the day came in which he was unable to respond to my questions or touch. I spoke to him soothingly, although I grew overwrought inside. Lord Robert sent his physician, but he could not help. And so, on October 28, my husband passed from my arms into the arms of God. We had been married but five months.

I did not leave his side until Anne Dudley quietly eased me away.

His body was prepared and laid out and I returned to him. I gently rubbed oil of rosemary, for remembrance, upon his face. "Thank you, William. You cared for me like a father, a teacher, and finally a husband. You found me as Elin, Wolf's daughter, and left me as Helena, Marchioness of Northampton." I bent down and kissed his cheek and then the coffin lid was closed, my girlhood carried away with him.

After the funeral, which by custom I did not attend, Her Majesty dismissed all but a few maids and pages and called me to her. "Are you well, Helena?" It was the first time she had ever used my first name.

"I am as well as can be expected, Your Majesty," I said. "Thank you for your many kindnesses."

"As William died with no issue, his estates reverted to the crown. Rest assured we shall ensure that you receive your portion and rents from Northampton's properties and everything that is now due you."

"Now due me, Majesty?"

"My good lady marquess, as the highest-ranking lady in the land you shall carry our train, you shall take precedence after ourselves and enjoy a host of other duties and privileges, including attending upon our person more often." At this she smiled, and for the first time in days I smiled back. I now understood why she was happy for herself as well as for William and me when we married, and it gladdened me; I was now of sufficient rank to be a close friend. It put me in mind of the evening when William told me that the queen had raised Lord Robert to earl so he was of a sufficiently marriageable rank. "Blanche can assist you in understanding," the queen finished.

I curtseyed and thanked her again.

She stood up and said, "And now, I've promised Robin that I shall best him at chess."

And then a thought crossed my mind and I reflected misery once more. A tear slipped down the side of my face and I wiped it away quickly and then curtseyed, face tilted downward, to hide my further sorrow.

"What is it?" the queen asked, bidding me rise.

"William and I often played chess. I shall miss that."

She rested a hand on my shoulder, tarried for a moment more, and then took her leave.

I would return to court a marchioness, foreigner or not.

# NINE

Years of Our Lord 1572, 1573
The Palace of Whitehall
On Progress
Kenilworth Castle

January: Year of Our Lord 1574
The Palace of Whitehall

T he year before had been one of mixed joy and
sorrow for me, and it had been for the queen
as well. Whilst I'd been celebrating my marriage,
the queen had been informed of yet another plot to
murder her, leaving her throne open for Mary,
Queen of Scots, and her secretly proposed husband, the Duke of Norfolk, he who had promised
to meddle no more in Mary's marriage.

One night at cards, Lord Ambrose Dudley, Lord
Robert's brother, explained to us what had
transpired. "The queen received a warning from
the Grand Duke of Tuscany that a man named
Ridolfi was working with Mary's ambassador to
the English court, John Lesley, to overthrow
Elizabeth and place Mary on the English throne."

"Isn't he the same man who commissioned
that pamphlet some years back calling for the
'restoration' of Mary to the English throne?" Anne
Dudley asked her husband.

He nodded. "Yes, in spite of Her Majesty's kind treatment of him and his mistress. In any case," he continued, "books and letters directly connected Lesley to Mary's involvement in the plot, and he divulged more when threatened with torture, including the use of papal money that was sent to the Marians in Scotland. Further investigation showed that Norfolk had been sending money to Mary's supporters in Scotland, too."

I couldn't believe how foolish Norfolk had been. Did he not think that he would be discovered, though he always was? Or did he not care? The plan was, of course, revealed, and Norfolk was arrested and tried by his peers. He was found guilty, and yet the queen was reluctant to sign his death warrant. To the frustration of her government, she'd signed—and rescinded—the execution warrants twice.

We sat in the queen's chamber some days later, the late sun filtering through the windows of Westminster Palace, watching barges sail up and down the Thames. I did my lacework, other women read, and some worked a needle to linen. Although I sat closest to the queen, carried her train, and had substantial grants of my own, none except Anne Dudley treated me with warmth beyond respect. I'd heard the word *Dane* muttered when I entered the room.

"What are you working, Helena?" the queen asked me, nodding toward my needle.

"I'm making the edge of a linen, Majesty. Would you like a turn with my needle?" I jested. We had indeed grown closer and the queen had given me liberties, within reason, since I'd become a marchioness.

She batted at me. All knew she was disinclined toward needlework.

"I've heard that your cousin Mary of Scots excels at needlework," I said, not looking up. "I've been told that she not only plies her own needle but that she fashions her own designs."

"Perhaps she, and other needleworkers, should spend yet more time in productive yield," the queen answered tartly before turning back to her lettering, terminating the conversation. I knew that I had reraised an issue in her sharp mind, though. At Norfolk's trial, there was much hard evidence, letters and communications and such, but there were also hints of treason of a more feminine kind. Norfolk was found to be wearing an engagement ring sent to him by Mary, and also in his possession was a pillow cover in which she'd embroidered a hand clipping off a barren vine—Elizabeth—so that a more fruitful one, Mary, may flourish. Underneath she'd sewn the motto "Virtue flourishes by wounding." Perhaps that safe pillow he'd sought?

And yet the queen was ill disposed to believe that Mary had plotted treasonously against her. Perhaps because she had so few Tudor family members, she wanted to believe Mary when she called the queen "my dear sister." There were none so blind as those who would not see. I thought back on my sister, dallying with my fiancé. I hadn't wanted to believe that she would seek her own good at my expense. But she had. Our queen was, perhaps, vulnerable to that very human, harmful desire to believe the best in others for far too long.

The queen did not alter her daily routine in response to the threats from within and without. She rode, she hunted, she walked, and she entertained without fear. In May, the French came to ratify the Treaty of Blois and she played the virginals herself to entertain them. I stood nearby, though she played from memory and had no need of a page turner. It did not escape my notice, nor anyone in the rooms, I'm sure, that the virginals had been decorated with a falcon and a tree stump, a mute remembrance of her mother's badge.

The music she'd chosen to play was wistful and slow compared with the lively volta we'd danced the night before. For those who listened, she foreshadowed. Comfortable with her new French treaty, she shortly thereafter issued the death warrant for Norfolk. This time, she did not rescind it.

I recalled a line I'd read in a book of poetry found in Her Majesty's library. It had been penned by Henry Howard, Norfolk's father, himself executed for treason some years before his son followed him to the scaffold: "Content thyself with thine estate, / Neither wish death, nor fear his might."

Lord Robert came to the queen's chambers late on June 2 to report to her. She dismissed all but a few who stayed for support.

"He wore black satin," he began, and I hid a smile that Lord Robert would notice what the condemned man wore, "and spoke well and nobly to the crowd. He recalled that 'through great clemency of Her Majesty, it has been strange to see a nobleman suffer in this place. It is my fortune to be the first, and I pray God that I may be the last.'"

How readily one may be raised in this realm and how quickly the ennobled may fall.

Would that Norfolk's prayer come to pass, that his noble death would be the first and last in uneasy years. He was a pawn wishing to be promoted to king, and minor pieces are oft sacrificed early in a game. The game, though, is always between the two most powerful pieces, queens.

Both could not win. One can never predict, however, if a given game shall go to the bold or to the prudent.

That summer, as always, the queen took the court on Progress. Cecil bemoaned the cost of moving the queen's carts all summer. The rest of us bemoaned not only the inconvenience of traipsing about the country with those hundreds of carts and litters but the lack of rooms for us courtiers, then required to crowd together like rabbits in warrens. But the queen would meet her people and have a summer of, mostly, an abatement from work. 'Twas hard to begrudge her that, and we enjoyed partaking of the lavish hospitality offered at each stop as well.

Things came to a fiery head, twice, in Warwick, however. Early in our stay a firework display was put on for her pleasure; unfortunately, balls of flame and hissing squibs fell into the nearby village, burning to the ground the simple house of a country man and his wife, who just escaped with their lives. The next morning, the queen had them brought to her.

They were still filthy with soot and smelled badly of spoiled meat; it was to Her Majesty's credit that she did not breathe into her pomander as she bid them come near. "My good man, we have heard that great damage was done to your home last eve," she began. Her voice was always quieter when dealing with commoners, gentling their nerves.

The man, kneeling before her, said, "Yes, Your Majesty. I'm sorry ta say that the house is done gone, and my bed and boots with it."

"And you, my good woman, are you well?"

the queen kindly asked the woman beside him.

"Yes, yes, ma'am," she stammered out. She could not meet the queen's eye.

The queen turned toward me. "My good lady marquess, would you be so kind as to take up a collection among the court for this couple? We should like to see their house rebuilt and relardered before we return to London."

"Certainly, Your Highness," I said. I set out to take a collection, and when I returned to the queen she was dictating a letter to her secretary. I stayed well in the background, repinning a brooch to my gown.

The queen stamped her ring into the hot wax seal and said to her secretary, "Please see that this letter gets to Mr. Thomas Gorges, who will deliver it to the Queen of Scots for me."

I dropped my brooch on the floor and the queen turned to me. "Are you well, Marchioness?"

"Yes, madam," I said, keeping my eye upon my brooch, not daring to meet her sharp gaze, as I knew she would see more in me if I did.

That week came an apocalypse, news delivered while we were out hunting with the queen. A messenger raced ahead to where the queen and Lord Robert rode in the lead. Within minutes, she had signaled all to stop. The hunt was being canceled and we were to return to Warwick Castle to mourn. The French king, perhaps at the urging of his mother, Catherine de' Medici, had authorized the assassination of some high-placed Protestants gathered in France for the wedding of Protestant Henry of Navarre to the French princess Margaret. Somehow, the French people had whipped themselves into a bloodthirsty mob and, in the end, murdered tens of thousands of common-born Protestant citizens.

It would not be inaccurate to say that the event turned many in court, and country, further against the Catholic faith and those practicing it.

That night, Eleanor Brydges and I worked together sorting through Her Majesty's ribbons. When Eleanor bent forward, I saw a beaded necklace tucked under her dress. Rosary beads. Outlawed Rosary beads . . . worn only by recusants, whose loyalties, of course, were now suspect.

"I see you wear something dear to your heart," I said quietly, not meeting her eye. "Rosary beads?"

"No!" she denied, tucking the necklace firmly under her neckline. Seeking to defuse the situation, I pulled out my own necklace, the locket of my mother and me. "I have shown this to but few, but I'd like to show it to you." She had been a constant, if not particularly warm, friend since I arrived at court.

"Lovely," she said, then turned away. "What do you think of the French matter?" she asked, quickly changing the conversation.

I shook my head. "There has long been talk, on

and off, of the queen marrying with the Duke d'Anjou." He, too, was a son of Catherine de' Medici. "All wish for Her Majesty to be married, but I question whether any could accept him now. Perhaps it will have to be an Englishman who provides our heir after all!" I finished merrily. I wanted nothing more than for the queen to be happily married, and in the end, I felt that could be achieved only with Lord Robert.

Eleanor did not comment. Maybe she was deep in thought about her own marriage, as she had just become engaged to a man we knew little about, Mr. George Giffard. I did not take mind of it. One thing everyone at court agreed upon was that the queen needed a successor and an heir.

Later that night, as I took off my own jewelry, I thought, *No matter her denial, she wore Rosary beads. For certain. And then she lied about it.* Should I have spoken out further? Was there someone I should tell? This was certainly not something I could ask Clemence, or anyone, and I did not know what to do.

Eleanor was married the next summer; she'd invited the queen to her wedding, of course, but the queen, buried with the work of her realm, sent me as her representative instead. Eleanor pretended that this did not bother her, but I knew it did. Her sister Katherine, younger than she, had married first a year earlier; Katherine was a great beauty and had captured the heart of William Sandys, Third Baron Sandys of the Vyne. The queen had attended that wedding.

Clemence noticed my silence that night. She'd been serving me for many years, and we'd grown close. "Was she unkind to you, then?" she asked.

I nodded. "I understand it, though. My younger sister was chosen, and honored, before I was. Eleanor's sister has married a man with a grand title, and she a man with no title at all."

"Don't be feeling sorry for that one," Clemence said as she helped me into my nightgown. "That family is oversown with bad seeds. Why, Eleanor's aunt tried to poison her own husband. He complained right sharply to Cecil. But Cecil, not understanding, mayhap, that the ways of women can oft times be more wicked than the ways of men, did nothing about it."

I looked at her. "Is this true?"

"Indeed, it is."

I let it go. The queen had settled some rents and small license on Eleanor as a wedding gift and spoken to her kindly; I well loved being Her Majesty's representative at weddings, and in her stead in other places.

As for marriage . . . I had been widowed for not quite three years and marriage was beginning to creep back into my own mind, though no one had roused my interest, save one, whom I had not seen for some time, though I'd kept watch for him.

• • •

Just after the new year, whispers passed like a baton throughout the court: Lord Robert was said to have secretly married his lover, the widowed Douglass Howard, Baroness Sheffield, and she was now with child. Elizabeth was too wise and well informed not to know of this, but she hid her feelings for a time. One of the queen's mottoes was "I see and say nothing." Perhaps she said nothing, but she always acted. Eventually it seemed that the grief over Lord Robert's whispered wedding could no longer be dammed and it whipped Her Majesty into a wondrous squall from which we all sought cover.

Poor Mary Shelton bore the brunt of it. In January she approached the queen to ask for permission to marry James Scudamore. The queen refused to give Mary, her second cousin, an answer, and soon enough Mary withdrew from the queen's presence whenever she could.

Word began to pass that Mary had already married Scudamore, assuming that the queen would grant her permission. When the queen found out she called Mary Shelton before her. "Strange news has reached us," she began, "that you have married James Scudamore without our permission."

"Yes, Majesty, I'm sorry, I thought not to trouble you with so trivial a matter."

"Thought not to trouble me?" She stood and in

one quick motion swung her arm around to Mary, striking her hand, hard.

That shocked all of us, apparently even the queen herself. She sat back down, indicated that Mary should come near her, and spoke to her so quietly that none of us could hear what she said. Mary nodded, said nothing, and fled the room.

Later, Eleanor told me she was leaving for Sudeley to assist her mother as the queen would soon visit. "The queen has used Mary Shelton very ill for her marriage."

I nodded my agreement; although I had served a princess who was not above offering a quick blow to her ladies, I'd yet to witness the queen strike anyone. I'd thought it was beneath her. I'd been wrong.

"She bought her husband very dearly," I agreed.

It could not have helped that Douglass Sheffield appeared about court flush in health and love and, perhaps, with the glow of pregnancy. In the days that followed, the queen exhorted all of us unmarried or widowed women to remain in the single state. Mary Radcliffe nodded and spoke her enthusiastic agreement, having already committed herself to a lifetime of virginity.

Those of us who were disinclined to celibacy kept our own counsel. As for me, I had special reason not to agree. I'd finally seen Thomas Gorges one day, riding at court. I trained my eyes on his fine form as long as I could keep him in view, then turned away from the window with a smile. I clasped my hands together and then unclasped them to smooth my hair.

He was clearly, then, at court again.

# TEN

We arrived at Sudeley Castle in the flush of spring, its gardens verdant and lush; they were well known for their beauty. Lady Dorothy had recently wed the son of Her Majesty's beloved but late Lady Knollys, Sir Francis's wife, so the queen had come to pay her respects. After attending to Her Majesty, I made my way to the Chapel of St. Mary. I knew William's sister Queen Kateryn was buried there, and I wished to pay my respects and to pray and meditate.

"Your brother was a fine man," I said aloud in the quiet stillness, though I knew Queen Kateryn was with the Lord and could not hear me. "And your stepdaughter, Elizabeth, she is a fine queen. You would be proud of her." William had told me that his sister had considered Elizabeth to be a daughter to her. He had also shared some unsavory details that Queen Kateryn's husband, Thomas Seymour, had tried to marry Elizabeth when she was still in her girlhood, to capture her throne, exploiting her vulnerability and desire to be loved and cared for.

155

Which of us did not wish to be loved and cared for?

Queen Kateryn had borne a child of her own, Lady Mary Seymour. The queen died of childbed fever and her child died of plague during the reign of King Edward as her governess was taking her to visit her grandmother. "I hope you are at peace, my lady, and your daughter, too," I whispered quietly, placing my hand upon her cold tomb before taking my leave.

William had also told me that Lady Dorothy, our hostess, was the aunt to his late wife Elisabeth Brooke. After dinner, as we were enjoying music and a cordial, I mentioned it to our hostess. "I know Lord Northampton had a particular affinity for Sudeley," I said.

"Really?" Lady Dorothy said. Her tone was cold. I began to see from where Eleanor inherited her lack of charm.

"Yes," I said. "Because, of course, it was home to his sister. And his wife Elisabeth Brooke, she was your niece, is that right?"

The room grew quiet, and I saw Her Majesty suppress a surprised smile, not a good sign in this situation.

"Yes, she was," Lady Dorothy said, and turned from me to take the arm of her much younger husband. It was ill mannered for her to turn her back on me, a guest, and one more highly titled than she, but I ignored it.

Later that evening, Clemence came to me. "Ma'am, I feel I must share something with you."

"Yes?" I said.

"Lady Dorothy, well, she, ah, she was, um, a companion to Lord Northampton before he met Lady Elisabeth Brooke."

"A companion, Clemence?"

"Yes, ma'am. In the . . . intimate sense. Then he left her for Elisabeth, whom he married."

Ah! Blood rushed to my face. I now understood. "Thank you for sharing that with me, Clemence. I'm certain it must have been awkward for you."

She dipped a little curtsey and went to get my gown ready for the morrow.

The next day, I was walking in the garden, near the chapel again, with Mary Radcliffe. Eleanor caught up with us. She seemed smug. "You have visited your sister-in-law?" She nodded toward the chapel.

"Yes," I said. "It would please William to know I'd done so."

She took my proffered arm, but I felt warned rather than warmed. "Did you always please William?"

I didn't know where she was leading. "Yes . . . I think so."

"That's considerate of you," she said. "Considering he was not, perhaps, dedicated to you alone during the many years while you waited to wed."

157

We stopped walking and I looked at her; Mary stepped back. "What are you speaking of?"

"Men are men," Eleanor said. "They do not set aside the lusts of the flesh simply because there is no marriage in place. They find other women to satisfy their drives."

"Do you know this in truth, this accusation you make?"

She didn't nod or shake her head, but she answered, "Not specifically. But I did long know Lord Northampton, and his character." I knew that she was speaking of his relationship with her mother, whom he cast aside without marrying. But that did not mean he was unfaithful to me—I did not believe it, though I'd admit, she'd planted doubt.

I withdrew my arm, angry that she would have so little respect for either my dead husband or my friendship. In my anger, I offered an intemperate response. "I cannot say for certain, of course, what William was doing when he was not with me. I can say, however, that he did marry *me,* and as soon as he could."

With that, I took my leave. Within a few days, we left Sudeley and returned to Whitehall.

The incident did put me in mind to think about men, though. I yet longed for one certain bold man, and though I looked for him among the players or other men about the court doing the queen's business, I did not see him again. I was beginning to wonder if we would ever meet again, and more important, why he had not sought me out. Surely he knew William had passed away some time ago; he'd said he made it his business to keep informed of court matters that concerned him.

A dark thought crossed my mind: Perhaps I was not a matter that concerned him any longer. Perhaps he had already taken another woman to wife.

All through the year the queen's "good sister," as she called herself, Mary, Queen of Scots, sent little gifts and presents to win the favor and affection of the queen. As I was in charge of receiving, caring for, and, upon the queen's orders, dispersing all of her gifts, I noted with small alarm both their increasing regularity and the queen's glee at receiving them.

Mary started by sending sweetmeats, which all knew the queen loved. To the consternation of Cecil and the man he'd appointed to have a care for the queen's safety and security, Francis Walsingham, the queen popped one into her mouth as soon as it arrived.

Next Mary sent a beautifully styled wig. Walsingham warned her not to put it on her head, but the queen dismissed his concerns. "I pay for her keep, whereby I've paid for this, I may as well enjoy it," she said. The next night Mary Radcliffe helped the Countess of Nottingham, Catherine Carey, style it on Her Majesty's head.

Mary soon sent a crimson petticoat, and the queen tried that on, too. She was wearing it while we played cards with her ladies after an early meal.

"I see you have on the dress of Mary, Queen of Scots," I said.

"Yes, it becomes us," she answered pertly.

I thought, but didn't say, that Mary would like some of Elizabeth's wardrobe in exchange, in particular, her crown and scepter.

We played several hands and the queen grew tired. "We shall retire to our bedchamber and read," she said. After Catherine Carey and I got her ready for bed, I said, "I, too, will retire to my reading."

"What are you reading, Helena?" the queen asked.

"Greek, Majesty."

"Oh!" She perked up at that, as she loved Greek. "What in particular?"

"Of the Trojans, madam. I am just now at the point where the city of Troy was besieged and taken by the gift of a horse."

She looked long at me, holding her face steady. I knew not whether she was holding back a smile or an ill humor. "Are you schooling us, Marchioness?"

I took her hand in mine and kissed her ring. "I

would never be so overbold, Majesty. I read Greek because I know it pleases you, and it pleases me to serve you in whatever ways I can."

At that, she smiled, and I took my leave.

Soon thereafter, the queen awarded to me substantial grants of land in Huntingdonshire, including the tolls of its markets and fairs, manors, and fisheries for the rest of my life, or until the queen revoked it.

Spring found the Countess of Nottingham, normally in charge of my lady's bedchamber and wardrobe, delivering a child. The queen appointed me to the task until she returned from childbirth, but she did not remove any of my other tasks. It was with some relief, then, when Eleanor Brydges returned to court and service.

"May we speak in private?" she asked me. I nodded my agreement, but did not thaw. We walked down one of the long galleries lined with portraits and she said, "I'm sorry for the sharp speech I offered to you at Sudeley. It's just that my sister, and then my mother, married noblemen while neither of them accepted my George. It's no excuse, I know. I now understand that one does not need to be married to the highborn in order to live a life of significance."

She looked so heartfelt and her speech was so unlike her usual reserve. I reached over and embraced her. "Consider it undone." She smiled and we walked together toward the queen's chamber.

"I must prepare the alms coin purses for Her Majesty, for the Maundy ceremony," I said. "Would you care to assist me?"

She nodded her assent and I told her where to find the material for the purses and their draw-strings. I would get the coins from the treasury myself. We sewed together till late in the night, talking, in my chamber. I could tell by the set of her face that Clemence was not pleased with this, but she said nothing.

I had ordered the seamstresses to make a new cambric apron for the queen, and a towel to tuck into it. I also had ordered a fine damask gown. It was tradition for the queen to give a gown to each poor woman who had been invited to present herself to court. As the queen was forty years of age this year, she would receive forty women and give thirty-nine of them a plain but well-made dress. One woman would get her "best dress"— the new damask made just for the occasion, threaded with gold.

I went to help the queen get dressed, but I'd forgotten some pins and also the purses. I turned to run back and get them, but Eleanor put a staying hand on my shoulder. "I shall fetch them for you," she said. "You have many more responsibilities than do I."

I nodded my thanks and went to assist the

queen. Within some minutes, Eleanor was back with pins, clothes, and the lacquered box of salves that I used to rub Her Majesty's aching shoulders and arms nearly each eve, which she would surely need after today's ceremony.

We finished dressing Her Majesty and then went to the great hall where hundreds were gathered. The poor women gathered were so inspired by the queen herself that I felt they would have been happy even if they had not been given purses of coins and a dress. The queen took time to greet each one of them with personal words and a heartfelt nod of affection. After the ceremony, we made our way back to her chamber. The mood, as was right for such a day, commemorating death, was somber. Shortly after we arrived in her chamber, however, Walsingham, unusually, joined us.

He stood in the center of the room emanating both concern and menace. Instinctively, we ladies backed away from him. The queen sat on her chair in the center of the room, holding her face in an impassive mask. I looked at her, but she would not meet my eye.

"Marchioness," Walsingham said. As I was the only woman in the realm with that title, of course, I knew he spoke to me. He beckoned me forward. I looked at the queen, and she nodded that I should obey him.

"I understand that it is your job to prepare

pomanders and scents and ointments such as the Queen's Majesty requires."

"Yes," I said. "Yes, that is right."

He pointed to my lacquered box. "Is that yours?"

"Yes," I said again. "I brought it from Sweden. I keep my herbal preparations in it."

He opened the box and lifted out a blue jar. "Do you use this rub on Her Majesty?"

I nodded.

"Open it."

I did, and I could smell the mint camphor I had blended in to speed the herbs through Her Majesty's skin for quicker relief, and to cover the scent of the valerian, which she disliked.

He stood very close to me; I could hear his ragged breath and see drops of sweat emerging through his beard, beading themselves on the rough hairs before sliding down them. He spoke clear enough for all to hear. "Can you please scoop out a large amount and liberally apply it to your own arms?"

I nodded and reached my hand into the jar, but just as my fingertips brushed the surface he clamped his hand down on mine and brought it back. He dismissed me to move back from the center of the room. As I did, he called forth another.

"Mistress Eleanor Giffard," he said. "Would you please come near?"

164

All eyes turned to look at Eleanor. She stood still and did not move at all. She looked toward the door, and then a look of peace settled over her face and she moved surely toward Walsingham. "Yes?" she demanded, her voice louder than his.

"Would you please scoop generously from the jar and liberally apply it to your arms?"

At that, she hesitated and seemed to lose her nerve. She looked me in the eye with neither a smile nor a sneer, but perhaps with a dare.

"The punishment for poisoners is death by boiling or by fire," Walsingham reminded her. At that moment, everyone in the room gasped. We understood what was behind his questioning and I better understood the whisperings against me from the birth of Edward Fortunatus to William's first wife. Because I had a gift with herbs I was suspected of being a poisoner!

Eleanor must have decided that whatever was in the preparation was a better death than boiling, because she reached her hand into the jar and smeared the contents over and into both of her arms. As soon as she did, she reached into her dress and pulled out her forbidden necklace and began to pray.

"Rosary beads!" someone hissed.

Eleanor turned toward me and said, "Yes, and Helena Northampton knew I wore them, and kept my secret. And then she invited me to assist her with the queen!"

Walsingham looked at me and I looked to the floor. She still sought to implicate me, and it may well have been effective. Within minutes Eleanor began heaving and gasping for breath. Walsingham called for two pages to assist her back to her chamber, and to call for her husband, who was somewhere at court.

"That's all," Walsingham said. He drew near to me. "You have had a difficult day, Marchioness. There are other ladies to attend upon the queen this evening. In the future, do not leave your preparations without guard, and be very certain you check each gift Her Majesty receives."

I could barely breathe myself, so unsteady was I, so uncertain of what had actually transpired. I did answer him, though. "I will, you can depend upon it."

He looked at me, not unkindly. "If you ever have reason to doubt or to question anything regarding Her Majesty's safety, you may confidentially seek me out. If you would have let me know about the Rosary beads as soon as you knew, I could have stopped this without anyone needing to die," he said, his gaze never wavering.

*As it is, this now rests upon your head and your soul,* was left unsaid but clearly heard.

I made it back to my rooms, and Clemence, who had already heard what had happened, was there to help me ungown. As she did, she accidently stuck me with a pin. I cried out.

"Sorry, ma'am," she said. I hurriedly pulled my gown back on, not taking time to explain, and ran from the room.

As I made my way back to the queen, I heard a series of low wails, like a flock of geese honking, then retching and shrill prayer. Eleanor. My heart wrenched for her. I did not stop, however, but flew into the queen's chambers, startling all.

"What is it, Helena?" the queen asked.

"Your pins, Majesty. Eleanor had charge over your pins. Do not move."

The queen stood still and I approached her. The men were dismissed from the chamber and I very carefully eased each pin out of her garment. Twice or thrice at first and then over again I stuck myself as I maneuvered the pins out of the garments in such a manner that they would not touch the queen in case Eleanor had dipped them in poison. All stared at me, watching to see if I fell ill or was slain by whatever evil may have been done.

Once the queen was out of her gown entirely, another lady came to help her dress, and I collapsed upon the floor, bleeding from the palm with pinpricks that were, thankfully, not poisoned, my head hot and floating. I felt anger and fear and revulsion and confusion all at once.

That night, when I had regained my composure, I asked Her Majesty if I might sleep at the foot of her bed. "As I did when I was a young maid," I said. "To comfort myself that you are indeed safe and whole."

She agreed.

"Here, Helena, I shall help you," Mary Radcliffe said, the first time she had called me by my given name. Over the course of the evening, and thenceforth, she made it clear by deed and word that we were now sincere friends. Anne Dudley, always a friend, came alongside as well. I had now, it seemed, proved myself completely trustworthy to them. They helped both the queen and me ready for bed.

Mary sat near me. "After the way Eleanor ill used you at Sudeley, why did you trust her?"

"I was willing to turn the other cheek," I said. "Once."

Mary told me that Walsingham had discovered correspondence indicating there would be Spanish poisons laced into the ointments while the queen and court all attended and were distracted by the Maundy service. Ground glass had been blended in to speed the toxins into the queen's blood. Instead, they had hastened Eleanor's death.

I lay awake long after I heard the queen and the two maids at the foot of the chamber breathing slowly, with my eyes wide open. Unbidden, a passage of Holy Writ that I had memorized only weeks before came back to me, from the prophet Isaiah: *Then the eyes of the blind shall be opened, and the ears of the deaf shall be unstopped.* It was not by chance that I had been directed toward that passage. I never heard another word connecting me and my herbs with poisons, and the warm hand of friendship was much more readily offered. It wasn't a title that brought true friendship and safety, but proven fealty to the queen. From that day forward, I applied ointments or salves on the queen only after assaying it first on my own skin in full view of everyone in her presence.

I had arrived on these shores nearly nine years earlier. I'd thought that William had brought me from girl to woman, but that night I had truly reached maturity. I had prayed for the queen, against her enemies in Spain and in France. But I understood for the first time, then, that the enemies with the greatest potential to harm were the ones closest at hand and to heart. My womanhood had been hard-won.

# ELEVEN

Year of Our Lord 1575
The Palace of Whitehall
Kenilworth Castle

The new year brought not Mary, Queen of Scots, in Her Majesty's fine garments, but I. The queen's miniaturist, Nicolas Hilliard, was painting a set of portrait panels for the queen. The queen sat to have her face painted but grew impatient after but a few hours.

"Helena," she said, "you favor us in feature, in hair color, and in build. Will you sit in our stead while the body is being painted?"

I nodded, thrilled. "Gladly! I do favor you; we could be sisters."

She indulged me with a slight smile and over-looked my impertinence. The queen took her leave, and some of the ladies brought Her Majesty's fine gowns and jewels into my apartment, just down the hallway, and helped me to dress in her garments.

"Begone, evildoers!" I said in my most regal, imitative voice when they'd finished.

"As you wish, Majesty," one of the maids jested, and pretended to kiss my ring. I waved them on and one of them let Mr. Hilliard into my chamber.

For the first portrait I was dressed in a rich black

gown with the finest gold embroidery. It was laced with pearls and puffs of cream roses. About my neck I wore the queen's jeweled flower choker, and pinned to my gown was a phoenix brooch. I thought about the phoenix as I sat. Only one phoenix lived at a time, and after its death, it mysteriously renewed itself from the ashes of destruction to bring forth new life. As such, it was a symbol of our Lord Jesus Christ, but also of our queen, who had arisen, magnificently, from the ashes of the destruction of her mother.

It put me in mind of an idea. "Master Hilliard," I said, "may I have a word with you after you are finished?"

"Certainly, Marchioness," he responded. "Please call me Nicolas." And a few hours later, among the tang of linseed oil and the buttery smears of paint, he kept his word.

"I would like to commission you," I said. "For two miniatures."

He cocked his head. "Certainly, Lady Northampton. Of whom?"

"You must promise to keep this to yourself. I understand that might be difficult for an artist, who surely paints for the pleasure of others' eyes. But I promise you that if you will keep this secret, it will be a commission that will be valued in a way none of your other works are."

He smiled. "I love mystery. When shall my subject sit for me? I leave for France after I finish these panels for the queen, and may not be back for some years."

"These subjects cannot sit for you," I said. "I must find something for you to work with. I shall set about it immediately, and when I sit in Her Grace's place for the portrait with the pelican device, I hope to have something for you."

A few days later, I excused myself from service for the day and made my way to Lambeth Palace, home of the Archbishop of Canterbury. After announcing my arrival, one of his men took me to his study.

He stood when I entered and bowed his head. "To what do I owe this pleasure, Marchioness?"

"May I sit, please?" I asked. I was not weary but he looked frail, and I knew he was ill but would not sit unless I did. He nodded toward a chair near the window and then drew one beside me.

Matthew Parker had been the queen's first choice for Archbishop of Canterbury and had served her whole reign. Moreover, he was the man whom Queen Anne Boleyn had charged with the spiritual care of her daughter, Elizabeth, just before Anne's execution.

"I wish to present something to the queen," I said. "And I believe you are the only one who can help me."

"Yes?" He nodded. "Continue."

"I wish to commission miniature portraits of the queen and her mother. However, I am not aware of any portrait of Queen Anne from which this may be drawn."

He agreed. "They were all . . . destroyed. Or hidden."

"I know. I wondered, perhaps, among your papers, might there be a sketch of some sort?"

He regarded me at length, wondering, I supposed, if I were to be trusted. I now understood that everyone was steeped in skepticism in the English court; it was perhaps our fifth humor here, in addition to the black and yellow bile, phlegm, and blood of which all were made.

"One moment," he said. He tottered out of the room, dignified but delicate, and returned nearly an hour later. He placed a palm-sized piece of paper in my hand. I looked at it and saw a raven-haired Elizabeth looking back at me.

"Queen Anne," he said. "Queen Elizabeth favors her mother as well as her father, does she not?"

I looked at her eyes, jet-black and yet warmed with humor and wit, her oval face, her intelligence. I could clearly see my own mother in my mind's eye, and wondered if the queen ever grieved that she had perhaps no vibrant memory of her mother. This thought encouraged me all the more on the path I'd set upon. "She does favor her, too," I said. "May I keep this?"

He nodded. "You may."

We made small talk for but a few minutes more and I could see he was tiring, so I thanked him again and rode, with my menservants, back to Whitehall. I was soon in contact with Robert Brandon, the queen's jeweler.

In May, just weeks after I had visited him, Archbishop Parker passed away, having fulfilled his duty to both Queen Anne and to her daughter, Queen Elizabeth.

Having mourned Parker, the queen had her master of revels hold several lavish and merry entertainments in the sunny month of early summer. At open court, the dancing spilled out onto the finely cared-for garden grass, so many were in attendance. The musicians stationed themselves so the dancers both inside and out could participate. I felt a hand upon my back and turned.

Thomas Gorges.

"Would you honor me with a dance, Elin?" he asked.

I couldn't speak for a moment I was so surprised and, I admit it, taken with the man. When I was able to again, I said, "I would be most pleased."

We were, of course, among all the other dancers, changing partners and dancing in line, but I could see that his eyes never left me. Although I took care to speak with and look at others, were they given leave, my eyes would have settled upon him alone.

We sat down, at long last, at a banqueting table. "*Du vack,*" he said to me.

I cocked my head, wondering if I had somehow misheard him as the crowd was still loud. "I beg your pardon, Thomas?"

He sighed. "You are beautiful."

I laughed. "Ah! *Du är vacker*!" Of a sudden, my eyes filled with tears. "It has been too long since I have heard Swedish. It is sweet to my ears."

"It has been too long since I have heard your voice. It is sweet to my ears," he said. "I was sorry to hear about the marquess."

I nodded; he meant it, I could see. "He was a wonderful man," I said. "He's been gone a little more than three years."

"I know," he said. "An appropriate mourning period."

We spent the evening talking, about his life, mostly outside of court, and mine, mostly within. He was a witty companion, and he asked after my thoughts twice as often as he shared his own. He was careful to make certain my wine was refreshed and that I had any of the sweetmeats that the queen's men passed. He joked, he spoke lines, he laughed loudly and well. I felt strength emanate from him and he drew me. "Why," I dared ask, "why have you not sought me out these many years if you had wished to hear my voice?"

He shrugged. "After you married Northampton, you became a marchioness. It seemed"—he recalled his turn as Endymion—"impossible to reach for the moon."

I nodded. He spoke truth. This could not be easily overcome.

"The queen has only just recalled me to more active service. She has not yet knighted me," he said. "But I have hope that as I grow in her favor and usefulness, she will."

Soon it was time for me to return to the queen, and as we stood up and he walked partway with me, he stepped upon my gown's long train, tripping me, and I fell headlong to the ground. I pulled him down with me and as we fell my hand was firmly, and indelicately, planted upon his thigh. Our faces were within an inch of each other; I could sense his desire to lean forward and kiss me, but he pulled away as others drew near.

"Oh, forgive me!" I said, mortified to have found myself in that position, with my hand thusly placed, and in public.

"No, it is completely my fault," he said. Others politely looked away and I hurriedly bid him good night, told him I wished to see him forthwith, and went to inspect the damage to my train. Truly, though, I was horrified to have made such an undignified spectacle of myself and my position.

The next day the queen was guest of honor at a play given on her behalf, and afterward, there was a banquet, but with fewer attending. As she circulated we saw Thomas with a large ribbon wrapped around his right leg.

She made her way to him. I shan't lie; I had

some concern over what he might say and how she might respond. "Cousin Gorges," she said. "What is that garment around your leg? And is that a medal tied to it? Are you a player again today?"

He drew near, grinning at me. "No, Majesty, I do not wear a costume. But last night I had the pleasure of a dance with the lovely marchioness. We were in the garden, and I stepped on her train, causing her to lose her balance. We tumbled and her hand fell upon my right leg. It was thus honored in a way I fear my left leg may never be, and it desired to boast its achievement to all. And—I know not if the good lady will forgive me for tripping her thusly."

The queen broke out in cheer and laughter. "We are certain in her kindness she will forgive you." At that she laughed again, put her hand fondly upon his face for a moment, and then her Robin came to lead her to dance, leaving Thomas and me alone.

"I did not discomfort you with my jest?" he asked, as if it mattered not.

I shook my head. "On the contrary, I am thrilled! No one has ever so boldly breached protocol for my favor. And you knew just what the queen would esteem, and," I added, "it brought pleasure and joy to my life, which can, sometimes, be one of lonely privilege."

"Have I won it, then?" he asked. "Your favor?"

"Yes." I nodded, my face hot with pleasure, his

eyes alight. "Yes, indeed. That was never in question." We spent the evening talking. I recited some poetry to him that I had memorized the night before, to please him. We danced till nigh everyone else had left, and at the end of the evening I asked, "Will you be coming on Progress with us next month?"

"I cannot," he said. "The queen called me to court to award me the dispensation of suits in the Court of Chancery," he said, "and collect and keep the many fees therein. It shall greatly raise my estate, though I shall be busy in London and then in the countryside on sundry duties for Her Majesty. Perhaps until the new year."

My heart dropped. "It's well that she thinks so highly of you," I said. "She will soon even better esteem you as you carry out these undertakings on her behalf."

"Yes," he said. "It will be to our advantage. If you'll wait."

In spite of the fact that she favored us both, I knew the queen would not be pleased when she found out the depth of Thomas's feelings for me, and mine for him. Perhaps this would raise him to knighthood, which she awarded infrequently. "I shall wait," I said.

Before we left on Progress, Her Majesty settled some new estates on me. She gave me all of the goods and chattel of William Barker, who had been attainted in the affair of Norfolk and Mary,

Queen of Scots. I was named first of the ladies accompanying her on Progress, a great honor and a mark of her friendship and affection, which I greatly esteemed.

The Sunday before we set out on Progress the queen honored the two composers of her court, William Byrd and Thomas Tallis, by accepting their dedication to her of their *Cantiones sacrae*, though the Church of England no longer used Latin in their services. It was the composers' understated way of asking if they would be permitted to quietly practice Catholicism, as they remained loyal to her. By her acceptance, she was showing that she allowed them the freedom of worship and continued to value their service to her. Court language was more often unspoken than said.

She was eager to set out. We were eager to set out. The gossip around court was that Lord Robert, having set aside Douglass Sheffield and claiming that he had not married her at all, was going to make one last, grand, romantic effort to win the forty-two-year-old queen's hand, and it was a distinct possibility that she would say yes. Queen Eleanor of Aquitaine, after all, had given birth to children into her forties.

When we arrived at Kenilworth Castle, the theme of the entertainments was immediately clear. The Arthurian Lady of the Lake greeted the queen, who arrived, of course, at the head of the four hundred courtiers and servants who came with us.

"This had been my lake and my abode, until your Royal arrival," she said. "And now that you are here, you are mistress of all."

"Thank you, good lady," the queen responded. "But withal we had understood that this castle was ours before it was given to you, and mayhap return likewise."

I hid a smile. Lord Robert had meant to make her mistress of all that was his, but she had gently rebuked him by reminding him from whom his largesse came. The queen gave, and the queen could just as easily take away.

Otherwise, she allowed herself to be refreshed in the mild countryside. Fireworks took place nearly every evening, and because the queen loved birdsong, Lord Robert had built a gilded aviary outside her apartment windows. Each morning when she awoke, she rose to the sweet song she loved, and she loved Lord Robert more for it. He joined her in her chamber each morning, and we left them by the window to talk.

"What else can I do to show my love to you, Elizabeth?" he asked. I knew of no other who called her by that name. "Shall I bring in other jugglers or finer jewelers? Gifted playwrights or poets who can better declare what is inside my heart than I can do with my ill-timed words and inadequate expressions?"

She shook her head and turned her back to us so we could not hear her response. But his face lit, and so he had hope, and so we who loved her did, too.

Lord Robert had players perform mystery plays of biblical miracles, hoping to show, perhaps, that nothing was impossible with God's help, and he surely felt God meant for them to be together. He had players act out Arthurian legends as an homage to Elizabeth's Tudor Welsh roots. He mostly had plays of romance and love performed, though, and very often, when it was a small group of us, he took the part of the lead so he could declare to her publicly what I knew he said in private. That softened her, and those same words softened me, too. Although I had been approached by other men of the court, some very highborn, I found them hidebound.

We stayed for nineteen days, and on the eighteenth, I dismissed her other women and said I would ready the queen for bed myself that evening. The married women welcomed a night with their husbands without duty and the others trusted me enough to know the queen's mind that they did not question me. The queen herself, though, was surprised when she returned from her bath. She dismissed her lady maid, though. I had served her trustworthily for ten years.

"I shall help you this evening, Majesty," I said, combing through her hair, which was still fiery, though beginning to be shot through with a few gray strands. I mixed up a small bowl of vinegar, honey, and fresh mill water, and then handed her a tooth cloth and golden pick so she could clean her teeth.

"Lord Robert has put on an amazing display for you, Majesty, these past weeks," I began. "He loves you well."

"And I, him," she said. I realized that she was not speaking in the royal sense, but woman to woman, using *I*.

"In like manner?"

I held my breath, wondering if a rebuke would be forthcoming, but none was. Blanche had told me that Kat Ashley had often been able to speak freely with the queen, as she had been as a mother to her. I hoped that the queen would take my rare, forthright questions as those of a younger sister who both admired and loved her well.

"They've said Lord Robert is ill suited for me."

"A finely bred falcon will not be best suited to a dove, madam, but rather to a high-flown hawk."

"And Lord Robert is a high-flown hawk," she responded.

I grinned. "Yes, madam. Or a peacock."

The queen laughed aloud. "Women commend a modest man but like him not."

"Though you are queen, you are a woman, too," I said softly.

"Yes," she agreed. And after a minute, "I have

known the love of a man. I have held the hand and heart of a man, but I have not known the touch of a man. The flesh and heart want what the mind forbids. I decided at a young age that my head must be that which rules, not my heart, lest I lose both."

I understood that.

"Do you not long for such a touch?" I dared ask.

"I have loved Lord Robert since I was a girl," she said. "I am given to him in all manner but one. I had, and have, passion. But I put it under glass, Helena, lest it set my kingdom on fire."

"Glass will snuff out a fire, Majesty," I said, brushing her long hair.

"As Saint Paul wrote to the Corinthians, 'There is difference also between a wife and a virgin. The unmarried woman cares for the things of the Lord, that she may be holy both in body and in spirit: but she that is married cares for the things of the world, how she may please her husband.' I am both virgin to the world and wife to my realm, and it is him whom I must first serve and please."

I glanced at her coronation ring, which she never removed, and recalled reading a script of her speech in which she declared, "I have already joined myself in marriage to a husband, namely the kingdom of England."

"Then what, my lady?" I asked.

"Within weeks of my marriage to Robin this

kingdom would fracture into factions like a shattered platter, never to be whole again."

My mind returned to the portrait Nicolas Hilliard had so recently painted, of the pelican that pricks its own breast to feed its children, sometimes mortally wounding itself in the process. "Does Lord Robert know?" I whispered, wishing I could somehow stanch that mortal bleeding for her.

She nodded, wiped her tears with the back of her hand, blotted out the deep misery etched upon her fair face. And then Elizabeth reverted back to queen. "We informed him tonight."

# TWELVE

Autumn: Year of Our Lord 1575
The Palace of Whitehall

Years of Our Lord 1576, 1577
The Palace of Whitehall

Autumn: Year of Our Lord 1577
Blackfriars, London

That September, we traveled to Woodstock, where Sir Henry Lee wrote a play, *The Hermit's Tale*, and then had it performed for the queen's entertainment. The story centered around two lovers who end up parting from one another due to her duty to her father and his dukedom. Elizabeth enthusiastically clapped throughout the play and at its end commended Sir Henry for his fine writing. Her duty came before her lover. He would not have dared perform it for her if he had not known it would meet with her approval. I began to understand even more about my mistress; as with the acceptance of the *sacrae* dedication, her support here was not only personal, it was strategic; it was a method in which she guided and ruled.

It would behoove us at court, I thought, to better pay attention to what she did and not only to what she said. She showed us all what she told very few.

I had one other occasion that year to ask to see the queen privately, just before the Accession Day celebrations in November. "Majesty, may I see you in private?" I asked. She indicated that yes, in the afternoon she would dismiss the others and speak with me. I arrived after the noon meal.

"Do you recall that I wear a locket necklace with a sketch of my mother and myself?" I asked.

She nodded. "Of course, Helena." She wasn't abrupt, but her tone said, "Do get on with it!"

I handed a golden ring box to her. "I commissioned this from Robert Brandon and Nicolas Hilliard."

She opened it up, and nestled within was the ring, gold and surrounded with rubies and pearls with a diamond *E* on the front. She drew in her breath and let true pleasure shine upon her face. "It's marvelous!"

"I know it's not typical to present gifts to you other than at New Year's, but I wanted this to be given in private, not public."

She nodded. "Yes, of course," she said. She lifted the ring out of the box and held it to the weak autumn light. The jewels shimmered. "This is a truly wonderful gift, Helena."

"There is a locket under the diamond *E*," I said. "I would be honored if you would open it." I held my breathing, hoping that I would please her beyond all measure, slightly worried that I had overstepped.

The queen opened up the locket to see a tiny miniature of herself on one side, and one of her mother, Anne Boleyn, on the other.

She closed her eyes for a moment, and as she did, a tear slipped from one of them, which she quietly brushed away. She opened her eyes to look at it again, and then closed the locket clasp before slipping the ring onto her slender finger. "Kept close, and yet hidden away," she quoted herself exactly from some years back.

I laughed. "Do you forget nothing?"

"No." She shook her head. "I do not." She drew me near and took my hands in her own ungloved ones, a sign of deep friendship and intimacy. "Our servants and favorites profess to love us for our good parts, but they all end in the same thing, namely, asking us for money. But not you. I shan't forget this."

From then on, she wore the ring continuously and smiled at me when she caught me looking upon it. It brought me great pleasure, perhaps as much as it brought her.

The next year passed quietly, almost without incident, and we were falsely lulled by a sense of peace we rarely enjoyed. At the end of September 1576, word reached court that Walter Devereux,

Earl of Essex, had died a violent death. The cause was dysentery, but the word circling round court was that Lord Robert had had him poisoned to clear the way to marry Essex's wife, Lettice Knollys Devereux. At the end, Essex charged that his children be transferred to the care of one of his kinsman, the Earl of Huntingdon, rather than be despoiled by their mother. His request was granted.

Few mourned Essex; he had once invited the Irish nobles to a peace feast and then had them ambushed and slaughtered. But I again heard the name of Amy Robsart whispered in dark hallways and at the end of long banquet tables. It was clear when you saw Lady Devereux and Lord Robert together that, having been spurned by the queen once and for all, Lord Robert's gaze lit and rested upon her beautiful cousin. It made me long for a loving gaze to be set and then rested upon me.

Thomas did not return to court, as the queen kept him abroad on minor business with the Spanish, but he did write to me, infrequently, so we did not draw curious eyes, I supposed. When he returned in the spring of 1577, I was the first person he sought. He sent a simple note by way of his manservant. My hands greedily opened the envelope. He'd scrawled, in bold script, "I've come for you."

I threw the letter into the air and laughed aloud,

followed by roisterous singing in Swedish, to the concern, I was sure, of my servants in the next room.

When we could do so without attracting undue attention, Thomas and I sat at the same table for cards, or met one another to walk in the galleries or gardens. We talked of his family, which had suffered some split when the church did, and of mine, though my family had, sorrowfully, begun to recede in my mind. Once I had made the decision to become English, to remain, I chose to focus upon my new home rather than pine for the old whenever the skies grew dark. Those skies were never dark, though, when I was with Thomas. We talked of his business, not only on behalf of the queen, but also at the London Exchange, which Her Majesty had established as a center of commerce and trade, to the health of the realm and the envy of the Continent. He asked about my herbal preparations, and I made some spiced scent for his wash water. I admit, I longed to press my face against his and draw in the scent of it as well as the feel of his skin.

One evening we sat in my apartments, Clemence quietly sewing in the next room, and he presented me with a gift. "I've been harried by guilt after ripping the train of your fine gown last year," he said.

"Oh, that." I waved my hand. "I am quick with a needle and Clemence quicker still."

He held out to me a heavy linen bag. "I've brought you a gift."

I cocked my head and eyebrow and took it from him. Inside were yards and yards of the finest silk fabric, shot through with gold, that I had ever seen. "It's like a cloud lit by sunlight," I said. "Thank you!" I reached over to hug him, and he wrapped his arms about me, both of us aware of Clemence humming loudly in the next room. He drew away for a moment, and then took my face in his hands and held my gaze with his fine blue eyes, asking my permission, silently, before continuing. I did not pull away.

He kissed me softly at first and then more insistently. I responded likewise. Within a minute he drew away and we both sat in silence, pink, restoring our breath. He stood up and pulled me to my feet. We held hands, facing one another.

"Let us see if you can think upon what occasion a gown made of that fine silk may be used," he said.

I nodded, and ran my hand through his hair. Nothing more needed, or dared, be said just then.

Spring fleshed out into early summer, and while the queen was busy with her counselors I was busy falling in love. One early evening a hundred or more courtiers were gathered in Her Majesty's gardens at Richmond, which were particularly beautiful, playing games upon the lawn. Thomas and I strolled about, he played bowls, and then one of his friends called to him.

"Gorges! Come along. We're to play Last Couple in Hell."

Thomas smiled and I looked at him wonderingly. "I have not heard of this game," I said.

"You'll like it," he replied, and followed his friend to a portion of the lawn perhaps a little farther away from the palace than some of the other games.

An area was divided into three sections, and there were three couples who played. One couple was assigned to the center square, called Hell; they must hold hands at all times. The other two couples were in the section to either side of them, and sought to exchange places while the couple in Hell sought to catch them as they ran through. If a couple was caught, they consoled themselves with a kiss, took one another's hands, and sang together the game's song:

> We two are last in Hell; what may we fear,
> To be tormented, or kept pris'ners here?
> Alas, if kissing be of plagues the worst,
> We'll wish in hell we had been last and first.

Then the other couples sought to run through and escape their grasp. After several rounds, Thomas and I were caught and had to remain in the center; he kissed me as we took our places.

"I suspect if you had your way, we'd remain here as long as you were required to kiss me," I teased.

"And, my fair lady, would you object?" he whispered, his eyes smiling.

"Not at all!"

We strolled back to the banqueting area that had been set up outside, lit with torches as the sun began to melt into the horizon. "I am twenty-seven years old. I've served the queen for eleven years, and it's been my pleasure. I served the princess for years before then. Although I've lived a life of satisfaction, I have never felt as alive and infused with joy until I met you."

He nodded. "I do not want to live without you as my wife. But you are a marchioness, and I am well born but untitled. I do not think the queen will suffer you to marry me. It's said that even in the best of circumstances, she is reluctant to let her ladies marry."

I shook my head. "No. I believe it's true that when her ladies marry she is, again, reminded of the fact that she will not, and the losses that entails. But she has arranged many fine marriages for her maids and ladies; do you think that if that were not so, noble parents would be rather reluctant to send their daughters to court? An advantageous marriage, after all, is what they seek for their girls. If they thought the queen would not allow or assist, surely there would not be mothers and fathers vying for their daughters to serve the queen. And there are."

He nodded. "I hope you are right."

"She worries, I know, that when one of her ladies marries she is allowing a little piece of her family to break away."

He pulled me into a quiet corner and took my hands in his. "I love you, Elin. I've waited so long. I do not want to wait any longer. Life is fickle, and my heart is given to you."

"And mine is yours," I said. Could I, a marchioness, really approach the queen and ask to marry Thomas, an untitled man? It was perhaps better to act, and ask forgiveness, as Mary Shelton had done. Then again the Grey sisters had acted without permission and the queen had never restored them to her affections—and had kept them separated from their husbands until they died. "I will think upon this forthwith," I answered, then reached up to kiss his lips, stilling the protest I saw forming upon them.

The queen was busy at court that season with one of her new favorites, Francis Drake, whom she had selected to head the expedition to sail round the world seeking gold and glory for God and Her Majesty. It was a way to both give the king of Spain a box on the ears and fill her coffers, two activities that pleased the queen as much as the bold explorer himself.

Thomas was good friends with Francis, so we

spent some evenings in his company and Thomas was among those who invested in the journey, hoping for a fine payoff. "I'm not just taking seamen," Drake told him one night. "I'm taking archers and players and gentlemen adventurers. Can I number you among them? It seems like just the kind of exploit you'd enjoy. There's certain to be riches and honor for us when we return to the realm, ships pregnant with booty for the queen."

Thomas shot a quick glance at me. "I'm afraid not, Drake, though my gold and prayers sail with you."

Drake looked from Thomas to me and back again and then broke out in delighted laughter. "Ah, I see now, the beautiful marchioness. We have both agreed to undertake a dangerous venture, Gorges, but I couldn't say which of us has the most at risk." At that he and Thomas both laughed, but I did not, perhaps understanding more than both of them what dangers might be dealt from the hand of our mistress.

The next week Thomas took me hunting after we'd secured permission from the queen to use her park. I was unpracticed with a bow, but he was an excellent shot. After some hours, I drew back my bow, taut and fresh, and shot a hart.

"My Valkyrie! Deciding exactly who falls in battle!" he exclaimed, and I was delighted to have pleased him, and felt flush and brave and, perhaps for the first time since I'd left Sweden, emboldened to let the strong woman I knew I was inside show herself through the court masque of obsequiousness and compliance.

We rode back to court, I pillion behind him, the first man I had ever clasped my arms around in intimacy on a horse, as William and I had always rode separately. I was engulfed in ecstasy.

We spent the summer on Progress, of course, and one evening the queen and I were alone playing chess, as we were wont to do. After I'd shared with her that I missed playing with William, she'd taken to inviting me to a game more frequently. My game had certainly become better as I sharpened myself against her, and as I had been well taught, I liked to think that I offered her a challenge as well.

I was pleasantly surprised one evening when she herself brought up the topic of marriage. I suppose I shouldn't have been surprised. "I see and say nothing" was one of her mottoes. I was glad she raised the topic, as it would have been indelicate for me to do so.

"What thinketh you of marriage?" she asked me.

"It's a holy estate," I said, "to those who are called to it."

She nodded and moved a piece forward, carefully.

"What do you think, Your Grace?" I moved a pawn one space forward to protect my queen.

"Likewise," she said. She considered the board, then stood up and moved back, looking upon it from afar. Once she sat down, she moved one of her knights. "With two knights available, it's best to make good use of both."

Within a week, I mentioned the game to Thomas. "I think she was affirming that I could marry twice," I said. "After all, why bring up the subject of marriage? Why speak of using two knights?"

Thomas looked skeptical. "I don't know, Elin. It doesn't sound very forthright, and Her Majesty can be as forthright as any man."

"But she's also as subtle as any woman," I disagreed; I did not want to see his skepticism or recognize the truth in what he said. Neither of us said more, but he sent word to the church near his London home that we wished to be married upon our return from Progress. I couldn't have been too certain of and at peace about Her Majesty's meanings about knights, as I did not seek her permission before marrying Thomas. In my heart, I strongly suspected she would say no and I was not going to risk that. It was one thing to act without her permission, but far more deadly to act against her stated will.

Thomas was willing to be bold for me, though of the two of us, he had the most to lose by angering Her Majesty. And yet, I would risk not only the perquisites and place I had at court but her friendship, which was dearer to me than almost any other. Almost.

In the end, I was firmly decided. I would be a Valkyrie for him.

Because most courtiers spent the summer away with the queen, the weeks following Progress were largely taken up by their tending to their families and personal affairs. So it was with little difficulty that I absented myself from service in late August. Clemence and I had spent some evenings stitching the cloud-like silk into an ethereal wedding dress. I could not take any of the ladies at court into my confidence and have them stand stead at our wedding; to do so would have been to put them at risk. Thomas asked Francis Drake, who was thrilled, as we knew he would be, to be included in a daring undertaking, and Clemence was a witness, too. Although I was fond of Clemence, her presence underscored, perhaps, how difficult and different this marriage was from my first one, wherein the queen had been witness.

Afterward, we returned to Thomas's home in Blackfriars. It was not, of course, on the scale of the palace or of any of William's homes, but it was tasteful and clean and well lit, with many rooms and a few servants.

"I have also bought a grand property, Langford," he'd told me as we'd discussed our plans before marrying. "It sits upon the River Avon, and while it is mostly ruins it has a magnificent presence and view. When Drake comes back and makes us all rich, we'll have money enough to build a formidable house."

I'd agreed, to make him happy, but in all truth, I was glad enough to be with him wherever we might be.

That night, we moved to his chambers upstairs. I bathed first, and when he emerged from the washing chamber he smelled of the spice preparation I'd made for him. He drew near to me and kissed me on the forehead, stroking my hair, and then my jaw, and then my lips. I pressed myself against him and drew in his breath as we were inches apart, face-to-face. Of a sudden, I had an idea.

I pulled myself back from him and firmly planted my right hand on his left thigh. "I had a promise to fulfill," I said. "From the night you tripped me. Now he need not feel unequal with his brother."

Thomas roared in laughter and came at me, tumbling me on the bed, and we sought each other in passion and joy.

Afterward, as he ran his fingers lightly up my spine as we lay nestled together, I thanked God for this night, the wedding night I had dreamed of, and more, since I was a girl. Thomas recited a poem, whispering it from behind me:

My love in her attire doth show her wit, It
    doth so well become her;
For every season she hath dressings fit,
    For winter, spring, and summer.
No beauty she doth miss when all her
    robes are on;
But beauty's self she is when all her robes
    are gone.

I giggled and turned to face him again.

We spent the days eating and laughing and
jesting and reading lines together until it was time
for us to return to court. We agreed I would go
first and share the news with Her Majesty, and
then Thomas would follow once the storm had
quelled, if there were one. Our new life put me in
mind of a Lyly line Thomas had once spoken to
me as we looked forward to our wedding night:
marriages are made in Heaven but consummated
on earth.

My trial *in regnis* was to be private.

"Come here, Marchioness," the queen called me
forward.

I stood before her, then dropped to my knees.
Not "Helena," nor even "My good lady marquess."
"Yes, Your Grace," I said.

She looked at me, her eyes cool obsidian. "Is it
better to be loved or feared?" she asked me,
quoting the Niccolò Machiavelli translation we

had read together a few months back. I had thought it to be satire, and had thought Her Majesty felt so, too, but now I was in doubt.

"Loved, Majesty," I said, answering for myself and not Machiavelli. "Or perhaps both."

" 'One would like to be both the one and the other,' " she quoted. " 'But because it is difficult to combine them, it is far safer to be feared than loved if you cannot be both.' "

I opened my mouth to speak but she put her hand up and silenced me. She called forth one of her pages and said, "Please take the marchioness's trunks from court and deliver them, and her, back to her *husband's* home, which she is not to depart from, on pain of imprisonment. Should she choose that, she can join her husband in the Tower."

Who had told her? Clemence? Surely not. One of Thomas's relatives? Drake? It was an unhappy reality of life at court that one never knew whom one could trust, though they be as close as linen to skin.

All the way back to Thomas's house I shivered in the early fall breeze, thinking, *He cannot have been delivered to the Tower.* But when I arrived his servant told me that was exactly what had happened. He had been arrested for marrying a noblewoman without the queen's permission and conveyed to the Tower with little but the shirt he wore. It horrified me, and when I saw his grooming tools in our chamber I burst into tears. I unpacked my trunks, numb. Clemence came to me; I was never so grateful that she was in my pay and keep and not Her Majesty's. She tried to cheer me, but I could not be cheered.

Late that night, as I lay alone in Thomas's large bed, I thought, *Yes. We are certainly the couple left in Hell.*

# THIRTEEN

Autumn: Year of Our Lord 1577
Blackfriars, London

Year of Our Lord 1578
The Palace of Whitehall
Hampton Court Palace
Blackfriars

Nan one came to see me, and every day I
expected a messenger from Her Majesty
either recalling me or stripping me of my titles
and rents. Neither happened. I ate but little at first,
but then I missed my monthly flux and, with a
bittersweet realization, understood that I was with
child. There was no way for me to share the glad
tidings with Thomas so I asked the Lord to,
instead.

"Lord Jesus, please," I begged in prayer. "Will
you not assist us?" The wry thought occurred to
me that, as in the case with my queen, I was
seeking comfort and absolution after the event
rather than guidance and permission before taking
the course of action. Perhaps I'd been unwilling to
risk hearing "No" from either sovereign. I did not
think I would act differently, though, if given
another chance.

After some time in quiet, I heard the whisper

of Holy Writ in my heart. *Can a woman forget her sucking child, that she should not have compassion on the son of her womb? Yea, they may forget, yet will I not forget thee.*

Within days, I knew what to do: write to my Lord Sussex, brother to my friend Mary Radcliffe, kinsman to Thomas, friend to me. He had been kindness itself when we stayed in his home upon our arrival from Sweden, a gentleman, still schooled in chivalry. I wrote him a letter and had it sent as quickly as I may.

> I urgently ask you (if sincere sorrow and contrition of heart, apart from any discomfort and inconvenience, is a sufficient punishment for an offense) if it might please you, in your merciful kindness, to help get back to the court. For if my cruel fate would add so much grief on me, neither the long suffering, prayer, repentance, or else can make good it, oh, my lord, in which utter despair I happen not then? Where should I direct my complaint? I cannot see any hope or consolation, but only utter despair on all sides. Therefore, if your worship pities me, an abandoned and banished creature, I beseech you to present my sad plight of Her Majesty.
>
> From my lonely abode in Blackfriars,

the 19 October, the most unfortunate Helena Northampton.

I signed it with William's surname, of course. Even though I was married, until and unless the queen stripped it from me, I retained my title and rank.

Sussex arrived several days after I'd sent a note pleading for his visit. I welcomed him with wine and comfit cake into the large reception room. He held me close for a moment. "Helena," he said.

I nearly broke down at the kindness in his voice. "You know I am exiled and that Thomas is—"

"Imprisoned," he said. "Yes, all know. Why did you not seek Her Majesty's permission for the marriage?"

I was able to be more honest with myself, and with others, after I'd had some weeks to reflect. "She would have denied it outright, and I deemed it safer to ask forgiveness than leave," I said. "It's apparent, now, how deep was my error."

"How can I assist you?" he asked.

"The queen trusts you well. She knows you are true to her and have served her faithfully. You're Thomas's friend and kinsman, and, well, you and your kind wife have been compassionate and benevolent to me since I arrived in this realm. Can you . . . speak for us?"

He shook his head. "I shall try," he answered. "She will not hear your name spoken. She truly loves you and grieves your absence more than any of her ladies, save perhaps Lady Knollys."

"What can I do?" I asked. "Am I lost? I can serve her at court; it need not be any different."

"But it shall be," he said. "And she knows it well. I will ask her to receive you."

"And then I will reassure her of my constant love and presence," I said, taking both of his hands in my own. "Thank you, my Lord Sussex."

"It's my pleasure, Marchioness."

Before he left, he turned to me and added something. "I've served the queen since she was but a child, and then a young woman, imprisoned in the Tower herself. During those years she, too, had to be abject and obedient to her brother, first, and then to her sister, who badly mistreated her. That is the way of rule. She does not ask of us what she has not required of herself, first."

"Yes, my lord. I understand."

As soon as he left, I fled the room and retched into the close stool, from anxiety or from the child, I knew not which.

The queen called me to court within a week. I put on a modest but becoming gown and applied some red to my white cheeks so I did not appear as careworn as I felt. The queen may have wanted to see that I was contrite, but she did not prefer the suggestion of ill health about her.

There were others in the room this time; Anne

Dudley gave a smile and it built my courage because she would know if the queen was going to dress me down, and would have warned me, I felt.

When the queen spoke her first words, my knees buckled in relief. "My good lady marquess," she said to me. "Come hither."

I came near and sank to my knees. She lifted me and indicated that I was to sit on the low stool next to her.

"Why did you not ask our permission for your marriage?" she said. "Have we so ill used you? Do you love us so little that you cannot bring yourself to be honest with us? To trust us to guide in your best interests?"

"Truly, Majesty, I trust you. You have never ill used me; on the contrary, you have offered nothing but kindness. I thought . . . I thought that the subject of marriage was one that brought you pain. So I did not raise it. When you raised the subject during our game of chess, and then indicated that each player may have two knights, I thought you were quietly sanctioning my second marriage, to Thomas."

I could see the puzzled look on her face as she sifted through memories. And then she laughed, not harshly, but neither with delight. "My good lady marquess, we were speaking of the proposal our counselors have urged us to consider for renewing the negotiations with the Duke d'Anjou for my hand," she said. "And how could we have possibly been speaking of Thomas Gorges? He is not even a knight!"

I flinched, then, at that insult, and was pleased Thomas wasn't there. It was then I knew that she disapproved of my marrying a man of so low rank, which she had, in fairness, made clear to all many times. Perhaps, I thought, she was angry at those who married for love, despite rank, because she herself could not do so, though she wished to.

"I beg your forgiveness, Majesty," I said. "I am as contrite as I may be, God as my witness."

She nodded and placed her hand upon mine. "We recognize this, Helena." She drew me near; perhaps the others could hear her, perhaps not. "I should be desolate without your companionship. Married women have children. My beloved stepmother, William's sister Queen Kateryn Parr, died a brutal death after delivering her child, as did my brother, Edward's, mother. Northampton, I knew, had not sired children, and therefore you were in no danger marrying him. But Thomas . . ."

"I understand, Majesty." This was not the time to tell her I was with child. I recalled Machiavelli, and the question he'd posed: *Which is better?* By loving me, she'd risked her heart.

She kissed me on the brow, a lovely, welcome, perfect gesture. "This is to send you off in your new marriage."

Tears coursed down my face, and I spied some in her eyes, too. And then, one by one, she kissed my cheeks. "We shall welcome our cousin Gorges back to court, whence you both may continue to serve us well, as you always have." She then smiled at me and quoted my phrase as I spoke it to Mary Radcliffe regarding Eleanor Brydges. "We, too, are able to turn the other cheek. Once."

Thomas was freed and welcomed back at court; Elizabeth had given him more responsibilities, which was a doubled-edged sword. It raised his income and his significance, but it would keep him increasingly busy at home and abroad for the queen. Given the choice, he would have chosen a player's life, I suspected. But which of us has such a choice?

We entertained some of his family before the Accession Day celebrations. He had joined me in my apartment at the palace, as my rooms were thrice the size of his, and more comfortably furnished.

I enjoyed meeting his Gorges relatives; William's sisters had both died before I came to England, and although the Herberts were, in a way, relations, they were nothing like the sprawling mass of Gorgeses, a few of whom were often at court.

After dinner, Thomas's brother William excused himself, and as soon as he'd left the room and but a few remained, Cousin John Gorges spoke up. I think he'd drunk too much wine, and I indicated to my servants to clear the goblets and bottles from the room.

"Well, Thomas, since you're highly placed now, I wonder if you can confirm something we've just heard: that Parliament desires to impose stunning fines for recusants and enforce that everyone in the realm partake of Protestant communion once per year. Truth?" He nervously twisted the ring on his finger; it was a strange design—I'd never seen one like it—a row of black beads encrusted upon a circle of gold.

Thomas nodded. "They did request that, but Her Majesty forcefully rejected it. She's said it before, and I'm sure need be she'll say it again: she has no desire to make windows into men's souls."

John covered his mouth with his fist, burped, and continued. "But the council has sent circulars to every diocese in the country asking them to name those known to be recusants."

"True, I'm afraid," Thomas said, quickly turning the conversation. "And now, my wife looks to be weary; I've heard that carrying a child will do that, and glad I am that I'll never know!"

At that, those remaining in the room broke out in laughter and relief. The servants tidied up and spread the ashes in the fire, and Thomas and I retired to our bedchamber.

We lay abed, his hand resting on my stomach, caressing our child though we could not, of course, feel him or her yet.

"And so, all is well with you and Her Majesty?" he said. "No residual storm from last month?"

"No," I answered. "And yet . . ."

He cocked his head at me.

"What is it?"

"I confess, I do love her as much as ever, and I know she senses that. But where I'd once thought her to be like the goddess Idun, now, perhaps, I think upon the tale of Frigga."

He turned toward me, player inside, courtier out, and urged me on. "Do tell the story, Lady Gorges!"

"Frigga is stately, majestic. She loves to dress in fine gowns and has exquisite taste in clothing and in her jewels. She inspires awe, both fear and love in those around her. But she is the goddess of the heavens, sometimes garbed in swan white, and sometimes deepest black, depending on her quickly changing moods."

He nodded his understanding. "Yes, yes, my love, 'tis apt. At least her clothing gives the standers-by a bit of a warning."

I smiled at that before continuing. "She's served by a number of maidens," I said, "but she's closest to her sister, Freya. Freya always helps Frigga as she prepares for the day, assisting with her ointments and cosmetics. She has charge over her jewels and golden shoes. She sometimes quietly advises Frigga on how to assist the mortals who apply to her for aid."

He rolled over. "And I suppose you, my love, are Freya?"

I smiled. "Elizabeth has many ladies who help her and whom she loves well. But only one of us is a Swede, so perhaps I may be as Freya to her."

He kissed me and then said quietly, "You've grown up, my love, as has your picture of our mistress, which is meet. Better to love the flesh-and-blood woman and not the taled goddess." He paused. "Do you think she has given me new tasks and undertakings for my sake, or for yours?"

This was the first in a series of questions, and years, I suspected, where I would have to intercede with my queen for my husband, or the other way round. "Both," I said. "She awarded Hurst Castle to you and the chancery before she knew we were in love, is that not true?"

He nodded, happy.

That New Year's, the queen received us both warmly. She gave me a gift of forty-two ounces of gilded silver, and Thomas, eight. The difference was certainly to be expected, but I could see it unsettled him.

Having reconciled herself to my own forthcoming child, the queen sent me to represent her at the christening of a courtier's child in February, a child to whom she'd promised to stand as godmother. As I was well ranked, I was welcomed as her deputy, and as I wouldn't attend, by custom, the christening of my own children, I was pleased to participate. 'Twas always a delight to present expensive gifts, too, especially when they hadn't been purchased from my own purse!

I knew the birth of babes reminded her of her own barrenness; she'd spoken of it to me. My gowns covered my growing child, and though I knew she was pleased for me, it was also a bit of ash in her eye. What made it worse were the whispers round court that her Robin was planning to marry her cousin Lettice some months hence, when her two years of widowhood were complete. She may see and say nothing, but she certainly heard all.

My Lord Sussex and other courtiers were with the queen and me one evening as we gambled. Suddenly, the conversation turned serious. Sussex was pressing the suit of the Duke d'Anjou again. Lord Robert, to no one's surprise, was against it.

"Majesty," Sussex said. "It is natural for us to wish for an heir from your own self. How glorious! How magnificent! How natural!"

At that, his sister and my friend Mary Radcliffe snickered. "Yes, brother, do tell, it is natural. I know it's been said that spinsters like myself are supposed to be paired up with apes in Hell; as for me, I shall take my chances on if that be true or not. For one thing is certain, to be partnered here on earth would be to assure such a husband!"

Sussex blushed; only his virgin sister could get

away with that stinging rebuke. We ladies hid our smiles behind our hands, and the queen quickly raised her white feather fan to hide her smile as well, rattling the long chain upon which it was clasped to her girdle.

"That's not what I mean," Sussex said.

"The people won't have it," Lord Robert declared, raising his voice.

"You mean *you* won't have it, Leicester, and your opinion in this matter concerns me not in the least!" Sussex shouted.

"Her Majesty will not partner herself with a French fop!" Lord Robert retorted.

Sussex looked Lord Robert up and down, noting his fine purple attire. "Nor an English one, apparently."

"Gentlemen," the queen said quietly. "I shall consider all you've said. And now, if you don't mind, I wish to play cards. Who will gamble against me this night?"

A cadre of her men agreed, and I thought, in cards and in life, it was the fool who gambled against Elizabeth.

Within days, the queen had signaled her approval for the negotiations to begin again between herself, at forty-four years of age, and Anjou, a man of but twenty-three who had, apparently, a novice's poverty of looks but a prince's riches in charm. She insisted in dressing again in the French fashion, which she much preferred anyway, perhaps as a token of affection to her mother.

Was it the rumors of Robin and Lettice that had made her turn aside from her declaration to me that she would remain married only to her realm? Or was it her realm that she was thinking to protect by aligning herself with France against Spain? A French husband would be a powerful antidote to the Scots' poison for her throne. In any case, I had learned to watch what she did, not what she said. Walsingham, too, was against the marriage. He was perhaps the most formidable foe any of the queen's enemies had, slithering as he did through country and court.

"I suspect Walsingham of fomenting public opposition to the French marriage," Thomas told me one night after he'd returned from a mission to the north for the queen. He loved when we could share a meal together in private, so I'd had one specially prepared and delivered to our quarters.

"Surely not!" I said. "That would border on treason."

"That's not how he would view it," he said. "But I am remiss to speak of matters of the realm. I'm more interested in the matters of my own hearth. How comes our child?"

"She comes soon," I said. "I sense her shifting within me."

"Her?" he noted with surprise.

"I'm certain it's a girl," I answered him. "Her Majesty has already agreed to stand as godmother and to allow us to name her Elizabeth, if that be all right with you."

I retired to Blackfriars with our own servants the middle week of May, and I didn't have to wait long until our insistent, red-haired daughter pushed herself out into the world. For nigh on twelve hours I cried out into a rag that I'd moistened with the helpful lady's bedstraw until the midwife held her, bloody and wailing, in the air in front of me.

"A daughter, my lady. Will your husband be disappointed?" she asked me.

I shrugged. Truly, I did not know. I'd been afraid to ask. The babe wailed for nigh on an hour and I could do nothing to stop her. But when she was cleaned and wrapped and Thomas brought in, he took her in his arms and she settled right away.

"You know how to charm the young ladies," I teased him as he bent over to kiss my sweaty brow.

"Seems I do," he agreed, and smiled back at me. "But I'm only interested in young, beautiful ones who favor you." I looked at them together and I knew that no matter what we'd risked to marry, it had all been worth it. Nothing and no one would separate us now.

# FOURTEEN

Years of Our Lord 1578, 1579, 1580
Blackfriars
The Palace of Whitehall
Hampton Court Palace

Our daughter was christened on June 4 at St. Dunstan's in the West by the very man who had married us not a year before. The queen gave us a double bowl of gilded silver in which the child was baptized, and then rejoined us at our small home to celebrate. I could not say for certain, but I think Thomas was slightly disconcerted by the size of our home because he brought up the topic of the ramshackle manor at Langford several times over the course of the evening. The queen, gracious as always, told him she felt perfectly at home right where she was.

I had not yet been churched after my daughter's birth, and therefore had not yet reappeared in public, when the queen left for Progress. She made a special trip to Blackfriars to see me and to ensure that I would join her midway.

"Yes, Majesty, of course. Perhaps I should oversee the effort to secure more sugar to be brought midway through the Progress."

She feigned annoyance. "Are you saying that we

are as a poor-quality wine, and can only be tolerated when well sugared?"

I laughed aloud, which she, like anyone who posits a jest, enjoyed. "No, no, Majesty. All know that you care not at all for the oysters, veal, mutton, anchovies, and eggs that are certain to be served to you as long as your confectionary course is well stocked."

She smirked. "I shall see you shortly and in fine health, my good lady marquess."

I settled back on my bed after she left, content that our friendship had been fully restored.

We were near the end of Progress, in August, when Sussex wrote again to the queen. One could not fault the man for his earnest devotion, and the queen credited that and much love to him, but he did not know when to leave a topic lie.

"Mary," the queen asked. "Would you please read to us the letter from your brother while I am gowned and my hair done?"

Mary nodded and Catherine Carey, the Countess of Nottingham, assisted Her Majesty into her gown.

" 'To marry Anjou, who is a most noble and worthy partner to yourself,' " she read, " 'would be to secure an heir from your own body, which is precious to all in your kingdom. It will also assist you as you seek to gainsay the Spanish and their continued attacks against the Protestants in the Netherlands.' "

The queen nodded for Mary to continue.

" 'You shall have a husband as a defender of all your causes present.' " None of us dared smile, but the thought of twenty-three-year-old Anjou protecting Elizabeth was one that, in another venue, would have brought loud, merry mirth.

"Well, then, it's settled," the queen said. "I'm to be married!"

I did not know if she jested, and by the discomfort in the room I suspected no one else did, either.

"There is more, Majesty," Mary said. "Shall I continue?"

"Yes, please do."

" 'There are, of course, a few disadvantages. Your own mislike of marriage, and the general mislike which Englishmen have to be governed by a stranger.' " He went on to convey that a popular pamphlet had begun to circulate in London, declaring, with admiration and affection, that Elizabeth was "a prince of no mingled blood, of Spaniard or stranger, but born mere English here amongst us."

The queen did not dismiss pamphleteers; she knew they spoke truth she was unlikely to hear in the gilded galleries of Whitehall.

Within a month of our return to court, the palace hummed with the news that Lord Robert had married his mistress, Lettice Knollys Devereux, at his house in Wanstead, two years after her husband Essex died, and three years after the queen had told him, with finality, that she would not marry him. Lettice's father, Sir Francis Knollys, was the unshakable witness. None dared tell the queen, and who wanted to be within arm's or ear's reach when she learned of it? And yet she would certainly find out.

The queen had sent Thomas abroad, to the Netherlands, as an emissary, and I sat companionably sewing by the fire with Mary Radcliffe one November night.

"My brother . . . ," she started.

"What is it?" I asked, handing a fresh needle to her. We both loved him well but knew his occasional intemperance of speech.

"He told the French ambassador of Lord Robert's marriage."

I set down my work. "I know he loves Lord Robert not, but the queen?" I marveled.

She nodded. "He believes it to be in Her Majesty's best interests," she said with a sigh. "Of course with Simier coming from France at the new year, well, it shan't be long till the queen hears of it. And we'll all be here as witnesses."

New Year's was the one time of year when all courtiers were expected to be present at court unless they were ill unto death or delivering a child. That meant Lettice would have to be there, too.

· · ·

As I was to take charge and then manage all gifts presented to Her Majesty, I was near her elbow and throne each New Year's, and therefore was close at hand when Lettice presented her gift to the queen at the beginning of 1579. The air between them was always disturbed, as they liked one another not, but as Lettice came forward and presented Elizabeth with a great chain of gold and amber with a small diamond, I detected no thunder in the clouds surrounding Frigga, so perhaps she did not yet know.

Elizabeth took the gift in hand and thanked her cousin graciously. "How does your family?" she asked.

Lettice looked perhaps a bit surprised. "My children are well, Majesty," she answered smoothly. She held her gaze equal with the queen, whereas most of us made sure our gaze was tipped slightly floorward. "My young earl studies well, and my daughters are thinking ahead toward marriage."

"Ah, yes, marriage," the queen answered. "We will take an especial interest in assuring that they marry in security, so please make certain we hear of their plans from their guardian, Lord Huntingdon, as soon as a possibility may be raised."

For those who cared to listen, there was a warning.

That year, as in many others, the queen received many gifts of gowns, fabrics, and other expensive clothing. Anne Dudley and I looked at one another with pleased satisfaction for the young maids of honor who would also benefit from this largesse. When the queen had to pay less for her own clothing, she presented more to her ladies and maids, many of whom served at their own expense, throughout the following year. Lady Mary Radcliffe, with little money of her own, almost always received a valuable piece or two of the queen's gifted jewelry.

Within weeks the d'Anjous' envoy, Simier, arrived at court. He was light of heart and step and had pretty words and tokens for all of us. As master of the duke's wardrobe as well as his "chief darling," he was authorized to speak freely on behalf of his master. After a year of tension, fear, and dull wit, I must say that whether or not one was in favor of the marriage, it was a pleasant diversion to have Simier at court.

"My master," he said to Her Majesty, "he is so very far away in France, and yet his heart, Majesty, is right here with you. May I send him a word, and perhaps a token, of your affection, something you yourself have touched?"

The queen, always engaged by courtly flirtation and wit, smiled and agreed. "A portrait of ourself?" she suggested.

"*Non, non, madame*, that will not do. Of course,

he has already seen of your beauty. But perhaps something that you have kissed and cherished and held dear?"

I was finishing the lace detail on one of the queen's handkerchiefs and I raised it slightly. She glanced at me and nodded. I finished off the edge and brought it to her. "Our perfume?" she said to me. I went to the lacquered box—which was now securely locked—and took out a crystal vial of the vanilla and rose scent she now favored.

"Majesty?" I held it out toward her and she unstoppered it, sprinkled the new handkerchief with a few spare drops and then kissed the linen before handing it over to Simier.

"*Oui, oui, c'est parfait!*" he exclaimed, bowing. And then, before any could stop him, he dashed into the next room, which was the queen's private bedchamber.

Alarmed, two of the men stationed at the door moved forward, but the queen lifted her hand to stop them. Within a minute, Simier came out with one of her lace bed caps in his hand.

"Monsieur Simier, what is the meaning of this?" she asked.

"I am sure that my master would like to have something not only close to your heart but close to your bed!" he insisted.

At that the queen laughed, pleased, I was certain, to be found attractive and desirable by a man twenty years younger than she. And perhaps, the jesting and acting were leavening in a court that often felt weighty and wearying.

Soon she had nicknamed Simier her "monkey." I looked at Mary Radcliffe, wondering, perhaps, if the queen was recalling the fable of virgins being forced to marry apes in Hell. Mary held back what seemed to be a tart retort as she responded to my glance, so I knew it was on her mind, too.

"May I always be numbered among your beasts!" Simier responded with diplomatic aplomb.

The courting soon turned to negotiations, however, and the forecast was not quite so bright. I heard Simier and Her Majesty discussing d'Anjou's terms, much more pointed than his compliments, as I was tending to her jewels with Mary.

"He must be crowned king immediately after the marriage," Simier insisted. "And he needs a generous allowance, as befits his position, paid annually throughout his life and which will be irrevocable."

The queen grew quiet before answering in flawless French that she would speak to her council on the matter.

Although Sussex and Cecil were strongly for the marriage, even they would not agree to those terms. Her other councilors, including Lord Robert and Walsingham, were strongly against it. Philip Sidney represented most Englishmen when he said the proposal would be unacceptable to her people regardless of the terms because d'Anjou was the "son of the Jezebel of our age," Catherine de' Medici.

The next Sunday the queen was forced to march out of the service given by her own minister, in her own chapel, who proclaimed, "Marriages with foreigners would only result in ruin to the country."

Thomas was back from his travels and greatly desired my companionship, but the queen was on edge and required it, too. That eve, before she retired, I rubbed her neck and shoulders with ointment of rose and valerian. By the time I returned to our chamber, having purposed to rub his shoulders as well, he was fast asleep.

I sat there, herbs nearby for a few moments, then quietly put them away. I slipped on my sleeping gown and, while he stirred some, he did not wake when I joined him in bed. I ran my hands over the back of his neck, craving his touch and, finding none, offering mine instead.

In September of that year John Stubbs published *The Discovery of a Gaping Gulf, Whereunto England Is Like to Be Swallowed by Another French Marriage, If the Lord Forbid Not the Banns by Letting Her Majesty See the Sin and Punishment Thereof.* Stubbs was rare in that he spoke for the common man but was also educated, in his case, at Trinity College, Cambridge.

When Elizabeth found out about this pamphlet, she demanded that both Stubbs and his publisher have their right hands cleaved off, and this was done, publicly, even after the book was banned.

After the bloody deed was accomplished, Stubbs was said to have raised his hat with his left hand and call out, "God save the queen!" before falling in a faint upon the platform.

The crowd watched in silent horror, but Clemence, who had attended the spectacle, told me that there were great murmurings of malcontent and unhappiness with Her Majesty afterward. I admit to wavering between admiration for her strength and revulsion toward the deed.

"The people, perhaps she does not know that their hearts can turn," Clemence told me.

Elizabeth knew.

Later that fall the council, still divided as to whether the marriage was good for queen and country, told her that, as they were split, they could make no recommendation at all.

We ladies loitered just outside the council chamber as was our duty, waiting for her to emerge, but we could, of course, hear the proceedings. Being closest to the door, I could see in as well.

Every man present looked down at the table as she began to cry and complain that she had expected them to support her marriage choice as a "surety to her and her realm . . . to have her marry and have a child of her own body to inherit, and so to continue the line of Henry the Eighth."

Sir Francis Knollys spoke up. "Majesty, there are none present, nor in your kingdom, who could desire less than perfect happiness for you and issue of your own body. But it is our learned view, and that of Walsingham, who has long resided in France and who is in communication with those across the Continent, that this marriage would enslave England to France."

"This is a fine way to show your attachment to us, who might desire, like others, to have children," she rebuked him.

Francis said nothing but, having been both a husband and a father to daughters, bowed his head in understanding. He deserved better; he had given his life, and his wife's, to the queen's service. The queen fled the room in tears and did not allow but a few into her presence for some days. I retired to Blackfriars, as I was near to giving birth to our second child.

Once at our small home, I relished being with my child, Elizabeth, for many hours during the day. She gurgled at me and shook her tiny fist as she walked across the floor with her small ball in her hand, holding it up to me to play with. I kissed those hands, her cheeks, her head, which had fine downy hair that would soon be twisted into curls. I took over many of the nurse's duties and enjoyed planning and ordering her wardrobe myself. We sat on my bed and I told her stories in Swedish and German, which she was learning to speak, though not well. They were rare hours that we spent together and I cherished them.

Thomas returned from court one afternoon much earlier than anticipated. He gently handed Elizabeth back to her nurse and then closed the doors to our reception room.

"Simier was sent back to France with the quiet understanding that if the queen's people did disapprove of the French marriage, she would not go forward with it. Simier, being no fool, knew that the English would never accept the duke. So, before he left, he insured that the queen had heard of Lord Robert's marriage."

"Oh . . ." I exhaled.

"Oh, indeed," Thomas said. "The queen has banished Lettice and Lord Robert from court. She's threatening to send Lord Robert to the Tower."

Nothing needed to be said to prompt our own memory of my banishment and Thomas's stay in the Tower. However, should Lord Robert be sent to the Tower, he was unlikely to enjoy a brief stay, as the wound his marriage would inflict upon the queen would be nearly mortal.

"What happened?"

"The queen called Lettice to stand before her. Lettice, of course, did not come humbly nor did she bow, ask forgiveness, or in any way abject herself. Instead she held her head high and came much nearer to the queen than was meet . . . or wise."

I shook my head. Foolish. There was a time for pride. This was not one of them. "She lashed out at her."

Thomas nodded. "Indeed. She boxed her on the ear and said, 'As but one sun lightened the earth, she would have but one queen in England.' She shouted to her men to remove the 'flouting wench' from her presence and said she'd never set eyes on that 'she-wolf' again. Then she sent for men to remove Lord Robert from court, back to one of his properties, where he may await her decisions. Word is that she intends to strip him of his lands and titles rather than see them benefit Lettice. And then imprison them so they may not meet."

"This is ill news, indeed," I said.

"And yet, it is not unreasonable that the man may want a son of his own to carry his name, and a wife of his own to companion him," Thomas finished. That was true, it was not unreasonable for Lord Robert to want such a thing; perhaps, as Lettice was the softer, younger version of her cousin the queen, he sought someone who favored her looks. My heart was entombed, I admit, from sympathy for Lettice. With a hundred or more men from whom she could have chosen, could she have settled upon any other?

Then my thoughts turned to poor Katherine Grey Seymour, separated from her husband, too, after marrying without permission.

A kingdom was complicated; a heart more so.

I ran my hand over my belly, which had begun to contract. "Quickly send to my Lord Sussex," I said. "He was able to speak wisely to her after she'd banished me and imprisoned you."

"Sussex?" Thomas asked. "He is no friend to Lord Robert."

"Which is precisely why Elizabeth will listen to him," I said.

My Lord Sussex did speak with the queen, and told her, gently but bluntly, that no one should be imprisoned for a lawful marriage. For my part, I prayed that although the queen had declared her desire to continue the line of her father, she would not continue his sins, punishing for personal vengeance and not for political right.

Lord Robert was not imprisoned, nor did he have his titles stripped. Lettice Knollys, however, was never again seen, or spoken of, at court.

We spent the days before our second child's birth playing chess together, rehearsing play lines, and reading passages of Holy Writ to one another. Some mornings our daughter, Elizabeth, would join us in our bed, her tiny hand reaching over to the table nearby to grab a piece of marchpane left over from the night before, stuffing it in her mouth, eyes wide with pleasure, while we laughed with her. Thomas indulged her and offered her another piece; I loved him even more for his devotion to her, and to me.

Our son was safely born and we named him Francis, in honor of Sir Francis Knollys, who continued to serve his queen well at great cost to himself—namely, the companionship of his wife while she'd lived. I did not return to court for six weeks, flourishing in the love of my family, suckling my babe for a week before turning him over to the wet nurse, and speaking German to young Elizabeth. Reluctantly, Thomas and I parted, and I returned to Whitehall.

The queen greeted me with affection and love. In private, one evening, I asked how she truly did. Her mask dropped, just a little, and I spied the frailty behind her pale, pulled white skin.

"To be a king and wear a crown is a thing more glorious to them that see it than it is pleasant to them that bear it," she responded quietly. I knew it cost her to be honest with me, and I cherished the trust she'd placed in me.

The year 1580 started off with more difficulties and dark concerns; the papal secretary of state had been asked if it would be a sin for someone to murder Queen Elizabeth. After discussing it with the pope, he answered, "Since that guilty woman of England rules over two such noble kingdoms of Christendom and is the cause of so much injury to the Catholic faith, and loss of so many million souls, there is no doubt that whosoever sends her out of the world with the pious intention of doing service, not only does not sin but gains merit."

Mary Radcliffe approached me one afternoon as we were attending to the queen's jewelry. "Whilst you were away, a new pamphlet was published, and a copy of it found here at court," she said. "In it, the ladies attending upon Her Majesty are urged to follow the example of Judith, and execute Her Majesty for the good of the Catholic faith."

Whoever wrote this must have known that the queen often slept under an eight-piece tapestry set of Judith and Holofernes. I shook my head. "Like Eleanor," I said quietly. "Where did you hear of this?"

"Walsingham," she said. "He wanted me to be aware." She looked at me for but a moment longer before turning away. I knew she trusted me; had I wanted to poison the queen I could have done it with the ointments or dipped her dress pins. Perhaps there was nothing at all behind the look. It was hard to tell.

Once the French marriage proposal was dead, the English returned to the love and adoration of their queen. Although they now understood, perhaps like my very own revelation, that the queen was flesh as well as spirit, most certainly did not want Mary, Queen of Scots, upon the throne.

In September, Thomas's great friend Francis Drake returned from the New World on his ship the *Golden Hind*. He had claimed new land for the queen and brought her back many novel and enjoyable tokens. After mooring his ship and securing it with booty and bounty aboard, he came to court to celebrate his victory.

"We welcome you!" the queen called to him as she raised him from his knees. He bent to kiss her ring and I daresay by the dip of her head that she was inclined to tickle his chin.

She spent six hours closeted with him, learning of his adventures, enjoying with a loud cry of delight the coconut he brought back for her. He cracked one open and personally served her some flesh and juice before asking if her confectioners could sugar the rest for her pleasure.

"Yes, all but one," she said, hanging on to one of the large, coarsely clothed fruits. "I shall have a silver cup fashioned in which this shall repose, in a place of honor, in my palace. It will remind all who see it of your exploits, Francis."

He grinned the devilishly charming smile of a pirate. "I do not want any to reflect upon me, Majesty. But if looking upon such a fruit can remind them that you, and your realm, have begun to dominate the world at large, yanking false claims from the Spaniards, then I am well pleased indeed!"

There had been some question as to whether Her Majesty, now that she had no shield in the French, should keep the booty stolen from the Spanish, but in the end, she kept it, as I knew she would. Francis Drake was made a wealthy man indeed and was knighted by the queen forthwith upon his ship.

Thomas and I profited, too, as investors. But late one night in bed, after we'd made love, he did not rest in the comfortable glow of marriage.

"What is it, Thomas?" I asked, stroking his cheek.

"I am well pleased for Drake," he said. "And yet I am restless; he is now knighted while I am not. I seek to serve Her Majesty well in all I do, whether it be at home, abroad, or the regular forfeiting of the companionship of my wife." I heard the notes of anger and restiveness in his voice, unusual for him.

"She may say nothing," I reassured him, "but she sees. Cecil has said that the queen's share of the bounty on the *Golden Hind* was more than the crown earned in a typical year throughout all other endeavors. She can hardly ignore that."

"Not that I want her to," he said. "But it's a shame if sure-and-steady service, though it be quiet, should be ignored." He kissed me on the lips before turning to sleep, but he seemed disquieted and perhaps overthoughtful. I tried to restart the conversation the next day, but he waved it away and turned the topic. There was nothing for me to do but comply.

Some months later our second daughter was born. We named her Frances after our friend, Drake.

# FIFTEEN

Year of Our Lord 1582
The Palace of Whitehall
Blackfriars
Windsor Castle

I n the spring of 1582 we entertained Thomas's
relations, many of whom were in town on court
business, and some who simply desired to visit the
markets of London, very near our home in
Blackfriars. I said a quick prayer for my own
family, and my mother in particular, as I tucked
my locket under my gown. Perhaps now that the
waters were mostly clear of Danes I could write to
her more regularly and expect to hear something,
anything, in return. Even though our home was
small, we still had a staff of nearly twenty-five to
assist us. I went to my children's chambers and
spoke with them before our guests arrived. They
wanted me to stay and tell stories but I could not.
I was as disappointed as their little faces showed
them to be.

Elizabeth was, as usual, playing with her dolls,
lining them up and speaking to them in an
authoritative tone of voice. Francis, who worshipped her, toddled nearby, while little Frances
slept under the watchful gaze of the baby nurse. I
kissed Francis on the head, and he felt warm to

me. "Has Francis been unwell?" I asked the nurse.

"No, ma'am, he has not, though he's been a wee bit tired. I shall watch after him," she said. There was no need to ask after Elizabeth; she was always ruddy and solid.

I made my way down to the great hall. The smell of roasting lamb filled the air, as did the aroma of the warm breads made of fine white wheat and the crisp scent of the parchment in which our fish had been baked. And then our guests arrived.

"Lady Gorges," Thomas's cousin John greeted me; John was often the first to arrive and last to leave. Thomas beamed; at court I was always the good lady marquess or the Marchioness of Northampton, but here at Blackfriars I was Lady Gorges.

Some of Thomas's Poyntz relatives, on his mother's side, came, too, and all told there were perhaps thirty people dining with us. I'd arranged for musicians to play from the upper choir level to soothe and entertain us as we ate. Toward the end of the evening the talk turned, as it almost always did, to court.

"I hear that Parliament has just passed a law that anyone who converts to Catholicism, or induces another to do so, faces charges of treason," one of Thomas's cousins said.

Thomas's brother William, a staunch supporter of the queen, disagreed. "That's only for those who withdraw their loyalty from Her Majesty, and surely, that would be cause for treason no matter what the cause."

"Then how be it treasonous to attend mass, for which the penalty is a weighty one hundred marks?" another Gorges cousin chimed in. "And if you don't attend the Protestant church, why, that's a burdensome twenty pounds to the crown from you. No man can afford that. Seems unlikely they're all treasonous."

I recalled a snippet of a letter I'd read in the queen's library once while searching out a history of the invasion of the Danes so long ago. It quoted the King Richard, second of that name. "This is a strange and fickle land," he'd written, "which never ceases to be riven and worn down by dissensions and strife and internecine hatreds."

The comments died away and then were replaced by talk of Drake's adventure; Thomas brought forth some of the treasures with which Francis had returned home. We had seen little of him in the last year; his beloved Mary had died and he kept mostly to himself and his sailors.

That night, after seeing our guests safely abed and checking on my children, a rare pleasure I was not afforded while I was at court, I went to our bedchamber, where Thomas stood looking out the window upon the dark street.

"What is it?"

"Nothing, love," he said.

I thought that perhaps he was disturbed by the

distressing conversation at dinner. "Your cousin John is a Catholic, isn't he?" I blurted. Then I wished I could take it back, because in truth, I did not want to know.

But Thomas nodded. "Yes, yes, he is. So are some others in my family, even in my mother's family, the Poyntzes."

I sat down on the bed. "How can that be?"

He came next to me and took my hand in his. "It's an untidy business in this realm, Elin. We were to be Catholic, and then not, and then so, and then not. Neither king nor queen can command what is subject to a man's own conscience and heart and faith, though they would, if they could."

I said nothing but looked at his face, still achingly handsome, by the light of the candles near our bedside.

"I want to please you," he said. "I want you to be proud of me. I am no marquess."

I gently squeezed his hand. "You joust with a ghost, my lord. I am your wife many times over what I had been to William. I am the mother of your children. I choose you above all others."

He shrugged and pulled away from me. "And yet, I am still not a knight."

I did not say that it did not matter, because we both knew it did. I was impatient for a moment, because he held me to account for acting with honor, and I had, from the time of our courting forward, always treated him with honor and respect, too—indeed, with a depth of love I had not developed with William. But I blew out the candles and sought to assure him of my love in the ways that only a wife might.

The next morning, Sunday, he told me to my surprise that he was unwell and could not attend St. Dunstan's with me and it would be better if I attended alone.

That summer, our son Edward was born.

"He favors you," I said, holding him toward Thomas, an offering of love that may come only from a woman to her husband. Thomas came near and kissed my cheek.

"He does indeed; he's a lovely boy," Thomas said. "Thank you, Elin." He held the babe for a while, but though we both wished otherwise, he did not have time to spare, as the queen had just honored Thomas by planning to send him to Sweden. There was no official ambassador, but she wished, in the current political climate, to remain friendly with all Protestant nations. She'd allowed me to retire from court for a week while I helped him prepare.

"I wish I could come with you," I said.

"I wish you could, too," he answered. "Do you worry that I shall not represent you, or Her Majesty, well?"

"No, no," I said, holding him close for a moment. I then disentangled myself. "It's only that I wish to see my homeland once more. My mother, my sisters, my cousins. The beech trees, the small strawberries . . ."

"I should capture all of them for you, if I could, and return with them." Thomas was beyond enthusiastic. "I shall comport myself well," he said, reassuring himself, I knew, and not me.

I laughed. "You shall indeed, was there ever a question? But beware; there are still debts outstanding from Princess Cecelia, and Johan, who was duke when he came here but is king now."

"Yes, indeed, I know," he said. He practiced some Swedish and German phrases with me, and our young Elizabeth came dancing into the room and corrected his pronunciation while shushing baby Edward, whom I reluctantly handed over to his nurse.

"I see how it is," Thomas declared, tickling Elizabeth's chin. "This young lass is going to correct her father's speech!"

"I shan't want you to say it incorrectly!" she insisted.

He turned her upside down and then sent her on her way.

"Me, too!" Francis raised his hands toward his father. Thomas, aware of Francis's delicate nature, tipped him upside down more carefully and then sent him gently on his way.

I saw Thomas off, watching him ride away until I could not see him on the horizon any longer and wiped tears away from my face. More often than not, it seemed, he was riding away from and not toward me.

I returned to court, where I was pleased that Her Majesty was negotiating in favor of the marriage of Francis Knollys's son to the rich daughter of Lady Rivett. The lady and young gentleman in question desired to marry out of love, and one might have expected the queen to oppose such a match. But, perhaps out of affection for Sir Francis and loyalty to the long-dead Lady Knollys, the queen intervened on behalf of the young lovers. Perhaps, too, it was a way to pay penance for the banishment from court, forever, of Sir Francis's daughter the she-wolf.

Illness came to London, and we were all gladdened when it passed by queen and court. However, Clemence came to get me early one morning, while it was still dark. "Lady Northampton," she called, knocking on my door. "Come quickly. It's Francis."

I was only partially awake and did not know of whom she spoke—Sir Francis Knollys? Francis Walsingham? Then it occurred to me that she would not refer to either man by his first name but that she spoke, instead, of my son.

We raced through the dark on horseback with a brace of my servants, but by the time we arrived my poor Francis was gone. His small, gaunt body was laid out on his bed with a thin white sheet covering him; his eyes, their lids darkened, had been closed. His soul was already with the Lord Jesus. That brought me some comfort, as did the continuing health of my other children.

I dismissed everyone from the room and wept over this fine, sweet boy, whom, I admitted, I barely knew though he had held me in highest love and esteem. I sang to him, quietly, till his body cooled, my heart wrenched within me. When I finally left the room, my young Elizabeth and small Frances took my right and left hands in their own small ones, and while it dulled the pain, nothing could erase it.

I had his coffin prepared, and before the lid was closed and he interred at St. Dunstan's, I put some of the first lamb's ears of the season in with him, for gentleness, and wished, for a brief moment, that I could join him.

The Danes had resolved their conflict with the English and with the Swedes, for now, and so Thomas was able to return home only months after he left. He departed the islands of Stockholm on August 14, stopped in Paris to pick up some dispatches from Sir Francis Walsingham, the queen's current ambassador to France as well as her spymaster, and then returned home.

I was at court when he arrived; he returned to Blackfriars and then came to see me. I excused myself from service.

"Please, take your leave, my good lady marquess," Elizabeth said. "We shall see you presently when our good cousin Gorges reports back to us of his trip." She knew I would want time to mourn young Francis with Thomas.

He was waiting for me in my apartments and I shut the door and then fell into his arms. "Francis . . ." I began, and the tears I'd held back since I buried our son came forth, unbidden.

He stroked my hair; he did not cry, for my sake, I know, but his hand and jaw trembled. "Shhh, there now. I have already been to Blackfriars. The governess informed me."

We sat together for an hour and mourned our son for some time. Then we spoke of his gentleness and humor and the way he won everyone to him, and the charming antics he played as a toddler, and we laughed, the first I had remembered him with joy since he'd passed away. Later that night, Thomas told me of his trip; I loved hearing of his travels, even when he rode within England. He'd loved Paris—and knew I would, too. He'd brought me back some silk and had been able to carry out some missions for Her Majesty there.

The next day the queen invited us to dine with her, privately, while Thomas recounted his trip.

"I was able to negotiate with King Johan," he said, "for repayment of many of the debts that are outstanding against your kingdom, Majesty, but to my regret, not all."

The queen leaned over and patted his hand. "In the letter the king had you deliver to me he commended you in all ways, Cousin, so we are certain that you achieved all that could have been achieved and more."

"He would like our backing in his war with Russia." Thomas looked uncomfortable.

"He has as many of our funds as he is likely to acquire," Elizabeth said shortly. "He may use them as he will."

Overall, though, she was pleased with Thomas's service and told him so. I asked for three days' leave and she agreed, though perhaps a little unwillingly.

"I have a surprise for you," he said as we rode to Blackfriars.

"A surprise!" I couldn't wait. When we arrived at our home, my surprise was awaiting me in the greeting chamber, surrounded by my children.

She came forward, and as she did, I recognized myself ten years earlier. She had the same red-brown hair, same eyes, same fair skin as I did. Her body was as mine, but perhaps more lithe as she had not yet borne children.

I cocked my head. "Sofia?"

"You recognized me!" she exclaimed in German, throwing herself at me and kissing my cheeks time and again. I had not seen her since she was a small girl nearly running off the dock as I'd left Sweden.

Thomas stood behind me, eager for my response. "I knew how you longed for family, and for Sweden, and I thought, what could I better bring to my love than both of those?"

"I hope, I hope you approve?" she asked.

My children, already enchanted, jumped up and down and said, "*Ja, ja, ja!*" Had she been speaking with them in German in my absence?

"Of course, Cousin," I said, and then turned to embrace, in gratitude, my pleased husband. I was thrilled to have someone from Sweden here, a friend, my very own family. "You are welcome to stay with us as long as you like." I turned back and kissed each of her cheeks softly; they smelled, somehow, of home.

"I plan to remain in England, Cousin, as you did!" she said.

"Yes, yes, of course," I said. "Have you settled into a chamber?"

"Of course. The servants were kind enough to assist me. Oh—and I have a letter from your lady mother."

At that, I grew truly excited. I had not heard from my mother in some time. Sofia quickly ran to her room and then returned with the letter in hand. "Can I help in any way?" she asked me.

I smiled. "I shall think upon it. Thomas and I will return to court, though we shall both be back and forth from time to time, he more than I. I'll ask the governess to assist you in finding an

English tutor to work with every day, and when the time is right, you can come to court, too."

She leaned over and kissed me. "Thank you, dearest Elin."

I wasn't sure why my given name grated on my ears from her tongue. "Here in England, I am known as Helena," I said.

"But Thomas . . ." she began.

"Thomas is different," I said firmly, then reached over and embraced her. "Welcome to our home."

I retired to my room and read the letter from my mother over and over again, rubbing my hand upon the page, which I knew her hand had touched, too. In it she asked after me and my family, told me she prayed daily for my well-being and that of my children. "Your Thomas is magnificent," she said. "All here were taken with him and it is clear that he is well read, well spoken, and well looked after! I daresay that Christina Abrahamsdotter was brimming with envy, as her husband is fat and old. Bridget ensured that Thomas knew whom to speak with and when, and translated from English to German when Latin wouldn't do."

Dear Bridget. I had a sudden pang, an uncharitable thought, wishing that Thomas had returned with Bridget and not Sofia. I repented of it; I had expressed my wish to him to see my family, and now he had provided it for me.

My mother concluded her letter by proclaiming her love for me over and over, then begging me to take care of Sofia, her sister's daughter, my cousin.

I would have, of course, even if she hadn't asked me to.

Thomas and I spent those three days playing with our children, listening to Sofia's stories, making love, and practicing the few Swedish words he had learned, which made me laugh when he spoke them, whereupon he began to laugh, too.

The queen held a banquet in honor of Thomas's successful journey to and from Sweden; she was always festive when monies were earned or recovered, or saved. The court musicians played German compositions in addition to her usual Italian and English pieces.

"Thank you, Majesty," I said after she had completed a dance and was watching others. "Thomas is blessed by your trust and attention, and I am, too."

"My good lady marquess, I am always pleased to laud my servants . . . and friends," she finished with a smile. She put her hand upon my arm. "Helena, who is yon woman?" She nodded toward Sofia, who, new to court, was at the center of a group of male courtiers, young and old. Her English was good and getting better each day.

"That is my cousin," I said. "She came back

with Thomas, hoping for a better life in England, as I'd found."

"And perhaps a husband, too, as you'd found. We see that she is busily assaying the selection," the queen said, not with malice, but perhaps with a note of caution. I watched as Sofia charmed the men around her. "She favors you," the queen said.

"Without the fat that bearing babies brings," I agreed, pinching a small amount on my still comely white hands. At that, the queen laughed.

That June we spent at Windsor Castle, I on constant attendance of the queen, Thomas sometimes at Windsor, sometimes at Blackfriars, sometimes on commission for the queen. We spent an odd day together now and then, mainly discussing the business of our family or our children, or making plans for the weeks and months ahead, but he was often sent on the queen's business and I was always in service. I sorrowed that there was little time for sharing walks and promised myself that, as soon as time permitted, we would bow hunt together again.

The queen loved Windsor with its mirrored ceilings and walls, its pretty-smelling privies, and the sense of security being ensconced in a fortress brought. As for me, I loved harvesting its gardens.

There was never a moment of rest from the Scots' ferment. Thomas and I had discussed in the preceding months and years the possibility that Walsingham saw shadows and specters where perhaps none existed. One night, during a rare dinner alone, he shared with me that perhaps Walsingham's fears weren't unfounded. "I listened to what the man had to say when I was in Paris for Her Majesty," he said. "And there are those surrounding the queen on all levels, and seeded into all corner of the realm, who would do her harm."

I mentioned to him the book that Mary Radcliffe had brought up to me, urging the queen's ladies to murder her. Thomas grew quiet but said nothing, simply nodding. "And I've heard that a wandering priest, disguised as a man who draws teeth for replacement, has been stopped by Walsingham's men. He was set free but his bag was seized, and in it, concealed amongst his equipment, were letters from those plotting with Mary against the queen."

"Will she never learn?" I asked.

"There's naught that says she's initiating these plots," Thomas warned me.

I hadn't expected that; I had thought to hear his concerns echo my own. "Whence did you learn of this?" I asked.

"From one of my Gorges cousins," he said. "And now, Lady Gorges, we shall finish our dinner and retire to a night alone."

I savored it, as we had so few days or nights together of late. I lay abed long after Thomas was asleep, though, my mind unquiet with thoughts of my children and their governess, whom I no longer wanted to engage but had not yet had time to find a replacement for, and Scotland.

I walked with the queen, just the two of us, trailed by some other of her maids and two ladies, the next morning in the rose gardens of Windsor. "Do you find what you need, Helena?" she asked me as I unlinked from her arm to snip some roses.

"I found some, Majesty. The gardens are not so lush as those at Richmond, but I shall find enough ripe roses that I may blend a linen water for your bedchamber and my own!" I said, snipping some longish stems and placing them into the basket I carried alongside.

The sun was out and the day grew warm so we soon returned to the queen's Privy Chamber, where she would attend to the day's paperwork from her council. I set the basket down near the marble table I'd work upon; Anne Dudley helped the queen into a more comfortable gown in which to work and then withdrew to arrange for the week's wardrobe to be requisitioned from the wardrobe stores at the Tower.

I arranged a small posy of rosebuds, both red blooms and white, to recognize Her Majesty's royal heritage, in a glass vase and placed it near where the queen worked so she could enjoy the scent throughout the day. I glanced at the paperwork before her; 'twas from the ambassador of

Scotland. "Thomas tells me they have caught a priest-spy from Scotland," I said. "And that your Tudor cousin foments against you once again."

"Thomas is particularly well informed for his position," the queen said.

"We are all concerned for your well-being, Majesty," I said. I slipped one more rose into her Tudor arrangement but had, apparently, neglected to snip off a thorn and it broke my flesh and I began to bleed.

"And I for yours. Be careful," Elizabeth said as she turned back to her dispatches. "Roses have thorns."

# SIXTEEN

Year of Our Lord 1583
The Palace of Whitehall
Theobalds
Blackfriars

Year of Our Lord 1584
The Palace of Whitehall
Sheen, Richmond

Shortly after the new year, King Johan sent a representative from Sweden to continue the bonhomie and diplomacy that Thomas had reignited the summer before. Count Eric Brahe, a friend of my family, came on behalf of the king and was awarded rich rooms at court for the duration of his stay. He delivered a packet of letters from my mother, and I spent as much time as possible with him and threw several entertainments in his honor. I'd heard that he particularly enjoyed jugglers, so I asked Thomas to query the community of players and find which performers were known to have the finest skills.

He found two men who performed together under the title A Deux, and we held an evening's entertainment in one of the large banqueting rooms, sumptuously and expensively decorated for the event.

The men began by throwing large rings at and toward one another—one would catch a ring and then toss it back to the other, arcing it high into the air, then back and forth again until there were more than a dozen rings in play. One by one the rings landed about the neck of one of the jugglers until he had a fair high cuff, which he paraded about with, imitating the high noses of the finely ruffed courtiers. The crowd roared and the performers bowed and we clapped. Then they performed tricks before and behind one another with pins and boxes, too.

By far the most exciting was the juggling of lit torches, perhaps a dozen between them spiraling through the air. One juggler called Thomas forward, and then he indicated that they wanted me, as hostess, to come forth.

"I?"

Thomas nodded. He took my hand and led me forward as the crowd hushed. The smell of the flame and ash filled the dead silence; the only noise was the whoosh of torches through the air. The players indicated that I was to run through the space between them. My eyes opened wide, but Thomas leaned over to me and whispered, " 'Tis safe, I've run through them myself."

I stood near the edge of their stage, praying that one or more of the torches would not light upon my expensive gown, and counted to five, at which point I dashed through the fire field. I could sense that they adjusted the speed of their throw and catch to accommodate my path, and, unbelievably, I made it through.

When I ran back once again and arrived safely at my seat, all in the room stood and cheered and whistled. Thomas looked pleased to have me so appreciated, more pleased than he had been with me for some time, which delighted me and made me think upon ways to encourage that. Although the queen did not stand she clapped and cheered very loudly indeed. Sofia smiled and raised a hand toward me, then soon took her seat.

Later, after the entertainments had concluded, Eric drew near to me. "I see your cousin Sofia has settled in well," he said.

I nodded. "I see but little of her, as I am in constant attendance upon the queen. I have tried several times to help her make her acquaintance with men of right standing, but so far, there are none she feels drawn to."

He sipped from his goblet. "Her fiancé in Sweden left her, you know."

I set my own goblet down on a nearby table. "I did not know that."

"She was set to marry him in September, but he found someone with more money and a better title and returned her dowry. Then your Thomas arrived and she spent quite a bit of time at court, and with your mother and sisters, during his stay. When Thomas mentioned how much you'd missed your family, Sofia offered to return to England with him to be a companion to you. She'd spent some time with the ladies who had returned with the princess, learning English and, I suspect, yearning for adventure . . . and wealth."

"And how does my sister Karin Bonde?" I asked with just the smallest bit of residual pain.

"She's well, and happy, with fine children, like yourself," he said softly. "All are glad that you met with such good fortune in England, the highest-titled woman in the land after Her Majesty."

"I am thankful," I said. Sofia had quickly excused herself from discussions with several squires and neatly positioned herself next to the eldest son of an earl. It hadn't taken her long to figure out who was most nobly titled.

"I take it there are no more marquesses in England right now?" Eric teased. "Or dukes?"

"Not presently," I said.

Eric looked again at Sofia. "She may find herself disappointed." Those same highborn men she sought soon disentangled themselves from her pretty company.

I enjoyed the visit from the Swedes, but in spite of the gift of exquisite horses that Eric had brought for the queen, the Swedish delegation had, once again, neglected to bring enough money for their own keep, much less anything more to pay back the debts that King Erik and Cecelia had amassed on two visits.

"I'm sorry, Majesty," I said as I rubbed ointment into her hands one morning before she slipped on her gloves. "I have paid, from my own purse, any debts that Eric Brahe amassed during this visit. But he told me that King Johan has refused to pay any more of his brother's debts, as he was known to be a madman."

"If he was known to be a madman, why did they try to foist him upon our realm and our person?" she sniffed. Then she flipped her hand over and squeezed mine. "We know that this is none of your doing," she said. "Be content. King Johan is well known to be vain, haughty, and unwise. You cannot undo that. And you are English now, my fiery marchioness."

"Do you refer to my hair, my temper, or my dash through the jugglers?" I asked.

"Why, all three!" she said. But she, known for her own fire, meant no harm but a compliment by the comment. I left anything else unsaid, lest I be considered disloyal to either King Johan or Queen Elizabeth.

The next month I was required to attend upon Her Majesty at Cecil's grand home, Theobalds, which he'd had built with perquisites from Her Majesty. Thomas was not to accompany me, as the queen had set upon him the task of assembling a team of players who would become her very own acting troupe, the Queen's Men.

"It's a great honor," I said. "You know how fond she is of entertainment."

He sighed. "Yes, I know she intends it as such. But perhaps assembling jugglers and players isn't quite the same as assisting in the greater matters of the realm."

"She trusts you, as you are such a fine player yourself," I said.

"I suspect Her Majesty does not knight those who assemble the evening's entertainment," he said with a grimace. "And I prefer that Blagrave continue as Master of Revels." I knew Thomas was disappointed that Elizabeth had not raised or rewarded him for his work in Sweden.

"And Walsingham is involved," he said. I thought it odd he would even mention that.

"Why?" I asked.

"Players travel," he said. "From home to home, throughout the country. They speak with servants, they learn things. I believe Walsingham truly enjoys the theater, but he lets no opportunity to sift information for the queen go by undisturbed."

After I returned from that magnificent manor, I retired to await the birth of our next child. "Do you want another son?" I asked Thomas one night, tentative.

He shook his head. "I do not know. It's not as if he can replace Francis."

I agreed. "I'm afraid that if it's a son, it will feel as though we're setting Francis aside in his favor."

Thomas laced his fingers through mine, a warm and lovely gesture he hadn't made for so, so long. I burst into tears and he drew me near.

"There, now, love, what is wrong?"

"I don't know. Should it be a girl, or a boy?"

Thomas took my face in his hand. "I don't believe you'll get to decide, now, will you?" He freely smiled, and I hadn't seen him do that for some time, either. It dried my tears and I smiled back.

"That's true."

"We'll take what the Lord sends," he said.

He sent a boy, in His mercy and wisdom, and our young son did not replace Francis in any way in our hearts, but he did remind me that God is a God of life, and that life follows death though we most often fear it may not.

"What should you like to name him?" I asked Thomas.

"Theobald," he replied as he readied himself to leave for the coast, and Hurst Castle. "A family name."

"Theobald?" It surprised me.

He left the next morning without saying good-bye, in a hurry, I supposed, to get on with his duties. I told myself that he hadn't wanted to disturb me so soon after childbirth, but oh, how different 'twas from the birth of our Elizabeth, when we slept together, chastely, every night, even before my churching, when I would be declared pure and able to return to church and community after childbirth. He did not wait for my churching to be complete before he left. In fact, we did not often attend church together of late, and it troubled me.

I looked out the window, hoping to catch sight of him as he rode off, but he was gone.

Later that month, before I left home to return to the queen, I made arrangements for an artist to come and paint portraits of my children, a large one of them together and then miniatures that I might take with me when I was away from them.

"I shan't want to sit for a portrait painter, Mother," Elizabeth said. "It shall be dull."

"I understand, love," I said. "But I miss you so dearly when I am gone."

"Then," she said matter-of-factly, "you must miss me all the time."

Sofia reached out and took my daughter's tiny hand in her own. "I shall sit with you and tell you stories of the north to pass the time."

At that, Elizabeth clapped, and Frances, who wanted to do everything her sister did, clapped, too. Young Edward and our newest son, Theobald, were too young to clap, but I had the sinking suspicion that if they were old enough they'd join in enthusiastically.

That November a man from Warwickshire made his way to London with a pistol and was heard to be shouting that he was come to see the queen, "a serpent and a viper," and that he meant to shoot her through and hoped to see her head set on a pole.

He'd so noisily informed all of his evil plans well before he reached the castle, and so was apprehended and was no longer a threat. However, that same month, a more serious plot for the queen's life was uncovered.

Francis Throckmorton, a man very close to the court, was arrested after six months of surveillance by Walsingham and his quiet minions. Walsingham's officials burst into Throckmorton's house, and he, still dressed in his nightcap and gown, raced up his stairways to attempt to set afire his correspondence.

"He was restrained," Walsingham reported to the queen shortly thereafter, while I was attending to her as she prepared for the evening ahead. He had a look of quiet satisfaction on his face, like a man who had eaten but not yet digested a particularly rich meal. "And we were able to acquire those letters."

"And what, pray tell, did they reveal?" the queen asked drily.

I was no friend of Walsingham—he gave me a shiver as though I had wet clothes on—but I did think the queen could be more gracious and thankful for his endeavors.

"He was midway through a letter to Mary of

Scotland advising her of English ports that would be friendly to a Spanish or French invasion on her behalf."

"A letter," she said. "That's all."

"May I press for more information, Majesty?" Walsingham asked. He emphasized the word *press*.

The queen's clerk of the council, Robert Beale, was a man of strong Protestant faith and he'd recently published a paper decrying the use of the rack as barbarous and illegal. He'd been largely ignored.

"Yes," the queen said. "And report back to us on what you find."

That night I told Thomas what I knew.

"I could hear a man being racked when I was imprisoned after our wedding," he said. "He began by moaning like a woman in childbirth, but by the end he was pleading for his mother, for his priest, for God and His angels to come and rescue him."

"Did he live?" I asked.

"I know not for certain," Thomas said. "But I think not. They wrung him like a rag and then threw him in the corner to die, untended by any but the rats, which are nearly as big as one of the queen's spaniels."

When Walsingham came to report to Elizabeth what he had learned from the racking, he proceeded to tell her in the Presence Chamber, in front of not only her councilors but her ladies and many who were about the court. He would dare not make so public a report without her implicit permission. What cause had she for making this so well known?

"He made a full confession, Majesty," Walsingham began, his black beard wagging. "He told that the Duke of Guise, Mary of Scots's cousin, was planning to attack England from the south."

I closed my eyes but for a minute. Did they never tire, these royals, of cousins?

"The goal was to deprive you of your crown and state, by which means, I daresay, to deprive you of your head."

The queen stood up, face flushed, and snapped shut her fan. "Go on."

"Ambassador Mendoza"—Walsingham turned and looked directly at the man himself—"has given his reassurances that Philip of Spain would aid and assist in any way necessary."

Mendoza did not shrink at all.

"Philip has been plotting for my throne for twenty-five years!" the queen shouted. "Since he could not pilfer it in my bed, he seeks to steal it like a common thief through the back door." She turned to Mendoza. "Return to your quarters, complete your tasks at hand, and pack your trunks to return to Spain!"

"They are already packed," he said, bowing,

showing that his spies had already told him what was to come.

That angered her further. She took a glance at one of her ladies, Bess Throckmorton, who wavered like a willow. The queen sat down again under the canopy of state. "And Throckmorton?"

Walsingham licked his lips. "He had written to Mary, and she responded to him, thanking him for his efforts and asking him how many English citizens could be counted upon to come to her aid when her cousin the Duke of Guise arrived on these shores to restore her rightful crown. Northumberland helped, too."

"Ungrateful! Impudent! Each year we pay for the upkeep and maintenance of her household, which numbers forty-eight presently. And even as we are working on her behalf to restore her Scots' crown to her unworthy and light head, she is plotting against us to take our crown instead and provoking the pope and other foreign potentates to attempt against us and our realm." The queen abruptly dismissed everyone but Cecil and Walsingham.

I came alongside Bess Throckmorton and took her cold hand in mine as we walked toward our chambers. I held it tightly to quell the tremor that ran within it. "Do not fear, Bess," I said. She was young, perhaps of the age that I had been when I had first arrived at the English court. "Her Majesty well knows that each family has those who serve her truly and those who are treacherous. She will not harshly judge you."

Bess squeezed my hand. "Thank you, Helena," she said. "Francis Throckmorton is my cousin."

Some months thereafter, her cousin Francis was executed at Tyburn. Henry Percy, the Eighth Earl of Northumberland, who had well served the queen for many years, was found shot through the heart in his simple Tower bed. Suicide was the official inquiry verdict. Murder, Clemence said some whispered, at the behest of the queen or her men.

# SEVENTEEN

Year of Our Lord 1584
The Palace of Whitehall
Sheen, Richmond

Winter: Year of Our Lord 1585
Wilton and Langford, Salisbury

That year found me with child again. Whilst it was not quite an immaculate conception, it was something of a miracle as it was a rare night that Thomas and I spent in one another's company any longer, and when we did, it was disappointingly perfunctory. I was mainly waiting upon the queen; as the Scots situation grew tenser she relied upon her principal ladies to keep her entertained and soothed. Thomas was often away, on the queen's business, though of late he did not share with me the locations of his destinations or how long he would be gone. He simply shrugged off my questions; hurt, I stopped asking and turned toward my own duties, keeping those details to myself as well.

One day, as I laid out the jewels the queen would wear that week, coordinating with the Countess of Nottingham, who was in charge of the robes, she noticed that my midsection had swelled.

"My grandfather Boleyn said once that his wife

brought him a child each year," she said to me, in a rare reference to her mother's family. She fingered the locket ring, in which hid her mother and herself; she never took it off and that brought me great pleasure these nearly ten years after I'd gifted it to her.

"I am apparently trying to keep up with your illustrious family, Majesty," I said. My back hurt and she noticed and bade me sit near her.

"How do your children?" she asked.

"They are well. Elizabeth is by turn a pirate or a lady, but she runs the household in my absence," I jested. I knew my daughter, though but one of many named after Her Grace, brought her pleasure.

"The others grow by turn, too," I said. I dared to broach a topic that had long been on my heart and mind and that Thomas had urged me to speak of with the queen. "Perhaps, Majesty, after this babe is born, I might be given leave to spend more time with them. They grow so quickly . . ."

"Of course, you should take the time to repose till you are churched," she said, smoothly moving beyond the request she knew I'd made.

I recalled Lady Cobham, an especial favorite of the queen and the mother of seven, recently hoping to get leave to rest her weary bones in the country, but the leave was denied. I felt for her as a mother, as a lady of the bedchamber, and also, as she was a relative of sorts to both of my husbands. We had grown to be friends.

I was both weary of court and wishing to spend more time with my family, and thrilled with court and its many intrigues and the hard-won friendships and fulfilling duties I immersed myself in each day.

Some months later, the queen called both Thomas and me into her Privy Chamber, alone. "We have a gift for you," she said. "We are giving you the former priory at Sheen, near Richmond Palace, as a residence for you, for life, so you may be nearer to your family when you wait upon us at court."

I smiled and leaned forward to hug her, which she seemed to tolerate but which I knew she truly enjoyed. "Thank you, thank you, Majesty. You know Richmond is a particular favorite of mine, with the gardens, and to live nearer by will be a great delight." I had always loved Sheen. It was the most important gift she had ever given me, and what's more, she gave it to both Thomas and myself jointly.

Thomas nodded with respect. "Thank you, Your Majesty," he said. But although he was perfectly proper, he was not as enthusiastic as I was, and I knew why.

"Are you not pleased with the gift?" I asked him later, in my luxe apartments at court.

" 'Twas kindly given," he admitted. "But by providing Sheen to us, for life or until she decides to revoke it, the queen is allowing the children and me to be closer to court, and you, but not giving you direct leave to spend more time with us."

"Still, 'tis a great honor. Many courtiers and foreign ambassadors have coveted lodging near Richmond for many years."

"I know," he said, and then looked beyond me. "I've got someone to meet shortly. Can we speak of this later?"

I agreed, and kissed him afore he left. He kissed me back, but not with passion. He closed the door behind him, and I sat on a chair, hands in my lap, for an hour, wondering why he couldn't be happy with the gift of Sheen and if I was wrong in feeling so.

We moved in shortly thereafter, and after some changes, we made an occasion to invite the queen, and her close circle, to our new home for one of the first performances by the Queen's Men.

I had been feeling remiss in my caretaking of Sofia; she had come to England to be a companion to me, and although I had provided company to her when I could, and for her English education, I had not had much time to spend with her. Apart from court, I had little time of my own. So I had a fine gown made for her of midnight blue silk shot through with gold and she wore her hair down, long and shimmering, as was her right as a virgin.

"Can I assist you with your clothing?" I asked Thomas, meeting him in his new chamber.

"No, thank you. Tobias has already laid out something suitable," Thomas said.

"Oh, all right." Tobias was Thomas's closest manservant. "Perhaps after dinner, then, I might return with you and we can discuss the events of the evening?"

He nodded politely. "Perhaps." Thomas indicated that he would meet me at dinner; Sheen was large enough that we each had our own bedchambers. They were near one another, but it was the first time in our married life that we did not sleep in the same bed each night when we were in the same house. I spent a moment wishing, perhaps, we were at the less-opulent Blackfriars instead.

There were a hundred or more courtiers already downstairs; our servants had made them welcome and I took time to greet each one once I made my arrival. As we were seated, Sofia made her way down the stairs, and I will admit that all male eyes were upon her for a time, but she had eyes for only one person present, the eighteen-year-old Earl of Essex.

"Who is he?" she asked me after dinner, before the entertainments were to begin.

"He's the son of the queen's enemy," I said with a smile, "who is forever banished from court. Essex is also one of her current favorites, along with Walter Raleigh." I nodded in the adventurer's direction.

"Ooh, that makes Essex ever more interesting,"

she replied mischievously in German. She'd taken to speaking German to me when she wanted to keep our conversations private. This was fine, but I knew that there were others at court who had a smattering of German and may be able to understand us, and they'd certainly understand the name Essex.

"Be careful not to be too loose in your speech," I said. She nodded but would have rolled her eyes, I knew, if she could have.

I took time to explain to her that Essex was the son of Lettice Knollys and her first husband, the Earl of Essex. "My first husband, William, was also the Earl of Essex," I said, "before he died."

"Wouldn't it be wonderful if we each married an Earl of Essex?" she said.

At that I stopped cold. I needed to return to my guests, but she had to understand that Essex was a high-flown young man; Lord Robert, his step-father, was placing him very carefully at court, for Lord Robert's benefit as well as Essex's.

"He's not within your reach," I said softly.

"'Who shoots at the midday sun, though he be sure he shall never hit the mark, yet as sure he is he shall shoot higher than who aims but at a bush,'" she answered. "Sir Philip Sidney's *Countess of Pembroke's Arcadia.*"

"Where did you read that?" I demanded.

"Thomas was sharing some of the court poetry with me," she said a bit saucily before moving on.

Thomas? My senses were alerted.

The Queen's Men were duly assembled. Although Thomas had initially seemed displeased, once they were at court, or here at Sheen, with splendid sets and costumes, he was proud of his work, and I of him. Courtiers had long had their own troupes, the Earl of Sussex's men, of course, and the Earl of Leicester's men, but for the Queen's Men to have been formed and perform regularly for Her Majesty meant that the stain of disapproval was removed from actors. Not only had she sworn them to her service; she allowed them to wear her livery, a high honor indeed. In so doing, she had made actors, before known as ne'er-do-wells if not outright cutpurses, into honorable entertainers. Playwriting, formerly looked down upon, became another high form of artistic expression, and lads, and some ladies, from the lowborn through the young Countess of Pembroke, took up their pens in new manners. Elizabeth was perhaps destined to be known as the Queen of Revels.

The play Thomas had chosen for them to perform that evening was another by his favorite, Lyly, who also was well thought of by the queen. This play, *Campaspe*, spoke of Alexander, who had traveled to Athens and fallen in love, unexpectedly, with a young woman. He loved her well and commissioned her portrait be painted, but the artist, too, fell in love with the charming young woman. He was so reluctant to let her go that he continued to mar his own painting day after day so that she would be forced to sit with him, continually, as he never finished his work.

The play was well under way and still Thomas had not made his way to sit next to me. I worried. Where could he be? The queen, justly proud of her men, was riveted by the tale of romance. Lord Robert, reinstated into her high favor, sat next to her. They still had an easy companionship and teasingly deep affections, but I sensed none of the sexual undercurrent of their earlier life; I credited this to Her Majesty as well as Lord Robert. She still loved him, but both recognized he was another woman's husband.

In the end, Alexander declared his love to be immortal and everlasting but came forward to set the young woman, his own true heart, free, so she may live with the artist with whom she had fallen in love. At this, young Bess Throckmorton turned to look at handsome Walter Raleigh, who shot a wicked smirk back in her direction.

*Ah, Bess, it has not been long enough since your cousin badly handled the queen for you to be thinking of Raleigh,* I thought.

As soon as the main player came near to the front of the stage, I could see who it was. Thomas! How had I not recognized him behind the paint and mask? I sighed with relief, reassured. 'Twas not that he was avoiding me; he had taken up a place as an actor. When he took his mask off along with the other players, everyone stood and applauded and he glowed in the triumph of having fooled them, for the moment, with his performance. Several glanced at me to see if I had been surprised, as indeed I had been!

Applauding loudly, too, but looking at Essex, was Sofia. She would not meet my eye, but instead made her way to the charming, handsome earl, who was not only the queen's darling but, owing to the tragic situation of his mother, which brought sympathy from all but the queen, the rest of the courtiers. He spoke with her kindly, but it was clear she was more interested in him than he in her. The queen caught my eye with a sharp, warning look. I would have to speak with Sofia again.

The second night, we had arranged for one of the Queen's Men to please her with a comedy, which she loved nearly as much as romance. Richard Tarleton, a witty jester, was one of Thomas's greatest discoveries. Tarleton mimicked and mocked and strolled and charmed. When someone from the audience threw a phrase out at him, he was able to twist it to both tease the shouter and please the queen with his banter. From the second he poked his head round the curtain, the audience began to laugh.

Midway through the performance, the queen's little dog escaped her grasp and ran upon the stage. Tarleton shrieked as the tiny spaniel came toward him, bewildered. "Majesty, Majesty!" Tarleton called out. "Please call off your mastiff or I am undone!"

Elizabeth laughed until she had tears, and at the end of his performance she said, "Take away this knave, lest he continue to force us to laugh in such an unregal manner!"

That night, after the guests had retired, I rubbed ointment into my husband's back and told him he had done a fine job. "I should not but wonder that she does knight you for plays and jesting," I said. "And that is not a bad service to offer to someone who is so often weighed down."

"Perhaps not," he said. "I know it is the way of things, but to see young Essex swaggering in his earldom does not sit well with me."

I was weary of his complaints and I did not hide that. He was weary of entertaining the court, and he did not hide that, either. We kissed perfunctorily and separated for sleep.

Shortly after our entertainments at Sheen, our good friend Thomas Radcliffe, the Earl of Sussex, died.

I made my way to Mary Radcliffe's chambers before I took my leave to prepare for my lying-in. I greeted her, both of us wearing black, with a long embrace.

"I am sorry for the loss of your brother, my

friend. The queen has so few good councilors, those who loved her long, and well, and put her interests above their own," I said. "I shall send a heartfelt letter to Lady Sussex before I leave court and keep you in my prayers."

Mary embraced me in return; though we were the same age, she looked older than I. Perhaps it was the loss of her brother, or the fact that she had no husband to comfort her in her sorrows. "She has spoken to me of his constancy," she said. "As, one by one, her trusted friends and councilors grow old, and infirm, she will rely yet more upon those of us who remain."

I took my box of herbal preparations with me and placed the queen's jewelry into the close care of the Countess of Nottingham.

"They'll be fine, Helena, don't fuss so," she said.

I thought upon who would carry the queen's train in my absence; who would have to decide who could enter the queen's Privy and Presence Chambers. In a very real way, I controlled access to the sovereign. Although I looked forward to going home, it would be untrue to say that I would not miss court, or my high place there, for the few weeks I was gone. I'd grown accustomed to, and enjoyed, being the second highest lady in the land, and the closeness to the queen.

The day before I left court came word that Prince William of Orange, in the Netherlands, had been betrayed by one of his servants on behalf of the Spanish and had been foully murdered. The Netherlands were engaged in their own struggle to free their Protestant nation from the grip of the Spaniards, and Philip of Spain had put a large bounty on William's head. The fact that access had been gained by someone close to the prince filled me with foreboding for my own sovereign.

The murderer was meted out a terrible penalty: burned with a hot iron, flesh torn from his bones, quartered and disemboweled while still alive, and finally beheaded, proving that neither side heeded the Lord Jesus' words: "Do unto others as you would have them do unto you."

I returned to my home to rest, attend to my family, and bear my child.

The second day at Sheen, I slept late before rising to spend time with my children and prepare for the birth of my child. The midwife was already in attendance, so I hoped to have some time to consider candidates for governess. I had already dismissed my children's current governess, who was not as well educated as I would have liked and tended to bend to my daughter Elizabeth's will, which would not do.

I sat in the front room, by the fire, writing a list of potential governesses and making note to ask the current nurse if she might recommend another, as we would need several new servants in the children's household with the addition of a new babe. I glanced up and saw, riding across the lawn and toward the stable, Thomas, with Sofia riding pillion behind him on the same horse, his bow tied behind them.

I had never seen anyone ride pillion with Thomas save myself.

I had not been able to hunt or ride with Thomas for some months due to my pregnancy, and though we'd enjoyed bow hunting in the past, we'd not had much time for that due to our court duties. I'd been surprised, actually, that he'd returned from the north so early in the week, but he said he'd wanted to be here for the babe's birth.

The two of them walked toward our house, and when they arrived, Sofia glanced at me, quickly, through her lashes and then retired to her room to ready herself for her instructor, who would arrive presently.

Thomas came and kissed me on both cheeks then placed his hands on my stomach, and our child. "Are you well?" he asked.

I nodded. "The babe will be here soon." I let a moment slip by. "I saw that you were hunting with Sofia this morning."

"Yes," he said. "She'd indicated she'd like to learn how, and I offered a first lesson as I was home this day. Is that all right?"

What could I answer? It was innocent enough, and she was given to my care. "You rode pillion?" I asked.

"Once we arrived at the park, she said her horse was not tame enough for her," he said. "I left him tied up and sent a servant for him afterward."

"Be that as it may," I said, "I shouldn't like to see that again."

He shrugged, and I went to speak with my cousin. "I see you went hunting with Thomas this morning," I said.

"Yes, it was very kind of him to take me," she responded, never averting her gaze.

"It's not appropriate for an unmarried woman to accompany a married man without escort," I said.

"Oh, surely I am safe with your husband!" She neatly turned responsibility from herself to Thomas, though I supposed there was blame to divide. Her eyes were wide and her smile well drawn, and I felt like a foolish matron striking out in unearned jealousy, though my heart told me otherwise.

Three nights hence my pangs grew closer and I knew our child was about to be born. I was a practiced mother by this time, and until the very end I was able to think upon other matters. Near the babe's birth, I made a decision to set about, with purpose, finding a husband for Sofia. Once I'd decided upon that, I felt peace and calm until I was engulfed in the pain of pushing my child into the world.

She arrived in silence, and for a moment, I thought that perhaps she did not live. But she did.

The midwife brought her to me and she looked at me with adoring eyes, and a silent smile. I named her Bridget after the truest friend I'd ever had, and Thomas agreed.

A month or so after Bridget was born, I engaged new nurses and a governess and then returned to court. Thomas was sent to Ireland on behalf of the crown; by now, preparing him to journey was a well-trod path. When he returned in November, I told him that we had been invited to Wilton, in Salisbury, the home of the Earl of Pembroke, just after the new year. The Wiltshire Nobility and gentry was holding a charity horse race; the home Thomas had purchased so long ago, Langford House, was just south of the city of Salisbury, eight miles from Wilton House. We were both fond of the Pembrokes; Henry Herbert, Earl of Pembroke, was the son of Anne Parr, William's sister. His wife, Mary Sidney Herbert, countess of Pembroke, was a niece of Robert Dudley. She was also the sister of Philip Sidney, the poet Sofia had quoted to me.

"I shall look forward to that!" he said, and took my hand. Pembroke's father-in-law, Sir Henry Sidney, was Lord President of Wales and an especially trustworthy friend to the queen. I thought perhaps Sofia would like to meet the poet himself, and the Pembrokes' Welsh friends and relatives were certain to be visiting Wilton for the event.

I wrote ahead and accepted the invitation, and added a personal, private postscript to Mary Sidney Herbert, who was a friend as well as a niece of sorts.

We both rode and took litters to Wiltshire. It was a long day, but we'd left the children at home, of course, with their nurses and attendants. It was difficult to pry myself from Bridget each time I left as she still yearned for me. The others kissed me each time I arrived and left and dutifully shared their lessons and devotions with me, but there was only premeditated affection. I wondered if I were as a specter to them, in and out, mostly at night and other unusual times, someone they knew but who had no substance or presence to them. How very unlike my own mother, who had been close to us all the days of our young lives.

I spurred on my horse, proud of my horsemanship, and caught up with my husband, who rode in the lead. Our servants and Sofia rode behind us.

"I should like to visit Langford while we are here," I said, and at that, his eyes twinkled, something I had not seen for some time. "And hear of your plans for it." He smiled at me and put his gloved hands to his lips and then extended them toward me in a sort of kiss. I returned the measure and felt, for the first time in some while, a sense of affection between us.

When we arrived at Wilton, which I had never

yet visited, I was stunned by its magnificence and beauty. I pulled my horse to a stop, and Thomas did likewise. "It's stunning, isn't it?" he asked.

I nodded. William's properties had been large and well staffed and gardened, but this house dominated the entire landscape. "I believe William's sister and her husband tore down the entire abbey and rebuilt the property from the ground up," I said. At the mention of my first husband, Thomas's face crumpled a little. I began to be irritated; he knew I'd been married but for a short time and that my heart now belonged wholly to him.

Didn't he?

Mary Herbert greeted us in her stately hall and found well-appointed chambers for each of us. "I shall speak with you later on the other matter," she whispered into my ear. I nodded and gave her another quick embrace.

It was a mark of honor and respect that they had assigned individual chambers for Thomas and myself, but I could not help but be a bit disheartened by that. We saw each other but little and I had hoped this would provide a time for us to rekindle our passion for one another, our heartfelt intimacy, and not simply attend to the pressing matters of the day.

The musicians were skilled and the banquet of a hundred courses competed with those at court in their splendor. We were not often in Wiltshire, though it were but one long day's journey from London, and it was pleasant to better know other neighboring gentry and noble families, most of whom I'd seen only in passing at court.

Sofia sat near the Welsh squire Mary Herbert had spoken to me of. "He's a good man from a good family," Mary had whispered, "but has a bit of spirit himself, so perhaps he is up to the task you've mentioned. His family, I believe, would welcome some interest. He's a middle son, so he won't inherit a title, but will have some wealth to speak of. And," she added, "like any man, he shall have to prove himself."

After dinner, Mary introduced me to the young man in question. "Aeron Upjohn, may I present Lady Northampton?"

He bowed and then met my gaze. "It's a delight, my lady. I trust it was your cousin who kept me in such fine company at dinner this evening?"

I was about to jest that if it had been fine company, perhaps it had not been my cousin after all, but that was unfair; Sofia was a fine companion when she was in a mind to be. "Yes, yes, it was. And I hope you found her amusing."

He smiled and winked. "I did. When I could keep her attention."

At that, I smiled back. He was clearly able to survey the land and had the wit to understand what he'd be up against if things progressed. But I liked him well, thus far. I wondered if Sofia did.

That night, I stayed up chatting with Lady Mary by the fire, and when I returned to my chamber, I'd hoped to find Thomas there, as I'd invited him to stay with me. But he was not there, and after some time, I allowed myself to fall asleep rather than hope that he would soon appear; hoping pained me too much.

The second day we rode out to the race Pembroke had set up. Each of the gentry and nobility had sponsored a horse in the race and bets had been placed. The winnings, and a silver trophy worth £50, would be awarded by Pembroke to the mayor who would then distribute it to the local poor. Thomas and I bet heavily, though we did not usually gamble much, knowing that the proceeds would help the area. Afterward, we planned to ride to Langford, which was just south of Salisbury.

"Shall I ride with you?" Sofia had asked me.

I shook my head. "I heard that young Upjohn was organizing some tournaments inside at Wilton this afternoon with some other young people. I thought perhaps you'd like to attend."

"Will there be nobility there?" she asked.

I held my face steady. "I am not sure; perhaps, if they are young as well."

"Or their sons!" she added. She looked at me for a quick moment, her face so sincere. "Thank you, Helena, for allowing me to come to England to live with you. No one could have asked for a better cousin."

I softened. Mayhap I had misjudged her; she was young, and far from home. "You're welcome, Sofia." I embraced her quickly. "Now, get on, and enjoy yourself."

I changed into a riding suit that I had made after bearing Bridget. It was dark blue and I knew it suited my red hair, which was beginning to be threaded with a few silver ones as well. The white ruff made my fair skin appear even fairer, and I knew Thomas found that lovely.

We met at the stables, and Thomas was magnificently dressed, too. "New riding boots?" I asked. I had not seen them before, and they did not appear to be by the leatherworker he'd always used.

"Yes," he said. His outfit was expensive, too. It was not proper for me to ask from where the money for this came, but it was unusually expensive for him. Perhaps because he was riding so much more often now, in service of Her Majesty? I looked at him, and the riding outfit, questioningly, but he did not answer my unspoken question, which made me even more ill at ease.

We rode side by side to Langford, and when we arrived, I endeavored to keep my face still. It was near the riverbank and the land approaching the property was beautiful, even in the bleak of winter, with ice shimmering like diamonds off the tips of barren branches. I could see that, in spring and summer, the land would be waving with grasses and flowers and humming with insects and birds. But the property itself was officially a ruin, and there was no better way to describe it.

He stopped his horse, dismounted, and then took my hand in his and helped me dismount, too. Once I was on the ground, he did not let go of my hand but tugged me along to see his treasure.

"I know it's not much, after Wilton," he said. "But it has real potential. The land is beautiful, the stones are there, and we could make this something of our own. For us. Something to pass along to our children, a country home of our own."

By "our own," I knew he meant not something that the queen had appointed to us, and could then withdraw at whim, should she so desire. But also I knew my man and he meant something we planned and built together.

"I would love for this to be our home," I said softly.

He turned toward me. "Truly? It is so far from court."

"Truly, Thomas." What I did not say was that I could not see where we could ever come into the money required to take this from heap to house. It was beyond imaginable. He knew what I'd been thinking, though.

"Cost," he said. It would take more fortune than our rents together could provide to restore other than a small portion of the ruins, in addition to caring for and educating our children.

I nodded and shivered; it was freezing out and now that we weren't riding I began to feel the cold bleed through my riding habit.

He nodded, too. "As long as I know that it's your desire as well."

I squeezed his hand to show him that yes, it was, then stood on my toes to offer a kiss. He kissed me back, warmly. Our shared breath brought steam to the air around us, and it gave me hope.

A month later, at Sheen, we entertained the Pembrokes, and as young Upjohn had not yet returned to Wales, Mary Herbert brought him with her. Sofia was pretty and polite, but lukewarm, which I told myself was better than cold. The young man, however, was smitten.

"He seems more taken than she is," I told Mary, who was younger, in actuality, than Sofia. However, she was already a mother to two and managed a large household and many estates.

"He's a horseman," she said with a grin. "He'd prefer someone with spirit to a tame mare."

Shortly thereafter I met my husband in his chamber as he prepared for a trip. "Come with me," Thomas said. "You shall see more of England, we will be together, and I should like your company." Thomas was to leave London to travel to the courts round the realm on behalf of the queen, though he continued to take tariffs only from the Chancery.

I shook my head. "I cannot. The trip is too long.

I've borne many children, and the queen has always given me leave for months at a time and I cannot presume upon that. Although she is always surrounded by courtiers, she has but few she truly depends upon and we, as you know, are dependent upon her goodwill."

This was all true; it was unlikely that she would smile upon another leave. I was honest enough to admit, though, that I preferred in some ways a warm court to the cold, wet ride that lay ahead. In any case, I knew for certain that the queen would not look favorably upon my request. I was loath to lose her friendship, the perquisites and incomes that she sent our way and that we needed, her goodwill, and truthfully, also my high place at the foot of her train. And Thomas and I had just spent time together.

Thomas turned his back, unwilling to see that I had valid points, too, but that I would miss him.

"You'll soon return and we'll be together again," I said.

He shook his head. "You needn't see me off, then."

"Please let me help you pack," I said, but he would not have it. I tried to dissuade him, but he would not change his mind, nor his heart.

My husband went north without me and I watched him ride away, second-guessing whether or not I should have gone with him. It was too late, in any case. I returned to service.

# EIGHTEEN

Year of Our Lord 1585
Windsor Castle
The Palace of Whitehall

I settled back into my responsibilities at court, taking charge over the queen's extensive jewelry and wardrobe, and controlling the ingress and egress of visitors who wished a word with her or to present her with a request.

Dear Blanche also had complete access to the queen at all hours of the day, but she was growing old, had difficulty seeing and walking. She spent her days assisting with letter writing and teasingly telling fortunes of the maids sitting about waiting for something to do for Her Majesty.

It was Blanche who delivered the news that the representative from the Scots' court had arrived, and also that there was, on his way and riding hard, a representative from Mary, Queen of Scots. I tended the queen's songbirds and thought how very much like them she was, in a gilded, jeweled cage, pretty as could be, but free to fly only within feet all round her.

The queen saw the Scotsman immediately.

"Your Grace," he said. "I come on behalf of my king, James. He wanted to ensure that you know that his mother, Mary, who is under your care, had

287

written to him of late, seeking to quietly ally herself with him against Your Grace. He wrote to her that he would in no way go against yourself and told her that even if he had the will to, he'd be a fool to align himself with one who was, as he'd put it, a captive in the desert."

"Come, come," the queen said to the envoy. She indicated for me to bring him some mead, which she preferred, though she drank sparingly, some cheese, and spiced wafers. "You must have ridden hard."

He nodded. "Indeed. My king instructed me to have a care to arrive as quickly as possible so you should not doubt his fidelity toward you."

"You may return to him with full assurance of my trust and affections," she said. "And now, I will have a chamber prepared for you to repose in for some hours."

Within days came a letter from Mary herself that Cecil purported to read to her before her council. The queen had us gown her in a splendid outfit and place many jewels upon her neck, fingers, and ears though it were daytime, and then she went to meet her councilors in private.

With the chamber doors open, we could hear her shout from down the hallway.

"So she says she shall find enough of heirs who will have talons strong enough to grasp what I may put in their hand, will she? What has she put in his hand? The head of his father? The instructions of a murderess? Her head should have been separated from her shoulders long ago."

Anne Dudley and I looked at one another. "Has Mary gone mad?" I asked.

"Yes, a long time since," she replied.

Within a few more minutes we could hear the queen's voice again; it rose high against the quiet rumble of her council.

"And yet she says that I need not fear for my life on her behalf, because"—there was a pause, perhaps so she could pick up the letter again— " 'as to any fear or apprehensions of such like accident, I would not take a single step, or say a single word more or less; for I had rather die and perish, with the honors such as it pleased God I was born to, than by pusillanimity to disgrace my life by prolonging it by anything unjust and unworthy of myself and my race.' "

Something hit the table, either the queen's hand, the letter, or both. "Indeed, dear sister, we find it strange that you should make such a claim as you have already proven that you are not only capable of devising such a plot but in marshaling others to assist you in carrying it out!"

She slammed shut the chamber door at that, but we soon found out that Elizabeth had appointed a new caretaker for Mary, a fanatical Puritan named Amias Paulet, who was unlikely to be charmed by Mary's pretty accent or winning manner.

And just like that, the queen turned that week from pain to pleasure at the knighting of Walter Raleigh. Afterward, the queen threw a banquet to celebrate his achievements, at home and abroad. The newly dubbed Sir Walter had insisted that Her Majesty need not open her purse strings for entertainment; he himself would provide them.

The queen, and we all, were intrigued. I took pity upon Sofia and brought her to court for the entertainment.

"Your chambers are so near the queen!" she exclaimed. We were at Windsor Castle; I do not think she had ever been there, an impressive and imposing structure high upon the hill. And 'twas true that my apartments were much closer to Her Majesty's here than at Whitehall.

Clemence was still in attendance upon me, but I also had three other serving women who cared for my personal belongings, my horse, and my person while at court, plus my secretary. I assigned one of the serving women to Sofia, but Clemence asked me if she might serve Sofia instead.

"Of course, Clemence," I said. I must have indicated my confusion.

"It's not that I don't want to serve you, ma'am. It's just that, well, perhaps it's better if I'm the one keeping an eye on Lady Sofia. I tend to do that when we're at home at Sheen, too."

I nodded. Sofia looked elegant and alluring in the dark green gown she'd selected to wear, and I loaned her an emerald necklace that William had given to me.

"Does Thomas mind?" she asked.

I looked at her in the reflection of my looking glass as my lady maid did my hair. "Does my husband mind what?"

"That he is so much more lowly placed, that you have more income, that you were once married to a man with much more money and of a higher rank?"

I gave her a stern, cold look for her impertinence, but I was not about to upbraid her in front of the servants, for their comfort, not hers.

We ate first; it was a longish affair with many courses, and included potatoes, which Sir Walter had provided from his journeys. When daubed with butter and salted they tasted strange, but not bad. I was seated near the queen and while she was taken with and focused on her new knight, she did glance up several times to see Sofia fairly chasing Essex.

*Milde makter.*

Some moments later, Lord Robert, who I am sure had grander plans for his stepson than my cousin, steered Essex toward another table. I looked at the queen and cast down my eyes in apology.

We made our way to the grand hall; the musicians were already playing and Sofia was dancing, thankfully not with Essex. I sat next to

Mary Radcliffe and we caught up on court gossip, of which she was fond, and the conversation turned, as it often did among her ladies, to the queen's safety.

"I feel that perhaps her enemies will take a respite from advancing their evils," Mary said with some relief.

"Why?" I asked.

"Paulet will not be simple to charm, and he is wise as a serpent. Getting correspondence through his hands will be like breaching Windsor."

"I doubt not the ability of evil to find a path wherever it so desires," I said.

"Other than Queen Mary's letter to her son, which is, I suppose, understandable, there has been no other cause for concern since Throckmorton," she said. "It has been relatively silent."

"One swallow does not make a summer," I said. "And perhaps the caged bird will take greater risks than he who may fly free."

Soon thereafter the music drew to a close and Raleigh drew near to the queen's throne. "Majesty!" he proclaimed. "You have seen the strange weed tabaco I bring back from the New World."

"Indeed, we have."

"I have, among my talents, the ability to weigh the smoke from this weed."

"Begone!" She laughed. "I shall wager with you, Sir Walter. Twenty pounds if you can do so, and if you cannot, you owe me twice that amount as a penalty for the boast!"

Raleigh called forth one of his men, who handed over a leather pouch and a set of weighted scales. He tapped some tabaco onto the scales and weighed it. Then he withdrew his pipe and, after stuffing some of the tabaco into it, he lit it and smoked, curls of aroma swirling through the air. He wiped the withdrawing end of the pipe with a fresh linen, then handed it to Elizabeth to smoke. All held their breath, wondering, perhaps, if she would choke or otherwise be taken ill by it. We needn't have worried. She drew in a smooth breath, and, with some relish, blew out the smoke in a thin, feminine stream before handing the pipe back to Sir Walter.

The court burst into applause.

After five minutes, Raleigh finished smoking and called forth the scales again. He tapped the ash onto the scales, subtracted it from the amount he'd put in, and then pronounced how much the smoke had weighed.

"And, Your Grace, I can, therefore, weigh smoke."

She shrugged teasingly and said she owed him £20.

"May I suggest another forfeit?" he asked.

"Proceed," she replied.

"I suggest that we name the land from which this delightful weed is harvested Virginia, in honor of history's most beautiful, and virgin, queen. May I have your permission?"

She looked down, truly stunned, I think. All thought because she spoke and struck boldly that she could not be taken by surprise. Though she was used to and even courted well-mannered compliments, she was still surprised by displays of genuine affection for her person.

"Yes, Sir Walter, you have my permission." Tears welled in her eyes. Few knew that retaining that virginity for the good of the realm had been charged to the account of her heart. It was a noble, apt gesture. She would not have a child named after her, but because she encouraged and launched her subjects in exploration, and not merely war as did many monarchs before and beside her, she would have new lands named for her.

He then presented some gifts to her from his journeys and travels, which she had encouraged and underwritten. Among them was a large basket of potatoes. "They are of an oblong shape, with a curious skin like burnt parchment, and truth be told, they smelled as such when baked and served," he said. All nodded; we'd noticed that when they had been served that night. "When broken open and served," he said, "they have a delicious soft flesh. And that is why"—he finished with a flourish—"they are said to encourage passion among those who partake of them."

"Sir Walter!" The queen stood with feigned indignance. "And you have instructed my cooks to prepare them for the whole court this eve?"

"Alas," he said, his head hanging, an earring looped through one ear. "It is true. Though if I could have instructed them to be served only to the ladies present, without drawing undue attention, I would have!"

"Well, then," she said, waving toward the musicians. "Play on. But we warn you—there shall be no immodest liberties taken at our court!" She bade us dance, and we did, with relish.

I did not dance as often as I usually did, missing Thomas, I supposed. Sir Walter, though he was the guest of honor, took a moment to come and speak with me. "Pining?" he asked.

"Mayhap," I admitted. "Thomas will be sore vexed that he missed this evening's entertainment. You are wonderful to watch and behold."

"I am sorry he cannot be here with us, too," he said. He bent and kissed my hand and, before leaving me to rejoin Bess Throckmorton, he pressed something into my hand.

I looked at it. It was a small potato he'd withdrawn from his leather pouch.

"A gift for you to share with your husband when he returns," he said with a mischievous grin.

I blushed and stammered out a thanks, which made him laugh all the more. I could not let him best me. "Perhaps I shall plant this, so many potatoes may grow, rather than consume it in one eating!"

"Touché," he said with a gallant bow.

That night, I dismissed the servants and called Sofia to my side. "I am well pleased to have you here," I began. "I know you took a large risk in coming to England, and no one understands more than I how difficult that can be."

She nodded. "I . . . I am a bit lonely," she said.

And when I thought upon it, I understood that she was, perhaps, even lonelier than I had been, as she was so rarely at court and there were but few at my house to entertain her but the governesses and the children. "Do you want to marry?" I asked her.

"Oh, oh, yes!" she said. "Perhaps Essex?"

I firmly shook my head. "Essex is out of the question."

"But for you, a marquess was not out of the question!"

"He sought me, not I him," I said gently.

"And yet the queen, she intervened on your behalf?" she persisted.

"For William," I said, though that was not strictly true. I had developed the bud of a friendship with Elizabeth by then, but Sofia was not the kind of woman she was drawn to in friendship; the queen enjoyed wit and charm in all of her courtiers but her true friends had a softness of spirit and, in some ways, a motherliness. We women are most often drawn to our opposites as friends. Perhaps they foil us, complete us.

"I can help you," I said, "find a good squire, a good man, a man with means."

"But no noble?" she pled.

"No," I said. "That I cannot help you with."

"That you *will* not help me with," she insisted, and at that, I grew tired. I stood and dismissed her.

"Good eve, Sofia."

She said nothing, but turned her back and went to the small chamber I'd assigned to her and then firmly closed the door.

I had hoped to have a respite of time with my husband, even if it were at court, after summer Progress, and had mentioned it to the queen.

"I had thought to send him to the Netherlands, as an envoy to Robert," she said. "I want someone I know I can trust to deliver sensitive material—and to report back to me, in all truth, how Leicester does."

The queen had finally decided to outright support the Netherlands as they sought freedom from their mutual foe, Spain. Where she had spent years, perhaps, her enemies might say, dithering and vexing herself about whether or not she would upset her powerful enemies, she had of late begun to strike with more courage and daring, leaning upon her council, of course, but mainly upon her own best judgment.

"Do you want to go?" I asked Thomas one night as we dined together, alone. "I shall miss your company."

"Do I have a choice?" he asked, his voice weary. "And we so rarely keep company together that I sense we have grown more accustomed to being apart than together. And yet, I am pleased that the queen honors me thusly. It's a mark of high esteem to send me to Leicester."

I had made a gift of the potato to him at an earlier meal and, while he had seemed charmed at the intention, it had not wrought the desired effect.

I went to bed alone and shed quiet tears for the truth that my husband had spoken. We were as comfortable, or perhaps more so, apart than together. I could not warm the linens that night and a steady rain cried down the window panes.

Shortly before he left, the queen awarded to us, jointly, the Manor of St. Ives, Hemingford Grey, and Hemingford Abbots, along with Houghton-with-Wyton and all their incomes. As typical, the reversion of properties and rents, when called, went back to the queen and not to our heirs.

I helped Thomas pack and sent special instructions with his servants to make sure that he ate well, as he seemed tired and weary of service. After he left, I wished that I had included a personal note of some kind in his bags. Truthfully, I'd been too busy to write one had I thought of it earlier.

After he left, I decided to look through his chests and coffers so that I might make an effort to mend any of his clothing while he was away. It wasn't that our seamstresses or tailors couldn't do it, it was more that I knew he would appreciate the touch of my own hand on his clothing, particularly his ruffs. I pulled open some drawers and took two or three garments in hand. In the fourth drawer, closest to the floor, of one of his chests there was a jewel case, and within the case nested a ring I had not seen before in my husband's possession.

It was gold, but all round it were fastened small jet beads. I sat upon the floor for a moment, wondering where I'd seen such a ring before, as I knew I had. I prayed and asked the Lord to bring it to mind and memory. Of a sudden, I could see Thomas's cousin John Gorges wearing the ring at a weekend's stay with us. He, too, wore the expensive leathers I'd seen on Thomas.

I heard footsteps coming down the hall and quickly snapped shut the case and stood.

"Are you well, Cousin?" Sofia asked me as I steadied myself.

"Oh, yes," I said. "I am looking after Thomas's mending." I curled my fist around the ring case, covering it with my hand, but I knew she had seen it. I don't know why I felt the need to hide it from her. But I did.

One afternoon as I sat in my chamber sewing with Mary Radcliffe, I decided to ask her what it was. She trusted me, and I her. I had taken it from the box and put it on a nearby table.

"Do you recognize this ring?" I asked her. She set down her linen work and took it in hand.

"Yes, yes, of course," she said, and looked at me suspiciously. "Why do you ask?"

"I found it in the great hall," I said, unhappy with the lie. "It's so unusual, I thought I should seek its owner and return it to him."

Mary shook her head and handed it back to me with as much revulsion as if it were a viper. "It's a recusant's ring."

"A . . . what?" I asked, genuinely confused.

"A Rosary ring. As Rosary beads are banned, recusants wear these rings privately so they may keep count as they recite the Rosary," she said. "I suggest you give it to Walsingham. It is not cheaply made. Whoever owns this ring has rank, and money, and is a traitor."

"I shall, indeed," I said, casually setting the ring back upon the table. I tried to pick my needlework back up, but my hand trembled so that I could not control the stitches. Without a doubt, Mary noticed, too.

That autumn, Parliament met, though they did not often do so during Elizabeth's reign. Before they sat, a group of loyal Catholic nobles and gentry appeared before the queen with a signed petition to assure her that they owed their loyalty to her and denying that the pope had any right to authorize regicide, which they declared to be "false, devilish, and abominable." Elizabeth received them graciously and said that she in no way questioned their loyalty, and reiterated that she had no wish to make windows into men's souls. "A clear and innocent conscience fears nothing," she reassured them. "There is only one Christ, Jesus, one faith. All else is a dispute over trifles."

'Twas not the first time, nor, I was certain, would it be the last, that I basked in the honor and privilege of giving my life's service to such a monarch.

However, Parliament's members made it clear that they felt very differently. They spent their sitting season closing up, among other items, holes in the recusancy laws. If an alleged recusant were able to avoid being served a summons, a notice was posted on the church door requiring him to show up in court. If he failed to show in court, fines were levied against him again and again, and his lands and monies could be forfeited, up to two-thirds of all he owned.

Additionally, anyone at all might be required to swear the Oath of Supremacy, declaring that the pope had no spiritual authority in England. Peers were assumed to concur, though others may be required to prove their agreement at any time, and peers were not exempt from protecting any known recusant.

I sweat a cold sheen. I, of course, was a peer. Thomas was not.

# NINETEEN

Year of Our Lord 1586
Windsor Castle
The Palace of Whitehall

At the New Year's celebrations that year, the offerings to Her Majesty were particularly thoughtful—and expensive. Lord Howard of Effingham, one of the queen's many cousins, the lord admiral of her navy, and a quiet Catholic, gave her a beautiful amulet of a phoenix emerging from a bed of ashes. Inside were eleven jeweled letters: *Semper Eadem*. Always the Same. It was a particularly touching gift, as *semper eadem* was also her mother's motto. She caught my eye and held it when she handed it off to me, then glanced down at the locket ring I'd given her and winked so only we two could see. I winked in return.

As I sorted through her gifts, deciding which would be passed along to others, which she would keep, and which she would soon wear, I said as I drew near, "This is a particularly beautiful prayer book, Majesty." The book, bound in gold, was strung with gold chains that could be securely fastened upon Her Majesty's waist girdle. "On one side is enameled a serpent, with a quote from the book of Numbers." I turned it over. "And on the back is the Judgment of Solomon." I read the passage from the book of 1 Kings quoted in enamel print: " 'Then the king answered and said, "Give her the living child, and slay not: for she is the mother thereof." ' "

"The first side rather puts me in mind of a story of Aesop I've told my young Elizabeth of late," I said as I clipped it to her girdle with her nodded permission. "And reminds me of your cousin Mary of Scots."

The queen, more sensitive than ever, said, "Indeed?" with the particular edge to her voice that alerted us to proceed with caution.

"Go on," Mary Radcliffe urged me.

"There once was a strong, benevolent lady who was walking through a frozen rose garden in the grievous chill of winter when her slipper brushed against something on the cobbled path. She saw that it was a snake, stiff with cold and nigh on dead, having run the fool's errand of leaving its own nest to seize a better one." The room grew quiet but I continued. "Forswearing her initial hesitation, the lady placed the serpent close to her bosom, where it quickly warmed. When it revived, the serpent resumed its natural nature, bit its benefactress, and poisoned her with a wound unto death.

" 'Why have you done this?' she cried. 'I have only sought to assist you!'

" 'You knew full well what I was when you drew me close to your heart,' replied the cunning viper.

" 'I am justly rewarded, then,' the lady sorrowed, 'for pitying a serpent.' "

There was no happy outburst at the end of my tale, as there had been when I'd shared of Idun. This was a much more serious matter and the queen knew I meant the lady in the garden to represent herself.

"And do you have a story at hand for the other side of this prayer book?" she asked with irritation as she flipped it over. "We have no doubt that you must, as you are rarely in want of something to share."

I heard the edge to her voice; she did not like to be instructed by anyone, though, in fairness, she could be counseled by almost anyone she trusted.

"Of course! The other side, of course, represents you, Majesty. Always the good mother, always willing to sacrifice yourself for the well-being of your child, England."

At that she smiled, because she knew that I had parried with a compliment to blunt the sting, but that I'd meant both.

The queen's councilors came then, and we ladies were dismissed. Before I retired, I heard Walsingham say that they had found the husband of Eleanor Brydges, she who had tried to poison the queen and had poisoned herself instead, involved in treasonous Catholic activity. He had just crossed to the Continent before they were able to apprehend him.

I retired to my own chamber, troubled. Was there a snake in my own garden? Where had Thomas come upon that ring? Was he, like so many of his family, still secretly Catholic at heart?

I would have said, "No, no, never, this is my husband and I know him well." But we had grown distant from one another. It had been two years since Bridget was born and we rarely slept together. We did not share a bed, we did not share dreams, and he did not often attend church with me, though he was bound by law to do so; and he did not tell me, any longer, to where he was riding or share details when he returned.

Perhaps he was a better player than I had ever imagined.

A person's leanings did not make him a traitor, and as had been proved with Norfolk and Mary, there needed to be hard evidence of action. Walsingham had once told me, with Eleanor retching from poison down the gallery, that by sharing my concerns I could forestall anything terrible from happening.

I could bring the ring to Thomas himself, but if he were truly given to the Catholic faith, and freeing Mary, I would only be warning him to be more cautious in his planning. And if Thomas had already acted and been branded a traitor, he would be executed. If I were in some way implicated by not bringing forth evidence when I knew of it, and I clearly now did, the law declared that I

306

could be executed as an accomplice. My children would be orphaned, their parents attainted. Francis Throckmorton, a good man caught up in sudden religious zeal and the charm of Mary of Scots, had neglected to consider what would come of his wife and ten-year-old son were he caught, and caught he was.

At the moment, I loathed England and its steady storms of treachery. My faith felt far and foreign to me, used by this side and that for nothing that resembled Christ at all. I had no idea if I could trust my husband, but I could not leave my children unsheltered. And perhaps, perhaps if suspicions were raised by Walsingham, whom Thomas respected and feared, there was time to warn him off from any foolery.

Some hours later, after wrestling with my conscience, I sent one of my lady maids to Sir Francis Walsingham with a note. An hour later, I heard a knock upon the door.

"My good lady marquess?" he said as he took a bow. I flinched, not only at the man, but at his appropriation of Her Majesty's nickname for me.

"Come in, Sir Francis," I said. "Please, have a seat."

I had dismissed my servants, so I served him a goblet of wine myself. "I have some . . . concerns," I said. "About my husband's family. And perhaps about my husband himself."

He nodded thoughtfully, stroking his long beard.

"You can rest assured in my confidence and concern, my lady," he said. "What you share with me will go no further."

I explained to him the many heated discussions that had taken place over the matters of faith, loathing myself as the words flew from my mouth. *Loyal, are you?* I scolded myself in my head. *In truth? Traitor. Liar.*

"Do you have any other concerns?" he asked.

"Well, after Thomas had left for the Netherlands, I found this in his drawer," I said. I handed over the recusant's ring.

"Yes, I'd heard you'd found one," he said.

At that I displayed my shock and he held back a smile. Who had told him? Surely not Mary Radcliffe, who trusted me implicitly after the Eleanor Brydges situation. But I had told none other.

Then I recalled, Sofia had seen me with it. Had it been her? Or had she told someone who told someone?

I said nothing, but as I handed it over to him I wondered what would have become of me if I hadn't called for him, since he knew I was cherishing this ring at my bosom.

"You have always proved most loyal to the queen," Walsingham said as he stood to leave. "That shall not go unrewarded, no matter the cost, and I shall keep the concerns of your family, and children, uppermost in my mind."

"I bring this to your attention, Sir Francis, so that you can defuse a wick that is likely not yet lit, if it even exists at all. You told me, during the Eleanor Brydges affair, that if I let you know what I knew, you could arrest ill will before it kindled at my door. I expect you to keep your word." I opened the door for him and drew myself up, head held high, and said with a trace of sarcasm, "You are like a master hawker, Sir Francis: breaking us all to hand, keeping a blind hood on us till you decide where you want us to hunt, and fly, and kill."

He laughed. "Well said, Lady Northampton. I, like you, hunt only and ever for one mistress: the queen."

"That's true, Sir Francis," I said. "I've been serving the queen for more than twenty years. And you?"

"Seventeen," he said, bowing stiffly before he took his leave.

After I let him out I sat upon my bed and cried, and then I was filled with cold dread; it sank in my belly and would not be dislodged even after I spent nearly an hour sobbing. How had it come to this? Had I just condemned my husband to death, or had I rescued him from folly? Had I protected my children from being orphaned and living with the curse of an attainted father and mother, or had I broken their home?

I sensed we had many deceptions between us

now. Each was like an inch, or a foot, or a mile that parted us. I considered for a moment the idea of telling Thomas of all this. But I could not. In my heart, I knew he would never forgive me for putting the queen's interests above his own.

I could only hope and pray that naught should come to pass.

If some had chanced upon me exactly ten summers earlier—when I was drunk with love for Thomas and he with me, we two, so ready to bear the wrath of the queen or anything else to be together—and told me that ten years hence our love would have grown cold, I should have laughed. I did not laugh now. Like a river that had been blocked of its natural course, our affections had taken a sharp turn, and though I stood in the middle and tried to redirect the flow, time and circumstance overflowed me.

I knew not why, but the queen had canceled her Progress that summer and we spent much of it at court in Windsor, her natural stronghold. I made provision for my children, but with the exception of Bridget they seemed to miss me not at all. They spoke nearly perfect German, thanks to Sofia, whom they conversed much with but heart-rendingly little with me as I was so often away. Thomas returned from the Netherlands in late June. In August, the queen sent Thomas north again.

"Shall I come with you?" I asked.

"Nay," he replied. I packed for him and we lay together but we did not make love; in truth, I could not remember with clarity the last time we had joined our bodies. As he rode away, his long blond hair pulled back in a queue, his body still fit and firm from riding, my own flesh ached for him. I shook it off and returned to court.

I'd been blending a perfume for Elizabeth when she sent for me to come to her council room. I set down my herbs and musk and then wiped my hands on a linen before tucking my hair back into obedience. And then I walked down the gallery.

When I arrived, she sat at the head of a long, thick table. Walsingham and Cecil were there, as were most of her other advisors; Lord Robert was still in the Netherlands. Standing at the end of the table was Thomas.

I nodded to him, shocked that I'd had no idea he had returned. I looked at the council faces; they were grim. He nodded back but did not smile, and I was overcome with fear.

*Lord Jesus, protect my husband.*

"We thought you would like to be present for this," Elizabeth said to me, indicating that I should sit upon a chair near, but not at, the table.

I sat down and Walsingham began. "As you know, Majesty, in the early summer months of this year, I had uncovered some correspondence from an English seminary student named Ballard, and

311

also Mendoza, lately rejected from this realm in the last plot against the Queen's Majesty by Mary of Scots, and now Spain's ambassador to France. Ballard asked what Spanish support there would be should English Catholics seek to overthrow you. Mendoza replied that there would be an invasion this summer to support it. Ballard recruited young Anthony Babington, a rich and well-born young Catholic man, and told him that while a Mr. Savage would actually carry out your murder, the plan would be successful if there were more men involved. And so our Mr. Babington, who had already served as a runner for letters and other goods from Mary to her supporters while she was at Chartley, agreed to recruit several others in this plot."

I looked at Thomas, but he would not meet my eye, which made me uncomfortable. I soothed myself that he was here before me and not in chains in the Tower, and so all must be well.

"Throughout the summer, Babington plotted and gathered supporters who debated the best way to murder you, whether it be in your litter, or while you hunted in a park, or perhaps even in your very own Presence Chamber."

The queen inhaled sharply, but she was no novice to plotting against her and waved her hand. "Continue, Sir Francis."

"In July, Babington, feeling certain that his communications were private, took Mary into his confidence. They were exchanging letters through waterproof pouches in the caskets of beer delivered to Mary, for her household, and paid for"—he looked at Elizabeth—"by Your Grace. Babington began by writing, 'My dread sovereign and Queen,' and then told her that there was a significant plot at home and abroad to kill Elizabeth and replace her with Mary, on the English throne." He looked down and read from a document " 'For the dispatch of the usurper, from the obedience of whom we are by excommunication of her made free, there be six noble gentlemen, all my private friends, who for the zeal they bear to the Catholic cause and Your Majesty's service will undertake that tragic execution.' "

I reached over, by impulse, and took Elizabeth's hand in mine for a moment, forgetting that we were among the men. She squeezed it kindly, and then withdrew it again to her lap.

"And Mary responded . . . ?" she asked. Though I knew she must have been briefed before this, likely many of the others did not know.

"She did not disagree with or protest in any way the plans laid for Her Majesty. Instead, she wrote, 'The affairs being thus prepared and forces in readiness both within and without the realm, then shall it be time to set the six gentlemen to work, taking order, upon the accomplishing of their design I may be suddenly transported out of this place.' "

Walsingham continued, "Plans were made to meet Mary as she hunted, for a party to greet her and secret her away to a place where she would remain safe while Your Majesty was being murdered. The men would then bring Mary safely to London, where she would be proclaimed queen. One of the men who had gained the confidence of Mary, and was among the plotters with Babington, was John Gorges."

I gasped and coughed. A page was sent for a glass of watered wine, and though I normally drank sparingly, at this I drank my full cup.

Walsingham brought his portion to a close. "Babington caught word of the breach and fled to London, where he colored his skin with the pigment of green walnuts and hid in the forest; he was caught and is now imprisoned along with many of his conspirators. Some, like John Gorges, fled to the Continent before they could be apprehended."

"Thank you, Sir Francis. And now, Cousin Gorges, I await your report of the capture of Mary."

I cocked my head and looked from Thomas, to Walsingham, to the queen. Thomas had apprehended Mary?

He stood and spoke, his voice clear and firm. "We rode out toward Chartley, but she had been told that there was a riding party waiting to meet her. She, along with her doctor, her butler, and some others, had planned to kill a fine buck that day. She'd dressed splendidly, assuming, perhaps, that this might also be the day of your death and her victory. Once she saw me, and not Babington, she grew alarmed.

"I approached her politely, on your behalf, and said, 'Madam, my lady the queen finds it very strange that despite the agreement reached between you, you have conspired against her and the kingdom, which she would never have thought if she had not seen the evidence with her own eyes. As far as she understands, some of your servants are involved. The rest will Sir Amias to say you.'"

So Elizabeth had already seen the letters. But of course. She saw them but said nothing. But Thomas had said nothing to me as well?

"Paulet, of course, knew we were to meet her there and ensured that many of her servants were with her. She began to shriek to her men that if they be any men at all they take up arms, immediately, for her defense and installment on your throne. And indeed, her secretary sought to knock me off my horse. But most of them, at that point, knew there was no use. Mary was conveyed to Tixall, nearby, and her secretaries to London. Her quarters at Chartley were searched by order of Sir Francis"—he looked at Walsingham—"and three large caskets of materials were conveyed back to your court."

This appeared to be the first time that Elizabeth had heard Mary's response. "She's a wicked murderess, and her treacherous dealings toward me, the one person who has been the savior of her life for many a year, are unforgivable!"

I, and Thomas, were politely dismissed as the queen and her councilors began to debate where Mary should be held, and when and how she should be brought to trial.

Thomas walked down the long hallway with me and I took his hand in mine. "Please, let me care for you. You've ridden hard many hundreds of miles."

He nodded. "I am tired unto death," he said.

I took him back to our chambers and sent a servant for hot water. I stripped him of his dusty riding clothes and bathed him. I rubbed his muscles with ointment and mint, fed him, and put him abed.

In the morning, we broke bread together and I tried to speak with him of his journey. "I am so proud of the work you have done on behalf of Her Majesty," I said. "I should have liked to have prayed for you. . . ."

He did not respond; I understood. It was a secret mission and he was not allowed to share the details. I was just so relieved that he was back, and well, and . . . not treasonous. "You're tired, I understand," I said. "We shall have weeks ahead to speak of this, and other things."

He smiled at me, but it did not seem genuine. If anything, now that this situation was over he seemed more distant to me than when he'd had a secret to keep. I was confused. I moved forward with affection, he parried me with distance. Soon enough, I let my overtures dwindle, confused but unwilling to be rebuffed again and again.

He rested on and off for more than a week, and I did not press him for more information. He seemed pleasant in my company, but cool. I wavered between being faint with relief that he had been in the employ of Walsingham and angry beyond measure that no one had thought to take me into such a confidence: not my husband, not the queen. In my better moments I understood that they had kept it secret to protect my husband from harm should word of his surprise appearance be leaked when he had clearly infiltrated the group, for information, through his cousin. I could hardly be angry, justly, with Thomas, as I had not taken him into my confidence, either.

But Walsingham, that was unforgivable. He let me believe, when I gave him the ring, that my husband might be guilty of recusancy, at best, or treason at worst, perhaps not trusting Thomas himself.

Did anyone at this court ever trust anyone else? Not husband, not mistress, not friend?

No sooner had Thomas recovered than the queen sent him north again. The council had wanted to convey Mary to the Tower, where Babington currently resided. "His wife fled," Thomas told me coldly. "Abandoned him and left their two-year-old daughter behind, rejecting her family in favor of the crown."

# TWENTY

Year of Our Lord 1586
The Palace of Whitehall

January: Year of Our Lord 1587
Sheen

T he queen insisted that Mary be taken to
Fotheringay Castle, and not the Tower, and
Thomas was to convey her there. She sent a letter
for Thomas to deliver; I was present as she
dictated it to her secretary: "You have, in various
ways and manners, attempted to take my life, and
to bring my kingdom to destruction and blood-
shed. I have never proceeded harshly against
you, but have, on the contrary, protected and
maintained you like myself. These treasons will
be proved to you, and all made manifest."

Some weeks later, after having returned, he told
me of their travel together. I was encouraged, as
he had stopped, some time ago, sharing details of
his journeys. I now understood why.

"She suffers badly in the joints, and rode for the
entirety of the four-day journey. She tried repeatedly
to charm and please me as I rode by her side,
another man on the other side of the carriage, each
of us with weapons lest her supporters try to find
another means of escape. She protested her

innocence to me. And I told her that I hoped it was so."

"She is guilty," I said.

"Beyond a doubt, a dozen times over. A cat may have nine lives, but she's spent ten, and she will not live out the year. She responded to the letter Her Majesty sent by saying, 'I am not so base as to wish to cause the death, or to lay hands on an anointed queen like myself.' "

I shook my head. "Those who are quickest to protest the wrongs of another are guilty of those wrongs themselves. She seeks to shame Elizabeth into commuting her death sentence."

"Will she?" Thomas said. "Will the queen allow her to die this time, if her trial proves her guilty?"

I inhaled, thinking of Elizabeth's mother, an anointed queen who was beheaded when her daughter was but a young child, the memory of which I knew still bedeviled her. "I hope so. But I know not." I turned toward him and put my hands on his face. "I am so proud of you. This was a difficult, dangerous task, one in which the queen and Walsingham must have thought carefully about before appointing the right man to carry it out."

He took my hands in his own for a moment, but not to hold them, rather to gently remove them from his face. Then he shook his head. "I am glad that the queen is safe, at last, from Mary and her bloody, wicked plans. But John Gorges is fled from his wife and children forever, and all know I am the cause of it. One of my mother's Poyntz relatives was involved, too. He apparently made his way to France. They had my assurance, as family, when they shared details with me and allowed me to get close to Mary at the end. I feigned recusancy. 'Twas one reason why Mary was not alerted until it was too late. In order to keep faith with the queen, I broke faith with my family, who trusted me. What kind of person does that?"

"You have chosen well," I told him. At that, he looked at me for but a moment longer than necessary, sighed before kissing my cheek, and took his leave.

I sat there, relishing the rare feel of his lips on my cheek until it faded into a memory and I could sense it no longer. I dried my eyes, and went back to service.

The queen knew that pamphlets had been used to sway the public she loved and who loved her. This autumn, ahead of Mary's trial, she asked the brilliant, hunchbacked son of Lord Cecil, Robert Cecil, to write one and have it circulated. It was to explain her reluctance to execute Mary. Robert Cecil did a brilliant job, though the queen needn't have worried. Most of her subjects were eager to have Mary, a traitoress many times over still suspected of murdering her husband, meet her Maker and explain herself to Him in person.

The queen's enemies, who wielded long forks and desired to help themselves to the meat of her realm, would prove a different matter indeed.

The trial commenced on November 15. Though it was held in front of only thirty-six peers, there was not a person at court, from the lowest maid in the buttery to the highest earl, who did not know, in detail, everything that was done and said at the great hall at Fotheringay. When Mary entered, she was said to have exclaimed, "Alas! Here are many councilors but not one for me!" She was not allowed a defense, but was able to defend herself well, with wit and courage. I found it disturbing that Babington and the other plotters were executed ahead of Mary's trial. Would it not have been prudent to call upon them for evidence? This did not trouble Walsingham, nor many others. There might well have been a chance that Mary had been misled, or that evidence had been contrived against her. But, as in my young Frances's favorite Aesop's fable, Mary had cried wolf once too many times with her deceits.

The thirty-six peers appointed to hear evidence were not allowed to deliver a verdict. They did reconvene, however, in the Star Chamber at Westminster and debate the evidence in front of others, including Thomas. All but one agreed that she was guilty of compassing, practicing, and imagining Her Majesty's death.

The queen thanked them for their nearly unanimous verdict, but still she was loath to write a warrant for Mary's execution. Perhaps she recalled the times when her own sister had been pressed to write out a death sentence for her but had stayed her hand. Elizabeth begged her councilors to consider how her enemies would look upon her if she agreed to have Mary executed. They already looked upon her as a bastard heretic. "When it shall be spread that for the safety of her life, a maiden queen could be content to spill the blood even of her own kinswoman, what shall they think then?" she asked.

"Majesty," Cecil objected, "they are not unwilling to spill *your* precious blood; in fact, as time shall prove, they are overeager to do so. Mary was wont to spill your blood and she did not care if it was done neatly, or if you were struck down while hunting in your own park!"

The queen wavered. She assured them of her love and her thankfulness for their caretaking. "As for your petition: your judgment I condemn not, nor do I mistake your reasons, but pray you to accept my thankfulness, excuse my doubtfulness, and take in good part my answer answerless."

Her council was nearly undone by her indecisiveness, but I felt it should be credited to her that she was not eager to execute Mary. Cecil said that if the queen could not come to a speedy resolution her people would call this a "Parliament of words but no action."

He did not have to wait long for relief. Soon thereafter the queen agreed that Mary was guilty of treason and she was sentenced to death on December 4. Bonfires were lit day and night in London as the citizens celebrated. All that remained was for the queen to sign the death warrant . . . which she did not do. It brought to mind her indecisiveness years past with Norfolk.

"Watch," she told me once she'd agreed with the verdict. "The vultures will begin to swarm, but they won't be wanting to pick from Mary's corpse, but ours."

From Scotland came word from King James that if his mother's life be touched or her blood be meddled with, he could no longer remain on good terms with the queen or estate of that realm. He continued by saying, "King Henry VIII's reputation was never prejudged but in the beheading of his bedfellow."

Elizabeth was livid. "It should not be my father with whom he concerns himself about the execution of a wedded bedfellow," she railed. "For his mother snuffed out the life of her bedfellow—his father, Darnley! Mayhap he should think upon that!"

From France came word that Henry III would "look upon it as a personal affront" if Mary was executed. Elizabeth took pen in her own hand and said that such words were "the shortest way to make me dispatch the cause of so much mischief."

And yet at night, when I rubbed her thin shoulders, the knots were not only felt but were visible. And she'd yet to hear from the greatest threat of all, Spain. "I have no will to see her executed," she said, standing near the cages of her quiet songbirds. "She has come to me as a bird that had flown for succor from the hawk."

Mary wrote, thanking Elizabeth for the happy tidings, expressing joy that she was about to be at "the end of my long and weary pilgrimage." She concluded by saying, "Yet while abandoning this world and preparing myself for a better, I must remind you that one day you will have to answer for your charge, and for all those whom you doom, and that I desire that my blood and my country may be remembered in that time." She sought, deviously, to undermine Elizabeth, threaten her, and cause her pain until the end. It was Mary and her ilk written about in the book of Jeremiah: "Can the leopard [change] his spots? Then may ye also do good, that are accustomed to do evil."

The queen wanted Lord Robert back from the Netherlands, and Lord Robert wanted to return. Thomas volunteered to go and convey her agreement to him, which surprised me, for he was nearly always gone now, and I'd thought he'd relish the opportunity to stay at home.

The queen told me, after he'd gone, that she meant to knight Thomas upon his return and appoint him as Master of the Wardrobe. I kissed her hand and prayed to God that would loose his demons forever.

I returned home for three days to set my household in order before the Christmas season. One afternoon I found a scrap of paper with a bit of a poem on it. I asked the tutor to my older children, "Do you recognize this?"

He took it in hand and within a minute said, "Yes, of course. The poet is Thomas Wyatt, and it is written in the hand of your cousin Sofia."

"Thank you," I said, hoping I hid my anger and dismay. I knew, at heart, that she had not meant this for Upjohn. As the tutor took his leave, I read it again before folding it up and securing it in my gold girdle purse.

> Pain or pleasure, now may you plant, even
>     which it please you steadfastly;
> Do which you list, I shall not want to be
>     your servant secretly.

After the New Year's celebrations had passed, the queen made good on her promise to knight Thomas. His accolade was held before our friends and other courtiers, but was solemn, and for Thomas, one of the most important days of his life.

I ensured that he was dressed splendidly in the finest fabrics and leathers we could find; the London merchants thrived under the queen and therefore it was not difficult to procure the best goods. One morning, after the queen, too, dressed in high finery, she had Thomas kneel before her on the knighting stool. I stood nearby, with our children: Elizabeth, who was nine and imperious and beautiful; Frances, seven, quiet and dignified and a scholar in the making; Edward, five, and Theobald, four, locking arms, the very best of companions and already steady horsemen; and baby Bridget, who was three, and the precious joy of all.

The queen rested the flat side of a jeweled sword on Thomas's right shoulder, then lifted it above his head and placed it upon his left. He then stood, thanked the queen, and kissed her ring, after which she presented him with his new insignia.

We made our way back to Sheen, where we were to sponsor some fine entertainment and celebrations that evening. The children teasingly called Thomas "Sir Papa" all the long ride home, and he reveled in tickling and teasing them. He sternly jested that there would not be any Lord of Misrule in his household, now that it was run by a knight, but Edward took exception.

"Nay, Papa, next Christmastime I intend to be the Lord of Misrule at our home!"

Thomas had smiled at me during the ceremony,

but he kept a margin of space between us and I wondered, to myself, what kind of home I would have by next Yuletide. There was much ill will betwixt my beloved and me.

Did he yet love me? I sorrowed as I realized, nay. Perhaps not.

Nigh on seventy courses were served for dinner, and we had mimes and puppet masters before the children went to bed for the evening, then there was music and dancing. The Pembrokes came, of course, and I had arranged for them to bring young Upjohn as well.

"Do spend some time with him," I urged Sofia. "If you do not show him some affections, there are other ladies waiting who will!" Indeed, there was a fair line of young women surrounding Upjohn, which did draw Sofia's interest and competitive nature. But she would not take her eyes off Essex, who would not take his eyes off the queen.

Mary Herbert, only a few years older than Essex herself, but settled, with a mature husband and children, not to mention a large estate and her own writing, came alongside me and slipped her arm through mine. After reassuring me of Upjohn's continued interest in Sofia, she said, "I see Essex pays mind to the queen whenever possible."

"Under Lord Robert's watchful eyes," I commented.

"Perhaps the attentions of someone beautiful and young, the flattery of being looked up to and wanted in spite of one's wearying life experience, makes one feel virile and desirable again," wise Mary said.

I looked firmly at her, surprised that she was speaking so boldly about Her Majesty when the queen was just across the room. Then it occurred to me that perhaps she was not speaking about Elizabeth and Essex at all.

Later that evening, before she retired, the queen drew Thomas and me near to her. "Sir Thomas, we are well pleased to be able to knight you at long last. We have recognized your faithful service in the past and we know we shall be able to depend upon you as the storms batter our coast," she said. "We thought it particularly apt that you be knighted in reward for service in regards to a Scotswoman. Your father was knighted at Flodden, fighting Scotsmen. We do not forget your family's long service to the crown."

Thomas looked pleased and surprised that she knew. "Yes, Your Grace, that is true. I am honored that you have remembered my father and me, and I will serve you to the best of my abilities until my last breath."

She smiled at him. "And now, Lady Northampton, if you will show me to my chamber for the evening, I will be well pleased."

Thomas bowed low, but before he did, I saw the smile flex to a frown. Later that evening, I tapped upon his chamber door. He opened it and let me in, though he was already prepared for sleep.

"I am certain that the queen will continue to promote you."

He nodded but said nothing.

"Thomas"—I took his hand in mine—"what is it?"

"She still calls you Lady Northampton," he said quietly. "I know 'tis the way of things, but no matter what comes my way, I cannot have one day without being reminded that my wife is more highly titled as the wife of another man."

"Long dead," I said, irritated.

He shrugged.

"Mary Herbert told me that Upjohn is interested in Sofia's hand," I said. "I'd like that for her."

"Does she want it?" he asked.

"I don't know," I said. "But it's time she's married and with a household of her own."

"One she likes to live in, with a man she wants, I should say," Thomas said, and then, perhaps realizing he had overstepped, continued, "but that is up to you. I shall take my leave tomorrow—the Rose Theater has officially opened in London. Pembroke's men and the lord admiral's men will be performing and I shall attend."

"I should like to come," I teased.

"No lady is seen at the Rose," he said. "Only women of low morals."

"Do you know such women?" I jested, perhaps a bit sharply.

He didn't answer. "And then Effingham has asked me to go up and down the coast recruiting sailors and making sure that the ports, including Hurst Castle, of which I am still governor, are secure."

"Spain?" I asked quietly.

He nodded. "Spain."

"Can we withstand them?"

"We can pray," he said. And then, perhaps moved by the thought that we may be under a siege from which we could not recover, he reached out and drew me into his arms for but a moment. I felt him fight with himself not to take me closer, but his will won and at length he withdrew. "Good night, Elin," he said, holding himself firm.

I'd been dismissed. My eyes filled with tears. "Good night, Sir Thomas." I despaired as I trudged back to my elaborate, rich chamber, where I lay alone in a beautifully carved bed.

My marriage was dead.

Thomas left the next day for the coast and I returned to court, a careworn, unwelcome pattern.

# TWENTY-ONE

Years of Our Lord 1587, 1588
Windsor Castle
The Palace of Whitehall
Richmond Palace

Y our children do you honor," the queen said to me some days later. "I enjoy them all but must admit that I am perhaps overfond of young Elizabeth."

"It's not a surprise that you might see her namesake reflected therein."

"Young Bridget is three years of age now, is that correct?" she asked as I pinned on her sleeves.

"I marvel, Majesty, how you never forget a date, a detail, or anything someone says. Do you know everything?" I teased.

"Perhaps," she said with a smile. "What happened to bringing Sir Thomas a child each year?"

I pinned for a full minute before answering. "That would require us to be in the same chamber, at the same time, willingly."

The queen said nothing, but she fondly patted my head as I knelt to complete my task. If she was not willing to open windows into men's souls, it was unlikely she was willing to open them into their hearts.

Her lord admiral, a quietly practicing Catholic, came to speak with the queen persuasively about the great danger she was in, a danger that would not be lifted, he felt, until Mary of Scots was executed.

Finally, she assented. On February 1, she asked Walsingham to have his secretary, John Davison, bring the death warrant for her to sign. She read each word carefully and, at the end, signed it with the swoops and loops her inimitable signature had become famous for. "She should be executed in the great hall of Fotheringay," she said calmly, "to preserve her dignity. She has asked that her servants be present, and that should, of course, be made possible. She will also want her priest nearby and that, too, should be accommodated."

She handed the document over to Davison, who took it with a bow. He turned, and just as he was about to leave the room she stood and shrilly called him back. "Mr. Davison!"

He turned. "Yes, Majesty."

"I wish . . . I wish to proceed upon another course first. I wish that you should write to Sir Amias, at Fotheringay, and ask if it be meet with him to take Mary's life in accordance to the terms of the Bond of Association."

Davison's eyes widened and Cecil and Walsingham could barely sputter out a question. We ladies, who waited outside the chamber to accompany her after her meeting, ducked back so we could hear but not be seen. After Throckmorton's threat some years back, the queen's faithful gentlemen across the realm had come together under the leadership of Walsingham and Cecil to form the Bond of Association, which was authorized by the queen and obliged all signatories to execute any person that attempted to or actually did usurp the queen's throne, or made an attempt upon or successfully took Elizabeth's life. If the queen were indeed killed, the signatories were required to hunt down the killer.

"Majesty?" Davison asked. "Ask Sir Amias to . . . murder Mary?"

"Not murder," the queen said dismissively. "Did he sign the Bond?"

"Yes."

"And has our cousin attempted to usurp our throne and take our life?"

"Yes, Majesty," he said quietly. "But I am sure he will not agree to carrying out such an evil deed."

We held our breath. He had just rebuked the queen.

"There should be no problem in carrying out a legal deed, if he is as good as his word."

Walsingham spoke up. "Are you so eager to give your power and authority to another?"

"Do you not see the danger, Sir Francis, in setting a precedent for an anointed queen to be executed by command of another monarch?"

There was a silence before he spoke. "Majesty, the monarchs of Spain and France would be glad to see you executed if they could but command it. Do you not see the greater danger in setting a precedent for murdering a crowned queen in her bed?"

I looked at Anne Dudley, a strong reformer, but nothing like the stout observer Paulet. "There is no way he will agree," she said, and I nodded. It was shameful that the queen would even ask, because most understood that the Bond's call for the signers to perform the death of a suspect was only obligatory after the successful murder of Queen Elizabeth. Otherwise, she was expected to act on her royal authority. But neither of us spoke of that.

Within days, the answer came back from Sir Amias. In tempered outrage, he refused to participate in any way. The queen raged, blaming "the niceness of those precise fellows who in words would do great things for her surety, but in deed perform nothing."

Davison apparently felt confident, after such a refusal, to carry forth with the document already entrusted to him and not retaken by the queen. On February 8, at eight in the morning, Elizabeth's "good sister" went to her death in the great hall at Fotheringay Castle.

Mary claimed until the end to be dying for her Catholic faith, though 'twas the queen's crown and throne she'd had designs for; had there not been persistent, treasonous attempts to seize those two, the strictures upon Catholics in England would not have been required. Among her last words on the scaffold, as the Protestant Dean of Peterborough sought to comfort her, were these: "My dean, trouble not yourself nor me, for know that I am settled in the ancient Catholic and Roman religion, and in defense thereof by God's grace mind to spend my blood."

She then turned to the ax man. "I forgive you," she said, and then, in Latin, "Into Your hands, O Lord, I commend my spirit."

It took two rough blows of the ax before her spirit was sent heavenward. When Mary's head was picked up, in a nightmare moment, the head itself fell to the floor and the poor man was left holding only her wig. Her little dog, a constant companion, scurried out from his mistress's skirts, whimpering over her prone body.

Elizabeth was informed, quietly, of the death, before Cecil could bring her the official word. I slept in her chamber that night; Mary Radcliffe slept at the foot of her bed. Neither of us trusted what she might do or say, that could not be soothed by one of the young maids typically on overnight service.

She slept fitfully, but morning brought the storm.

"I did not authorize this!" she shrieked. "I did

not tell Davison to deliver that warrant after Paulet refused to honor his word with the Bond of Association. Who instructed Davison to have that carried out?"

"The council met, Majesty, and we thought, with your signature and no other recourse, that was your wish," Cecil said quietly. He had served her faithfully for many decades; indeed, I think she looked upon him as a father.

"Who chairs this council?" she demanded.

"I do," he said quietly. His decades of steady service did not save him for the moment. He was banished, and Davison sent to the Tower.

The queen quickly dictated a letter to James, in Scotland, saying she had not authorized the execution and promised to look into the matter to the fullest and punish the wrongdoers, up to and including hanging Davison without a trial if need be.

The queen's ambassador from France sent a communication saying, "I never saw a thing more hated by little, great, old, young, and of all religions than the Queen of Scots's death, and especially the manner of it. I would to God . . . she had died and no more." He followed up by saying that great throngs of people were calling for Mary's canonization. Walsingham finally stopped sharing the communiqués with the queen, as they only increased her anger against her council, and Cecil in particular, who was still banished.

Within weeks, though, the queen's anger began to subside and her appetite returned. She was sleeping well again, and though none doubted her sincere discomfort and regret over Mary's necessary death, I began to wonder if she, too, were a better player than most credited her for.

"Has James sent word of his anger, or of forthcoming war?" I asked her one morning.

She shook her head, and again quoted Machiavelli to me. "'Men sooner forget the death of their father than the loss of their patrimony.'"

It was the closest she ever came to naming a successor in my presence.

After the French fuse had burnt out and James had seen a safer way to claim the southern crown for his head than his mother had inheriting it, the Spanish were still left to be dealt with.

Mendoza, who could not keep himself from meddling and perhaps had a vendetta against the queen, wrote to Philip, "As God has so willed that this accursed people, for His ends, should . . . against all reason commit such an act as this, it is evidently His design to deliver those two kingdoms into Your Majesty's hands."

Walsingham had intercepted this communication before it was passed to Philip. But it was not news.

"With Mary alive, Philip could not overlook her claim to your throne," Walsingham said. "But now that Mary is dead, he has nothing and no one holding him back from claiming it for himself."

"Which he has long desired," the queen agreed. "Is there news of an imminent invasion by Spain?"

"They are building up their fleet for such," Walsingham responded. "A mighty armada."

"Then we shall have to consider whether to strike first," Elizabeth said.

I turned to her in marvel and joy. She, who had always tried to forestall those who would come after her and her realm, appeasing them with charm, with offers of marriage, or with diplomatic dissembling, was on the brink of declaring outright war. I told her so, later.

"We are no craven king," she lightly rebuked me.

"Never, Majesty, never have I thought this. It's just that, perhaps—perhaps you should take up jousting!" I teased. "Who could face you on the tiltyard?"

She smiled, but she did seem stronger, bolder. "I know I have the body of a weak and feeble woman, but I have the heart and stomach of a king, and a king of England, too, and think foul scorn that Parma or Spain, or any prince of Europe, should dare to invade the borders of my realm; rather than any dishonor shall grow by me, I myself will take up arms!"

I stood back and we ladies all applauded loudly.

"You must tell that to your men, Your Grace,"

Anne Dudley said. "They will be heartened by it, as we are."

In April, it was reported to her, "The pope is daily plotting nothing but how he may bring about your utter overthrow. . . . The King of Spain is busy arming and extending his power to ruin both you and your estate. Will not Your Majesty, beholding the flames of your enemies on every side kindling around, unlock all your coffers and convert your treasure for the advancing of worthy men for the arming of ships and men of war to defend you?"

She nodded. "I shall. And if he attempts to penetrate my shores, I shall meet him myself."

The air was unstable round us as it is before a storm. Elizabeth recalled Raleigh from his expeditions, understanding that she would have need of his fleet.

Drake, too, was on his way back to England; he sailed into Cadiz harbor, where, he said, he "singed the King of Spain's beard" by destroying thirty-seven galleons gathering to form an armada against the English. He made his way to a Spanish fort, which he captured, and harried all of the Spanish vessels he could find along the way, perhaps as many as a hundred, burning their cargo, including all materials needed to make water and larder caskets for the entire Spanish fleet. He told the queen, "Philip will be hard-pressed to replace these in an expeditious manner, which means they will have to store their food and water in unseasoned timber, which will bring rot on quickly."

And, at the last, Drake captured the *St. Philip*, a Spanish merchantman laden with spices, bullion, jewels, and expensive fabrics, just before arriving, hailed as a hero, in Plymouth.

"Her Majesty asked me to meet Drake, knowing we are friends, but also to inventory the haul for her," Thomas said to me one morning. He showed me the letter he'd received from the council.

> You shall first deliver our letter to Sir Francis Drake and acquaint him with your instructions: you shall see the bills of lading of the prizes taken: you shall see what is best to be conveyed hither by land or sea, and what to be sold locally: you shall consider the safest means of transport: you shall cause all coffers and boxes you judge or know to have gold, stones, jewels, etc., to be opened before Sir Francis Drake and yourselves. . . .

"The queen will take her thirty-five percent and then the rest shall be divided upon the investors. And Francis is rich," Thomas said, but with no rancor. All England loved the man we knew to be our own pirate; men wished to be like him, women wished their husbands were. I simply wished for my husband to return to me.

The queen sent Thomas because she knew him to be meticulous to the penny; she knew where every cent in her kingdom was, to whom it was due, and what was due her. Although she would treat Drake fairly, she never gave anything away without necessity. "Drake's actions will delay Philip as he must restore his lost fleet, if he can, and will give England more time to prepare. But it will also spur him on to brutal war if he can; he is no man to be tweaked by a woman, queen or no."

I had not brought up the topic of the Wyatt poem with Thomas; what would I have said? There was no evidence at all, except the fear that lodged in my heart like a bone in the throat, that told me it was meant from Sofia to my husband. With war imminent, it did not seem a likely time for me to try to solve the problem of Sofia's potential marriage or my own. And so, like the hulls of those burnt galleons, Thomas and I drifted.

Whilst Thomas was at Plymouth, the queen met with her councilors to plan fortifications against the Spanish. And then, in the midst of things, came a package, by sea, from the czar Ivan the Terrible of Russia.

We were at Richmond when the queen received an emissary of the czar. The queen met him in a private chamber flanked by me, Anne Dudley,

Mary Radcliffe, and some other ladies as well as some of her noblemen.

"My master would like you to consider his gifts, and perhaps, his hand in marriage," the envoy said, which brought a fit of giggles from the maids in the back of the chamber and a stern look from Her Majesty. At fifty-four, she was flattered to be still considered matrimonial material. Mary and I opened his packages in the presence of the queen; he gave her four pieces of Persian cloth of gold and two whole pieces of cloth of silver, a fair large Turkish carpet, one hundred black, very rich sable skins, and two gowns of white ermine.

The queen was gracious and instructed me to find some suitable gifts to return to Ivan with his servant, but she had no intention of marrying him.

Later, in her chamber, we ladies wrapped ourselves in the black skins and the queen in her gown of white ermine. I taught her a few words of Russian, which I had learned as a girl in the north, and as she ably mimicked me, we ladies burst out in laughter.

It was a much-needed moment of lightheartedness, as it came clearer each day that war was upon us.

The months passed and we prayed against and prepared for the Spanish. Thomas spent much of his time working for Lord Howard of Effingham, the queen's cousin and lord admiral, and even

Essex, as he prepared Hurst Castle and all ports north and south to withstand Spanish attack if they could.

War was upon me at my home, too. The queen spent much of early 1588 at Richmond Palace, which was rare, but which I relished, as I was able to stay in my own home and enjoy my children as we were but a few feet away. One evening, as I bent down to retrieve a ball that Edward had rolled down a long gallery and into Thomas's room, I spied something under Thomas's bed frame.

I leaned down and picked it up. It was a dainty, jeweled slipper. Sofia's slipper. I sank to the floor and bade Edward to play with his brother for a moment.

*What must I do?* I prayed. *What can I do?* I recalled the story I'd shared with Her Majesty, of the bosom serpent in the garden.

It only took one serpent to destroy Eden.

And then a second thought: it also took two willing participants.

I wrote to Mary Herbert.

# TWENTY-TWO

Spring: Year of Our Lord 1588
Richmond Palace
Langford House

Summer: Year of Our Lord 1588
Whitehall Palace
English Coast

I decided that I had to find out for myself if there was deceit afoot in my home or if I was, in my weariness, threading together unrelated incidents. Thomas had not yet returned from Hurst, but he would that evening; to that end, his secretary was already at Sheen.

"Could you please write a note for me?" I asked him.

"Certainly, Lady Northampton," he said, wary. I had my own secretary, after all.

"Please just pen, 'If you want to make plans together, privately, meet me tomorrow evening in the large closet off of the long galley,'" I said. "Half nine. And then sign it, 'Gorges.'"

He cocked his head. "Not Northampton?"

"No," I said brusquely. "I am a Gorges as well, am I not?"

He nodded. "Yes, of course." He sealed the note

and stamped it with Thomas's seal, as that was all he had at hand.

"Please deliver this to my cousin Sofia," I said. "But speak nothing else to her, on pain of termination." I could tell that concerned him; I was easy mannered most of the time.

I checked on my children after they had dined; we had been so often at Richmond that they had thawed to me and clamored for my attention after dinner. It was all the sustenance I needed; besides, I was too worried to eat. Sofia had taken dinner in her chambers. Perhaps she'd sensed my mood, or perhaps she was planning for a rendezvous.

Thomas returned home the next day, weary. I did not meet him or speak to him, even after he sent for me. Once I had my servants ensure that he was abed for the night, well before eight, I took the slipper and Wyatt poem in hand and went to the closet, where I waited, alone, in the dark.

It had not escaped my attention that I was here in a closet confronting a woman, a relative, who desired to tryst with my man. The first time, with Karin and Philip, I had been but a girl who was willing to overlook the ill done her. This time, I was neither a girl nor willing to ignore or excuse treachery.

This time, I would fight.

At exactly half nine the door crept open. I could see her, because of the torches still lit in the hallway, but she could not see me.

"Thomas?" she called into the dark as she moved forward. She had dressed most becomingly, perhaps most unseemly for an unmarried woman, and had brushed her hair to a shine.

As she grew closer she saw that it was me, and not Thomas. She recoiled.

"You were mayhap expecting to see someone else?" I asked. I held up the slipper and the scrap of paper to her. I didn't need to ask anything else; her face betrayed her.

"I meant no harm," she said. "I was often alone. Thomas was often alone. We became . . . companions."

"Companions!" I shouted, not caring who heard me, though the children's chambers were on another floor, and this wing was far from them.

"I have no one," she said. "You have left me bereft and alone."

"You came here on my good graces, at my good pleasure, and my long hours of service have kept you these many years while you plotted against me: to take my home, my husband, and my children."

"It's not hard to rob the house that goes untended," she retorted.

I held my hand at my side so I would not strike her. Was she void of remorse or conscience? It put me in mind of one of Master Lyly's lines: all is fair in love and war. I would not give her the man she wanted, a nobleman, so she'd determined to take mine.

"I have made arrangements for you to travel to Wales," I said. "Lord Pembroke is now governor of Wales, and they reside at Ludlow. Young Upjohn is nearby and is still willing to take you to wife, though I cannot understand why."

"Wales?" she shrieked. "What is in Wales? Nothing. Barbarians!"

I lowered my voice. "The forebears of the Queen's Majesty come from Wales. Is she, too, a barbarian?"

At that she shrunk. She knew I would not fear to tell Elizabeth of those sentiments.

"You could return to Sweden," I said, "in shame. Your choice. You have until tomorrow morning to let me know which you choose. You have been an instrument of trouble in my home, and you are no longer welcome here."

She dipped a saucy bow and left the room. I waited until she left and then I followed behind her and walked into Thomas's chamber unannounced. I stood near his bed. "I should like to speak with you," I said, waking him.

He rolled and turned toward me. "Now?"

I picked up a vase that was next to his bed stand and threw it at a wall that was not hung with tapestry. It shattered and water dripped down the wall, leaving the blooms askew on the floor. Truly alarmed, he got out of bed, put on some breeches, but remained bare-chested to delay, I gathered, our conversation no more.

"Have you bedded her?" I asked quietly.

He looked at me bewildered, but sleep-drunk no longer. "I do not know of whom you speak," he said.

I reached over and took his quill and ink and threw them against a wall. "The pretty miss you recite such fine poetry to," I said, shaking the scrap of poem at him. "Wyatt?"

He looked confused. "I recite poetry to no one," he said, "but you."

"Have you bedded her?" I asked him quietly. I held up the slipper. "I found this under your bed."

He looked at me without flinching. "No. But she's asked me to, more than once. She came to me at night and sat on the foot of my bed, whereby, I suppose, she left a slipper. I didn't bed her. But I considered it."

I went forward to strike him and he caught my wrist in his hand before I could. I stood there, trapped, and when he was sure I was not going to strike him he let go of my wrist and backed away.

"And what if I had bedded her, eh?" he asked. "Would that be something to run and tell Walsingham? Perhaps he could have me followed and flogged for it."

I grew cold. "Walsingham . . ."

"Oh, yes," Thomas said. "You went running to him with the recusant ring instead of asking me, your husband, what it was. He was so proud of you, of your loyalty."

"Mayhap if you'd told me first, I would not have had to run to anyone!" I shouted. "Where's the loyalty in *that?*"

"I trusted you to understand that I would always have your best interests in mind and there was no way I was going to risk *you,* or our children, until the plot had been defused!" He ran his hand through his hair. "All of this!" he continued. "The missions, the fortress, the envoys, the courts, the errands, the ultimate betrayal of my family and the risk of my life. *All* of it," he said, "I do for you. So you would have pride in me, and be not ashamed that you had taken me, untitled, as a husband. And what is my thanks? Bearing tales to Walsingham."

He sat down on the bed, silent. "All of this, Elin," he finally said, "I've done for you. But you are never here. A man wants a wife who carries his name, who is home to greet him when he returns, who hunts with him and reads with him and plays chess with him. Who warms his bed. Is that so hard to understand?"

I crumpled onto the floor. "No," I said. "In truth, it's not."

"You're gone more often than not," he said. "Sofia is here more often than gone." He looked at me. "But I haven't bedded her. I swear that to you. I haven't bedded her."

I put my head in my hands and began to cry. He came from the bed and sat with me there, on the floor. "Elin," he said. "Elin. Do not mourn so."

"How did it come to this?" I asked. "Not so long ago you and I held one another, defying the queen, promising to love one another and let nothing and no one come between us. And here we are, with nothing left to bind us together."

He held my hand and clasped his finger over my wedding ring and then drew my hand to his lips. And then he put his lips on mine and kissed me softly. I kissed him back and before many more moments had passed he picked me up from the floor and helped me from my gown and moved me to the bed.

I spoke many languages at court, and Thomas did, too, but there was one language that he spoke only with me, and I with him. We used no words to reassure one another in that language that there were yet many unshakable bonds of love between us.

Afterward, I did not sleep, nor did he.

"Where did the Rosary ring come from?" I asked him, touching the wedding band of gold on his finger.

"My cousin," he said, voice still sorrowing. "I had to win them to confidence, misleading them into believing that I was a Catholic so they would share the plans they had with me, plans not for good, but for evil, for overthrowing the queen and replacing her with Mary. I regret deceiving them, but there was no other way."

"Is that why you hadn't gone to church with me?"

He nodded. "I worshipped in private, though."

I slid nearer to him. "You do not have to explain yourself to me. It was my error."

"And perhaps mine," he said. "I could have shared more, but, well, we were grown apart and you are always with the queen and—"

I put my finger to his lips. "I have told Sofia that she can choose between Wales and Sweden."

"Will Upjohn have her?" he asked.

"I believe so. I've been honest with Mary about my concerns all along, and she told me that Upjohn was taken with Sofia, as he preferred a spirited woman."

"I well understand that," Thomas said.

I looked at him with surprise and hurt.

"Nay, nay, love, not Sofia, never." He kissed me. "A spirited woman."

I sighed and settled back. "And yet, even with her gone, that shan't solve our problems," I said.

"There is no solution." He looked away.

I lay my head on his chest. This was my moment, perhaps my last chance, to show my husband what he meant to me. I had made many missteps along the way, but I would not make one now.

"I shall leave Her Majesty's service," I said. "Not altogether. I shall be present from time to time, but in the main, I shall be with you and the children."

He sat up, dislodging me. "What?"

I sat up and drew the coverlet about me. "I shall leave her active, constant service." Lady Knollys, after all, had worked herself to death in service of the queen, to the detriment of her husband and children.

Thomas had remembered that, too. He shook his head. "It cannot be done. If she would not allow Lady Knollys to leave her service for but even a short time, nor Lady Cobham, she will certainly not allow you to leave. She depends upon you. She loves you. She craves your comfort and companionship."

"So do you," I whispered as I took his head in my hands.

He pulled me to him so I would not see the tears that I felt instead. "I do. But she will not abide it. She will disallow it."

"She can hardly throw me in the Tower," I said, trying to jest though I did not feel like it.

"No, she can do worse," he replied. "She can strip us of our lands, our titles, our commissions, our rents, our offices, our grants, our gifts, and everything we need to raise our children, educate them, and marry them well. We could be left with no preferment at all. Look at poor Davison. He sits, still in the Tower a year later, for lawfully carrying out her order."

"I am willing to risk that if you are," I said.

He drew my ear near and whispered in it.

" 'Tangled I was in love's snare, oppressed with pain, torment with care, of grief right sure, of joy full bare, clean in despair by cruelty—But ha! ha! ha! full well is me, for I am now at liberty.' " He looked me in the eye. "That's Thomas Wyatt. And it be only for my wife." He pulled me toward him and we made love again while the sun rose.

As I got dressed, he asked, "When shall you tell her?"

"After the war with Spain is over," I said. "If you agree."

He nodded. Neither of us wished to abandon her at the most difficult hour in her rule.

I called Sofia to me later that day.

She spoke but one word. "Wales."

"Prepare your belongings," I said. "I shall take you to Salisbury and you shall be met there by some of the Pembrokes' menservants, who will take you to Upjohn. I shall give you a lady maid as your wedding gift."

At that, she softened, perhaps expecting nothing at all. I did not wish to ruin her life. I merely wished for her to not ruin mine.

I sent word to the queen that I would not be at court that day but requested an audience with her that evening, and word came back that the queen had agreed.

My husband and I spent the day bow hunting, he

behind me, his arms around me, and I cared not at all if I killed a stag because I had recaptured the only thing that mattered. It put me in mind of a saying: a bow long bent at last waxeth weak. My marriage was bent to the point of breaking, and I must repair it.

We spent the late afternoon in one another's arms, again, in my chamber, because on the morrow I would leave for Salisbury and he for Dover as the country prepared for war.

"If something should happen . . ." I began. In truth, I knew not which something I meant: war, the queen, an untimely death.

"If something should happen, Elin, we are already whole," he said, kissing me into silence.

*"Hans mun är idel sötma, hela hans väsende är ljuvlighet. Sådan är min vän, ja, sådan är min älskade."*

"It has been long since you have spoken Swedish to me. What say you?"

"From the Song of Solomon," I said. " 'His mouth is most sweet: yea, he is altogether lovely. This is my beloved, and this is my friend.' "

"Come, Helena." The queen beckoned me forward. "You seem weary."

I looked at her pointedly; it was not that she did not care for her ladies; we all knew that she well loved us. But it was true that I was not accustomed to her asking after my well-being. I wondered if her instincts, sharp as a broken shell, had picked up on the shift in my mood.

"I should like a few days' leave, Majesty," I said. "I wish to travel to Salisbury."

"Salisbury?" she asked, surprised. "Yes, of course, but whatever for?"

"My cousin Sofia is to be married to a young Welsh squire. We're to meet some from the Pembrokes' household at Wilton and she will travel with them to Wales."

The queen softened and sat back in her large chair. "A marriage? Are there congratulations to be offered? It seems hastily arranged."

"My cousin was corresponding with my husband," I said bluntly.

The queen leaned forward again, shocked. "Surely not Sir Thomas! He did not involve himself in an unchivalrous manner?"

"Nay, Majesty, despite her vigorous efforts otherwise."

She eased again. "Well then, a young and lovely cousin who favors you and desires the man you've chosen for your own. What shall we do? Have her thrown into the Tower?"

I smiled, appreciating that these many years after her Robin had married Lettice she was able to jest about it, though the "she-wolf" had never been forgiven. I now understood her torment in a most personal manner.

"Do not tempt me, my lady!" I teased back. "I shall return in but a few days."

"See that you do, my good lady marquess," the queen said wistfully. "I shall miss your companionship while you are gone. I cannot do without you."

And yet, she must do without me. My heart and mind filled with foreboding, and while my back was firm, my knees were not.

I left Sofia at Wilton, in good hands, and then rode out to Langford with some of my household's men and six craftsmen I had hired in London.

We came upon the ruins, and I indicated that I wanted them to begin to make some part of the house habitable.

"A kitchen, of course, and the privies. The hall and some chambers, and the library." I had counted the cost before leaving London, using some of the money we'd earned on Drake's last journey as well as many of my own rents I had been saving. I had not told Thomas. It was to be a gift for him after the war. Our living area would not be grand; it would be small, a yolk of life surrounded by ruins, but it would be ours. I took one of the stones with me; they were unique, pinkish brown.

I made my way back to London before the fleet sailed, and sent the rock to Thomas. He would know it had come from Langford, and though he did not know what I was about, he would understand that I was sending him a bit of our home.

He had a messenger deliver a gift to me, a gold salamander brooch with a ruby eye. The queen spied me wearing it and smiled. Salamanders were the gift of lovers, designed for heat.

But lovers come in tamer varieties, too, and that spring and summer the queen dined often, and alone, with Lord Robert. There was nothing improper between them, of this I was sure, as I was still on constant attendance. But when the heat between them had withdrawn, it left a warm field of affection and companionship. Lettice Knollys was never at court, but rumor had it that she was sharp with Lord Robert. I knew not if that were true, but I heard its opposite, merriment and pleasure from the queen's dining chamber and I saw Lord Robert and her, many a night, heads down over a chess game.

Watching them together, wondering what might have been had they married, put me in mind of a chess move—the willful sacrifice of a queen made to strengthen the realm's overall position. Each day she paced her chambers waiting for word from her men on the coasts. When the missives arrived, she read them, quickly, and fired back instructions.

Lord Howard of Effingham had letters sent to the coastal towns, instructing them to arm themselves and prepare for battle. Walsingham had certain information that the Spanish were preparing to attack within months. They had 138 ships prepared, many more than the 61 that the queen had in her fleet. But their ships were bloated, oceangoing vessels, heavy and self-important like the Spanish king, whereas the English fleet was made up of galleons that were made for piracy: sleek and sharp and able to quickly respond and redirect when necessary, like our queen. More important, they carried two thousand cannons, more than twice the number that the Spanish carried, a gift that her father, King Henry, fascinated by artillery, had bequeathed to his daughter. I couldn't help but think he would be proud to see her, in her red-haired glory, facing the Spanish head-on.

Too, there was a certain wry satisfaction in the fact that many of the newer cannons had been made by melting down bells from confiscated Catholic church property. The pope, the queen's declared enemy, had financed some of her firepower.

The last day of May, her lord admiral set out with his fleet for Spain but was driven back by strong winds. "We have danced as lustily as the most gallant dancers in court," Howard wrote to Walsingham, who conveyed it to the queen. Walsingham set down the letter. "But he is eager to get back to sea as soon as possible."

"Tell him to wait," the queen said, pacing in her Presence Chamber.

"Wait, Majesty?" Walsingham looked worried. "Why?"

"We have . . . a premonition," she said. "We have a deep concern that the Spanish shall outmaneuver him and make for our shores."

Walsingham did as he was told and sent the letter, but Lord Howard wrote back immediately and said, "I must and will obey; and am glad there be such at court as are able to judge what is fitter for us to do than we here; but by my instructions which I had, I did think it otherwise."

The queen, able to discern and follow sound counsel, backed off and told her lord admiral that he should do as he saw best.

By the middle of July the Spanish had made it to the English coastal waters. Due to strong winds and the hand of God, most said, the English fleet was able to slip past and surround them, the winds at their back.

Thomas and Essex were in Dover and rode hard back to court to apprise the queen. Things were at a tense but anticipatory standoff.

"Our men danced on the shore as the Spanish came into sight," Thomas said.

"And Drake finished his game of bowls before boarding his ship," Essex finished with not a little admiration. But board Drake did, and at the beating of his drum, his crew and the others mustered for battle.

Lord Robert begged the queen to come to inspect her troops at Tilbury. "You shall, dear lady, behold as goodly, as loyal, and as able men as any Christian prince can show you."

Walsingham disagreed and begged the queen not to go, fearful for her safety. Those of us who knew her well could see that the idea of riding out to war with Lord Robert was something she was unlikely to pass by.

Her Robin promised that he would guarantee her person to be as safe as it would be at St. James's Palace, and staked his life upon it.

"We agree!" she said. Before she left, she wrote to Lord Howard and asked how things progressed.

"Their force is wonderful great and strong," he replied, "and yet we pluck their feathers little by little."

Thomas, who had ridden nearly the entire shoreline to prepare the towns for battle, reported that bonfires had been lit all along the coast to spread news of the armada's sighting.

"It's the English way," he said. Seventeen thousand men had been readied in the south-east. I imagined that the Spanish, approaching the realm and seeing those bonfires, may have thought that they had misjudged the strength or determination of the little isle.

I helped the queen pack her trunks before she

left, in August, to Tilbury. Although she was fifty-four years old, she wore a silver breastplate over her white velvet dress, and held a truncheon in her hand.

"A truncheon instead of a scepter, Majesty?" I asked.

"Each in its own time is required for rule," she answered. She rehearsed her speech in front of us ladies.

"My loving people," she began. "We have been persuaded by some that are careful of our safety to take heed how we commit ourself to armed multitudes for fear of treachery; but I assure you, I do not desire to live to distrust my faithful and loving people. Let tyrants fear. I have always so behaved myself that, under God, I have placed my chiefest strength and safeguard in the loyal hearts and goodwill of my subjects, and therefore I am come amongst you, as you see, at this time, not for my recreation and disport, but being resolved, in the midst and heat of the battle, to live or die amongst you all, to lay down my life for my God and for my kingdom and for my people, my honor, and my blood, even in the dust."

I wanted nothing more than to mount a horse and ride alongside her.

Lord Howard ordered some of his ship's hulks to be laden with pitch and gunpowder, then set afire and sailed into the Spanish fleet anchoring at Calais. The fleet, once ablaze, became disoriented and panicked. The Spanish then headed north, taking a more dangerous and roundabout way home. In the end, only half of the armada made it safely back to Spain. The great crusade to which the pope and several Catholic nations had contributed ended in humiliation at the hand of a brave queen and her Catholic admiral.

The war was won, and England rejoiced, but the queen's Robin was unwell. I saw him as they returned to court; he was said to have been ill since the eve they dined together in his tent after the queen's speech at Tilbury.

She worried on his behalf. When they returned to Whitehall, I thought he looked ill unto death. Selfishly, I wondered, should he die, could I find the courage to leave her, too?

# TWENTY-THREE

Summer and Autumn: Year of Our Lord 1588
The Palace of Whitehall

Lord Robert was heavier than I'd ever seen him—perhaps because he could no longer ride and hunt often due to pain in his legs and back. His face was reddened though he drank but little wine any longer, and after the briefest exertion his breath came in short puffs and bursts like a woman giving birth, which took him ever longer to recover from.

He'd been commander in chief of the home forces, but now that there was no longer a need for land defense, his own defenses buckled some. I noted that he had difficulty standing while reviewing the troops at Whitehall, at the end of August, and after he and the queen applauded as Essex tilted against the Earl of Cumberland, he left for Buxton, at the queen's command, to take the healing waters. As soon as he was gone, she was sore vexed.

I think she knew.

Perhaps she'd long known, which is why they'd spent so much time together over the summer, dining together, riding together, and meeting Spain together.

Shortly after Lord Robert left the queen, she

asked me to fetch a pouch made of cloth of gold and bring it to her. I did, and when everyone had left her bedchamber save myself, Anne Dudley, and a few maids of honor, the queen went to her chessboard and put the ivory king and queen into the pouch and then drew the strings closed and kissed it.

"Call Master Tracy," she instructed me, and I sent for someone to fetch the young messenger.

"Please ride hard to deliver these to the Earl of Leicester," the queen commanded him.

Tracy, no fool, did as he was told. Within a few days, he returned to the queen with a letter. She opened it up as soon as it arrived, excusing herself from her councilors who waited, with the post-Spain business of the realm, for the queen to sort out her affections.

I judged her not. Shall governance of the heart always submit to governance of a kingdom?

She instructed me to ask her apothecary to blend something to be sent to Woodstock for Lord Robert, and then she returned to the council.

I fell to temptation and read the bottom part of the letter, which she had left on her writing table. I told myself I wanted to know what his symptoms were so I could better instruct the apothecary.

"I would know how my gracious lady does, and what ease of her late pains she finds; being the chiefest thing in the world I do pray for, for her to have good health and long life. I have partaken of the medicines you had prepared for me, and find it helps more than any other thing that has been given to me." He finished, "With the continuance of my prayers for your Majesty's preservation, I humbly kiss your foot . . . P.S. even as I had written this much, I received your Majesty's token by young Tracy."

I wondered what went through his heart and mind, after he'd sent this back with Tracy, when in private he opened the golden pouch with the king and queen nestled together, inside.

Word returned to court that Lord Robert had stopped at Cornbury Park to rest, his fever having grown stronger, his ague more pronounced, and a deep cough setting in. Being with the queen at the marshes at Tilbury had certainly done his heart good, but his health mayhap suffered ill for it.

On September 4 came word that Robin, having loved Elizabeth for forty-seven of his fifty-five years, had died. He had been an able horseman, a defender of church reform, a noted linguist, and a wise counselor all the years of her reign. But mainly, he had been her love.

Upon hearing the news, the queen burst into tears and withdrew to her bedchamber and locked the doors to the world outside her, with the exception of a maid who assisted her with a portable privy. Within a day she let Blanche in, and Blanche, perhaps, coaxed her into letting Mary Radcliffe in with food after three days. Mary invited myself and Anne Dudley in a day later.

I worked hard not to show my shock at how she looked. Her skin was taut and for the first time I saw that it hung in small pouches below her black eyes, which were swollen and dull. The lines on her forehead and above her lip folded into pronounced wrinkles, and she set off an air of hopelessness.

"Come now, I've brought some ointments and oils to soothe," I said, though I knew the touch of loving hands would work better wonders.

"Thank you, Marchioness," she said, using my formal title. She often referred to her ladies, even beloved ones, formally when she sought to maintain her composure. There was no shrieking, or outburst, and perhaps this concerned me most of all.

I rubbed her shoulders and her neck and her head and her hands, one by one, as she switched Lord Robert's last letter to her from one hand to the other, never letting go of it entirely.

"We didn't respond to this letter," she mourned.

"Did he receive your token?" I asked, feigning ignorance of the letter's contents.

"Yes." She nodded. "He indicated that he did."

"Then he needed no answer, Elizabeth," I said, using her name for the first time in twenty-three years of friendship and service. "The heart needs no words to understand what has been long unspoken but understood."

She held my hand then, for but a moment more.

"You will rise from these ashes," I said.

She nodded. She knew she must. Her country waited to rejoice with her over the defeat of Spain.

Before I left her chamber that afternoon I personally replaced the linens on her bed, ensuring that they were scented with soothing oils. As I gathered up the older ones I noticed small, soft haystacks of red and red-gray hairs upon them, the sum of those which had fallen out over the previous few nights.

A month later, I knelt at the Royal Chapel and recited "A Prayer for Men to Say Entering into Battle," written by William's sister Queen Kateryn Parr. I had asked Mary Radcliffe to see that the other ladies and maids left the queen and myself alone as I spoke with her after the noon meal. Mary, true to her word, did as I'd asked.

I approached the queen as she sat at her writing table, preparing, I supposed, for the victory celebrations that would be held across the realm and, in particular, at her Accession Day festivities. France was no longer a threat; congenial James seemed ready to please the woman he assumed, right likely, would pass her crown to him upon her death. Spain was licking its wounds. Queen and crown had prevailed.

She looked at me as I entered and the other ladies followed Mary, which drew the queen's attention.

"I have an important matter to discuss with you," I said.

"Yes, proceed," she said abruptly. She did not like surprises, and Mary's clearing the others from the room alerted her that this would be an unusual audience.

"I need to retire to my home, to take my leave," I said. "To Langford."

"Yes, yes," she said, gesturing at my filled-out gown. "In anticipation of the baby. We understand this. But Langford? 'Tis crumbling, and so far away when Sheen is near at hand."

"My husband prefers Langford, Majesty, though he does not yet have the means to finish it. After the baby is born, I wish to remain with my husband. And my children."

She put down her quill. "Remain? For some weeks? Through the new year?"

I knelt before her. "I wish to retire from constant service."

She stood then, towering over me. "One does not retire from service. We shall never retire from service. Our Lord never retired from service. We have never had a lady leave our service, and we shan't have it now!"

"I would yet walk into the lions' den for you, and I bear you all manner of love. But you must understand that my husband desires me to wait upon him, as well. Your realm is secure. My house is not."

"We thought you sent your cousin to Wales."

"I did," I said. "But that does not mean I am not still needed."

"We need you," she said, looking weary again. "Especially at this time!"

I hoped that I had not toppled her from the unsteady balance she had only recently regained after Lord Robert's death. "I understand your grief, Majesty, but your kingdom and responsibilities are grand in scope, and constant. Although Lord Robert's loss was great, I fear that for a queen, these challenges shall never cease. You are well able to meet them, though, if I may dare say."

"No, you may not dare say anything!" she said. "Is this the reward we deserve for the kindness we have always shown you, from your arrival here in our realm, from the sponsorship of your marriage to a marquess and then the acceptance of your marriage to a squire? Have we so ill used you that you must now repay us in kind?"

"No, my lady," I said. "I have always sought to serve you with the honor, dedication, and fealty you deserve."

"Then what of our needs now?"

I stood up and took her hands in mine, taking care to first hold the hand upon which she wore the locket ring I had given her many years since, and then the one upon which she bore her coronation ring.

"You once told me, Majesty, that you are both virgin to the world and wife to your realm, and it is him whom you must first serve and please. Then you spoke Holy Writ to me, which I know you hold in highest esteem, as do I. As Saint Paul wrote, 'There is difference also between a wife and a virgin. The unmarried woman cares for the things of the Lord, that she may be holy both in body and in spirit: but she that is married cares for the things of the world, how she may please her husband.' "

I took a deep breath and steadied myself as I could feel her hands tremble in anger. "I am not married to England, Majesty. I am married to Thomas Gorges."

She pulled her hands away from me then, catching the locket ring on the sleeve of my gown. "Begone, then!" she said. "If you care nothing for the preferments, the perquisites, and the goodly offerings we have shared with you these many years, nor the affections and love we have settled upon you, you may leave court altogether!"

I was going to plead with her to reconsider, but she stalked into her bedchamber, leaving me to look at her back, before she closed the door.

I withdrew, not knowing if she would make good on her subtle threat to take from us all she had given. I saw Mary Radcliffe as I made my way down the gallery to pack my apartments.

"Be you all right?" she asked.

After a quick embrace, I hurried down the hallway before any should see my tears.

# TWENTY-FOUR

November: Year of Our Lord 1588
Langford House, Salisbury

Spring: Year of Our Lord 1589
Windsor Castle

We arrived at Langford in November; it was windy and cold and our quarters were cozy but not large. The children, used to Sheen and its grandeur, made polite comments but I could tell they were surprised and perhaps a little afraid because the ruins still surrounded us.

"No stories of specters," I teasingly warned the nurse, who still tended to them from time to time, and she agreed with a grin. I had brought a midwife with me from Salisbury, as the babe was soon due and, as I had already given birth so many times, this one was likely to come quickly.

Within a week, some of Thomas's men arrived from Hurst Castle, of which he was still governor, to say that a Spanish galleon had been found wrecked in its waters and they wanted to know what to do with it.

Thomas looked at me. "I need to ride out there and see for myself."

I nodded. "The midwife is here to attend me, and we have servants." He kissed my forehead and instructed the children to be obedient and then he left. I lay very still upon my bed, trying to forestall the child's birth until Thomas returned, but it was of no use. Within hours the babe came, and before long, I heard the sturdy squall of my young son. He had dark hair, not like Thomas's fair or my red. For a moment, he put me in mind of a Gypsy, and I recalled that Lord Robert, so recently passed, had once been teasingly called "the Gypsy" by his enemies for his dark good looks.

I had borne Thomas four sons; three of them yet lived, but he had not named any son for himself. I knew that I wanted to name this child for the queen, because in spite of her harsh remonstrance, I knew she loved me well. But I could not ask that of Thomas.

He returned home in two days, and sat near me. "The wrecked galleon is loaded with silver and gold," he said. "I've sent some guards out in skiffs to surround it till I hear back from Her Majesty on what she wants me to do with it."

"What do you think she'll say?" I asked, holding our new babe tight to my chest.

"I suspect she'll ask me to account for everything and then send some of her men to Hurst to convey it to the treasury," he said. "But I do not know. She has not written to me since we left court some weeks back. She may relieve me of Hurst, and the Wardrobe, Chancery, and everything else."

I nodded. "It's well that you asked her," I said. "And here is your fine new son." I handed the wrapped babe to him and he drew him near and then kissed the baby's soft cheeks.

"Have you named him?" Thomas asked.

"Without you?" I said. "Never!"

He teased, "You had named our last babe Bridget without me, though you feigned that you had not thought of it well ahead of time."

"It is good to be known," I teased. But then I grew more serious. "We have not named a son after you, dear husband."

"And yet . . ." he said.

I shrugged. "With Lord Robert's death, I thought, I thought perhaps we would name him Robert."

He laughed. "Placating the queen?"

I nodded and smiled. "Perhaps. But freely offered as well. And the next babe will be named Thomas. I promise."

He agreed with me and I asked my secretary to please take a letter in which I told the queen that I was safely delivered of a son, and asked her to stand as godmother. This, then, would be the true test of whether she had forgiven me or not.

Within a week came a note from court saying that although the queen wished that she could attend the christening of my child, she could not leave court just then because it was nigh unto

Christmas. It was too rough and cold for the queen to travel, but she would send Lady Mary Radcliffe in her stead.

Thomas had not yet heard back about the wrecked Spanish ship.

When I arrived at Windsor the next spring for a visit with Her Majesty, I found that my quarters had not yet been reassigned but that the queen had saved them for me. I sent a quick note asking if Thomas and I might bring our young son, her godson whom she had not met, with me as I presented myself to her. She sent word that yes, I might.

I dressed him in satin and we three made our way to her chambers, where her pages let me in. I saw instantly that Anne Dudley, who had no children, and Mary Radcliffe, who had not married, were now her principal ladies and it would be a mistruth to say I minded not. But as my babe wriggled in my arms, I knew I'd made the right choice.

I handed the child to Anne, who kissed and cuddled him, afore I knelt before the queen.

"I wish for you to meet my son, Majesty," I said, taking him in hand again from Anne Dudley. The queen held out her arms and took the child in them; I had seen her talk to children and tease and banter with them, but I had never seen her hold a child. "His name is Robert."

She looked at me, her black eyes soft. "We should have liked to have had a son named Robert."

"Yes, Majesty, I know that," I said. "It is my gift to you."

She held him for but a moment longer, drawing in his baby scent. The child did not flinch from her, nor cry, but looked her straight back in the eye.

"You shall have to teach him better manners," she teased. She handed him back to me, and as I drew near to take him, she kissed my forehead, which filled my heart.

"You have another fine son, Thomas," she said, beckoning my husband to draw near. "We thank you for your continued work on our behalf, at Hurst and elsewhere." I could see her suppress a grin and wondered what she could possibly be about to say.

"It is my privilege and honor, Majesty," Thomas said.

She nodded before continuing. "We are gifting to you, and to Lady Northampton, jointly and permanently, everything aboard the sunken ship you reclaimed off Hurst Castle."

Thomas stood up. "Majesty, please excuse me, I must have been remiss in conveying exactly what was aboard. It was loaded with silver and gold. I remitted the contents to your treasury. I shall endeavor to find out where the bill of contents was mislaid." All knew that Her Majesty kept a firm grasp upon her purse.

"We are well aware of the contents, Sir Thomas. You are to use them to build your house."

I looked at Thomas and he nodded at me before we bowed before her. There would be money enough to rebuild Langford entirely.

"We are awestruck and grateful, Majesty," he said. I could hear the quiver in his voice. "I know not what to say."

She grinned. "In light of the fact that you have ever made your fortune by boarding foreign vessels, we see no reason for you not to persist withal." At that she laughed aloud, giving us permission to do likewise and the loving tease she was so well known for. We all laughed with her and then I stood, unbidden, and kissed her hand and she ran it over my hair once before I returned to Thomas's side.

"Thank you, thank you, Majesty, for the gift of the galleon," I said. "I shall never be able to repay you of that. Words to express my thanks toward and love for you cannot be found." I bowed my head again and she raised it.

"The heart needs no words to understand what has been long unspoken but understood," she replied, quoting me from just after Lord Robert's death.

"We do not forget those who serve us well," she said, turning toward Thomas again. "We should like for you, and your wife, to attend upon us from time to time at court throughout the year."

"Indeed, we shall," Thomas agreed.

"That was not a request, Sir Thomas, but a command." I could see her restrain a smile.

He bowed his head in acquiescence and as he did, she burst out in laughter, and then Mary Radcliffe joined her in it, and Anne, and me. Thomas looked at us, wondering, I supposed, about women and the inability to truly know what to expect from us, and left us in the chamber.

We stayed at court for nearly two weeks, then took our leave as the queen prepared for Progress. Just before I left, the queen called me to her.

"Helena, I have a gift I should like to give to you, a token to take back to Langford."

"No, Majesty, you have given me too much already!" I protested.

"One does not contradict one's sovereign," she said. "Follow me." I walked after her down the long hallway, and soon I saw where she was taking me. To her aviary.

She called for one of her servants to bring forth a gold and jeweled cage in which were two songbirds.

"Since we know you so enjoyed caring for our songbirds at court, we thought it right for you to take some to Langford," she said.

Songbirds. *Milde makter.*

I forced a smile, and then I saw the twinkle in her eye. She knew!

"Do you know everything?" I asked, as I had oft done.

"Perhaps," she yet replied, with a smile.

# EPILOGUE

Early Spring: Year of Our Lord 1603
Richmond Palace
The Palace of Whitehall
Westminster Abbey

I returned to court for the new year, 1603, and did not leave as expected. My dearest friend Anne Dudley had taken ill; her beloved husband had died some years before, but she had served the queen as a widow since. Although Anne had rallied some, the queen was in need of ladies to assist, because another beloved friend, Catherine Carey, Countess of Nottingham, had taken ill as well.

When Lady Nottingham passed away in February, we could see the life flicker in Her Majesty, who was now a frail seventy years old. I had not thought to live to see the day when her spirit wavered as well as her body, but that day had come.

"I have never seen her fetch sighs," Lady Nottingham's brother, Robert Carey, told me after the funeral for his sister. "I have not heard her sigh so since Mary, Queen of Scots, was beheaded."

I agreed with him; it worried me, too.

Within a few weeks, Her Majesty was having trouble swallowing and grew yet more faint. I did

381

not think she ever recovered from the death of Catherine Carey, but she was not afraid of her own death, either. When, so many long years back, Parliament had hoped to scare her into naming a successor by discussing her death, she had responded, "I know I am but mortal and so therewhilst prepare myself for death, whensoever it shall please God to send it."

By mid-March she would not take remedy or even food. She lay, prone, on her pillows in a withdrawing chamber and would not move. She rarely spoke, though in a moment with less fever and pain she would grace us with a smile. Finally, Lord Howard of Effingham, her lord admiral and dear friend, coaxed her to her bed, where she reclined with her ladies surrounding her.

Robert Dudley was gone, Sussex was gone, Lady Knollys was long gone, Essex was executed, and Kat and Blanche were both long dead. Anne Dudley was ill unto death. Elizabeth had secured her kingdom. She knew she could die in peace.

We sent for the Archbishop of Canterbury, himself no young man, and he prayed at her bedside for hours, shifting from bony knee to bony knee in his discomfort. She would not let him leave, indicating with a squeeze of her hand that she wished for him to remain. I softly rubbed sweet-smelling oil into her thin hand skin, and willow bark near her jaw, which ached.

She spoke no more to us, but as the night grew

on, her face turned from gray to white again, but not the white, at first, of death, but of an ethereal quality. Between two and three in the morning, she slipped from mortal life to eternal life, one of her courtiers later said, "mildly like a lamb, easily like a ripe apple from the tree."

Of all the honors that came with my high rank, there was one that brought me true satisfaction. As the highest-ranking woman in the land, it was my position to be Chief Mourner for the queen.

I stood near her coffin as arrangements were made for it to make its way by lit barge down the Thames. She had not wanted her body to be prepared, but I tucked one bay leaf near her head, to represent a laurel of sacrifice and victory. I knew she was at peace and with those she best loved: in the embrace of the Lord Jesus, then next, perhaps her Robin, and then finally, finally, resting enfolded in the arms of her mother.

I quoted Holy Writ, and the queen herself, as her men closed the casket. " 'And have ye not read this scripture; the stone which the builders rejected is become the head of the corner: This was the Lord's doing, and it is marvelous in our eyes.' "

# Parr Family Tree

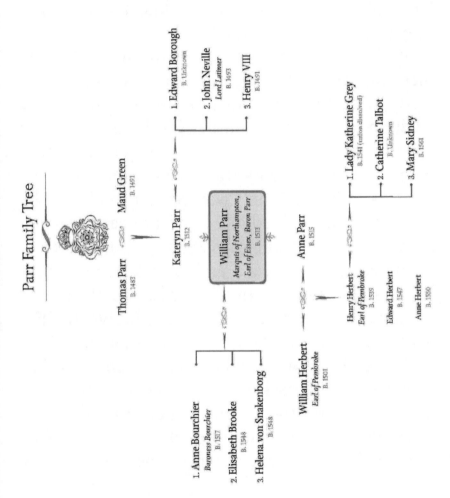

Thomas Parr
B. 1483

Maud Green
B. 1491

Kateryn Parr
B. 1512

1. Edward Borough
B. Unknown

2. John Neville
Lord Latimer
B. 1493

3. Henry VIII
B. 1491

William Parr
*Marquis of Northampton,
Earl of Essex, Baron Parr*
B. 1513

1. Anne Bourchier
*Baroness Bourchier*
B. 1517

2. Elisabeth Brooke
B. 1548

3. Helena von Snakenborg
B. 1548

Anne Parr
B. 1515

William Herbert
*Earl of Pembroke*
B. 1501

Henry Herbert
*Earl of Pembroke*
B. 1539

Edward Herbert
B. 1547

Anne Herbert
B. 1550

1. Lady Katherine Grey
B. 1541 (union dissolved)

2. Catherine Talbot
B. Unknown

3. Mary Sidney
B. 1561

# Gorges Family Tree

**2. Sir Thomas Gorges** ◦◦◦  
B. 1536

**Helena von Snakenborg**  
*Marchioness of Northampton*  
B. 1548

◦◦◦ **1. William Parr**  
*Marquis of Northampton,*  
*Earl of Essex, Baron Parr*  
B. 1513

**Elizabeth**  
B. 1578

**Francis**  
B. 1579

**Frances**  
B. 1580

**Edward**  
B. 1582

**Theobald**  
B. 1583

**Bridget**  
B. 1584

**Robert**  
B. 1588

**Thomas**  
B. 1589

# AFTERWORD

Did Elizabeth really hate other women?

I don't believe she did, though some still think so. I started this series wanting to know more about the hearts and innermost thoughts of the queens I was writing about, and I approached each story through their closest friends, those who principally served them, their ladies. It was a much different task to write about a queen consort than a queen regnant, though, and not only *a* queen regnant but perhaps the most famous queen regnant of all. Would I find a woman who was a true, lifelong friend to Elizabeth Tudor?

Indeed, I found more than one.

Because of her sovereign position, she was never really able to be an "equal" with anyone, and while she clearly enjoyed her power, I think she keenly felt the loss of the kind of intimacy that we all desire. Elizabeth adored Katherine Knollys, her cousin and perhaps half sister, as well Kat Ashley and Blanche Parry, who were like mothers to her. Catherine Carey, the Countess of Nottingham, was also a cousin; she died shortly before Elizabeth did and it was said that her death was the loss Elizabeth was unable to bear.

The author Antonia Fraser said, "Her [Elizabeth's] household resembled a large family, often on the move between residences, and as a family it had its feuds when factions formed around strong personalities. It was not out of malice that Elizabeth opposed her maids of honor's plans to marry, but because marriages broke up her own family circle." Happy marriages and babies born did remind Elizabeth of her loss, but perhaps the greater loss was the breaking up of the "family" she'd built, and rebuilt, for herself, having been denied a family of her own.

Elizabeth liked bold friends. The story is told of Sir Walter Raleigh writing on a window where the queen would see it, "Fain would I climb, yet fear I to fall." She responded, underneath it, "If thy heart fails thee, climb not at all." I also believe that Elizabeth chose her closest friends from among those who were a foil and balance to her personality, those who were softer, and perhaps motherly. And in truth, who among us can count more than a handful of very close friends over the course of a lifetime?

While Elizabeth did not allow her women—or anyone!—to meddle directly in her kingdom, she took counsel from those she trusted, among them Cecil, Walsingham, Lord Howard of Effingham, and, I believe, the women she relied upon. Cecil, who loved and admired her so much that he dedicated his whole life to her service, once said the queen was "more than a man and, in truth, something less than a woman." She had to be able to rule like a man and relate like a woman, often at the same time. No easy task, and I think she might have communicated more overtly with the men in her council and more subtly with the women in her chambers.

Then in 1566 came Helena von Snakenborg.

How had I missed her in a lifetime of reading the Tudors? I stumbled across Helena's tale while writing the second book in this series, focusing on Kateryn Parr. I have had to infer some into the friendship between Helena and Elizabeth, but I did try to keep all known facts. The queen did intervene, unusually, with another monarch in order to allow Helena to remain in England, and she who was as famous for counting her pennies as was her grandfather Henry VII, awarded, unusually, rooms, a servant, and a horse to Helena within months of her arriving in England. Helena was known as never being able to be bribed for access to the queen. According to several sound sources, Elizabeth did allow Helena and Thomas to keep the silver and gold from the wrecked Spanish ship, though she'd had Thomas count every last yard of silk and pound of spice from Drake's voyage. Although parsimonious, Elizabeth could be generous with those she loved.

Elin von Snakenborg's journey to England is even more fantastic than I described in the book. It took ten months, mostly over frozen land, as they tried to dodge the Danes. For a heavily pregnant princess and her mostly young female attendants, it was a bold journey. It does seem that, once Elin arrived in England, Parr fell immediately in love with her. I believe that he came to love her for her person, though he may have been instantly attracted to her physically, as she looked like his second wife, who had not been dead for long.

I do not know why Helena decided to stay in England, but she did. She didn't seem to have a gold-digging personality, so although Parr's title was attractive, I'm sure there had to be a bit more behind it. Her sister Karin did marry Philip Bonde, and as much of the story was about personal betrayal, the motivation of a fiancé who loved her sister, who loved him back, seemed to fit.

It is uncertain whether Gorges and Helena married in 1576 or 1577; I chose 1577 to fall in line with my story and also because I believe that a punishment of months was more in line with Elizabeth's treatment of favorites who irritated her (Lord Robert, Cecil, even perhaps Mary Shelton) rather than years or forever for people who threatened her crown or whom she simply did not like (Katherine Grey Seymour, Lettice Knollys, Bess Throckmorton). Thomas was imprisoned, though, and Helena banished, and Sussex really did have to intervene for them.

Thomas's role in the arrest of Mary, Queen of Scots, is absolutely true, though I do not know if he feigned his faith; I do not know the story behind the other Gorges and the Poyntz who were arrested in the Babington plot, either, but there was one of each, according to records that can still be accessed. And, of course, Thomas's mother was a Poyntz and his father a Gorges.

Helena did name her first child Elizabeth, and the child she bore just after Robert Dudley died, Robert. And there was a long gap between the children she "brought every year" that can be explained by physical and emotional estrangement, which was resolved before the conception of baby Robert Gorges. It's interesting to know that Thomas and Helena's daughter Elizabeth eventually married the man who would be the first governor of the state of Maine; the current Duchess of Norfolk is also one of Helena's descendants. Thinking upon Helena's encounters with Norfolk in this book only makes that more satisfying! The current princes William and Harry are descended through their mother from Amias Paulet, the stern Puritan guard finally in charge of Mary, Queen of Scots. I'm sure there are many other connections; it would be fun to find them all.

Sixteenth-century England was a century of religious turmoil. I used the words *Protestant* and *Catholic* in this book simply to make it easier on the modern reader, although other words and terms were in play during that era. Thirty years after taking the throne, Elizabeth said, "When I first came to the scepter and crown of this realm, I did think more of God who gave it to me than of the title, and therefore my first care was to set in order those things which did concern the Church of God, and this religion in which I was born, in which I was bred, and in which I trust to die not being ignorant how dangerous a thing it was to work in a kingdom a sudden alteration of religion."

Her father had wrested his realm back and forth between religious approaches, and her brother had been far to the end of the Protestant spectrum and her sister far to the end of the Catholic one. She wisely chose to steer her nation down the *via media*, the middle way. Elizabeth was a uniter. She did not let Catholics take over her realm, nor the far wings of Protestantism—Puritans and Calvinists—though she had beloved friends and councilors amongst all three.

She was a woman of quiet faith; Elizabeth's prayers are rich, detailed, humble, and sub-missive. She refers to herself repeatedly as a "handmaid," she is abject and penitent, she is personal. She asks for help, she offers praise. She—amazingly—writes her prayers out in many languages: English, French, Italian, Latin, and Greek. Her prayers reveal the fact that she, like others in the sixteenth century, clearly recognized a firmly established hierarchy. She understood that she was to be abject and humble before God, and that she was dependent upon His mercies and grace. But she also understood that her courtiers were to be humble and, when required, likewise abject before her, and their subordinates to them, all the way down the ladder. There is no democracy in the kingdom of heaven, nor was there in this one on earth.

Elizabeth was very fond of bawdy jokes; I think she and her whole court enjoyed the wit and the wordplay and the teasing repartee they brought— it was a kind of flirty intellectual jousting. In fact, those kinds of jokes are replete throughout the literature of the time. Shakespeare himself was the master of them and they are as much a part of this multidimensional queen as her faith, her temper, her affections, and her strength.

I tried to use actual poems and plays from the sixteenth century; I attributed them in the book where it would naturally fit in, but that wasn't always possible.

I'm not one who thinks Elizabeth was having a daily melodramatic meltdown. Biographer Alison Plowden says, "Elizabeth had learnt to conceal her innermost feelings before she grew out of her teens, and as she grew older she either 'patiently endured or politely dissembled' her greatest griefs of mind and body." I think she had a temper and she used and lost it from time to time, but she had an amazing ability to control herself, too—when she was in the Tower, when she faced the Spanish with only a little blink, and with the restraint of her physical passions.

Was Elizabeth a virgin?

Of course, this has been debated for centuries and I'm sure will continue to be throughout the ages. For me, it comes down to personal integrity. She insisted throughout her life that she was a virgin; to believe that she was not a virgin would be to believe that she lied, regularly and consistently, to her people, her courtiers, her friends, and to God. Should she have dallied with someone and then later reclaimed celibacy, she was smart enough to figure out a way to have stated that without lying. She said, to her Parliamentary delegation, "It would please me best if, at the last, a marble stone shall record that this Queen having lived such and such a time, lived and died a virgin." I'm just going to take her at her word. It makes her sacrifice more poignant as well.

Some of the stories herein may be apocryphal. It's not certain that Raleigh brought the potatoes or not, but it's plausible and makes for a good story. No one (thus far!) knows where the famous locket ring came from, but I like to think it came from someone who loved her and knew of her desire to keep her mother close to her heart, and the timing was right. Some say that both faces in the locket are of Elizabeth, but lockets, then and now, are known for keeping a portrait of oneself and a loved one close by; it was unlikely that anyone would keep two portraits of themselves in a locket. It's clear that Elizabeth kept mementos of her mother about, but subtly, and this would have fit right in. It was fun to invent a provenance. The girdle prayer book I described was most likely to be owned by Elizabeth Tyrwhitt; it exists still in the British Museum and you can see it online. However, all highborn women had highly decorated prayer books attached to their girdles. I have tried throughout to keep the integrity of the dates as much as possible, but births, marriages, and deaths are not always clear nearly five hundred years on, so there may be some unintentional variations.

I don't know the whole story of poor Eleanor Brydges; I do know that her aunt was accused of poisoning her husband, that Eleanor appeared at court with her sister but then disappears from the record, and that her husband was caught fleeing to the Jesuits in the year that Mary, Queen of Scots, was apprehended. I built upon that for those truths, with apologies for any wrongly taken liberties in her story.

I do not know if Helena retired from more active service, or if the queen would have allowed for that, for certain. But I do know that her ladies wished for it to be so; evidence remains of the letter quoted in the book from Francis Knollys to his wife, the queen's beloved Lady Knollys. The

Earl of Leicester reported that Lady Cobham wished to visit her husband at his country home "to rest her weary bones awhile, if she could get leave," but he didn't think it was likely that the queen would allow her to go. So it was certainly an issue among her ladies. Elizabeth had a firm will but always was willing to bend when it made sense, especially for those she loved; and because I wanted to explore this angle of ladies in waiting, the storyline made sense to me.

Although James I had Tudor blood, of course, his reign was the beginning of the English Stuart years and Elizabeth's is considered to be the concluding reign of the Tudor era. In a Renaissance century rich with intelligence, intrigue, faith, factions, passion, and drama, nearly five hundred years on, she truly stands out, the marvelous daughter of Henry VIII and Anne Boleyn.

To quote Elizabeth herself, though she was not speaking of herself at the time, "The end crowneth the work."

# ACKNOWLEDGMENTS

Writing a book is truly a team sport, and I feel thankful and blessed to have a number of wonderful people who graciously contributed their many talents.

As with each of the Ladies in Waiting books, I relied on the magnificent gifts of Lauren Mackay, historical research assistant and an author in her own right. She always knows exactly where to put her hands on the right material, trims over-wrought language, and can dig through a heap of history five hundred years old to suggest the exact fact the book requires. This time around, Jessica Barnes, a talented longtime friend and trusted, gifted editor with Story-Driven Editorial, also stepped in to assist with her invaluable story-depth and character-development insights. The exceptional Jenny Q of Historical Editorial brought her knowledge base and amazing, intuitive plot analysis to the completed manuscript. Laura A. Wideburg, PhD, lead teacher at the Swedish Cultural Center in Seattle, Washington, was an invaluable resource of all things Swedish Renaissance. Thanks very much to Susan Hageman and the Royal Horseguards Hotel, a beautiful property located in the Whitehall district, near and dear to all British history lovers.

I truly appreciate Danielle Egan-Miller and

Joanna MacKenzie, simply the best and brightest agents in the world, and their wonderful assistant, Shelbey Campbell; my confidence is bolstered knowing that they are in my corner. Thanks, too, to the great team at Howard Books who help bring these books to life and to market. Debbie Austin, as always, deserves high praise for her abilities to keep me, and the many thousands of facts uncovered, organized, and properly presented.

I could never have written this book without my astonishing husband, Michael, who did everything from reassuring and encouraging to hand-translating an entire book from Swedish to English online. Thanks, too, to my kids, Samuel and Elizabeth, who bring joy and meaning to my life. Finally, all honor and glory to God, who makes all things possible.

# PRINCIPAL WORKS
# OF REFERENCE

This is by no means exhaustive, and some of these books I relied on extensively while some only provided helpful tidbits. I love to look up books and resources when I read historical fiction, and I thought it might be enjoyable for others to do so, too, if they wish.

Sjogren, Gunnar. *Helena Snakenborg*, 1973.

Bradford, Charles Angell. *Helena, Marchioness of Northampton*, 1936.

Bell, James. *Queen Elizabeth and a Swedish Princess*, 1926.

Gorges, Raymond. *The Story of a Family Through Eleven Centuries: Being a History of the Family of Gorges*, 1944.

Somerset, Anne. *Elizabeth I*, 2003.

Plowden, Alison. *Elizabethan England: Life in an Age of Adventure*, 1982.

Plowden, Alison. *Elizabeth I*, 2004.

Doran, Susan. *Queen Elizabeth I*, 2003.

Borman, Tracy. *Elizabeth's Women: The Hidden Story of The Virgin Queen*, 2009.

Somerset, Anne. *Ladies in Waiting*, 2004.

Marcus, Leah S., Janel Mueller, Mary Beth Rose, editors. *Elizabeth I: Collected Works*, 2000.

Doran, Susan. *Elizabeth I and Religion 1558–1603*, 1994.

Doran, Susan. *Monarchy and Matrimony: The Courtships of Elizabeth I*, 1996.

Secara, Maggie. *A Compendium of Common Knowledge: 1558–1603: Elizabethan Commonplaces for Writers, Actors & Re-enactors*, 2008.

Sim, Alison. *Pleasures and Pastimes in Tudor England*, 2009.

Picard, Liza. *Elizabeth's London: Everyday Life in Elizabethan London*, 2003.

Gristwood, Sarah. *Elizabeth & Leicester: Power, Passion, Politics*, 2007.

Doran, Susan. *Mary Queen of Scots: An Illustrated Life*, 2007.

Fraser, Antonia. *Mary Queen of Scots*, 1969.

Mattingly, Garrett. *The Armada*, 1989.

Arnold, Janet. *Queen Elizabeth's Wardrobe Unlock'd*, 2001.

# READING GROUP GUIDE

*Roses Have Thorns*
*A Novel of Elizabeth I*

Sandra Byrd

## INTRODUCTION

When Elin von Snakenborg visits England with a royal entourage from Sweden and decides to remain, she drastically alters the course of her life. She marries an English nobleman and becomes one of Queen Elizabeth I's most trusted ladies in waiting, a position that draws her deep into the intrigue, danger, and treachery of the court.

## TOPICS AND QUESTIONS FOR DISCUSSION

1. If you were Elin, would you have wanted to return to Sweden or remain in England? What factors would have influenced your decision? Would you have changed your name, as she did?

2. Helena admits that she is fond of William but not in love with him, nor is she physically attracted to him. Is this any different from other engaged, highborn women of the time; for example, her friend Anne Russell? How did the

system of marrying for dynastic and financial concerns help or hinder women of the time? Is our current system of choosing husbands always better? Why or why not?

3. Right before Princess Cecelia departs for Sweden, she maliciously tells Helena that William is already married. What were William's reasons for withholding this information from Helena until it was too late for her to change her mind? Did it damage his reputation for high integrity, or did his past marital history honestly lead him to believe this would be a quickly solved problem?

4. When Helena first enters Elizabeth's employ, the queen is polite yet distant. How does Helena go about creating a place for herself in the royal household? What are several factors that account for the deepening of their friendship? Why does Helena commission the locket ring for Elizabeth? Was it a game-changer for their friendship?

5. Discuss the role that ladies in waiting play in the queen's life versus servants in the lives of every highborn woman, royal or not. What is your opinion of the way Elizabeth treats the women in her household? That culture certainly believed that the perks that come with the coveted position outweigh the negatives. Would it have, for you, had you lived then?

6. How does Helena use myths and tales, such as the legend of Idun, to convey her thoughts and opinions to Elizabeth? Why does she seek to influence the queen in this manner rather than in a more direct way? How else do the ladies in waiting "persuade effectively by softer manner"?

7. When Helena shares the story of the frozen rose garden with the queen, what is she really advising her about Mary, Queen of Scots? Was Elizabeth justified in ordering her cousin's execution? Why does Helena believe the monarch waited so long to have the deed carried out despite the evidence against Mary? Why do you believe Queen Elizabeth waited so long? Would you have acted similarly? How or how not?

8. What are the greatest threats facing Elizabeth I and the stability of the English throne? In what ways is religion—specifically religious differences—a significant factor in the unrest during her reign? What parallels can be drawn to religion in our time?

9. What is your opinion of Elizabeth I as a monarch, as seen through Helena's eyes? What characteristics and qualities do you think made her a successful ruler? How does Sandra Byrd's portrayal of Elizabeth I differ from those in other historical novels you've read or that you've seen

in films? Are we likely to get a more complete picture of any one person by looking at him or her from different perspectives?

10. In two different instances Helena is suspicious of Eleanor, once when the other woman reveals something she could not possibly have overheard and the other when she catches a glimpse of Eleanor's Rosary beads. Was it Helena's history and personality that compelled her to keep quiet, or fear, or circumstance? How is Eleanor's death a turning point for Helena personally? In what ways does it alter her association with the other ladies in waiting?

11. Why did Elizabeth allow Helena's marriage to William but likely would have denied permission for her to wed Thomas? Were Helena and Thomas right to marry in secret? What other couples married in secret during the Elizabethan era, and what were the consequences? (Consider Mary Shelton and Bess Throckmorton, both mentioned in the book.) Helena claims she thought the queen had discreetly sanctioned the union because of a comment made during a chess game. Does she honestly believe this was the case, or is she using the incident as a way to diffuse the queen's anger?

12. After Helena finds the Rosary ring among Thomas's possessions, why does she take it to Sir

Francis Walsingham rather than confront her husband? What were the benefits and risks to her and her children by taking it to Walsingham? What could have happened to Helena and her children if she had not gone to Walsingham, and he found out she was withholding treasonous information? Considering all that is at stake, what would you have done in her situation?

13. Helena balances serving the queen with marriage, motherhood, and managing her own household. What similarities does she share with present-day women who juggle careers and family? How is her situation different?

14. The first two books in this series were set during the tumult of the Reformation, when the protagonists were perhaps more zealous. How is faith lived out, albeit more quietly, by the protagonists in this book?

15. At one point Helena believes her relationship with Thomas is over. What accounts for the erosion of their marriage during the course of the decade? What was the turning point that allowed them to rebuild their marriage?

16. Why does Helena not act sooner on the misgivings she has about Sofia? How does the earlier betrayal of Karin and Philip factor into

how she deals with her cousin and her character arc? Was she too harsh on Sofia or not harsh enough?

17. "Court language was more often unspoken than said," writes Sandra Byrd. Why is Helena successful in navigating the intricacies of Elizabeth's court, even more so than many of the queen's countrymen and women? Is it more to her benefit or her detriment that she is a foreigner? What qualities are necessary to succeed in a royal court?

18. Do you feel that Elizabeth was, indeed, the capstone of the Tudor Era? Why or why not?

A CONVERSATION WITH SANDRA BYRD

**Q: Was it difficult to write about someone so well known, and both fiercely loved and scorned, as Queen Elizabeth I?**

A: It was certainly intimidating, challenging, and exciting. I have a large print of Queen Elizabeth I in my office and every morning she'd be there, waiting for me. Because she is so well known, people have strongly formed opinions of her and her reign, and I do, too. She lived a long, rich, complicated life, so in the span of this book I was only able to show one perspective, Helena's point of view as I'd imagined it and drawn it from history. It was a thrill to write, and I hope I have done her justice.

**Q: When you came across a mention of Helena von Snakenborg while doing research for *The Secret Keeper*, did you know immediately that she would be the protagonist for a novel? Why do you think the myth that Elizabeth I had no female friends has been so widely perpetuated?**

A: I did have an epiphany of sorts when I came across Helena. I'd been hoping all along to tell the story of a real lady in waiting, but one whose story had not been often told. I was grateful to uncover Helena. The fact that she served Elizabeth I for so long, and so closely, made her an excellent point-of-view character. Her May-December marriage to Parr, the mysterious gap in her child-bearing, and the fact that the queen had actually "exiled" her and thrown her second husband into the Tower made for a rich canvas upon which to imagine. Plus, the fact that Thomas Gorges actually led the party to arrest Mary, Queen of Scots, was too juicy to pass up!

Elizabeth was known to keep tight purse strings, so when good sources indicated that she very well may have given Helena the silver from the wrecked galleon, I knew I had a lady that Elizabeth had loved.

Elizabeth was not a woman's woman—she couldn't have been, or she'd not have been able to govern her kingdom in a time when women were not expected to be strong and effective rulers and John Knox was publishing his "First Blast of the Trumpet Against the Monstrous Regiment of Women." There are accounts that on the rare occasion when she did burst into tears her male councilors tended to look uncomfortably at their knuckles until it passed. The myth that she didn't promote marriages for her maids of honor was effectively put to rest for me by one of her biographers who concluded that, had that been the case, families would have stopped advocating their daughters for that position shortly into Elizabeth's long reign. I think she knew she could trust very few people, and so she did.

She was jealous, I suspect, on some level, of those who had husbands and children, but she was also a lifelong flirt, something a married woman could not be. I think she had deeply loved friends, among them Katherine Carey Knollys, Anne Russell Dudley, Catherine Carey Howard, and of course Helena.

**Q: "In a very real way, I controlled access to the sovereign," muses Helena in _Roses Have Thorns_. How unusual was it that a foreign-born woman like Helena would become the**

**highest-ranking of Queen Elizabeth I's ladies in waiting?**

A: In the days of Queen Katherine of Aragon, there were many high-ranking Spanish women who had traveled to England with her, held significant positions, and also married into English nobility. One of note is Maria de Salinas, a lady in waiting to Queen Katherine of Aragon. She eventually married William Willoughby, eleventh Baron Willoughby de Eresby, and they had a child, Katherine, named for the queen. This Katherine grew up to marry Charles Brandon and became a well-known reformer who played a memorable role as the friend of Queen Kateryn Parr, and guardian of Parr's baby Mary Seymour, in the last Ladies in Waiting book, *The Secret Keeper: A Novel of Kateryn Parr.*

However, most ladies in waiting were drawn from established English families. Rank, of course, comes from birth and marriage, so what catapulted Helena to the top of the heap, as it were, was her marriage to William Parr, Marquess of Northampton. Helena retained his title and rank throughout her life, even after her second marriage.

Sovereigns do raise their favorites to make them more fitting for close friendship. Henry VIII raised Anne Boleyn to Marquess of Pembroke before marrying her to make her of a more suitable rank. Elizabeth I raised Robert Dudley to the peerage as Earl of Leicester, in 1564; some suspected that was so he would be of a more marriageable rank. Helena gained her rank through marriage, of course. But although she was nobly born, her position as Marchioness of Northampton made her even more fitting to be close to the queen.

**Q: A vivid scene takes place early in the novel when Helena grabs a bee flying around Princess Cecelia. Why did you decide to include this in the story? What does it reveal about Helena's character?**

A: I wanted to encapsulate Elin's bravery and her fealty with one action, something that could be reflected upon, later, when her courage and loyalty toward Queen Elizabeth, and even Helena's own husband, Thomas, would be questioned. Our impulse as humans is to flee danger—including stinging insects—so to show her acting against that instinct in service to another demonstrates exactly what kind of woman she was.

Later, of course, that action is echoed in a much more dangerous situation when Helena removes the potentially poisoned pins from Elizabeth's gowns, sticking her hand, again, in the process.

**Q: The rivalry between Queen Elizabeth and her cousin Lettice Knollys was quite contentious. What happened to Lettice after Robert Dudley's death? Did Elizabeth ever soften toward the other woman?**

A: No, Elizabeth never did soften toward the woman she called "the she-wolf." Once she married Robert Dudley, Lettice Knollys was banished from court forever. It seems that their lack of affection for each other began long before Lettice became involved with Dudley. In some senses, Dudley and Lettice are sympathetic—each should certainly have been able to marry whom they chose, especially after the queen made it clear she would not be marrying Dudley. However, the more I read about Lettice and her older children, the less likable I found them to be.

I do have compassion toward her for the loss of her and Dudley's child, affectionately known as The Noble Imp. I'm sure that was difficult all around. One of Lettice's other sons, the Earl of Essex, became a favorite, and then a treasonous heartbreak, for Queen Elizabeth toward the end of her life. But that is another story!

**Q: One of the most intriguing aspects of *Roses Have Thorns* is the view it gives of the inner workings of Elizabeth's private chambers. How important was the role of the ladies in**

**waiting in protecting the queen and keeping her from harm as well as in safeguarding her reputation?**

A: Sleeping arrangements in that era were nothing as private as what we would expect now, and the queen, in particular, always had a maid of honor or one of her ladies sleeping on a small bed in her room. The maid of honor would be there to serve her if the queen needed something in the night, but also to protect her: physically, if someone tried to breach the bedchamber, and from gossip that might insinuate that the virgin queen was not sleeping alone.

I think the greater role that her ladies played was that of companionship and providing care and affection. As I mention in the Afterword, Elizabeth had no mother, no father, no siblings, no husband, no children, and all of her cousins were in some way rivals for her throne. That made for a lonely and guarded existence, and was one reason, I believe, why she could be somewhat needy and reluctant to let them go.

**Q: Elizabeth allowed Catholics the freedom to worship in private. Can she be considered an early proponent of religious freedom? At one point in the story you reveal that the Papal Secretary of State sanctioned the queen's murder, which is rather shocking. Was it**

**routine or extreme for the Vatican to take this kind of overt action against a monarch?**

A: Elizabeth has always said she had no desire to make windows into men's souls. In other words, she was willing to let them worship according to their own consciences and inclinations as long as it did not veer into treason. She made it clear that she was born and bred in the Church of England, but as long as her Catholic subjects remained loyal to her politically, she allowed them the freedom of choosing their own religious path. Once an action became a threat to her kingdom, it was a matter of state and not of soul, and she took action.

The Papal Bull calling for her execution was shocking. It was a time when there were people on both "sides" with pure motivations to protect what they felt was true Christian faith, and people who used the faith issues of the time to gain political power; scratch the surface and they had no good intent. Sorting out which was which was, then as now, difficult.

**Q: Tell us about your travels to England. What places associated with the Tudors made the greatest impression on you?**

A: All of it felt like a pilgrimage of sorts, to be honest. I loved visiting The Tower, Hampton

Court Palace, Allington Castle, and Hever Castle. I have not yet made it to Sudeley, but I will! Standing by the monument in Westminster Abbey where Queen Elizabeth I rests atop Queen Mary I, one can only hope that they are at peace with themselves, and each other, at last. Mary, Queen of Scots, by the way, is interred just down the aisle from them.

**Q: "They were burning my bones to get out and onto paper," you remarked in an interview about the Ladies in Waiting stories. Do you plan to keep writing about the Tudor era, or will you venture into another historical time period?**

A: I read dozens of books while writing the Ladies in Waiting books, so for now, I feel satiated with the era. I will continue to read Tudor fiction, because I love it and there are so many skilled novelists writing good books. However, there are other eras and genres in British fiction I am itching to explore as a writer, and I am eager to begin!

ENHANCE YOUR BOOK CLUB

1. Buy a lavender sachet or herbal candle for each member of your club to hand out at the end of the meeting.

2. Serve a feast using recipes in the International Cooking section on Epicurious.com in honor of Helena's adopted country, along with Swedish fare in a nod to her heritage (www.epicurious .com/recipesmenus/global/scandinavian/recipes).

3. Elizabeth was well known to have loved sweets, especially marchpane, which we now call marzipan. Pitted fruits, such as plums, were also popular at court. Prepare this recipe, and serve it at your meeting for dessert: www.epicurious.com /recipes/food/views/Plum-Tart-with-Marzipan-Crumble-103654.

4. Have a look at Queen Elizabeth's locket ring, the model for the one Helena gives her in the novel. Typically kept tucked away at the British prime minister's country residence, it can be seen here: www.thetudorswiki.com/page/ARTIFACTS +of+the+Tudors.

5. Pair your reading of *Roses Have Thorns* with one or both of Sandra Byrd's other novels centered on royal ladies in waiting—*To Die For: A Novel of Anne Boleyn*, which features Queen Anne Boleyn, mother of Elizabeth I, and *The Secret Keeper: A Novel of Kateryn Parr*, which features Queen Kateryn Parr, stepmother of Elizabeth I.

6. Visit www.SandraByrd.com to learn more about the author, her books, and Tudor tidbits like a royal timeline.

**Center Point Large Print**
600 Brooks Road / PO Box 1
Thorndike ME 04986-0001 USA

(207) 568-3717

US & Canada:
1 800 929-9108
www.centerpointlargeprint.com